THEN HE KISSED HER

MacRorah had been kissed before, but never in the way that this dark stranger, who had visited her in her dreams and who had saved her from certain death, kissed her.

His tongue explored her mouth and his hands explored her body.

Her arms were around his neck, and for the life of her, she didn't know how they'd got there. Desperately, she tried to rationalize what was happening to her by reminding herself that the only other time she'd seen this man, she'd been in a heightened state of emotion, which probably explained why she hadn't been able to think about him since then without a certain tremor of excitement. And now that he was actually here—actually touching her, actually—

Oh, my mercy . . .

SLOW SURRENDER

"Bronwyn Williams has an earthy, rare and glorious understanding of romance."

—Elizabeth Lowell

SLOW SURRENDER

Bronwyn Williams

A TOPAZ BOOK

TOPAZ
Published by the Penguin Group
Penguin Books USA Inc., 375 Hudson Street,
New York, New York 10014, U.S.A.
Penguin Books Ltd, 27 Wrights Lane,
London W8 5TZ, England
Penguin Books Australia Ltd, Ringwood,
Victoria, Australia
Penguin Books Canada Ltd, 10 Alcorn Avenue,
Toronto, Ontario, Canada M4V 3B2
Penguin Books (N.Z.) Ltd, 182–190 Wairau Road,
Auckland 10, New Zealand

Penguin Books Ltd, Registered Offices:
Harmondsworth, Middlesex, England

First Printing, December, 1995
10 9 8 7 6 5 4 3 2 1

To all our fans, friends, and family in the beautiful town of Elizabeth City, North Carolina. Thanks for all your support and encouragement.

Chapter One

☙

1 8 8 2

Don't be a goose, Sara Ball, it's entirely up to you whether you want to be a doormat for men to wipe their feet on, or whether you want to take your life into your own hands and shape it to your liking."

"Oh, MacRorah, don't start preaching again, *please!*"

The conversation had to do with obedience. The response around the marble-topped table in Gilbert's Ice Cream Parlor included one groan, one solemn nod of agreement, and a halfhearted rebuke, which was no more than she'd expected. At least it was better than being called a seditionist simply for advising her friends that wearing long drawers and hose, a chemise, a corselet, a petticoat, and a bustle, and all that under a skirt and an overskirt, when the temperature hovered near the century mark—well, it was excessive, to say the very least.

"But Mama says all a lady has to do is make herself pleasant to a gentleman, and he'll take care of everything," ventured soft-spoken Sally Lee Winslette.

"Your mama is absolutely correct. He'll also take possession of her personal funds and see that she never again expresses an opinion of her own. He'll make certain she kowtows to his every wish, and if she dares to speak out, he'll make certain she doesn't sit down for a week, nor leave the house without a heavy layer of face powder and a veiled hat."

There were several horrified gasps. MacRorah suspected her friends knew of her father's uncertain temper. There were few secrets in such a small town, but no one with a scrap of breeding would dream of saying anything about it. Nor would MacRorah have done so save that it helped her to make an important point.

"Look at you! I'm ashamed of you all! Are you just going to sit there like a row of pincushions and allow your papas to sell you to the highest bidder?" she challenged. "I assure you, once I come of age, I have no intention whatsoever of ever again living under any man's thumb."

MacRorah shifted uncomfortably on the round veneer chair in order to spare her bruised behind. It occurred to her that if she'd only waited a little longer to leave off her extra petticoat and ruffled horsehair bustle, she might not be suffering quite so much now. Her father had fair whaled the living daylights out of her when she'd refused point-blank to accept Marvin Leaks's suit.

She took pride in the fact that she had not shed a single tear. Small she might be, but she refused to give him the satisfaction of knowing he could hurt her. Her father called it muleheadedness. MacRorah preferred to call it pride.

Leaving the shop, they strolled the seven blocks along Main Street, past the courthouse, past Miss Harvey's big magnolia trees, past Judge Charlie's house, exchanging greetings with several acquaintances along the way.

"Are you and your family going to the beach next month?" Sally Lee asked as they reached the wrought-iron gate in front of her elegant three-story home.

"We're going week after next. When are you going, Carolyn?"

Red-haired Carolyn Stevens shook her head. "Mama can't make up her mind."

The four young women, flowers of Elizabeth City society, discussed the annual pilgrimage to Nags Head, where the families of each had cottages along the same stretch of sound side. Sally Lee wondered aloud if Seaborn Adams, generally considered to be the handsomest man in town, would be spending any time at his family's cottage this season.

Seaborn, at nearly twenty-four, was some half dozen years older than MacRorah, the eldest of her set. Over the years she had come to look on him as a sort of honorary older brother. Whenever Sally Lee took to sighing over him, MacRorah always felt vaguely guilty. She was the only one of their group who didn't have a crush on the man, yet she was the one he had chosen to propose to on her fifteenth birthday, nearly three years ago. And at regular intervals since then.

It was a big joke, of course. Sea teased her about it whenever he wanted to get under her skin, saying he was only waiting for her to grow up, and if she ever decided she couldn't live without him, why, then, he would just have to sacrifice his freedom and marry her for her money, as he doubted her looks would ever improve beyond the merely passable.

MacRorah knew she was pretty. She was hardly blind. But she appreciated Seaborn's gentle teasing, because there were times when she needed a friend who accepted her for what she was and not for the way she looked or for the wealth her family represented.

And what she was just happened to be a strong-willed, outspoken, rebellious young woman who was more often in trouble than not.

When her little sister, Rosa, had died unexpectedly four years before, it had been Seaborn who had comforted her. Her mother had been prostrate with grief, hardly speaking to a soul for six months. Recovering, she'd thrown herself into charity works that some had described as bizarre and others had called disgraceful, ignoring her husband and her remaining daughter alike. For the first time in her meek, timid life, Jean MacRorah Douglas had set the town on its ears, and to everyone's amazement, her husband had not uttered a word of protest.

That had been when the 41 Pecan Street project was born. It had begun as a shelter for pregnant, ill, or retired prostitutes. Since then it had expanded to take in disabled seamen.

Chalmers Douglas, not surprisingly, had reacted to the loss of his youngest daughter by drinking himself into oblivion and then leaving town for an extended stay with his harness-racing friends in Virginia. Which was the only reason, MacRorah was certain, that Jean Douglas had been able to get the bit between her teeth, so to speak.

She sighed. Sometimes she almost wished she could bring herself to accept Seaborn's offer, but it would never do. He was worlds better than Marvin Leaks, but he was still only a man, after all. Men held one standard for themselves and another for their wives. It was that double standard that drove MacRorah wild. If there was one thing she could not abide, it was unfairness.

As she neared the white three-story house that had once belonged to her maternal grandfather, old Gregory MacRorah, her steps began to drag. Chances were excellent that her father would be there. She wished he would leave town for another extended stay. When there was no one at home but her mother and herself and whatever unfortunate young women happened to be working for them at the time, they got along just fine. It was only when Chalmers came home, bringing with him his snide remarks, his uncertain temper, and his bullying ways, that everyone walked on tiptoe and spoke in whispers.

According to Polly, one of her mother's projects who was in an interesting condition and wise beyond her years at the ripe old age of fifteen and a half, a man beholden to his wife was worse than a harness-galled ox. Kitchen gossip, which MacRorah knew she shouldn't listen to—only how else was a body to learn anything?—held that Chalmers had married Miss Jean for her money, only to be foiled by old man MacRorah's lawyers. Polly said it was no wonder Mr. Chalmers was mean as a hard-shelled crab.

MacRorah didn't understand all the details, nor did she dare ask, but she did know that if there was one thing a reformed prostitute would know all about, it was men.

Besides which, MacRorah happened to know her father had wanted a son. Instead he'd been stuck with two daughters, one of whom had died in childhood and one who'd been blessed with her grandfather's cast-iron will. MacRorah didn't remember the grandfather for whom she'd been named, although she'd heard stories attesting to both his formidable wealth and his even more formidable stubbornness.

She readily admitted to being stubborn, if that meant she found it impossible to give in when she knew she was in the right. And while she preferred to call it pride, she could see how some might call it willfulness.

Sighing, she poked at a broken stay that seemed determined to stab her to death. One more week, she thought longingly, and she would no longer have to wear stays. She could dress as she pleased to go fishing and crabbing and bathing in the surf—she could even go gigging for flounders with a lantern at night once her mother was safely asleep.

But best of all, her father wouldn't be shoving Marvin Leaks under her nose every time she turned around!

Chalmers Douglas had a habit of slicking back his pomaded hair with the flat of his hand and then rubbing his two hands together. That very morning, he'd declared, "What you need, missy, is a husband to keep you on a short rein. Women ain't happy unless they've got a good man to take 'em in hand."

MacRorah had seen little enough happiness in her parents' marriage. She doubted that her friends' parents were all that deliriously happy, either, for all they might pretend in public. Carolyn's father, she happened to know, had run off with his wife's sister, although everyone in town pretended he'd simply gone on an extended trip. As for Sally Lee's father and Sara Ball's married brother, they were both known womanizers. MacRorah had that from an unexceptional source. There was no better source on who was philandering and who wasn't than the ladies at 41 Pecan Street, several of whom her mother had taken into her own home to train as cooks and housemaids so that they could improve their lot in life. Without them, MacRorah wouldn't know half of what she now knew. It was her opinion that every girl owed it to herself to become educated in the ways of the world.

The following week, MacRorah had yet another run-in with her father over the subject of marriage to that spineless worm, Marvin Leaks. It had ended in her being confined to her room for four days. On the very day her punishment had ended, she'd been astonished to learn that both Marvin and his mother had left town suddenly on an unexpected journey to St. Louis for an extended stay with Mrs. Leaks's family. MacRorah almost collapsed with relief.

Her father, of course, was furious when he found out, but it was her mother's reaction that puzzled MacRorah the most. Once or twice she caught a look of what almost appeared to be triumph on Jean Douglas's face.

MacRorah was on her way to the pantry for the starch bag to dust her white canvas shoes in readiness for the beach trip when she happened to overhear a conversation between her mother and that odd Mr. Gritmire from 41 Pecan Street. Jean was saying that something or other had not been precisely blackmail, with which the peg-legged ex-seaman had concurred, and then she'd mentioned that the whatever it was had cost her a tidy sum, but had been worth every penny.

But the most puzzling thing of all was the mention in the same conversation of the cost of a pair of one-way tickets to St. Louis.

Thoughtfully, MacRorah took her shoes and the

bag of cornstarch to the backyard, where she beat starch into the nap of the canvas until the worst of the smudges disappeared. By the end of the season they'd be ruined, of course, for ladylike or not, she still managed to ruin at least one pair of shoes whenever she went near the beach.

Blackmail?

How extremely odd. Jean Douglas was a quiet woman, rather plain. Until just recently, she'd been completely under the thumb of her domineering husband.

Or so everyone thought.

Lately, MacRorah had begun to wonder.

It was after three when Jean and MacRorah Douglas set out to the dressmaker for the final fitting of their new summer gowns. Three apiece. Not that MacRorah was all that interested in new gowns— lately she'd been far more interested in talking her mother into allowing her to attend Chowan Baptist Female Institute with a view to becoming a teacher. But for the past two summers she'd worn the same gowns, and although she hadn't added an inch to her five-foot-two inches since she was thirteen years old, her bosom had grown too full to stuff into her bodice without endangering the seams.

Besides, she had learned just recently that unless her mother spent her quarterly allowance from Grandpop MacRorah's estate down to the last penny, her father usually managed somehow to gain access to what remained. Invariably, he would drink it all up

or gamble it away on horses or dogs or roosters or
some such foolishness.

It occurred to her for the first time that the house
at 41 Pecan Street just might be an excuse to keep
that very thing from happening. After all, there was
only so much a woman could squander on clothes in
a town the size of Elizabeth City.

Mrs. Baggott's dress shop on Poindexter Street was
crowded, mostly with women who would be leaving
for Nags Head within the next few weeks. July and
August were the preferred months, but June had
been such a scorcher, everyone was panting for relief.

MacRorah exchanged news with the friends she
had seen just yesterday while her mother stood on
the stool for a hem adjustment. Then it was
MacRorah's turn to take the stool while her mother
gossiped with several friends from her church circle.

The others at first paid little attention to the two
new women who came through the door, other than
to notice that they obviously didn't belong there on a
Thursday afternoon. But shielded by a trio of half-
clad dressmaker's dummies, MacRorah stared, fascinated, at the pair. Their costumes and makeup were
certainly excessive for a simple fitting at Mrs.
Baggott's.

Conversation resumed as Jean Douglas told one of
her oldest friends that, indeed, she intended to take
her new maid to the beach with them, for she could
hardly leave the poor child alone, and she wasn't *that*
far along, after all.

Turning slowly on command, MacRorah listened absently to the usual chiding remarks about her mother's scandalous charity, which was tolerated because everyone knew that for all her advantages, Jean Douglas had never had an easy time of it.

"Well, I must say, the cook you sent me is a dab hand with pastries, and she don't cost much above half what I paid my last girl," declared Miss Ella Pomphrey. Which was one of the reasons, MacRorah suspected, why her mother got away with taking such women into her own home to train as cooks, housekeepers, and maids: Miserliness was another of her father's defining traits.

There was tea in the kitchen, cold lemonade for those who preferred it. Thursdays at Mrs. Baggott's were generally set aside for the so-called best families, with Tuesday evenings reserved for those poor women who were forced to work for a living. MacRorah had often wished she could be a fly on the wall some Tuesday evening. Working women were sure to be more interesting than those of her mother's set.

"Come look at this lavender taffeta, Jean. Now, tell me the truth, do you think it makes me look sallow?"

"I can't decide on the buttons. Belle, what do you think? Jet or pearl? Of course, for summer . . ."

". . . soft crabs on toast, and they were . . ."

". . . taking a Sunday School group for two weeks in July, and I told her . . ."

"Whaddya think of these earbobs Chalmers gave

me last night, hon? He says if I'm a good girl, he'll give me the matching necklace, too." One of the newcomers, a redhead, was speaking in a voice that was brash and a bit too loud.

"Just how good does he want you to be?" The giggling response of her companion fell into a sudden pool of silence.

"Better than Daisy, I reckon. She didn't last no time at all once she started putting on airs. Chalmers said he got enough of that at home, poor dumplin', but they do say his wife is—"

Snatching the half-pinned skirt from the assistant's hands, MacRorah jumped down from the stool just as her mother dashed out the door. The redhead stared after her, one hand covering her mouth. "What happened?"

"That was his wife, you fool!" snapped Mrs. Baggott, who knew every scrap of gossip in town, but had the good sense to keep it to herself. "This is *Thursday!*"

"My gawd, but I never meant to—"

MacRorah shoved the flashily dressed female out of the way and raced off after her mother. She had almost reached the street when the henna-haired courtesan caught up with her and grabbed her by the arm, spinning her around. "Please, miss—I never meant no harm, I swear! All I wanted to do was leave off this negli-jay to get it sewed up, and I thought—"

If the woman's eyelashes hadn't been so heavily layered with paint, they would have been singed by the look MacRorah gave her. "Kindly remove your hand from my arm, if you please."

"Miss—I guess it's Miss Douglas, ain't it? Honest to God, on my mother's grave, I swear I never set out to hurt nobody's feelings. I wouldn't embarrass your ma for all the diamonds in Fred Harmon's Jewelry Emporium. Why, every one of my friends has a real tender spot in their hearts for your ma, 'ceptin' maybe Darcy O'Briant. He ain't no friend of hers, I can tell you that much! But Jean Douglas!"

"Don't even speak my mother's name," MacRorah hissed.

Clutching MacRorah's yellow dimity sleeve with her ring-laden fingers, the woman continued to plead her case. "Chalmers said his wife didn't care— honest to God, he said she didn't want nothing to do with him no more, and he was to find himself a nice lady friend, so me and him—"

MacRorah, oblivious to several curious passersby, glared at the woman who clutched her sleeve. "I'm warning you, madam, if you don't release me this instant, you will regret it!"

Looking close to tears, the gaudily dressed woman continued to plead her case. "You're young yet, Miss Douglas, but one o' these days you'll understand that it's a man's world, and a lady's got only so many good years." As MacRorah pulled away, the woman's voice rose shrilly. "If she don't make the most of them, she'll more'n likely end up in the gutter. There ain't too many places like that house your ma runs down by the docks."

Blinded by tears of sheer fury, MacRorah snatched her arm free and whirled around, leaving the wretched creature wailing excuses after her. Intent on finding her mother, she had almost reached the street when she was suddenly snatched off her feet, captured by a pair of steely arms and slammed up against what felt like a stone wall.

"Whoa, there—easy does it." The voice came from somewhere above the crown of her straw skimmer. It took several seconds to realize that she was being held in the unbreakable embrace of a stranger who was staring down at her with a look that shifted quickly from amusement to speculation to something almost predatory.

Oh, my, he was dapper! Never in all her born days had she seen a man quite so flawlessly dressed. He smelled of soap, tobacco, and some light, crisp masculine scent. Belatedly filling her lungs with air, MacRorah was suddenly keenly aware of everything about him. Except for Seaborn and her father, she had never before been so close to any man.

He was dark in the way of a man who spent considerable time in the sun, his hair nearly black, his face lean and angular, while his eyes were deep-set, hazel—sparkling with gold and amber and sunlit green.

Sparkling with wicked amusement, more likely!

"Well, well, what have we here?" Even his voice was different, his accent clipped, yet velvety soft.

Belatedly coming to her senses, MacRorah glared at him, for all the good it did. He grinned down at her, his eyes dancing like sunlight on a shallow creek. It occurred to her only then that she was still suspended in the air, held in the arms of a strange man right there on Poindexter Street in the middle of the afternoon, where everyone in town could see her.

Oh, my mercy, she thought dazedly. Jabbing him in the chest with a finger, she demanded to be set down. "We do have laws around here, you know," she warned. "You can't just go about accosting people!"

"Not even when they're about to walk into the side of an ice wagon? No, I suppose not even then," he said with a sigh that seemed oddly out of place from such an outrageous man.

Slowly, ever so slowly, he lowered her to the sidewalk. It struck her, in the brief moment before she wrenched herself from his embrace, that there was a look of sadness, perhaps even bitterness, in those remarkably changeable eyes of his.

"Yes, well . . ." She brushed down her skirt, which was only partially pinned up. Not quite daring to meet his eyes, she muttered her thanks, resettled her hat, and offered her knight in black serge a curt nod before crossing the street at a sedate march.

Was it possible for a pair of eyes to bore a hole in someone's backside? She could still feel the heat of his gaze.

But the man was soon forgotten as MacRorah searched for a glimpse of her mother. Merciful heavens, as if she needed this humiliation on top of everything else!

* * *

Some five minutes later, Seaborn sauntered up to the place where Courtland Adams waited. "Sorry, Court—they were out of double coronas, can you believe it?"

The two men set out together to where Seaborn had left the buggy. Earlier they had driven along the waterfront so that Seaborn could point out the new depot and sidings beside the Pasquotank River's horseshoe bend where Adams-Snelling's lumber boats would come in through the narrows from Alligator Lumber Mills and offload directly onto the Elizabeth City & Norfolk siding.

Courtland had stopped off to send a wire to his father while his cousin Seaborn had gone to pick up a box of cigars, after which they had planned to return to the Adams home to wind up their business. From there, Court planned to catch a southbound train to explore additional timber sources before heading back to Connecticut, where the northern branch of the family-owned business was located.

Now, staring down the street past the clutter of carriages, buggies, farm wagons, and pedestrians, he asked, "Did you happen to notice a young lady crossing the street a few minutes ago? A girl, I should say, for she's certainly no lady."

"When? Where?" The gelding shied as a hound loped across the street, and Seaborn gave over to cursing all stray dogs.

"Forget it," Court muttered. The last thing he needed now was to let himself be distracted by a lightskirt, even one so delectable she hardly looked the part.

She *was* a lightskirt, wasn't she? What else could she be? There was no question about the redhead's profession, and the two of them had been carrying on quite a conversation, right out on the street. No decent woman would even recognize a whore, much less speak to her.

She was a lightskirt, all right. But God's teeth, she was delectable! New at the profession, from the look of her. Still, judging from the company she kept and from the few words he'd overheard, there could be no doubt of what she was.

If she had a handler, he mused, and if the blighter had half a brain, she'd make him a mint. She had the kind of fresh, innocent seductiveness that would enable her to play the professional virgin for a good long time if she was a halfway decent actress.

Over dinner, followed by a generous sample of what his cousin described as Buffalo City swamp juice, imported from a nearby county, Court allowed his mind to wander while Seaborn rambled on about some local belle he called Mickey. "Named her after her grandpa, poor kid. Thought it would open the moneybags, but old Gregory was too smart for that. Poor little devil, she has it rough at home. Her old man's a shabby piece of business—lives off his wife and treats her like dirt. Mickey, too, not that she ever says anything. Damned sight too plucky for her own good, if you ask me. Stands up to Chalmers every

time he swats her down—sticks her chin out and
gives back as good as she gets."

"Sounds as if she's lacking in brains."

"Oh, Mickey's plenty smart. Trouble is, she's just
too young to know how the world works."

"So marry her and teach her," Court suggested,
not particularly interested in a small-town drama
that had nothing to do with him. He had enough on
his own plate without borrowing trouble.

"Damned if I wouldn't marry her in a minute, only
she won't have me. Got some bee in her bonnet
about liberating womankind from bondage, or some
such claptrap. 'Sides, Dad would pitch a fit. Like I
said, her ma's good family, but her old man's a scoundrel. No breeding. Dad says Chalmers Douglas
would cheat at solitaire if he was fool enough to play
against himself."

But Court was no longer listening. Instead, he was
remembering the incredible way the little trollop had
felt in his arms. He wished he'd asked her
direction—hell, whatever she charged, it would have
been worth it! One sweet memory to take back home
with him. . . .

For a minute there, he could almost swear she'd
responded to him. But then, it had been so long
since he'd been free to hell-raise when and where it
pleased him that he'd all but forgotten how sweet it
could be.

"I think I can get logging rights to that acreage in
Tyrrell County without having to buy it outright.
Good farmland, once's it's cleared and drained. By

the time you come back through here on your way north again, I'll know how much it's going to cost us."

Court nodded absently. Logging rights. What did he care about logging rights? He'd been well into his second year of law studies at Yale, excited at the possibilities open to him, when those same possibilities had been snuffed out like a candle.

"Sounds good to me." Shoving his unfinished drink aside, he stood up and yawned, stretching his lean six-foot frame. "If you want to stay up all night, cousin, you'll have to do it alone. I've got a train to catch in a few hours."

"Maybe on your way back through town, I'll ask Mama to invite Mickey over for dinner. You'll like her, Court. Leastwise, you won't be bored."

Court murmured something appropriate, not overly excited at meeting the small-town belle who had his cousin dancing to her whim.

Chapter Two

Three days before they were to leave on the packet boat for Nags Head, Jean Douglas suffered a heart attack. She had woken up with an aching arm, eliciting from Chalmers several nasty remarks about whining, complaining females. Finally, to everyone's great relief, he had sent word for his gig to be set to and brought around, ordered his bag packed, and left for some undisclosed destination in Virginia.

By midmorning, it was obvious that Jean suffered from more than a mere muscle cramp. Her face was pale and damp and there was a look of panic in her faded blue eyes. MacRorah sent Polly scampering down the street to fetch the doctor.

"Get Teeny," Jean whispered, grabbing at MacRorah's hand as she stroked her mother's damp brow with a towel. "Must tell him—"

"Shhh, Mama, don't worry about—"

"Please!"

Teeny was Mr. Gritmire—that strange, wooden-legged giant who lived at 41 Pecan Street and acted as servant, driver, and protector whenever her mother left the house.

"All right, Mama, just as soon as Polly comes back with Dr. Meyer, I'll send Gordy to find him. There, now, whatever needs doing, you'll be up and taking care of it yourself in a day or so. It's this awful heat. Once we get to the beach, you'll feel much better."

In the massive tester bed, Jean Douglas's slight form scarcely lifted the covers. Her blue-shadowed lids slowly lowered. She seemed to be having trouble breathing, and MacRorah fought off the panic that had threatened all day. Her mother was *never* ill. For all her delicacy, who else in this town had the courage to walk the streets day after day, collecting those poor unfortunate creatures and seeing that they had a roof over their heads and food in their bellies so they wouldn't have to sell their poor bodies?

MacRorah didn't know all the particulars about the selling of bodies—she wasn't supposed to know anything at all about her mother's project, but it was impossible not to hear things. Thanks partly to Polly and partly to that awful woman at Mrs. Baggott's, she now knew far more than she cared to know.

Her own father! Oh, he'd made no secret of his gambling and drinking, but she had never even suspected the other. Although she supposed she should have guessed. More than a few otherwise respectable men, it seemed, had the morals of a tomcat,

while their wives were expected to look the other
way.

Clutching her mother's cold hand, MacRorah
prayed as she hadn't prayed since she had watched
her baby sister fade away before her very eyes.

On learning of the seriousness of Jean Douglas's
illness, thanks to Polly's quick tongue, the neighbors
wasted no time in bringing cakes, hams, and pots of
soup and greens. MacRorah's friends came that first
day in twos and threes, looking solemn and uncomfortable. Seaborn came as soon as he heard, and
MacRorah sent him to track down Mr. Gritmire. She
had no idea why her mother set such great store by
the ex-ship's carpenter. Nor did she know what her
father would say about the matter when he got
home, but if her mother wanted Mr. Gritmire nearby,
then nearby he would be, if MacRorah had to tie
him down and sit on him.

It didn't quite come to that, although the blond giant seemed about as comfortable in the stately house
on West Main Street as a cat in an ice house. However, he quickly made himself useful.

"There's furniture to be moved, Mr. Gritmire,"
directed MacRorah. Though he lacked a limb, Teeny
Gritmire was turning out to be more useful than
most men of her acquaintance. "I'll need a cot and a
larger washstand brought down from the attic, and
the canvas tub moved into Mother's dressing room.
Gordy from the stable can help you."

Three days later Jean was resting far more comfort-

ably under her daughter's watchful eye. The household quickly settled into a routine. When MacRorah
could stay awake no longer, Polly took over bedside
duties. Teeny Gritmire left word of his whereabouts
with Evelyn Espy, the manager Jean Douglas had recently hired to oversee the Pecan Street operation,
and then hurried back to the Douglas residence, moving into the tack room with young Gordy, son of one
of the residents of 41 Pecan Street, who served as the
Douglases' stable hand.

It was two weeks later that word came from Chalmers that he'd taken the Saratoga & Syracuse line
north with a group of friends and would return in a
week or so.

Pockets to let, MacRorah had no doubt. Her father had long since established a pattern of winning
a bit at cards, risking it on something else, and
then—when and if he managed to accrue a big
enough stake—joining his more affluent friends of
the horsey set.

After living on hopes and prayers for almost three
weeks, it was growing obvious to all that Jean Douglas was not recovering her strength. Each day she
seemed to fade a bit more. MacRorah saved her
tears until her mother was asleep. Her panic she
managed to forestall altogether, for it was upon her
shoulders that the management of the household
had evolved.

For something to do while she hovered at the bedside, she made lists. Lists of things to do, lists of

things for others to do, lists of amusing things to tell her mother when she recovered.

But composing lists couldn't keep her from knowing how unlikely that was—couldn't keep her heart from breaking by slow degrees, as she watched her mother grow weaker each day.

Polly, a bustling, straw-haired, freckle-faced country girl with a growing lump under her apron, proved to be a godsend, as did Teeny, who brought a woman from 41 Pecan Street to help out in the emergency. Mrs. George was a buxom female with a jaundiced complexion and an unlikely crop of hair that left her scalp as a muddy shade of tan and ended up the color of marigolds. The effect was rather startling when screwed up into a tight knot at the back of her head. The bright pink gowns she favored ill became her, but regardless of all that, she had proved to be an excellent plain cook.

Still, no matter how delicious the nourishing broths Mrs. George prepared, Jean Douglas continued to fail. "You'll be eighteen years old in another few weeks," she whispered one morning as Mac-Rorah urged her to take just one more spoonful. "I never got around to telling you—"

"Shhh, you can tell me later, Mama. Polly's going to bring up some fresh strawberries with cream in a little while, and I expect you to scrape the bowl clean right down to the daisies."

Jean's eyes filled, as did MacRorah's. That had once been Jean's favorite admonition to both her daughters. The nursery dishes had been decorated with a pattern of daisies, and Rosa had wept for days when she had accidentally broken the matching chocolate pot.

Sweet little Rosa. With wispy fair hair and eyes the color of an April sky—blue with just a hint of gray—she'd been a miniature image of their mother. MacRorah wondered why she must lose everyone in the world she loved. Then, chiding herself for harboring such a selfish thought, she leaned closer to catch her mother's faint voice.

"Must tell you, Rorie—you'll be a wealthy young woman. Papa left it all to you, you know, and once I'm gone, you must know how to—"

"No, Mama—don't even think about such things! I won't let you leave me! Why, we'll be going to the cottage soon—I told Teeny to see the captain and have him stand ready as soon as you're feeling strong enough."

A transient look of beauty colored Jean's wan face as she gazed up at her daughter. "Thank God you took after Papa," she whispered. "He'd be so proud of you."

"I'd rather be like you, Mama. No one really suspects how strong you are, do they? Who else would have had the courage to fly into the face of propriety to help all those poor creatures down on Pecan Street?"

"You—" Jean seemed to be having more difficulty in speaking than usual. MacRorah tried to shush her, but her mother was not to be shushed. "Don't let all I've done go to waste, Rorie. The account books are

. . . in my desk. Lease in the safe in Mr. Marshall's office. Teeny will tell you—he'll show you what needs to be done. Mr. Marshall will—"

"Shhh, I know, dearest, I know," MacRorah interrupted. "Mr. Marshall will take care of everything. If there's anything I need to know, I'll certainly ask him until you're on your feet again and can take the reins back into your own hands."

Those hands, so frail they seemed translucent, were twisting the bedclothes now. There was something else her mother wanted to say, and MacRorah knew she wouldn't rest until she got it said.

"You must promise me . . ."

Her heart aching, MacRorah waited, but her mother had fallen into the light sleep that had claimed her more and more frequently.

Two days later, Chalmers returned, smelling of cologne and strong spirits, slapping his driving gloves against his palm, a sure sign that he was displeased over something. Either he had lost whatever funds he'd wagered, MacRorah concluded, or he was disappointed to find his wife still malingering, as he called it—or both.

Probably both. MacRorah found it almost impossible to remain civil to the man, despite the fact that he was her father. Occasionally she found herself studying him, wondering with growing alarm if she would become more like him as she grew older.

She had certainly not taken after her mother. They were both small in stature, but where Jean was fragile and soft-spoken, MacRorah was healthy as a horse and too outspoken for her own good. Instead of her mother's pale blond hair and blue-gray eyes, Jean had inherited from someone—her grandfather, she supposed—plain brown hair and ordinary light brown eyes. Eyes that Seaborn had claimed, in one of his more poetic moments, to be the exact color of the water in a cypress swamp.

Less than a week after he'd come home, Chalmers announced his intention of leaving again. By then, MacRorah was more than ready to shove him out the door and bar it against his return. They had argued almost continually since he'd returned from his trip north.

First about Mrs. George. "Another of those damned tramps your mother insists on filling my house with!"

"It's Mother's house," MacRorah retorted before she could stop herself. "Besides, Mrs. George is an excellent—"

"Hush your mouth, girl!"

"At least she can cook, which is probably more than can be said for that—that orange-haired strumpet I met at Mrs. Baggott's last month!"

"I warned you to hush you mouth!" He lifted a hand, and MacRorah, with long years of practice, stepped nimbly back, putting a chair between them. "You don't know what you're talking about, girlie," he muttered.

"I know more than you think I know." She was

dying to take him to task for his philandering, but something about his expression kept her from it. For just a moment when he'd come out of his wife's bedroom earlier, he had looked almost . . . anguished.

Which was a sure sign that she was overwrought, MacRorah told herself. The only time her father looked anguished was when he'd overspent his allowance and tried, unsuccessfully, to wheedle more from his wife.

"If you'll excuse me now—*sir*—" she said through clenched teeth, "I'll just go and see if dinner is ready. Will you be dining in or out tonight?"

"Damn you, I'll lock you in your room again until you learn to honor your father!"

MacRorah bit back the immediate response that came to mind, knowing that it was no empty threat. Head held high, she repeated, "Will you be joining us for dinner—Father? We'll be dining upstairs in Mother's room, of course. I had a table moved in."

Muttering something about a house of pestilence, Chalmers wheeled about and stalked out of the room, bellowing for someone to pack his bags.

His was a carrying voice. MacRorah followed him as far as the hall to see Polly, elbows pumping and hair every which way, scampering for the stairs, rolling her eyes heavenward.

"I'll do it," growled Teeny, clumping in from the carriage house through the side door. "Git on in the kitchen, girl, I'll take care of the ol'—" He clamped his mouth shut and lurched up the wide stairway, his peg leg clicking his disapproval loudly against the polished oak.

Less than an hour later, Chalmers departed, muttering something about "... business ... Norfolk ... steamliner to London."

As if he could possibly scrape up the money for passage to London. He couldn't afford passage up Knobb's Creek!

It wasn't until three days later that MacRorah learned her father had not gone alone. Rumor had it—and rumor generally had some basis in fact—that he had taken his mistress with him. That same henna-haired female who had accosted her in the street that day she'd almost walked into the side of the ice wagon and been rescued by ...

Tiredly, she allowed herself to speculate on the identity of the dark-haired stranger with the sparkling hazel eyes. Strangers were hardly unusual in this small port city, yet as a rule, they kept to the waterfront.

This one had stood there in the middle of town, looking as arrogant as if he owned the world and all in it. Including herself!

Who was he? What was he doing in town? Was he married?

Not that it mattered one whit. All the same, she couldn't help but wonder. If Sally Lee had caught a single glimpse of him, she would have clean forgotten about poor Seaborn.

MacRorah arranged the flowers Miss Ida had brought just that morning and thought some more about the stranger, and then she thought about her father and wondered if he could really be so heartless as to go abroad while his wife was lingering at death's door.

Not that anything the man did came as much of a surprise anymore. Her chief concern at this point was to keep the news of his latest disgraceful behavior from her mother. As desperately ill as she was, it couldn't help to know her husband was off flaunting his fancy piece before the whole world.

Toward the end of the week, Jean seemed to rally. The entire household was jubilant. Teeny picked every flower in the garden, and Polly crammed them into vases and tiptoed clumsily into the sickroom to place them on every available surface.

Mrs. George baked a batch of rich peach cream tarts, and as the encouraging news spread over the back fence via Polly, who had a double-hinged tongue where gossip was concerned, neighbors began calling in droves, bringing all manner of gifts.

Meanwhile, MacRorah's eighteenth birthday had come and gone unheralded. She still spent every waking hour at her mother's bedside. Dr. Meyer came by each morning on his way to his office, and Teeny brought a variety of small gifts from the ladies and gentlemen at 41 Pecan Street—crocheted doilies, pen wipers, stamp cases, and a beautifully embroidered wall pocket, suitable for bedside use.

But it was the letter case made by a bedridden seaman who had crushed his spine falling from the rigging that brought tears to both Jean's and MacRorah's eyes. Beautifully carved of some rich, burled wood, it was inlaid with scrimshaw, the worked ivory forming the words, GOD BLESS YOU, J.D.

That night her mother seemed more restless than usual, though not in any great pain. MacRorah read to her and held her head while she sipped a watery broth and weak tea, but she seemed more eager than usual to talk.

"Mama, it'll keep," MacRorah murmured, holding the limp hand outside the cool linen sheet.

"No, no—I heard—heard about Chalmers and his traveling companion, and—"

"Oh, Mama, no! I'm sure it's all a mistake. Father wouldn't—"

"He would, my dear. We both know your father's a weak man. Not bad—well, not precisely—at least, not when we first wed. You see, he's been disappointed in life." Her eyes closed, and MacRorah waited, willing her mother to sleep, suspecting she wouldn't until she got whatever it was that was bothering her off her mind.

"Who told you?" she asked when she once more felt her mother's faded eyes upon her face.

Jean managed a smile, her first in days. "Remember when I asked you to open the window this morning before you went down for my breakfast tray? Polly has a habit of visiting with Ida Winslette's maid over the back fence when they hang the laundry."

"I'm sorry, Mama. I wouldn't have had you know for anything."

"Child, you can't protect me from this world—it's far too late for that—but perhaps there's still time to protect you."

"I don't need—"

"Yes, my dear, you do. Listen, now, for I've little time to waste. When I married your father, he was a handsome, charming scoundrel, and I loved him dearly, even though Papa threatened to shoot him and send me to a convent."

"A convent! But we're not even—"

"I know. A little thing like logic never bothered your grandfather, Lord love him. He was a strong-willed man, my father was—as honorable and upright as a steeple. I'm glad you took after him instead of—"

Her voice had faded so that MacRorah was forced to lean over the bed to hear. "Well, never mind that now. The thing is, dearest, Papa was right. Chalmers is still a scoundrel and a weakling, but he loved me. I know he did. And I loved him. A long, long time ago, he made me feel . . ."

"Oh, Mama—" MacRorah didn't want to hear this. It was easier to hate her father. She didn't want to have to try and understand him after all this time.

"When Rosa was born, he was so disappointed. We'd wanted a boy—and then I took the childbed fever and nearly died. Dr. Meyer said I shouldn't have any more babies, and Chalmers—ah, Rorie, he wept, he wept on my bosom."

I don't want to hear this, Mama. Not about Father!

"From that day until this, he never touched me

again, and yet I know he loved me. In his own way, he still does."

Jean might believe it. MacRorah had her doubts. Nevertheless, she knew better than to argue with her mother, especially now.

"Looking back, I believe it was when he found out how Papa had left his money—a small allowance to him and the bulk of the estate to be paid directly to me in quarterly allotments through Mr. Marshall— that he started to change. It did something to his pride. That's when he started gambling, you know."

MacRorah patted her mother's hand. She suspected her father had been gambling since he was in short pants. It was seldom a fever that came on a man late in life.

"Like I said, he began to change. It was almost as if using brute strength made him feel more manly. Looking back, I believe his conscience was hurting him, and he simply wanted to hurt back. Then, too, he had already taken up with loose women, and that made him feel even more wretched after he—after one of our disagreements."

"Oh, Mama, please don't," MacRorah whispered.

Jean smiled, a wan effort that brought tears to her daughter's eyes. "Men—men are different from us, Rorie."

"Mama, don't talk anymore. Rest now. By next week, or the week after, we'll be setting out for Nags Head, and you can lie on the porch and watch the seagulls feeding, and the children playing about in the water, and—"

"With you leading the pack, I don't doubt," said her mother with a feeble imitation of her old sweet smile. "You've grown into a beautiful woman, MacRorah. Someday soon, you'll be tempted . . ."

Her voice trailed off, and MacRorah patted her hand gently, praying she would sleep.

"No, don't stop me, dear, for I must get this said. I must warn you—about the web that can entangle an impressionable young woman before she ever learns what life's all about."

"Mama, I promise you, I'm no impressionable young woman," MacRorah assured her mother, laughing through her tears. "I don't think I ever have been."

"Nevertheless, there comes a time . . . when a girl believes she's found love." A vision of a certain dark face with deep-set hazel eyes flashed before MacRorah's mind. Ruthlessly, she blocked it out.

Suddenly Jean gripped her daughter's fingers with surprising strength. "Listen to me, Daughter—don't *ever* let yourself get tangled in any man's web, no matter how tempting. It's a man's world—"

It's a man's world. She had heard those same words quite recently.

"—and I never want you to have to go through what I've gone through. Marriage—" Jean closed her eyes momentarily, her lids crepelike and darkly shadowed. "Marriage for a woman is the cruelest form of indenture, for death is the only release."

Tears ran freely from MacRorah's red-rimmed eyes. "Rest now, Mama—please don't do this to yourself. We can talk again when you wake up, but rest now . . . please?"

"Hush, now. Don't argue. You were always so willful, MacRorah," said Jean, and MacRorah couldn't help but smile through her tears.

"If I had it to do over, child," Jean said fervently, "I would never have married any man, no matter how greatly tempted I was. I'd be mistress, never a wife, for with no legal ties to hold them together, a man must constantly court his mistress if he wants to keep her."

"Oh, Mama, I doubt if being a mistress is all that wonderful. What happens to a woman when a man tires of her? How many of the women at 41 Pecan Street started out that way, thinking their protector would be around forever?"

The small sound that issued from Jean's colorless lips was only a ghost of laughter. MacRorah's heart quietly broke in that moment. "My poor innocent child, you were not even supposed to know about such things as mistresses and protectors—yet I suppose you must. Promise me, Rorie, don't let any man ruin your life." Jean whispered urgently, and MacRorah, lifting that pale, cold hand to her own wet cheek, would have promised her own life. They had never talked openly of such things before. MacRorah told herself it was a mark of her own maturity that her mother now felt free to discuss such matters.

She refused to believe it was a mark of her mother's desperation.

* * *

Three weeks after MacRorah's eighteenth birthday, Jean died quietly in her sleep. The minister asked after her father, and MacRorah, distraught, promised to write to him, although she had no notion of where to direct a letter. Then the Reverend Mr. Bricklaier was shown out and the family lawyer was shown in.

"Would you please try to find my father, Mr. Marshall?"

"Most assuredly, I'll see to it right away. We must talk, Miss Douglas," the elderly man said. "I haven't wanted to bother you while your mother was so ill. However, your grandfather's will is rather, um . . . unique, in some ways. I do believe—"

Just then, Seaborn was shown in by Teeny, who was acting in the unlikely capacity of butler. "Mickey, I'm so sorry—I just heard. I've been out of town and I came over as soon as Mama told me the news."

The lawyer accepted his hat from Teeny, but lingered for a final word. "The service has been arranged for the day after tomorrow, I believe, Miss Douglas. Perhaps I can call on you one day next week. Good morning, Adams. My best to your father."

MacRorah stared unseeingly as Mrs. George went around lowering the window shades. The two men spoke a few more quiet words, and then the lawyer murmured condolences and edged out the parlor door. MacRorah, wishing the whole world would disappear and allow her to curl up in a ball and cry forever, hung on to her composure by a thread.

The moment they were alone, Seaborn gathered her into his arms. Needing desperately to be held, she went willingly.

"I stand at your service," he said quietly, and she nodded against the scratchy surface of his navy serge coat.

"The minister and Mr. Marshall have made most of the arrangements. Mr. Winslette helped, too, and everyone's been s-s-so k-kind, but Sea, I just d-d-don't know what I'm going to do," she wailed.

It was only a momentary weakness. The instant she felt Seaborn draw a deep breath, felt his hand began to stroke her shoulders, MacRorah tensed, wondering if he was about to reissue his standing proposal. It had been a running joke between them since she'd turned fifteen, but as greatly as she valued his friendship, this was not the time for a proposal of marriage, even one between friends. In her present condition, she might even weaken and accept, and that would never do. Sea would never ruin her life, but she had promised her mother. . . . oh mercy, what *had* she promised?

"Ride with me to the church for the service, Seaborn, will you do that? If I'm going to fall apart, I'd rather you were there to help scrape up the pieces and put them into some semblance of order before I show my face in public." She moved back, a watery smile on her face, and to his credit, Seaborn Adams didn't press his advantage.

"Send that big bruiser who's waiting to show me out if you need anything at all, love, but tell him to leave his knife behind."

MacRorah shook her head in gentle remonstrance, knowing that Seaborn still had a hard time accepting the type of people Jean had collected around her. Not that he'd ever spoken a word of criticism. "Teeny's as gentle as a lamb. Mama found him soon after his leg was crushed, when he had nowhere to go and no one to care for him while he mended. He would cut out his own heart sooner than hurt one of her friends."

"If you say so," Seaborn said, and after kissing her on the forehead, he left.

To anyone who didn't know Jean Douglas, her funeral might have seemed an odd affair. At MacRorah's right side stood Seaborn, looking somber and several years older than his twenty-four years in his funeral attire.

On her left side stood Teeny Gritmire, who had transferred his allegiance from Jean Douglas to her daughter. For the sad occasion he was fitted out in an assortment of black garments from the Women's World Relief Missionary Barrel and a new leg neatly turned from red Honduras mahogany. The knife he habitually wore at his side was conspicuously missing, his battered face suspiciously damp. From time to time, a sob shook his massive shoulders, which was nearly the undoing of MacRorah.

Black did not become MacRorah. Despite the

weeks of indoor nursing, traces of an unfashionable suntan lingered on her face, making her look sallow in the black silk, quickly run up by Mrs. Baggott from a pattern in the pages of *Harper's Bazaar*. Nevertheless, Polly had done her best, pinching her mistress's cheeks and pawing through Jean's jewelry case to find a pair of simple jet earbobs.

"Hmph! Not much to choose from," she'd said at the time, but MacRorah had paid no attention. Under her gown, she wore Granna MacRorah's pearls for comfort, not for beauty.

The front half of the church was filled with Elizabeth City's founding families, as was only fitting for the funeral of the daughter of old Gregory MacRorah.

It was just before the service began that the contingent from 41 Pecan Street began to file in. Heads turned. Gasps were heard quite clearly. Everyone knew about the rambling, ramshackle old house wedged in between the oyster houses and salons near Tiber Creek down on the waterfront, but it had not occurred to any of them that "those people" would dare attend a respectable funeral.

Beside her, MacRorah felt Teeny stiffen. Seaborn twisted around to glance over his shoulder as the murmur of whispers grew louder. "Dear God in heaven," he breathed softly, and just as the organ wheezed to life, MacRorah herself turned to see what had caused all the commotion.

Directly behind Judge and Mrs. Camden, their son and daughter-in-law, and their two elder grandchildren, sat the Winslettes, the Balls, the Pooles, and the Stevenses. The next few rows were filled with acquaintances, including Mrs. Baggott, and the greengrocer, Mr. James, and old Mrs. Garnette, who had hemstitched half the linens in town.

Then, as MacRorah watched, the entire back row began filling with women garbed in the most remarkable splendor. Bedecked in beads, feathers, and glittering paste jewels, they settled themselves with a self-conscious flurry. Numbly, MacRorah noted that three were in an obvious stage of pregnancy. Another one looked far too pale to be in good health, but all had put on their finest feathers to pay their last respects to Jean Douglas.

Immediately behind the colorful row of reformed ladies of the evening sat half a row of the roughest, most battered-looking men anyone had ever seen west of Water Street. The most cursory glance summed up two eye patches, half a dozen earrings, one set of crutches, one notched ear, and a remarkable variety of scars and facial hair.

Against all reason, MacRorah's heart suddenly swelled with pride in her mother. Though most people had considered Jean Douglas timid and frail, surely no one had ever made such a difference in the lives of those poor unfortunates whom society would prefer to sweep under the carpet.

Let the town gossips have their field day. As for MacRorah, just knowing that her mother had been so well loved was more comforting than all the fine words the Reverend Mr. Bricklaier was even now preparing to speak.

Ignoring the shocked and disapproving expressions on the faces of her neighbors, she stood and turned to face the congregation. Gazing out over the heads of people she had known all her life, she smiled her welcome to everyone, including all those in the two back rows.

Suddenly her heart felt lighter. She felt as if she had made an important stand—a beginning. The Lord only knew what would come next, but she stood ready to meet it. For her mother's sake, she would take up the reins and go forward.

Chapter Three

ℰ

As summer wore on, life, at least on the surface, gradually returned to normal. The brand-new Elizabeth City & Norfolk chugged noisily in and out of town hauling freight and passengers. Packet boats set out almost daily for Nags Head with a full load of passengers, furniture, and servants, accompanied by enough livestock to see them all through the summer.

Along West Main Street, with the temperature reaching sweltering temperatures by midmorning, bees droned lazily on the mock orange bushes, the produce carts began to hawk the first watermelons. A prominently pregnant Polly clashed with Teeny at least once a day. First he insisted she not lift anything heavier than a broom. Next, he ordered her to confine herself to the first floor, which quite naturally ruffled her feathers. As a result, she spent more time than ever huffing up the stairs, supporting her rapidly increasing bulk with one hand, determined

not to be bested by any ham-fisted, one-legged, meddlesome son of a sea cook!

As for Teeny, he had more or less taken over the
running of the two households. Wooden leg ringing
out sharply on the polished oak floors, he made his
rounds, overseeing the stables, the supplies, and the
security of both houses. If he felt any longing for the
seagoing life he had left behind, it never showed in
his stolid demeanor.

MacRorah refused to allow herself to dwell on the
guilt she felt over her relief at her father's continued
absence. She had done all she could on that front.
Cables had been sent to the U.S. Embassy in London, and almost daily she expected his return. On a
fast ship, he could have been home long before now.

Most of their neighbors had already left for the
beach, but those who remained still called to offer
sympathy and advice. To each caller, she served lemonade and a tray of Mrs. George's best cakes, and
when the talk turned, as it invariably did, to the dangers of a young, unprotected woman living alone, she
murmured that her father would be home most any
day now.

She made lists of things to be done: Her mother's
clothing was sent around to the ladies of 41 Pecan
Street; her keepsakes were packed away until such
time as MacRorah was able to deal with them without falling apart.

For the most part, she managed to keep busy, but
sometimes, when she least expected it, the memory
of a pair of deep-set hazel eyes would return to taunt

her. Devilish eyes. Laughing eyes. Surely she had only imagined the look of sadness and bitterness?

Oh, well. She would never know, and that, perhaps, was for the best. If there was one thing her mother had taught her and taught her well, it was never to allow herself to fall under the influence of any man. Especially not a man who was more fantasy than reality.

A frequent visitor was Sally Lee's grandmother.

"You're more than welcome to come stay with us, MacRorah. Your mother would have wanted me to look after you," said the elder Mrs. Winslette, who despised the beach and stayed on in town when the younger members of the family made their annual pilgrimage.

"That's kind of you, ma'am, but I'd better stay here and look after things. Father will be home any day now."

Unfortunately, she had no choice but to stay. She had wanted to buy a small house of her own and become her own mistress, but under the terms of her grandfather's will, her inheritance was to remain invested, the interest to be deposited quarterly into her new bank account in the form of an allowance. And because of the promise she had made to her mother, she would be spending the bulk of that allowance on the tenants of 41 Pecan Street. The rest of the money, unfortunately, would hardly support a separate household.

After seeing Mrs. Winslette out the door with a promise to consider her offer, MacRorah sent Gordy around for the gig. Perhaps by now Mr. Marshall had heard something from her father, or at least found some loophole in her grandfather's will that would enable her to invest some of her capital in a small cottage and thus establish her independence.

In the second-floor office of the firm of Marshall, Petree, and Gobble, Mr. Marshall, who habitually expressed disapproval by tapping his fountain pen on his desk, was beginning to sound like a teletype machine as he assured her that no such loophole would ever be found in any document prepared by the firm his father had established two years before the War Between the States.

"But men can invest in real estate. Why can't I?"

"That is entirely different, Miss Douglas."

"Then there's no way, unless I go against my mother's last wish, that I can afford to live independently, is that correct?"

"Out of the question, young lady. In my considered opinion, your mother's generous heart simply overcame her common sense. That—that *place*"—tap-tap-tap—"should be shut down immediately!"

"Because it costs too much to operate?"

"Well, now—harrumph! Miss Douglas, no decent, umarried girl"—tap-tap-tap—"has any business consorting with the dregs of society. I feel it's my duty to advise you to allow me to buy your way free of the lease." Tap-tap-tap. "In which case, you might eventually find yourself in a position to look into the possibility of, er—ahem! That is, if your father agrees, I feel sure we could work out some arrangement."

"My father has nothing to say to the matter, sir. You, of all people, should know that it was arranged between my grandfather and old Judge Charlie, that the only MacRorah property he can lay hands on is his quarterly allowance and whatever Mama gave him."

"Yes, well, as to that—"

"Was it MacRorah money that leased the Pecan Street property?"

"It was, but—"

"Is it MacRorah money that keeps it in operation?"

"Yes, of course, but—"

"In other words, everything that belonged to my grandfather was left in trust to Mama and to whatever children she should have, or at least that's my understanding of the matter."

"Well, yes, technically, that is true. However, we cannot be entirely certain that an actual court challenge would—"

"Has anyone ever challenged either will?"

"Well, now, as to that, I believe there is a clause that discourages your father from—"

"Precisely! So it's unlikely that anyone will upset the apple cart at this late date. In which case, I have no intention of turning all those poor people out into the streets again. They depend on me now."

"Yes, yes, but if you was to marry, your husband—"

"Bother my husband! I don't intend to marry!" MacRorah wanted to tell the musty old stick that it was none of his business, but unfortunately, it was, as he had managed her family's affairs for years.

Even more unfortunately, she couldn't afford to alienate the man who doled out her allowance and held in his possession the lease on 41 Pecan Street.

Horace Marshall removed his wire-rimmed spectacles and polished them with a small square of flannel. Carefully, he replaced them on his nose and then cleared his throat several times while MacRorah fidgeted. "Your dear mother, bless her, was too softhearted for her own good. I often told her that. You'll do well to allow yourself to be guided by older and wiser heads, Miss Douglas." He smiled as if afraid his withered cheeks might crack. "A young lady in your position simply cannot take such—such *people* into her own home. It simply won't do, my dear. Why, you could end up murdered in your own bed."

"I could end up walking into the side of an ice wagon and breaking my neck, too, but the chances are, I won't," MacRorah said dryly.

Ice wagons! Where on earth had that thought come from?

"Mr. Marshall, would you answer one more question?"

"Miss Douglas, I've been your mother's lawyer since the day she married your father. My father before me served in the same capacity for your grandfather MacRorah."

"Fine. Now—isn't there any *possible* way I can keep 41 Pecan Street and still buy a very, very tiny cottage? I don't take up much room, and it doesn't have to be in the best neighborhood. Even some-

thing out in the country would do." She endured a
barrage of pen-tapping while she waited, taking silent inventory of the rows of leather-bound books on
the far wall. Surely there was one law among the
thousands written there that would give a woman do-
minion over her own affairs.

Ah, but the laws were written by men.

"Well?" she prompted when the throat-clearing
and the pen-tapping threatened to drive her into
doing something drastic.

"I'm afraid that would be impossible, Miss Douglas."

She drew in a deep, steadying breath, praying she
could escape without breaking a chair over someone's head. "Then thank you very much, Mr. Marshall. I believe that covers everything." Rising
gracefully, she smoothed her black, lightweight
worsted skirt over her hips and gathered up her driving gloves, her reticule, and her parasol, which she
carried in honor of her mother's often expressed wish
that she stay out of the sun long enough to lose her
unfashionable tan.

"Now, to another matter, Miss Douglas, I'm
pleased to inform you that just this morning we sent
off a cable to our embassy in Paris, as we've never
heard from London, inquiring after the whereabouts
of your father. The moment we have word—"

But MacRorah was already gone. Out on the sidewalk, she expelled her breath explosively, tugged the
high collar of her broadcloth blouse away from her
throat, and untied her horse.

"Men!" she muttered under her breath. Furious at the double standard that allowed men to—to *use* those poor women and cast them aside, yet forbade their wives and daughters from even acknowledging their existence, much less attempting to help those in need, MacRorah was more determined than ever to carry on her mother's good works.

Although she still wasn't entirely certain what constituted "use" in such cases. Her mother had refused to explain the intricacies of the relationships between men and their mistresses and whores. She wasn't even certain what separated one calling from another, but evidently there were degrees of wickedness known only to the initiated.

Which MacRorah wasn't.

However, anyone with a grain of sense could tell when a woman was weak, ill, hungry, and in dire need of a helping hand. Wickedness had nothing to do with it.

"Wake up, Nellie, it's time to go home," she snapped at the elderly mare, one of the two left in her father's stable. The good Lord only knew where Chalmers's gelding was. A showy piece of horseflesh, he'd won it in a poker game and, for all she knew, could have sold it to pay his passage to England. Or lost it in still another game of chance.

She had just turned onto East Main Street, headed west, when she caught a glimpse of a familiar face tooling past in a hired gig. Nearly dropping the reins, she turned to gawk as the dusty vehicle turned off onto Martin Street.

Could it possibly be?

Surely not. Not after all this time. If he'd still been in town, she would have run into him before now.

Nevertheless, the single glimpse of a half-remembered face was all she needed to fuel another spate of daydreams, and if there was one thing MacRorah prided herself on, it was her down-to-earth common sense.

Which made it all the more implausible that at least a dozen times in the next twenty-four hours, she found herself falling still in the middle of some task or another, reliving a moment out of time.

Was this what it felt like to be in love?

Merciful heavens, no! She didn't even know the man's name. It probably hadn't even been the same man she'd just seen. And besides, love had no place in her plans for the future.

Yet there was no denying that something unusual had happened to her all those weeks ago. As startled as she'd been at the time—as upset over the scene in Mrs. Baggott's—she distinctly remembered feeling a disturbance in the region of her heart when she'd found herself swept off her feet into the arms of a dark, handsome stranger. Not a twinge, precisely— more like a flutter.

A windy digestion from too much cabbage and sweet potatoes? That was far more likely than love, she told herself as she set about polishing her grandmother MacRorah's sterling coffeepot, which was heavy enough, even empty, to herniate the staunch-est servant.

* * *

The very next day, MacRorah insisted on being given a complete guided tour of 41 Pecan Street, a rambling onetime boardinghouse right on the waterfront that was in the process of being renovated after a recent fire—the third such fire in the past year. She was determined to settle into a comfortable routine and forget all her foolish whimsies.

"And this here's the sewing room," Teeny said proudly, gesturing at the newly refurbished attic. "Them there tables is for cutting patterns and such like. Mr. Weisel provides patterns, and once the wimmen passes muster, so to speak, Mrs. Baggott takes 'em on until they moves out on their own."

She was shown the classroom, where Mrs. Espy conducted lessons in reading, writing, and simple bookkeeping; the kitchens, where instruction in plain and fancy cookery was held daily; the dormitorylike bedrooms, plainly furnished but scrupulously clean; and the nursery, where several children from cradle to rocking horse age were being looked after by a very pregnant woman with improbably blue-black hair.

Teeny drew the line at showing her the men's quarters. "Naught but bunks, hammocks, lockers an' a washstand. It ain't fittin' fer a lady to see where a man sleeps, ma'am. This here porch I shut in is where they spend most of their time. Some does woodworking and some does fancy work."

"Fancy work?" The only fancy work MacRorah knew of was needlework, at which she was an abject failure. Under her less than skilled fingers, thread tangled, needles broke, and scissors invariably were lost and ended up wedged down beside the cushion of her father's favorite chair, through no fault of her own.

It seemed that a few of the ex-seamen were skilled at the unlikely art of crocheting, but as Teeny explained, "A crocheting hook ain't that different from a fid or a nettin' needle. Them that can splice and net can work line to most any pattern."

MacRorah's interest in the home for reformed prostitutes and disabled seamen did not go unnoticed among the townspeople. The waterfront was considered no place for a lady, but friends of long standing made allowances. Twice a week, MacRorah ordered her mother's gig put to and drove herself to the home, where she spent an hour or more. She told herself it was her duty to see to the needs of the residents, particularly the children, but suspected it was partly a desire to prove something to the world.

Although just what it was that she wished to prove, she could not have said.

In addition to the standing arrangement with Mrs. Baggott to take on qualified seamstresses, there was another arrangement with a local agency to place qualified cooks and housekeeper. No attempt was made to disguise the background of the would-be hirelings, but such was Jean Douglas's reputation that few applicants failed to be hired.

There was still talk, of course. Especially as

MacRorah made no bones about her activities. "Miss Emma's card party?" she responded one day to an invitation from Sally Lee. "Thursday? Oh, what a shame. Thursday's my day to take my ladies to Dr. Meyer."

"Honestly, Mickey," Sally Lee said, "I don't know how you can stand to associate with those—those—"

"Women?"

"You know what I mean. Why, there's no telling what kind of diseases they have!"

"According to Dr. Meyer, Crystal has a cyst on her elbow that needs lancing and Georgette suffers from swollen veins and bunions. And of course, Eulalia's due to deliver—"

"MacRorah!"

"Well, for heaven's sake, everyone knows where babies come from!"

"Yes, but not everyone goes around talking about it."

"Perhaps if more people did, fewer babies would be born to women who can't look after them properly."

Predictably, Sally Lee gasped. MacRorah tried to look knowledgeable and superior, but too well she remembered the time before Rosa was born. She'd been so excited about the prospect of having a tiny baby to play with that her mother had taken her by the hand and allowed her to feel the baby's movement.

"Did you feel that, darling? She just kicked her little foot."

Aghast, MacRorah had backed away. Then she'd run and hid in her room, where she'd cried for hours, thinking her mother had somehow eaten their baby.

She knew more about such matters now. Not a great deal more, to be sure. However, it was knowledge she was never likely to need, as she never intended to get close enough to any man to catch a baby.

That evening, Seaborn came by to see her. For the sake of propriety, he insisted they sit outside on the porch. MacRorah was uncomfortably aware that she should have been the one to insist on such a move, but then, the proprieties had never ranked very high with her.

"I've been out of town for the past few days," he said, seating himself in the slatted swing. "Adams-Snelling is going to own half the South, at this rate. Timber rights, at least."

"Does it bother you? All these carpetbaggers coming down here and buying up everything in sight?" MacRorah seated herself beside him, and they set the swing in motion.

"War's over, Mick. Besides, you forget—Dad's folks came from Connecticut. I've got a passel of kinfolk up there. Got a cousin in particular I want you to meet. He comes through right often—just left town, matter of fact."

MacRorah nodded, not really interested in Seaborn's northern kinfolk. "Mr. Marshall still hasn't been able to locate Father. I reckon he's lying low, trying to escape some gamester he cheated out of his shirt," she said with more than a little bitterness.

There were few secrets between the two friends. Although neither MacRorah nor her mother had made a habit of talking about their situation, MacRorah suspected that the neighbors had a fairly good idea what went on in the tall white mansion on West Main Street. There were days on end when Jean Douglas had not kept a single engagement.

MacRorah's punishment for an offense, real or imagined, had usually been confinement, but more than one of her friends had seen her flinch from a light touch on her back. Usually she claimed a bad case of boils, or perhaps a strained muscle from playing tennis.

"That brings me to my reason for dropping by," Seaborn said, touching his necktie before smoothing his sandy blond hair. "Mickey, you, uh—that is, we've always been friends. And now that you're alone, it seems only reasonable to me that—"

"Sea, if you're going to ask me again to marry you, I beg you not to." In the warm, fragrant dusk, she couldn't be certain of his expression, but she prayed he wasn't going to get sticky about the matter. "The thing is, I like you too much."

"Then there you are—for I like you, too."

"You don't understand." She placed her hand on the back of his, and he reversed his palm to clasp her fingers. Her hands were small, but surprisingly strong. "I never intend to marry. If Mama taught me one single thing, it was never to place myself under any man's rule."

"Rule! As if I ever would." Then, with a wry grin, he added, "As if I ever *could*! Mickey, you scare the bejabbers out of most folks, and them you don't scare, you shock speechless. A little supervision might do you a world of good. Not that I'd ever try," he added hastily, seeing her expression. "But you might as well know, folks are talking. It was one thing for your mother—what I mean is, for an older, respectably married woman, to uh . . . consort with people like that."

"Consort? Are you saying my mother *consorted*?"

"Your mother was a saint, but Mickey, we both know that you've lifted half the eyebrows in town, what with one thing or another. Trouble is, you've always been a—a tad outrageous."

Biting back a reluctant chuckle, MacRorah jabbed him gently in the arm. "Just a tad?"

"All right, a great gob, then. And it don't help, knowing you're living here all alone with only that one-legged brute and two prosti—uh, unmarried women of questionable virtue."

She could no longer hold back the laughter. It bubbled forth, easing the sudden tension, but she remained adamant. She refused to marry, she refused to move in with Seaborn's Aunt Clara, whose whole house reeked of the weeds she burned to ease her asthma, and she refused to get rid of Polly, Mrs. George, and Teeny and let Mrs. Adams find her some respectable help from the agency.

"What would I do without them, Sea? They're my friends. Mrs. George mothers me, Teeny watches over me like a great big guard dog, and Polly's the dearest little thing, though she's led an unfortunate life. Of course, she does have a tendency to gossip."

"A tendency! Her tongue's likely sunburnt from hanging out all the time. I swear, when she and that girl that works for Ida Winslette get together over the back fence, sails start flapping all the way out to the narrows!"

MacRorah laughed, hoping the question of marriage had been laid to rest once and for all. If she were ever going to marry any man, Seaborn would probably be her choice. He was kind, easy to manage, and she trusted him—which was more than she could say about most men.

"It would be so easy, Mickey. Your father would understand. Your mother and I always got along real well. She'd have understood, too."

Sighing, she leaned her head briefly on his shoulder. "Sea, I like you entirely too much to wish myself off on you. I'd make a horrible wife, and then you wouldn't be my friend any longer. Let's leave things the way they stand, shall we?"

"You're probably right. You lead me around by my nose as it is. If we were married, you'd likely end up running Adams-Snelling and I'd wind up wearing ruffled aprons, but who's complaining?"

"If I thought there was a chance of taking over your father's company, I'd marry you in a minute," MacRorah said with a soft, husky chuckle. "Do you

know how many careers are open to woman?" Before
he could reply, she ticked them off on the fingers on
one hand. "And that doesn't include prostitute,
whore, mistress, and—"

"MacRorah!" Seaborn slapped a hand on his brow.
"All I can say is, your papa had better come home
before it's too late—if it isn't already."

A week later, the town was abuzz again. This time,
it was seeing MacRorah marching down the street to
Dr. Meyer's office, a whimpering infant in her arms
and a lady of obviously dubious gentility following
along behind, weeping gullies through the thick layers of paint on her sagging face.

"Hush up, LaFrance! This child needs a doctor's
attention. After that, we'll see about getting you
sorted out!"

She had gotten word of the woman and her baby
from one of the ticket agents down near the depot.
Aging, although obviously not too old to give birth to
a child, the woman had been evicted from her room
over one of the saloons after being forced to work
more and more hours for less and less money, leaving
a crying infant alone for long stretches of time.

MacRorah had not taken time to argue. Instead,
she had given the woman an ultimatum. Rather than
risk losing her child and being sent to jail, LaFrance
Murphy had meekly packed their few belongings and
followed the angel of vengeance to whatever fate
awaited.

"Shush, now, love, don't cry so," MacRorah whispered to the infant. "Soon we'll have a dry napkin and a belly full of nice warm milk, and then the world will look entirely different."

"Ma'am, I needs a drink somethin' awful." The orange-haired woman hurried to catch up, but fell behind again after one searing look from the avenging angel. "Mebbe later," she muttered.

Teeny would have his hands full keeping this one on track until she dried out. Some of her girls were like that until they were made to understand that if they wished to turn their lives around before it was too late, they must follow the rules, and rules number one and two specified no men and no alcohol.

MacRorah knew she lacked the patience that had made Jean Douglas the patron saint of the fallen and downtrodden. What she lacked, however, in patience and saintliness, she more than made up in determination.

Two women, friends of her mother's, gasped at the unlikely parade, then crossed the street rather than pass her on the sidewalk. Both pointedly averted their eyes. Sara Ball Poole and Carolyn Stevens ducked into the nearest store, which happened to be White's Feed & Seed Store, which MacRorah ventured to guess neither one had ever patronized before.

Mr. Hawthorne, enjoying a cigar outside the newspaper office, caught sight of MacRorah and her companions and nearly strangled on cigar smoke, causing his companion, Henry Adams, Seaborn's father, to take off his spectacles, polish them, and make a show of putting them on again in order to glare at her more effectively.

Jouncing the squalling infant in her arms, MacRorah wheeled into Dr. Meyer's office, which was located between the offices of Adams-Snelling Lumber Company and the newspaper office, her head held high. "In here, LaFrance. Now, try to stop shaking. No one is going to hurt you. Once we get you straightened out, you're going to feel better than you've felt in years, and so is this little dumpling. I do believe he has your eyes."

Two men watched as the odd trio disappeared inside the narrow brick office building. From a nearby alley, one dapper young man in a garish plaid suit spat on the cobblestones and swore. Darcy O'Briant had thought his troubles had ended when Jean Douglas had popped off. He hadn't figured on her meddlesome young chit taking over, but he'd figured it was only a matter of time before she lost interest and he could once more do business without losing half his girls before he could even get them broken in.

"Damn the bitch and all her kind," he muttered. "Who the divil appointed her to rescue every damned whore in Pasquotank County?"

The son of a waterfront whore who had left him behind when she'd headed west, Darcy had started with nothing and worked his way up to where he now controlled all but a handful of prostitutes in the small riverfront town. Before he was done, he intended to be the biggest procurer on the East Coast.

At the tender age of twenty-four, he was already one of the most powerful men in town, respected by both his whores and the gentlemen they serviced. With his reputation at stake, he wasn't about to let some sass-mouthed little chit spoil his game.

Three fires, and not a damned one of them had done the trick! And that was even before the old broad had turned up her toes. As for the girl, he'd thought all the gossip would have made her back off, but to see her prance by with her nose in the air, she didn't even know she was the talk of the town.

Darcy didn't invent all the rumors—he didn't have to. But he sure as hell helped fan the flames. Trouble was, both the Douglas females had the nerve of a brass monkey and more friends than a Quaker meeting house!

And though it galled him to admit it, when he wasn't cursing her, Darcy often found himself applauding her guts. By damn, wouldn't he like to have a plucky one like her in his string?

Even so, one way or another, he was going to have to get rid of her. But first he would have to find some way to separate her from that great hulking watchdog, and that might not be so easy to do.

From the opposite side of the street, where a gig had halted to allow passage of a funeral procession, another man watched intently. Courtland Adams looked older than his twenty-six years, older than he had looked only a few months before when he'd first laid eyes on the small, enchanting lightskirt.

Dammit, he *felt* older! That last scene with his father had been brutal. Their relationship—never more than coldly cordial, from the time he'd been sent off to school at the tender ago of nine until he'd left law school after the death of his older brother—had deteriorated steadily. Sometimes he wondered why he didn't chuck the whole thing and start fresh on the West Coast—anywhere where he wasn't constantly reminded that he was the youngest son, the wild one—the cuckoo in the nest, if his own growing suspicions had any basis in fact.

But although it killed him to have to admit it, his father needed him now. Court took what small pleasure he could find in knowing that even more than he hated doing the old man's bidding, the cold-blooded bastard hated having to ask him. If that made him an unnatural son, so be it.

For his mother's sake, Court knew he couldn't walk out on his responsibilities. The lumber business wasn't so bad. It was a far cry from what he'd envisioned for himself, but when he chafed at the bit too much, he tried to put himself in the position of a pair of aging businessmen who had staked their lives to build a multistate empire, only to lose both their heirs.

Snelling still had a daughter, Diana. Court's father was left with him. The dynasty would continue. He owed his parents that much.

He owed his late brother, Rick, that much. If

Court hadn't been laid up on the weekend of the annual regatta, and if Rick hadn't agreed to fill in for him, both Rick and Andrew Snelling's only son, Junius, might still be alive today. Rick would have married Diana Snelling, and the two young men would have slipped into the harness, leaving Court free to pursue his own dreams.

Following the progress of the woman who had unexpectedly captured his imagination a few months ago, Court wondered if the pressure wasn't getting to him. The last carriage of the funeral procession rolled past, and he wondered how she could have possibly had a child and still retained that look of virginal innocence. He wondered if she even knew the father's name.

As his eyes slid past the raddled old hag trailing along behind the young whore and her child, he wondered why the hell he was wasting his time daydreaming about an amber-eyed fancy piece when he had a perfectly good mistress back home who was paid to take care of his physical needs.

He sighed. And then he swore. Willing or not, it was time he quit dragging his feet and got on with his wedding plans.

Chapter Four

𝒞

As summer slowly waned, MacRorah almost forgot about her father. She still grieved for her mother, but she dealt with her grief in her own commonsensical fashion by staying as busy as possible during her waking hours so that she usually slept as soon as her head hit the pillow. After the first week, she dried her tears for good, telling herself that tears never mended a broken teapot. If her heart ached and her life sometimes felt hollow, so be it. At eighteen, she prided herself that she was in complete charge of two households and making a good job of both.

Although there were times when her staff was more hindrance than help. She was dressing to go out on what she had come to think of as her morning rounds when they started in again, this time directly underneath her open window.

Polly had evidently gone outside to hang the light wash. Teeny, seeing her struggling with the small basket of wet clothing, had gone charging to the rescue.

"Damn fool woman, ye're bound and determined to strain yer goozle! Here, gimmee—"

"I'll goozle you, you one-legged pirate! Gimme back my clothes basket!"

"Maybe I ain't got but one leg, but I got more brains in me big toe than you got under all that frizzled yaller hair!"

"Brains! I'll show you brains! You drop them clean clothes an' get 'em all muddy, and you'll be scraping what little brains you got up off'n the floor in a thimble!"

"Pipe down, woman! Now leave me be! I'm gonna tote this here basket out to the wash line, elsewise you're gonna pop a gasket and launch that young'un o' your'n here in the yarb patch, an' Miss Mac, she don't need no more little bastids to worry 'bout!"

"Why, you self-righteous son of a she-buzzard, you might call yourself a butler's mate since you pushed yourself in on Miss Mac's good nature, but you ain't no more'n a washed up old souse who ain't good fer nothin' but flappin' his tongue!"

"You're a good one to talk about tongue-flappin'! Damned if you ain't wore my ears plumb down to the headbone with your prattling! The bigger yer belly gets, the more yer tongue clatters!"

"Yes, well, I might be swole up some, but leastwise I ain't—"

"Swole up! You look like you done swallered a blasted dinghy, oars an' all!"

Polly was independent to a fault, a trait which MacRorah could not but admire. Teeny was equally determined to protect the small, pregnant ex-prostitute, and MacRorah could only wonder whose pride suffered most in their frequent battles.

Grimacing, she adjusted her straw cartwheel and collected her reticule. Half the time she forgot to wear a hat at all. She'd long since left off all but a single lawn petticoat, but just lately she'd felt it necessary to pay a bit more attention to the conventions. With half the people she passed no longer seeming to recognize her, and a few of her male friends going so far as to leer and snicker among themselves, she was beginning to think perhaps she had gone too far in leaving off half her undergarments and unfastening the top two buttons on her shirtwaists.

She was on her way out the front door, Gordy having brought the gig around, when Seaborn strolled up the front walk. "Not now, Sea, for pity's sake," she grumbled into her reticule as she searched for her driving gloves. He had come to plague her again about living unchaperoned and Lord knows what other offenses. Honestly, for a man of twenty-four, he was almost as starchy as old Mr. Marshall!

"Caught you just in time," he greeted cheerfully. "Want to ride out Riverside Drive? They say Mrs. Pickett's whatchamacallits are blooming up a storm."

"Crepe myrtle, and no, thank you, I've errands that need doing."

"Errands that just happen to be down around the

waterfront, no doubt. Mickey, Mickey, what am I going to do with you?" he asked with mock despair.

"You might try giving me credit for being able to manage my own affairs."

"People are talking, Mick."

"People always talk. As a rule, it's the male pillars of society that give rise to all the gossip."

Which was a topic neither of them cared to pursue, as Chalmers Douglas was a prime example of the species.

"Ride with me," MacRorah offered impulsively. The truth was, no matter how hard she tried to pretend otherwise, she was still uncomfortable in the Pecan Street neighborhood, with its wharves bustling with seamen, its oyster houses bustling with fishermen, and its saloons overflowing night and day. The fact that Teeny was usually somewhere in the vicinity keeping an eye on her didn't always save her from speculative looks and impertinent remarks. Word spread quickly along the waterfront among the newcomers that Miss Douglas was off-limits unless one wished to have his head squashed like a beetle on a melon vine, but that word sometimes did not spread quickly enough. Now and then she heard the most peculiar rumors about herself—which, of course, no one who knew her would ever believe.

"Are you going past the office?" Seaborn asked cautiously, and when MacRorah admitted that one of her errands was a quick visit to Dr. Meyer's office to collect a bottle of digestive salts for Mrs. Espy, he shoved his hands into his pockets and hunched his shoulders. "Reckon I'll pass, then. Dad wouldn't appreciate seeing me out gallivanting when I'm supposed to be hard at work arranging the shipping on a load of Alligator River juniper."

Or more likely, MacRorah thought as she watched him saunter off down the sidewalk, old Mr. Adams wouldn't appreciate seeing his son and heir off gallivanting with the shameless Douglas girl. She hadn't missed the disapproving looks the old man sent her way whenever she took one of her charges downtown to visit the doctor.

The narrows were crowded with traffic. Produce-laden sloops, schooners, and sharpies—hulking lumber boats bound for points north and south. Now that the season was winding down, packet boats made almost daily trips between Nags Head and Elizabeth City, carrying the late-goers to the beach for the last few weeks of summer, returning with those who had gone forth at the very beginning of the season.

Which made it rather odd, come to think of it, that Sally Lee, Sara Ball, and Carolyn had not been around to see her. She was almost certain she'd caught a glimpse of them going into Mr. White's Feed & Seed store just yesterday.

Yes, and now that she thought about it, the few friends she had run into lately had seemed rather . . . cool? Yes, decidedly cool. Of course, it could be that they were simply uncomfortable around someone who was still in mourning, although MacRorah had put away her black, which was unbearably hot, and gone to grays and lavenders. Still, some people felt a certain constraint around the bereaved.

In the gazebo out behind the Adams mansion on Church Street, Courtland and Seaborn Adams sprawled out in the comfortable rattan chairs Mrs. Adams had recently had covered with bright chintz cushions, sipping their after-dinner drinks. Iced tea on Court's part—something rather stronger for Seaborn, who had reached the maudlin stage.

"D'I ever tell you about this girl I'm half in love with? Name's Mickey—naw, not Mickey. Name's MacRorah. Crazy name to pin on a girl, ain't it? To my way of thinking, names make a man. Woman, in this case. Now, you take Sally Lee—sweet little name. Girl's a reg'lar wilting lily. Never say boo to a goose."

Seaborn finished his drink and poured more from the decanter on the dark-green-painted rattan table. "Court? Y'sleep?"

The older man stirred, frowned at the half-empty glass in his hand, and sighed. "No, I'm not asleep. Tired, I suppose. Too much traveling." He had just gotten into town again the night before.

"This girl I was telling you 'bout? You gotta meet her, Court. You'll like her. Thing is, she looks like a Chris'mas tree angel, but don't you b'lieve it. Ol' Mick's f'rever up to some rig that'd make your hair stand on end."

"Hmmm," was the enigmatic response.

"D'I ever tell you 'bout the time she blew up the cemetery?"

Court lifted one of his dark, straight brows in an unspoken invitation. He'd been too caught up in his own affairs to pay much attention, but he'd always been fond of his younger cousin. The truth was, this Mickey creature sounded a hell of a lot more entertaining than the woman he was about to buckle himself to for life.

For Seaborn's sake, he hoped so. There were probably worse things in life than being bored, but at the moment, he could think of very few.

"Blew the whole dang thing to kingdom come—leastwise, that's what all the santi—sanc—ti—monious old biddies thought when they came spilling outta church after Wednesday night prayer meetin'. Didn't actually blow it up, o' course."

"Of course not," Court murmured obligingly. He wondered what Diana was doing at this moment. Getting dressed to go out on the town, no doubt. For a woman with all the personality of a dressmaker's dummy, she led an exhausting social life.

"Thing was, Mickey, she'd got ahold of these fireworks—bought 'em with her Sunday school c'lection money she'd been squirreling away instead of droppin' it in the basket, so by the time Halloween rolled around, she had buckets o' the stuff, all ready to set off from th' bottom of a fresh dug grave—can't remember who passed away, but as I was sayin', Mick—she was 'bout ten years old as I recall—real pistol! Wanted to do it all herself.

'Course, we all knew about it. Too good to keep. We were hid out all over the cemetery, crouched down behind tombstones when the thing blew, and I mean, there was mud *everywhere*!"

"She sounds like a wonderful woman, I'm sure," Court observed, thinking the female sounded as if she should be put away for the good of the town.

"Nobody snitched. Not even when the paper wrote it up—young barbarians, they called us. Said we was a threat to the very pillows—um, pillars—o' society. Li'l ol' Mick in her pigtails and pinafores, a threat to the pillows o' society! Nearly split my sides laughin', I can tell you."

"Hmmm," was all Courtland could come up with. He might need to have a word with his Uncle Henry about this radical female who seemed to have entrapped his gullible cousin.

On the other hand, every generation should have the privilege of making its own mistakes. God knows, he wished it for himself.

Even though it was hot as blazes in the kitchen, MacRorah had lately begun taking her meals there, much to the disgust of her outspoken staff. She could tolerate the heat a lot better than she could tolerate dining alone at a table for twelve in the formal dining room where her only company was the echo of cutlery, china, and crystal.

The kitchen was far more comfortable. Here there was no protocol. Mrs. George served the table directly from the range, and then they all served themselves. They were just finishing the lemon fig ice cream, compliments of Mrs. George's recipe and Teeny's good cranking arm, when the doorbell sounded.

Teeny excused himself, dragging his napkin, which fell to the floor. Polly muttered something about clumsy old fools and started to retrieve it, and MacRorah, laughing, reached out and caught her shoulder, shoving her back into her chair.

"Don't you dare! If you tip over, we'll never get you back on your feet again. I'll get it."

"Old fool coulda picked up his own napkin," the maid grumbled, her freckled face flushed from even so small an effort.

Teeny's return was heralded by the distinctive click-stomp of a boot and a wooden peg, which he polished nightly with lemon oil and beeswax. "Mr. Adams come to call, Miss Mac. *Ag'in!* I done tol' him to wait out on the porch."

Rising, MacRorah shook her head in resignation. Her own mother could not have been more solicitous of her reputation, she thought, hurrying through the hall to the wide front porch. She supposed she should be grateful to her self-appointed protector. "Good evening, Sea, would you like a dish of ice cream? I don't think the temperature has dropped a smidge since the sun went down."

Seaborn bobbed to his feet, clasping the brim of his summer straw in his hands. "No, thanks. I—uh, wanted to talk to you, Mickey." His usual grin was absent. He seemed oddly ill at ease.

"It's probably cooler inside," said MacRorah, holding the door open in invitation.

"This is just fine."

"Goodness, I've never seen you so fidgety."

"Yes, well . . . Mickey, did you ever think about running off and getting married?"

"Married? Why on earth would I want to do that?"

Raking his fingers through his carefully groomed hair, Seaborn snapped, "Why would anyone want to do that? To—to be together, you goose!"

"Me? With *you*?" Closing the door behind her, she joined him in the wide-slatted swing. "Honestly, Sea, would you be serious for once in your life?"

"Dammit, MacRorah, I am serious! I'm proposing to you, aren't I? That's about as serious as a man can get!"

"You've proposed to me before, and we both know if I'd accepted, you'd have run screaming off into the night."

He eyed her sourly. "Don't be too sure of that."

MacRorah blinked several times and composed herself, hands clasped in the lap of her lavender liberty-print skirt. It wasn't like Seaborn to swear. It wasn't like him to call her by her name, either. She'd been Mickey to him ever since she'd lost her baby teeth. When she wasn't MacTrouble, or MacRumpus, or Mac-something even worse.

"It's my father." He gripped the brim of his hat until she was sure the straw would snap.

"Your father? Mr. Henry's ill?"

"There's nothing wrong with him, only he says I have to stop hanging around you so much."

MacRorah was silent. What could she say? Henry Adams had disapproved of her ever since he'd caught her trying to make wine in his carriage house from grapes she'd stolen from his vines.

Leaning back, Seaborn set the swing into motion. He hadn't planned to come here tonight. If she'd said yes, he didn't know if he'd even have the nerve to go through with it, but she needed him. And he'd always cared for her. "He's wanting me to spark up Sally Lee because he thinks she'd be a good influence," he said with a look of desperate misery on his normally placid face. "Thing is—well, you know Dad. Anyway, I sort of promised him I'd give it a go, but now I don't know. If I thought you'd have me . . . that is, I thought I'd offer you one last chance. I mean, if you're interested."

"You and *Sally Lee Winslette*? Good Lord, Sea, you can't stand her! You always said she was so sugary sweet, she made you break out in spots."

"Yeah, well . . . Sal's not so bad now that she's grown up."

"Is it the money? Is it because her family owns half of three counties?"

"Oh, hell, Mick, if you must know, it's you! You've been running wild all your life, and since your mama died and your old man ran off—well, it just don't look right, you living here all alone and messing around with those—those you-know-whats."

MacRorah's usually soft, full lips thinned dangerously. "What's the matter, Sea, is your father afraid I'll catch a bad case of immorality and pass it on to his precious only child?"

"You can joke all you want to, but Dad said if I didn't break it off with you, he'd write me out of his will. I thought Court was in a bad fix," he said morosely, "but I'm not in much better shape than he is, poor devil."

"Court?"

"Cousin. Adams and Snelling. Connecticut end of the business. Look, the thing is, Mickey, I don't reckon the old man'd actually go s'far's to cut me clean out, but still, you see what kind of a fix I'm in, don't you? I just wanted you to understand that if I don't come around much from now on, it's not that I don't still care for you, because I do. Always did, more's the pity—probably always will. It's the company you keep. Folks are talking. Now, me, I know there's not a lick o' truth to it, but all the same . . . Thing is, I've warned you. You're just too muleheaded to take good advice when it's offered."

With a dignity that could only be called queenly, MacRorah stood, her back poker-straight, her neck rising swanlike from the high, lace-edged collar of her lilac voile shirtwaist.

Seaborn stood up too quickly, setting the swing into reckless motion. "You do understand, don't you, Mick?" he pleaded as the swing whacked him on the back of his white-flannel-clad legs. "I'll always be your friend, it's just that . . ."

Looking down her short nose, which was quite an

accomplishment as he topped her own five-foot-two inches by at least half a foot, MacRorah said, "I understand perfectly, Seaborn. Don't give it another thought. Oh, and if you're on your way around to the Winslettes', please give Sally Lee my best. I'd do it myself, but whenever I happen to see her, she's always in too big a hurry to stop and talk. But then, I suppose it's no wonder, now that I'm officially beyond the pale."

Swallowing an ache so big it threatened to choke her, MacRorah thought of what she knew of old Henry Adams—that he'd kept a mistress for years right under his wife's nose. And as for Mr. Winslette, it was an open secret that half the children on that farm of his down near Weeksville had his red hair and the Winslette nose.

So much for friendship. She might have known that Sea was no more faithful than the rest of his sex!

For the next two days, MacRorah stayed home. It rained incessantly, which brought relief from the heat but didn't help her attack of the dismals at all. She sipped Mrs. George's remedy for the monthlies, a toddy that was more sugar and spice than liquor, but which comforted, even so, and she fumed about the injustice of it all. Men! Casting stones right and left, when every single one of them lived in a glass house! She scribbled endless lists. She plotted.

And then she sent for Polly.

By the next afternoon, once the rain had cleared

away and clothes were once more being hung out on backyard lines, the news was already sizzling through town. Miss Douglas had hired a private investigator down from Norfolk to look into the affairs of a certain gentleman whose identity she preferred not to mention.

The consequences were laughably predictable. MacRorah took some small comfort from knowing that half the men in town would be scrambling to cover their tracks, thanks to a preponderance of male hypocrites suffering from a guilty conscience.

Let them squirm. They deserved it! She'd have given anything to be a fly on the wall inside the best men's club in town. Lacking the opportunity, she ran as many errands downtown over the next few days as she could drum up, making separate trips to the apothecary shop to buy each item on her shopping list. Downey's Bunion Cream for Mrs. Espy and Dr. Thompson's Eye Water for Mrs. George, and then another trip for a jar of Mrs. Ruppert's Face Bleach for Polly's freckles.

It wasn't only her imagination, she thought as she gleefully clucked Nellie into a respectable plod. Half the men looked at her as if she were a pestilence sent down from on high to test them. The other half regarded her with looks that could only be called guilty.

Something else she had noticed—a few of the women who had snubbed her only last week had smiled at her today. Poor timid little Margaret Doyle, whose father drank like a fish and whose two older brothers were overbearing bullies who chased after anything in skirts, if gossip could be believed, actually found the courage to clasp her lace-mitted hands over her head and give a soft cheer.

Things were looking up. Oh, my, yes!

The very next afternoon, Sara Ball and Carolyn came around to invite MacRorah to go out for ice cream and stop in Mr. Weisel's to look over the new fall patterns.

MacRorah canceled her plans to go with Teeny to take LaFrance and her baby for their weekly visit to Dr. Meyer. Teeny was certainly capable of managing without her, and only now did MacRorah dare admit how very lost and lonely she had felt ever since her friends had abandoned her.

It was one thing to appear brave and independent and carefree.

It was quite another thing to feel that way.

"MacRorah, tell me it's just another of your pranks," Carolyn Stevens said as soon as they set out.

"I'm sure I don't know what you're talking about."

"A private investigator? A *certain gentleman*? Honestly, even my mother was singing your praises, and she's never been your greatest fan. Admit it—you did it deliberately to prick—"

"Every hypocrite in town. I never saw so many men in church as last Sunday," Sara Ball said, giggling. "Every single pew was filled, and everyone was cutting their eyes around, trying to figure out who the *certain gentleman* was."

"Really? I wasn't there—I wasn't feeling quite the thing." MacRorah had been afraid of being snubbed again, if the truth were to be known.

Carolyn leaned closer. "You want to know what I think? I think it's the best prank you've pulled since you blew up the graveyard."

Sara Ball skipped to catch up. Only four-foot-eight, she was at a disadvantage, but made up for it with her bustling energy. "Not only that, since you left off your stays—oh, yes, you did, because Polly told Miss Ida's Ella Mae, and she told Ophelia, who does our laundry—"

"Get to the point, Sara," interrupted Carolyn. "What Sara's trying to say is that half the women in town have decided not to wear stays between June and September, because even though they might squeeze in your waist a few inches and push your bosom up so it looks bigger, they cause such a miserable heat rash, and Patsy Coltrain fainted the other day right on the courthouse steps from squeezing herself up so tight, trying to make people think she wasn't in an interesting condition."

"And Mama told Daddy right to his face that if he didn't like it, he could just wear one himself, because he was just as fat as she was, and she was tired of suffering alone."

The three young women giggled their way through large dishes of Mr. Gilbert's French vanilla ice cream with tutti-frutti on top, and for a little while

MacRorah almost succeeded in convincing herself that nothing had changed since the last time she had sat at the same marble-topped table with her two best friends.

It was a clerk in Mr. Marshall's office who was responsible for leaking the news, even before the lawyer had had time to call on MacRorah and prepare her for the latest blow. Within hours, it was all over town.

They said that word of poor Jean's death had chased Chalmers Douglas from London to Brussels and finally caught up with him in Paris, months after the fact. They said that, hounded by guilt and knowing that his daughter would never forgive him anyway—everyone knew what had happened that day in Mrs. Baggott's place when that painted tart had blabbed his name out right in front of Jean and MacRorah—Chalmers had up and married his redheaded mistress.

Before Mr. Marshall had even finished telling her the news, MacRorah felt her temper begin to simmer. It couldn't be true. Not even her father would be so unfeeling.

But there it was, spread out on the table before her, the words fairly jumping off the paper as she picked up the cable to read it again.

"Bereaved? I'll just bet he was bereaved," she seethed, crushing the thing in her fist. "So bereaved he went right out and married that—that—"

"I believe her name is—was—Miss, um— Chartreuse Flowers."

"Of course it is. And mine is George Washington! Can he do that, Mr. Marshall? So soon? Is it legal?"

"I'm afraid so, my dear."

"Oh, God, I hate him!"

Chartreuse Flowers—Chartreuse Douglas now. Oh, she couldn't bear it, for her mother's sake! To think that there was now another Mrs. Chalmers Douglas who was without doubt the very same painted trollop who had accosted her outside Mrs. Baggott's shop.

What had she said then? That a lady had only so many good years, and it behooved her to make the best of them?

"Lady, ha! She might think she's ended up on easy street," MacRorah said under her breath as she came from showing the lawyer out. "She'll change her mind soon enough. Being a mistress is one thing. Being a wife is quite another."

Chapter Five

D id I happen to mention that I've decided to become a mistress?"

MacRorah dropped the bombshell in the middle of the monthly meeting of the West Main Street Young Ladies' Sewing Circle while they worked busily at patching quilts for the church bazaar to raise money for the poor starving orphans.

Orphans in other countries, that is. Naturally, the local variety was exempt. Ignoring the gasps, she jabbed her needle angrily into the hashwork she was making of joining a square of yellow foulard to a triangle of pink cambric.

"A mistress!"

"A *what*?"

"MacRorah Douglas, you shouldn't say such a thing!"

"Honestly, Mickey, you'll do anything for attention, won't you?"

Was that truly all she was doing? she wondered,

anger dwindling into a defeated sort of misery. She'd conceived of the notion the day after that blasted cable had arrived. Still numb with impotent fury, she'd happened to overhear a conversation between two gentleman concerning the demands of their respective mistresses, one of whom insisted on her own bank account, the other on having a cottage in her own name.

The road to freedom had suddenly been emblazoned before her very eyes. She'd had her life all neatly arranged until news of that blasted cable had hit town! Well, sauce for the gander was sauce for the goose!

"We know you're only teasing about being a you-know-what," said Frances Gilbert, Ice Cream Gilbert's granddaughter. She'd been the first to recognize the familiar glint in MacRorah's eye when she'd first arrived that afternoon. "You're only saying it to get back at your father, aren't you? When's he coming home, have you heard? He's not bringing that—" here her voice dropped off to a whisper, "that *female* with him, is he?"

"Oh, he wouldn't!" Sally Lee cried.

"Not in a million years," put in Sara Ball Poole. "Mr. Douglas might be—that is, he might not be— well, you know what I mean, and I'm sorry, MacRorah, but we all know how your father is. But surely he can't expect the decent people of this town to accept that *creature,* with Jean Douglas, bless her sainted heart, not even cold in her . . ." Her bright pink face clashed with her carrot-colored hair. "Well, you know what I mean."

But MacRorah was no longer listening. Swallowing the lump in her throat, she tried to put aside her sewing only to discover she'd stitched the blamed thing to her skirt. "I'm sure I couldn't care less if the pair of them are run out of town on a rail," she said airily, trying surreptitiously to break the threads. "Father can do whatever he blessed well wants to do, for I've already made up my mind. First thing tomorrow, I'm going to advertise for a lover, and he'll set me up in a cottage all my own and give me everything I ask for."

There was another outburst of gasps.

"A lover!"

"Advertise! In the *North Carolinian*?"

"Mickey, not even *you*—!"

Lifting her miserable face, MacRorah pinned on a look of haughty disdain. "My dears, can you think of a better way to gain the same kind of power over a man that men have over every single one of us? We all know—and don't pretend you don't know what I'm talking about, because in a town like this, everyone knows everything about everybody. We all know that men spend money like water on their—their lightskirts. You all saw those earbobs that creature was flaunting in Mrs. Baggott's shop, but did you know that Father all but cleaned out Mama's jewelry box? I daresay that's what the pair of them have been living on all this time."

There was another round of horrified exclamations, and then one after another, the cream of Elizabeth City's young feminine society leaned forward to confide some real or suspected offense committed by a male member of a the so-called best families.

". . . and both of them naked as a pair of herrings, right there in the carriage house!" whispered one shocked voice.

"Oh, my mercy, I never! But did you hear about . . ."

"Yes, but wait till you hear what Martha Dillard told Miss Vinnie Hatcher while they were sitting in Dr. Meyer's waiting room last week."

"Oh, I knew all about that, but can you guess who was seen sneaking in the back door at Sadie Varney's social last Tuesday?"

"Lordy, did you about hear that, too?"

Few male citizens escaped condemnation, whether directly or by association. Feeling vindicated, not to mention considerably more determined than when she had first made her proclamation, MacRorah took center stage once again. "So there you have it. Just cause for a woman's revolution. If you can't lick 'em, join 'em, I always say."

"I never heard you say that," Sally Lee murmured.

"Hush up, silly, it's a figure of speech," put in Sara Ball. "What I want to know is, what are you going to say in your advertisement, Mickey?"

"Oh, well, I—That is, I never said I was planning to place an actual advertisement in the newspaper. I thought perhaps an unsigned notice on the bulletin board at the Riverside Club would serve."

"But Mickey," wailed a horrified Frances, "our own fathers belong to the Riverside!"

MacRorah shrugged. "Shall we say the Royal Flush, then?" The private club, located just across the river, catered to the town's up-and-coming young businessmen. It was a place where they could entertain out-of-town guests away from the dampening influence of the elder generation.

"But how will you ever manage? Women aren't allowed there. At least, ladies aren't." Frances looked horrified.

"Ladies aren't allowed much of anywhere, are they?" MacRorah shrugged. "I do believe it's time someone turned the tables, don't you?"

"Yes, but—well, that's all very well, but—"

"What Frances is trying to say," put in Carolyn, "is, how will you go about it? I mean, how will you choose? The richest? The handsomest?"

Thus challenged, MacRorah quickly invented a set of rules. "I'll write down a list of all my requirements, and then I'll simply hold auditions. Whichever man comes closest to meeting my standards—and, my dears, those standards will be exceedingly high, I assure you—why, then, I'll consider accepting him as my mister."

"She means like a male mistress, Frances," snapped Sara Ball, who was liking the notion more and more. "Golly, I wish I had the courage. . . ."

"Papa would kill me, he'd absolutely wring my neck!" squealed one of the younger members of the circle.

Head high, MacRorah smiled her most enigmatic smile. "But then, I don't have that to worry about, do I? Lucky me, my father's ashamed to show his face in this town."

Her head was still high when she left a few minutes later, feeling angry, embarrassed, and more than a little afraid of what she'd gotten herself into.

MacRorah Douglas, however, was no quitter. One way or another, she was going to teach this town and every man in it a much-needed lesson in equality!

Having just returned on the 5:44 after looking over the company's new timber acreage on the Tar River, Courtland caught a ride to the Adams home and walked straight into a heated debate between his Uncle Henry and his Cousin Seaborn. An extremely uncomfortable reception after an extremely tiresome journey was the last thing he needed. The train had been crowded, the club car too noisy and smoke-filled for comfort. Court had stepped outside and spent the last part of the journey east watching the rails spin off into the distance and dwelling on the untenable situation at home.

Cutting his father a resentful glare, Seaborn apologized to Court. "Sorry, old man. Meant to collect you from the depot, but the time just slipped up on me."

Henry Adams grunted something about whipper-snappers.

"Don't give it another thought," Court said blandly.

The atmosphere in the walnut-paneled library was

even thicker than the cigar smoke in the club car had been. Perhaps, Court thought with bitter amusement, it was the fate of every man to quarrel with his elder. Some obscure generational, or perhaps territorial, rite of passage common to all male animals.

Personally, he'd found travel helped ease the tension. While it might not solve the problem, at least for a little while it allowed one to escape a father's unspoken condemnation, a mother's silent misery— or a fiancée's chilly indifference.

Seaborn rubbed a hand over his sweaty forehead, looking embarrassed. "Say, if you want to go over what you found out, Martin Stone's your man. He handles all our rights agreements. You remember old Marty? Might be a good idea to run over things with him while the meets and bounds are still fresh in your mind. You can probably catch him out at the Royal Flush. You remember that place across the river where we had supper last time you were in town?"

Court remembered. As tired as he was, he would rather have gone straight upstairs and slept the clock around, but if his presence in the Adams household was an embarrassment, he'd do better to take himself off and allow his two southern relatives a chance to cool down before he reported on the details of his journey.

"Then, if it won't inconvenience you, I believe I'll change clothes and take supper at the club. May I borrow your gig, Sea?"

"Here, take my membership card, too—you'll need

it to get in. Word of advice, though. Don't drink with Sam Quincy and don't play poker with Joe Harvey."

Seaborn looked as if he would have given a box of Havana's finest cigars to go with him. Court gave him a thumbs-up sign behind old Henry's ramrod back and headed upstairs for a hasty wash and a change of clothes.

The sun was just setting some thirty minutes later when he tooled down Main Street, turned left on Water Street, and headed for the ferry over the narrows.

The Royal Flush catered to a rowdier set than the more opulent Riverside Club. It occurred to Court that he could do with a little rowdy company before he headed north again.

It also occurred to him that this just might be his last chance.

By the time he'd greeted Stone, his uncle's secretary; passed a few words with several other men he half-remembered meeting on earlier trips south; and done justice to a fine meal of baked shad, washed down with what Martin Stone termed Buffalo City swamp juice, which was considerably more powerful than the scotch Court usually enjoyed in moderation, he'd forgotten whom he was supposed to avoid drinking with and whom to stay away from at cards.

Fortunately, no one seemed interested in getting up a game.

Talk was general, mostly business and baseball, turning only later in the evening to women. It didn't take long for someone to bring up the infamous notice some female whose identity seemed to be an open secret had smuggled into the club and posted on the board in the foyer. The note had been promptly removed, but not before several of the men had seen it and spread the word.

"Unsigned, you say?" Court found it mildly amusing—hardly more. "How is a man to know where to apply, supposing he's interested?"

"Didn't sign her name. Left her initials though, and there ain't but one woman in town with the initials McR. D. Ol' Chalmers is gonna have that young'un's scalp when he gets back to town," said Stone.

"*If* he gets back to town," said an older man whose name Court couldn't remember. "If I was him, I'd keep an ocean or two between me and that crazy daughter o' his."

Court sipped his drink and tried not to dwell on what awaited him at the end of this particular journey. "A bit light under the bonnet, is she?"

"Not by a long shot! Too damned smart for her own good, 'f you ask me. Joe Harvey here was the first one to see the notice go up. Happened to be three sheets to the wind on account o' losing that contract with Grabe Shipping, so what did the poor fool do but march himself around and apply for the position."

There was a general round of laughter. "Heard she sent you packing, Harve. What's the matter, not up to her weight?"

"Can I help it if I had to shore up my nerve with

a few drinks first in case that one-legged giant o' hers tried to bust my noggin for me? I don't care what you say, a man ain't at his best when he's got too many drinks under his belt."

Amid the laughter and Joe Harvey's indignant disclaimer, Court was in danger of slipping back into his earlier mood of melancholy. He roused himself to the present to decline any interest in trying his luck. "Sorry, friends. I never mix drinking and whoring. Dangerous practice."

"Hey, we're not talking about whoring. Mick's no tramp, she's just wild as a buck."

Mick. Now, why did that name sound familiar? Probably because the woman was infamous, Court mused. With only half a mind he listened to the others' idle talk while he thought about what awaited him at home.

"She's always up to some rig. You remember, Billy, when she . . ."

"Remember! Hell, Billy was the one who . . ."

"Mumps! God, I never laughed so much in all my life!"

Another round of drinks was served along with another round of stories about the redoubtable Miss McR. D. Wild or not, it was clear to see she was a favorite with the local men. "Are you telling me a respectable female actually advertised for a—what did you call it? A *mister*?"

"I wouldn't exactly call her respectable," said Billy. "I mean, she is, but she ain't, if you catch my drift."

Court didn't. But then, he'd be the first to admit

that his brain was well on the way to being em-
balmed in the local beverage of choice. "Yes, but . . .
a *mister*?" he repeated.

"Male mistress," replied Joe Harvey. "Tol' me so
herself."

"The mind boggles," said Sam Quincy, signaling
for service. "Drink up, drink up, man, this is just
plain ol' swamp juice, it won't hurt you."

Court shook his head, which felt as if it might
float free at any moment. Which an improve-
ment, come to think of it, on the head he'd brought
in with him. He finished his drink and allowed himself to be served another. Then, judging the strength
by the color, he rose and added additional water after
the waiter had moved off. He was grinning. It occurred to him that he had been grinning for some
time. "Male mish—mistress, hmmm? Shounds
inter'shting."

"Who's next to step up to the plate? Ol' Harve
here struck out," said Sam with a leer. "What about
you, Billy? Scared Mary'll break your bat over your
head? Say, you're not married, are you, Court? Dare
you to have a go at it. Hell, man, if you strike out,
you can skip town and leave your shame behind you.
We'll never breath a word of it, honest. It'll be our
little secret, right, boys?"

There was considerable raillery and more whiskey
consumed than was perhaps wise, with Courtland
taking care to water down his own drink each time.
But then, on a Friday evening, in a private club for
gentlemen, that was the rule rather than the excep-

tion. He failed to notice the winks that passed behind his back each time he added a generous portion
of white lightning to the brown-colored juniper water
in his glass.

Thus it was that Courtland Adams, for reasons
that seemed excellent at the time, found himself
crossing the narrows again and being driven to a
handsome house in one of the town's more select
neighborhoods. The same neighborhood, unless his
eyes were playing tricks on him—a very real possibility, he admitted ruefully—which he had left earlier
that evening.

Supported as far as the front door by his compatri-
ots, he was propped up and left there with a few
snickers, a few words of advice, and one or two remarks that led him to wonder if at least one of the
men wasn't beginning to have second thoughts.

"Don't worry, Billy, Mick can take care of herself."

"Yeah, better save your worryin' for our Yankee
friend here. Think maybe we ought to warn him?"

"Nah, let her have her fun. Once ol' Chalmers
gets back, she'll have little enough o' that."

His escort drove off, harmonizing an off-key
bawdy ballad and promising to return later to collect
his remains and load them onto the next northbound
freight. Even before the echo of the doorbell faded
away, Court was beginning to regret the whole
damn-fool affair.

Had he actually bet twenty dollars on whether or
not he could get into a woman's bloomers on the first

try? God, that was pretty damned disgraceful, even if she had asked for it!

There'd been a time, back in his undergraduate days, when such a lark might even have appealed to him, but that had been another lifetime. The Courtland Adams of today was a twenty-four-carat stick-in-the-mud, everyone knew that. A real sober-sides. No fun at all. A Gloomy-Gus who, through absolutely no choice of his own, carried the weight of the world on his shoulders.

Where the devil was *that* Court Adams when a man needed him?

He sure as hell wasn't standing on a strange front porch in a strange town, weaving like a willow in a high wind while he waited for some flighty little baggage to put him through his paces.

Leaning on the doorbell, Court closed his eyes and hoped he wasn't going to disgrace himself by being sick.

MacRorah called herself several kinds of a fool. She wondered if she would get away with pretending it had all been a silly prank, a dare. She'd had trouble getting to sleep even before the sound of the doorbell startled her wide awake again.

Normally, Polly or Teeny would have answered it, but Polly had been fretful all day. She'd gone to bed early after complaining of a backache. Teeny was evidently still out. Sometimes he stayed late playing checkers with the men at 41 Pecan Street, and let himself in with his own key. Since the weather had turned cooler, he had made himself a place in the attic, which he called his crow's nest. He must have forgotten his key.

Reluctant to disturb poor Polly, MacRorah grabbed a wrapper, flung it over her shoulders, and hurried downstairs. Lifting a finger to her lips in a signal for silence, she flung open the door and then reeled back on her heels as a man in rumpled evening dress practically fell on top of her.

During the few seconds in which she stared up into a face which she had never expected to see again, it occurred to her that he was not nearly as handsome as she remembered, yet he was a thousand times more attractive. How on earth was it that after only a single glimpse, she still remembered those deep-set hazel eyes?

They were a bit bloodshot at the moment, yet they still held that remarkable combination of sadness and amusement. To add to the confusion, his lips were twisted in a smile that was both mocking and remarkably sweet.

"You advertised for a mas—a mister, m'lady?"

At the sound of his raspy drawl—oh, yes, she knew that Yankees didn't drawl, but the effect was the same—MacRorah's face flooded with hot color.

That blasted notice! Why on earth had she done something so incredibly stupid? At the time she remembered thinking that taking a lover would be as easy as shelling butter beans. Men did it all the time, didn't they?

Lovers, not butter beans.

And if the women involved were smart, they stood to reap untold benefits, she had reasoned.

On the other hand, there were the ladies at 41 Pecan Street. . . .

On still another hand, she thought distractedly, there was that awful creature her father had married.

But Joe Harvey had said they'd taken her notice off the bulletin board right away. He'd also told her she was making a fool of herself and that there were tales going around town which no one really believed, but he'd warned her to behave before people began thinking she was fast. Which she'd fully intended to be, only she hadn't known exactly how to go about it.

She should have thought of all that before she'd posted that stupid notice!

The stranger swayed in the doorway, blinking owlishly while MacRorah tried desperately to decide whether to back out or to go through with her plan. Aware of her lamentable lack of knowledge, she had asked Polly only this morning for a brief description of what occurred between a man and a woman once the bedroom door was shut.

"You hush your mouth, Miss Mac! Miss Jean would whale the living daylights out of you was she to hear you talking thisaway!"

MacRorah had played on her sympathy. "I don't have a mother to tell me about these things, Polly. What if I need to know in a hurry and you're not there to advise me?"

"Oh, I don't know, Miss Mac . . . it don't seem

right, but—well, there really ain't much to it, I guess. Mostly you don't have to do nothing but be there, but if you feel like joining in, why, I reckon it's sorta like milkin' a cow."

After which revelation, the maid had shouldered her way out to the backyard with a basket of laundry, leaving MacRorah more mystified than ever.

And now here was her ice-wagon hero, come hat in hand, so to speak, to apply for her favors, which she had publicly announced that she intended to dispense at her own discretion. Her first impulse was to slam the door in his face.

But then she took another look at those sad, bitter, beautiful eyes and that crinkly half-smile.

"Don't tell me I'm the first," he said with a leer. Having righted himself after a hasty entrance, he was more or less draped over the hall tree, looking impossibly attractive even though he was obviously potted to the gills.

"You're number seven," MacRorah lied. "And as it's so awfully late, I'm afraid I'll have to ask you to leave."

"Can't."

"Must," she snapped, and then, irritated because she was terribly tempted to brush his untidy hair off his forehead and lead him into her parlor, she tried to turn him toward the door. "Please?"

"Can't." He beamed down at her, patting her hand. "Buggy gone home, lef' me here."

"You mean you sent your buggy away? Don't you think that was a bit hasty?"

He nodded, winced as if in pain, and MacRorah heard, not for the first time, the sultry whisper of temptation. *What do you have to lose? After all, you've already told everyone you were going to do it, haven't you? They'll never in a hundred years believe you didn't.*

And he was, after all, a stranger, not someone like Joe Harvey, who had known her all her life. With a stranger, it might not be so embarrassing. She could start out with a set of questions and lead up gradually to—The Other. She wouldn't even have to get to The Other tonight. Or even at all, if she didn't want to.

Inhaling deeply, she nodded her head, drawing a rather startled look from her tipsy guest. "Would you care to come into the parlor? I'd offer you something to drink but you look as if you've already enjoyed ample refreshments."

Trailing her yellow lawn summer wrap majestically behind her, she led the way to the parlor, pausing to light two lamps. It was one thing to take a serious step toward the equality of womankind; it was quite another to have some strange man trip over a footstool in the dark and break his neck in her front parlor.

MacRorah indicated a wing chair. Her slightly unsteady guest gestured grandly toward the satin-covered Biedermeier settee. Nodding graciously, she seated herself, spreading her skirts gracefully about her, thinking that even drunk, he was obviously a gentleman.

Now. What questions would be appropriate for such circumstances? she wondered. She had made out several lists and then torn them up when she'd lost her courage.

Age? Irrelevant.

Name? But then he might ask hers, and she would just as soon he didn't know at this stage. Sooner or later, of course, he would have to know. *If* she kept him.

Marital status?

Did it matter? She would hate for his wife to be hurt. On the other hand, men did this sort of thing all the time, married or single. One had to start somewhere if one wanted to strike a blow for the emancipation of womankind.

Just as she was thinking she should have taken the time to think things through more thoroughly and establish a few rules, her would-be lover reeled down onto the settee beside her, offering her a smile of such ineffable sweetness that she completely lost her train of thought.

Chapter Six

Ⴒ

Damned if it wasn't his little perennial virgin! Bemused, Courtland stared at the woman seated beside him, marveling at the good luck that had caused Seaborn and his father to get into a wrangle just as he'd arrived back in town, exhausted after a long journey—which had led him to escape to the club. Where, partly because of the unusual potency of the local drinks and partly because his mind had been otherwise engaged, he'd gotten himself involved in a harum-scarum prank that had tumbled him out on the doorsteps of the very woman who had embedded herself in his imagination like a hardwood splinter.

And all at a time in his life when he rather desperately needed a distraction.

In the candlelight, she could almost pass for an innocent. There was even a faintly ethereal look about her in that wispy yellow thing she was wearing, with her golden brown hair spilling over her shoulders and her golden brown eyes, set in dense beds of golden brown lashes, staring up at him as if she'd never seen a man before.

But of course, he'd seen her with her child. He had seen the sort of company she kept. And besides, no real innocent would receive a gentleman alone at this hour of night, dressed in her nightclothes.

What was it they'd said about her? That she was wild? Outrageous? That she was smart?

Whatever she was, Court was in no mood to quibble. For months now, ever since he'd first seen her, she had flitted in and out of his dreams like a beautiful, elusive ghost. Lying in his narrow bed in the small back bedroom that had always been his in his father's large stone mansion, he had brooded about Diana, the woman his brother was to have married— the woman who was soon to become his own bride—only to fall asleep and dream about an amber-eyed houri he had held in his arms but once, and that only briefly, on a busy sidewalk in some little backwater southern town.

And now here he was again.

And here she was.

And all he seemed able to do was to sit here grinning like a frog on a turtle shell.

Court wished he were sober, but if he'd been sober, he wouldn't be here. At least he was sober enough to know he was drunk. That was an advantage. Wasn't it? His head was still soaring, but not quite so high as it had been earlier. If he was very lucky and very persuasive, he might still manage to come though this business with a few memories to carry with him on the northbound train.

He touched his cravat, cleared his throat, and very carefully leaned closer, breathing in the faint sweet scent of her skin. "Trees," he said suavely. "Came south to see 'bout some trees. Never 'magined I'd wind up in th' Garden of Eden."

Her skin was like porcelain, like one of the delicate figurines his mother collected, all garbed in porcelain swags and ruffles, their tiny faces adorned with simpering smiles and vacant eyes.

He wondered if she would feel cool and smooth and hard, like porcelain, or warm and soft and yielding, the way she had felt for one brief moment when he'd held her in his arms.

"I beg your pardon?" she said, her voice husky, as if she'd just woken up from a deep sleep.

Court blinked owlishly. She was good. If he didn't know better, he might even believe she was as innocent as she looked.

"Warm. That is, I meant to say, trees. M'business. Trees t'build houses, trees t'build ships, trees t'build . . . baseball bats!" He grinned broadly and waited for her approval, proud of the fact that even drunk as a lord, he could converse intelligently on any number of topics.

MacRorah nodded warily. The man was either completely under the hatches or he was a fool. She hated to think he was a fool, for that would mean she had wasted all those dreams.

Taking a deep breath, she smiled and allowed her

hand to slide ever so casually from her lap to lay on the seat between them. Purely as a scientific experiment. To see what would happen next.

She had no particular interest in spending an evening discussing trees, even with this fascinating stranger, but it might not be wise to become intimate—that is, to reach the hand-holding stage— too quickly.

On the other hand, a mistress's work, like that of any other laborer, she supposed, was created from a demand. She had been studying a book on economics recently in an effort to better serve the needs of those poor souls at 41 Pecan Street.

However, nothing in *Barton's Treatise on Economics for the Coming Century* seemed applicable in this particular case. The truth was, she hadn't the least notion of what was expected under these circumstances. She wasn't eager to exchange names, but it might be pertinent to know where he lived and how long he expected to be in town. And whether or not he was married. And how much money he was accustomed to spending on his mistresses.

The possibility of his having a wife at home bothered her in spite of what Polly had told her—that ladies of the evening were doing wives a favor—that most wives considered the whole messy business of performing their wifely duties to be a chore and a bore.

Which didn't sound particularly enticing, now that she was considering making it her life's work. However . . .

Stealing a look at his rather angular face, she followed his gaze to the hand that was lying on the seat between them like a hapless living sacrifice. After a bit of fumbling, he hooked his little finger over hers, causing the strangest feelings to sizzle all the way up her arm. Light seemed to flare under those dark, level brows, but even as she watched, it was quickly banked.

Controlling her breathing with great difficulty, MacRorah glanced away, praying he wasn't going to pounce on her. It occurred to her that for once in her life, she just might have bitten off more than she could chew.

What if he became . . . aggressive?

Oh, my mercy! The nearest vase was on the other side of the room, the fireplace tools were stored for the summer, and the whatnots on the piecrust table beside the settee were too small to inflict much damage.

What she needed was a cane or an umbrella. Unfortunately, they were all in the stand out in the hall.

It was while she was still toying with various methods of self-defense in the event that it should become necessary, that her midnight caller lifted her hand to his lips.

All thought of umbrellas fled. MacRorah braced herself for the next stage, torn between the need to escape and the need to see what would happen next.

What happened next was not so very extraordinary, although she had to admit that the effect was like nothing she'd ever experienced. He kissed the inside of her wrist. Then he kissed each knuckle, which she thought was rather peculiar, yet not at all unpleasant.

And then he began to suckle her fingertips.

Feeling as if a flock of sparrows had suddenly taken flight in the pit of her stomach, she stiffened. This was not a part of her plan! This—this whatever it was that was happening to her. Somewhere along the line, she seemed to have miscalculated rather badly, because it had never occurred to her that something so simple as a man's touch would affect her physically.

This was distracting! How could she possibly think straight while he was doing what he was doing to her fingers?

She wasn't even certain it wasn't depraved.

Why should any man want to suck on a woman's fingertips? She had half a mind to make him stop it this very instant! And she would, too—just as soon as she could catch her breath.

As a wave of dizziness passed over her, MacRorah reminded herself that this entire exercise was supposed to be about power.

A woman's power over a man.

Not a man's power over a woman!

The sensible thing to do, now that she'd discovered the flaw in her plan, was to hand him his hat and send him on his way until she could rethink the entire business.

On the other hand, she could consider tonight merely an exercise in learning. In which case, now that she'd come this far, why not go just a bit further and see what the next stage was?

Purely as a matter of intellectual curiosity.

Pondering the matter, she closed her eyes, breathing deeply through her mouth as she felt his tongue touch the sensitive space between her fingers. Goose bumps raced down her left flank. Was this what mistresses did?

Really, it was a most bizarre experience. Polly had said nothing at all about finger licking.

Goodness! She was certainly gaining a liberal education in mistresshood. However, as long as she remained in control, she should be safe enough. Polly was sleeping not far away, Mrs. George was in the little room off the kitchen, and Teeny should be coming in most any moment now. Besides, as soon as she grew bored, she would simply send the gentleman packing.

Thus, in the interest of scientific experimentation, MacRorah relaxed and continued to examine the remarkable variety of sensations emanating from the place where a man's tongue came in contact with a woman's skin. Curiously enough, the effects were entirely different from those created by her own tongue, when she'd sucked on a cut or licked honey from her fingers.

Entirely different!

Suddenly a bolt of lightning streaked clean through her body. Emanating from the palm of her hand, it sizzled its way up her arm and then down through her stomach, as if a swarm of ants were marching through her insides. Gasping, she curled her fingers over her damp, quivering palm.

At the sound of her sharply indrawn breath, the dark-eyed man lifted his head, bringing his face entirely too close to her own. Before she could gather her wits to push him away, she felt his warm, whiskey-scented breath on her face.

Then he kissed her.

MacRorah had been kissed before. Out of curiosity, she had made Seaborn stand still and let her practice on him the summer she'd turned fifteen. They'd been picking scuppernongs in the Adamses' backyard at the time, and dropping his bucket, he'd reached up and grasped the arbor to brace himself. By the time she'd grown bored with the whole procedure and resumed picking grapes, he had turned red in the face and somehow managed to pull half the grapevine down around their feet.

This kiss, however, was nothing at all like that. In the first place, this wasn't Seaborn, it was the same dark stranger who had visited her in her dreams—the man who had caught her in his arms and saved her from certain death.

Or at least from a thorough dust-up.

While his tongue explored her mouth and his hands explored her body, MacRorah stared wide-eyed at his left ear and tried vainly to maintain a scientific objectivity toward the cataclysmic happenings that were taking place inside her body.

Words such as *power* and *control* flitted through her mind, then winked out like lightning bugs, only to be replaced by a Fourth of July display of fireworks.

Her arms were around his neck, and for the life of her, she didn't know how they'd gotten there. Nothing about this entire bizarre business made sense. Desperately, she tried to rationalize what was happening to her by reminding herself that the only other time she'd seen this man, she'd been in a heightened state of emotion, which probably explained why she hadn't been able to think about him since then without a certain tremor of excitement. And now that he was actually here—actually touching her—actually—

Oh, my mercy . . .

As he nuzzled her throat, she instinctively lifted her chin to give him better access, then stiffened as he found a particularly vulnerable place. So *that* was what this particular portion of her neck was for, she mused.

It couldn't be safe, she thought distractedly. How could a woman ever hope to gain the upper hand when a man insisted on doing all these extraordinary things to her person? Polly hadn't said anything at all about—

"Ohhh—ahh," she gasped long moments later.

Whatever he was doing to her was not only affecting her body, it was playing havoc with her brain! How else could she explain finding herself flat on her back on the settee, one slippered foot braced against the rolled arm, the other touching the floor, while a perfect stranger knelt beside her, holding her in both his arms and kissing her naked breast?

Her naked breast?

"Oh, heavens, you can't kiss me there," she cried, struggling to crawl out from under the weight of the body that was wedged against her thigh and pressing down on her chest.

"Nectar of rosebuds," he murmured, drawing the sensitive tip of her breast into his mouth again.

Shocked to the marrow of her bones, MacRorah tried to shove his head away, her fingers tangling in his thick, dark hair. It was warm. He was warm.

She was burning up!

"You're right," he whispered hoarsely. "Need more room."

"Indeed you do!" she quavered. "I—I'll thank you to remove yourself from my presence immediately!"

"Mmm, tha's good," he murmured softly, sliding his hand up under her nightgown along the silken flesh of her inner thigh.

Snatching her arms from around his neck, she grabbed at his wrist with one hand and tried to shove his head off her breast with the other, but heads were heavier than she'd realized, and he was not be-ing at all cooperative.

And then suddenly he touched her . . . *there*.

A soft sound exploded from her lips. To her horror, she recognized it as a sigh. "This can't—you can't—Oh, my mercy, what are you *doing*?"

The clock in the hall bonged eleven times, wheezed once, and subsided. MacRorah lay paralyzed, enthralled by a power she didn't even attempt to understand. Who would ever believe that a body could have a mind of its own?

His head was still heavy on her breast, one arm flung across her shoulder. His right hand had settled on an area of her body that had not seen the light of day since she'd snuck off to go swimming naked in the creek during a church picnic at the age of five.

Before she could work her foot into position to kick him, she heard the sound of a horse turning off the street and into the carriageway. Teeny!

"Please! Whoever you are, you've got to get up now! This has gone far enough. Please?" she whispered plaintively, struggling to crawl out from under the dead weight lying across her body.

On the verge of kicking whatever part of his body was in reach of her foot, she heard the sound of a gentle snore.

A *snore*?

"Oh . . . balderdash," she muttered, practically in tears.

By the time Teeny, seeing the strip of light under the parlor door, called out softly to ask if she was all right, MacRorah was on her feet, her color suspiciously high, but her clothing once more in order. There was no way on earth she was going to be able to explain this.

"Miz Mac? Are you all right?"

"I'm perfectly all right, Teeny, but I'm afraid the gentleman who—who came by unexpectedly to—to see Father is a bit under the weather." She avoided looking directly into Teeny's big, battered face as he peered through the open door. He was gentle as a kitten, but he could be quite ferocious if he thought she was in need of protection.

"A—a friend from out of town. He just dropped by to—to—well, I suppose the best thing to do is to take him to the hotel and leave him. If you'll help him into his coat, I'll write a note—" She shrugged. It would have to do. She couldn't face an inquisition tonight, no matter how well-meaning.

Even for the massive ex-ship's carpenter, a dead weight of some six feet of solid muscle was an awkward burden. Teeny managed to sling the man over his shoulder, and with one last look at MacRorah that promised questions to come, crammed the envelope in his coat pocket and set out to hitch up the gig again.

Hotel! He wasn't about to introduce himself to some high-rumped night clerk and try to offload this bag of bilge. A hammock at 41 Pecan Street would serve well enough. Hell, he could have the Queen's Boo-dwar, for that matter, which was what the inhabitants called the only room in the rambling old waterfront boardinghouse that had yet to be done over.

Friend of her father's, was he? What the devil was that little tartar up to now? Miz Jean would've had a conniption fit!

Ten hours later, Courtland opened one eye experimentally. Squinting up at a stamped tin ceiling that showed signs of rust stains through a particularly nauseating shade of pink paint, he wondered just where the hell he was.

He wondered who had left all the lamps in the room burning. The glare was killing him!

He wondered who had stuffed his mouth full of dead moths.

Last of all, he wondered why a crew of gandy-dancers insisted on working over the inside of his skull with their pry bars.

All that was before he came aware of the revolution taking place inside his belly. "God, if I'm already in hell, kindly finish me off and put me out of my misery," he groaned.

An hour later he was afraid he might survive. After having emptied his gut of whatever poison he had consumed, he had ducked his face several times in the washbowl and taken bleary-eyed stock of his surroundings.

This was definitely not the well-appointed guest room in his uncle's house. In fact, it looked more like a two-bit flophouse. Or worse.

Wondering if his belly would accept a gallon or so of black coffee, Court struggled into his rumpled coat and opened the door just as a few disjointed memories flashed through his swollen brain.

A ferry ride across the narrows. A club. What was it called, the Flash in the Pan? The Royal Something-or-other?

He half remembered dining with a handful of

rogues, some of whom he dimly recalled meeting on a previous trip south, most of whom were strangers.

What the devil had be been drinking? Two scotches on top of whatever wine he consumed with his dinner was his absolute limit. More often than not, he worked too late into the night even to indulge himself to that extent. And come to think of it, he distinctly remembered watering down his drinks as soon as he began to feel the effects.

A blowsy-looking female in a hideous gown sidled past with a mop and pail in her hand, sending him a curious look. Her hair was the color of the ink in his new fountain pen—black with a distinctively purple cast. Her eyes were . . .

Amber-colored eyes?

Where had that come from? The whore's eyes were blue. A faded, tired-looking blue.

A whorehouse. God, he'd spent the night in a blooming bawdy house! And a waterfront bawdy house, at that. Even in his wilder days, he'd had sense enough to be more selective.

But where was that satin-covered sofa? Where was the walnut wainscoting, and the dinky little table full of thingamabobs? Had he dreamed all that?

Judas priest, he was supposed to be on a train, wasn't he? A northbound train? *Can't go on running forever, old man. Time to go home and face the music.*

Where had that thought come from?

Court shook his head, then grabbed it with both hands and groaned. He needed coffee. What he really needed was to turn the clock back and start the day over again. Not just the clock—the whole damned calendar!

Hair like warm brown silk—lips that tasted of honey—

Oh, boy. He had really managed to screw up this time. How long had it been since he'd done anything this stupid? Three years? Four? The last time he could remember was the night he had finally made up his mind to forget the life he had planned and give in to his father's demands. For his mother's sake, not his father's. He owed her more than he could ever repay—owed them both. For Rick.

A vision of hauntingly beautiful, hauntingly familiar wide golden brown eyes drifted in and out of his consciousness and he lurched back to his room and dropped heavily into the room's only chair, a gaudy gold satin affair that clashed horribly with the pink-flowered coverlet on the rumpled bed.

Her name . . . what was her name?

He couldn't even remember the name of the whore he had shared the bed with. The last thing he remembered clearly was hiring a hack to drive him from the depot to his uncle's house and walking in on a wrangle that had reminded him a little too much for comfort of the kind of wrangles he endured at home.

Yes, and he remembered going to that place across the river. He'd been there once before with Seaborn. Vaguely he remembered being warned not to play poker with someone or other, and not to drink with someone else.

Judging from the evidence, he must have disregarded the last warning, if not the first one. Rising unsteadily, he felt in his pockets, coming up with a wallet and a train ticket. At least he hadn't been rolled. Now all he had to do was swallow enough coffee to get him to the depot. In case he hadn't already missed his train.

Hearing a medley of sounds outside—a barking dog, the distant sound of a train whistle, and the more immediate sounds typical of a busy waterfront—Court was sorely tempted to bury his head under the pillow and sleep until his world righted itself and things once more began to make sense. He might be a bit hazy on the details of the previous evening, but he did know that drinking himself into oblivion wasn't something he did on a regular basis.

At the moment, he could recall only three times in his entire life when he'd found himself unable to deal with what had to be dealt with. Each time he had drunk himself into a stupor, suffered the usual punishment when he'd sobered up, and then set about dealing with whatever it was that had to be dealt with.

Had he paid her? He'd better leave a few bills on the dresser in case he'd forgotten. With that in mind, he took out his wallet again, laid a ten spot on the scarred dresser top, then impulsively added another bill.

It was then that he saw the note, addressed only "To the Gentleman of the Evening."

Gentleman of the Evening? Curious sense of humor for a bawd, he mused. Had he actually been so crass as to call her a lady of the evening? Normally, he would have had more tact.

Amused in spite of his physical misery, Court ripped open the envelope, stared at the several bills that fluttered to the bald carpet, and then scanned the few scrawled lines. And then he read them over again.

> Sir:
> *Please accept this small sum of money in*
> *exchange for your time. I regret to inform you*
> *that you failed to rise to my standards, therefore*
> *your services will no longer be required.*
> *Yrs. in haste,*
> McR. D.

Not until several hours later did Court manage to rid himself of one hellacious headache. As for his pride, that would take considerably longer.

What the hell had she meant, he'd failed to rise to her standards? Who did she think she was?

It had gradually come back to him in disjointed snatches of memory just how he had spent the previous evening.

The woman on the street.

Against all reason, it had been his amber-eyed houri, that exquisite perennial virgin of his dreams, who had greeted him at the door of that run-down waterfront bawdy house.

Funny, though—the place had looked entirely different at night.

But then, all cats looked gray in the darkness, a truism that obviously applied equally to cathouses.

There had certainly been no mistaking where he was in the harsh light of day. Nor had there been any mistaking the grim intention of that damned old madam when he'd attempted to find his amber-eyed houri again. The old biddy had threatened to call the law on him if he didn't leave the premises at once.

Even though he still suffered a slight dyspepsia from his evening of debauchery, Court tried valiantly to piece together the confusing events of the previous evening. She had greeted him at the door wearing a few wispy layers of something designed to entice. No heavy perfumes, no painted face, though. She'd looked so clean and wholesome that he'd found it almost impossible to believe she was what she obviously was.

No wonder he'd been unable to forget the little witch.

The trouble was, dammit, he couldn't remember having her!

He remembered her hands, which were small, square, and firm. He remembered her breasts, which were small, high, and firm. He remembered her lips. Her scent. Her taste . . .

But that was all he remembered.

Had he or had he not performed up to his usual standard? He had never before had any complaints.

On the northbound connection out of Norfolk late

that evening, Court took out the crumpled note and read it over again for the hundredth time. God, the little witch had a nerve! If it was the last thing he ever did, he was going to make her eat every snide word she'd written.

At least he hadn't taken her money. He'd left that, along with his own, on the dresser. If the old bawd with a bucket ducked inside the room and snatched it up first, it would serve the arrogant little baggage right!

By the time the northbound train pulled out of the station at Washington, D.C., Court had gone through and discarded at least a dozen plans for revenge. On his next trip south—he'd think of some reason to go back—he would find her if he had to dig up every damned cobblestone and tear down every damned building on the waterfront!

And once he found the little strumpet, he fully intended to buy her services for a solid week, exhaust them both with his "performance," and then inform her that she had, unfortunately, failed to come up to his standards.

But God, she had!

At least, he thought she had. . . .

Next time, he was going to imprint every enticing, delectable morsel of her sweet little body on his brain. He still couldn't believe he'd had all that and couldn't remember it!

By the time his train pulled out of Grand Central on the last leg of his homeward journey, Court had half decided to take her out of that wretched old house on the river and set her up in a neat cottage somewhere in a quiet section of town. Once he was married and settled down, he'd be able to travel as often as it suited him—and unless things changed drastically with Diana, it would doubtless suit him frequently. A mistress in the town where the southern portion of his business was centered would be a luxury he could easily afford.

As for his wedding vows . . .

Oh, hell, his marriage was strictly a business arrangement. That had been understood from the first. Besides, his own father had mounted a mistress for years. Most men who could afford it did. As his mistress, the girl would want for nothing.

He would show her performance! Perhaps after a few years, if she suited as well as he expected her to, he might even move her to Connecticut. Not, of course, to the town where he'd be living with Diana and whatever children, if any, they happened to produce, but close enough for convenience.

He'd been tempted to confide in Seaborn and ask his assistance, but in the end, pride had won out. Pride and conscience. A man on the verge of marrying—with every intention of being a good husband, no matter that the match had not been of his own making—had no business making an alliance with another woman. It could wait until his next trip south.

Instead, he'd spent the last few minutes at the depot in Elizabeth City, while waiting for the train to board, going over details of a pending business deal.

"I'll look after things," Sea had said, handing him a newspaper to read on his way north. "Sorry I was tied up last night."

"Perfectly all right. Glad to see you two sorted out whatever it was between you."

"A woman. Dad doesn't approve of her. Half the time, I don't approve of her myself. Trouble is, I've loved her since she was a snaggletoothed little ragamuffin, climbing fences, getting caught in blackberry thickets, and yelling for me to come save her."

"Sounds exciting." Court grinned, hoping he didn't look as hellish as he felt.

"Yeah, well—that's just it. After Mickey, every other woman seems tame as wet bread. Better get on aboard, or you'll have to lay over till Tuesday. Don't reckon your Diana would like that too well, would she?"

Court could have told him that his Diana had probably not even noticed that he was gone. Now, as the miles rattled past, he folded the newspaper, closed his eyes . . .

And there she was again. Smiling at him. Taunting him. Damn her wicked little soul!

What the devil had prompted him to go out looking for that kind of entertainment in the first place? He could've sworn he'd outgrown that sort of thing when he'd left law school and gone to work at Adams-Snelling.

Looking back, he seemed to recall some fuzzy-minded notion that he could create a few warm memories to look back on over the bleak years ahead.

Some memories. He'd already forgotten the best parts!

Chapter Seven

𝕮

During the night it began to rain. MacRorah heard the first few drops strike the window, heard the shift of the wind. Heard the branches of the giant water oak slapping the side of the house. She stared sightlessly up into the darkness, wondering where *he* was. She'd been afraid to go out yesterday for fear of seeing him again—had half expected him to show up again last night in spite of that curt note she'd had Teeny leave with him at the hotel. The money should have been enough to pay for his room.

Actually, she considered it a rather generous gesture, but she'd been afraid the hotel would refuse to take him in without payment in advance, and Teeny could hardly be expected to go through the man's pockets right there in the lobby.

Still, she could have left off the note. Even men had their pride, she supposed.

The clock struck the half hour. She thought about

her father and wondered if he ever planned to come home again. And then she wondered if she even wanted him to. He was her father, after all. Her mother had once loved him enough to defy her own father to marry him. As his daughter, MacRorah knew she was supposed to love him, too, only it was hard to love someone you despised.

After a while she had begun to accept the loss of her mother and to pick up the threads of her life again, but it was downright scary, the way a person's entire life could change so quickly. Only yesterday she'd been content to lark about town with her friends, raising the occasional eyebrow, but secure in the knowledge that the only cloud on her horizon was her father.

And even he had been no real threat. The occasional paddling, the occasional slapping around, did no lasting damage, she supposed, although it was humiliating in the extreme. What hurt even worse were his harsh words and the way he was forever putting her down. She had proved to them both that in that arena, at least, she was more than a match for him.

Then, over the course of a single summer, everything had changed. She'd been forced to grow up. In some ways, she admitted reluctantly, she'd made a royal muddle of it.

By the time a watery sun broke over the horizon to filter through the white lawn curtains at her window, MacRorah was groggy from a lack of sleep, yet sleep still evaded her. She heard the first produce wagon rattling in from the country. Just as it reached the corner, she heard Miss Lupe call out from across the street for a mess of greens and half a dozen of the best sweet potatoes. Heard the muffled sounds of her own household stirring to life.

Yawning, MacRorah sat up and rubbed her itchy eyes. If there was one lesson she should have learned over a long and varied career of mischief-making, it was never to lose sleep over what couldn't be undone. Yesterday she had kept herself busy turning out closets, going over household accounts for both houses, and settling disputes between Polly and Teeny over whose task it was to haul out ashes and whose to scour the flagstones clean of moss; doing anything and everything to keep from dwelling on her single disastrous attempt at mistresshood.

But two sleepless nights were penance enough for any crime. Today she was determined to work until she was fit to drop, at which time she fully intended to sleep until hunger drove her from her bed.

Dressed in a gray poplin that was unbecoming, but suited her frame of mind to perfection, she hurried down to the kitchen, to be greeted by a harried Mrs. George. "Miss Mac, I done sent Teeny to fetch Maude Squires. Polly, she's down in the back again. Ask me, her young'un's fixin' to get 'imself borned, ready or not."

"The midwife? But it's not time, is it?"

"Seven month, nine month—young'un can't count no better'n a mealie worm."

"I'd better go see about her, poor child. Teeny warned her she was trying to do too much."

"You'll do no such thing, missy! You'll set right down and have your breakfast. I got fresh-boiled coffee, Abner's peaches off'n his late trees, hot buttermilk biscuits, an' a bowl of clabber with 'lasses, all set out on the table."

Still standing, MacRorah reached absently for a biscuit. She didn't have time to worry about food now. Sometime during the night she had reached a major decision concerning the future course of her own life.

Only first she must see about Polly. "I'll be back as soon as I—"

"Set!" Mrs. George, though she'd been on the streets for half her life, knew how to use the authority of her superior age.

MacRorah sat. Meekly, she allowed herself to be served, but only after being assured that there was nothing she could do for Polly's comfort at the moment, and that she would only embarrass the child. "Ain't no place for an unmarried girl, no matter how smart she thinks she is. Your own ma wouldn't let you within a mile of any birthin'."

"Mrs. George, I'm eighteen years old. I'm certainly no young innocent. Who do you think looks after the women at 41?"

"Not who you think does, I warrant," the older woman snapped.

Which made MacRorah wonder, not for the first time, if there was a conspiracy afoot to protect her in spite of herself, perpetrated by the very ones she was supposed to be looking after.

Well, all that was about to change. According to her mother, a lady had only four choices in life. To seek employment—but who in this town would hire her? To remain a spinster and under the thumb of a father, which was unthinkable in MacRorah's case. To marry, and put herself at the mercy of a husband, and with the example of her parents' marriage, that, too, was out of the question.

Or to become a mistress, trading her favors to a man of her own choice, free to leave at her own discretion. Which sounded all very well, but as she'd quickly discovered, there were hidden dangers involved. Not all the power a man could wield over a woman consisted of brute strength.

Which was why MacRorah had chosen to try yet another course first. As a woman of means, subject only to the terms of her grandfather's will—and as her father seemed disinclined to return—she was totally independent. Free to devote herself, as her mother had done the last half dozen years of her life, to good works. When and if she learned more about this mistress business and decided to become one, she would simply do it. If, on the other hand, she decided to further her education and become a teacher instead, why, then, she would pursue that course. She had no one to please except herself.

Now, *that* was *freedom*!

She still could not fathom why any woman, particularly one who was already an established mistress, should want to trade her position in on a wedding ring. Surely even a woman of minimal intelligence would know she was letting herself in for a life of bondage, at the very least.

It had been the news of her father's shameful remarriage that had pushed her into making a stand, however reckless and ill-conceived. The minute all her friends had started ladling sympathy over her head like so much cream gravy, she'd said the first thing that had popped into her mind, just to shut them up.

But then, one thing had led to another, and before she'd had time to come to her senses, she had dashed off that awful note and offered Jimmy Lea Robbins a penny to slip in and pin it on the wall at the Royal Flush.

She had never actually intended to go through with it. At least, she didn't think she had. At the time, she had simply wanted to strike out at something, and that had been the most outrageous thing she could think of.

Besides which, she purely hated being pitied by her friends. Better to be outrageous than to be pitied.

Joe Harvey had been the first one to come around. She rather thought he'd been put up to it by some of his rapscallion friends, because he'd blushed and stammered until she'd finally got out of him what he wanted, which was to apply for the position she'd advertised.

She'd known Joe Harvey forever. He would never have done something like that on his own. Even so, she had managed to dispatch him without overly embarrassing either one of them. And then Henry Calvin had come by. She'd always liked Henry, so she'd told him right off that she'd done the whole thing on a dare and asked him please to remove the notice.

"It's already been torn down, Miss MacRorah. Heck, we all knew it was something like that. Some of us just thought we'd go along with it, same as we did with that graveyard thing and the sack full of cats you let loose in the church that day Warren Broughton married the senator's widow. No harm intended."

"And none taken, Henry. Tell your mama I appreciate the turnip greens she sent 'round last week. That was real thoughtful."

And then, just when she'd thought it was all over and done with, *he* had turned up at her door. It was probably the shock of seeing him again that had caused her to weaken and let him in. She didn't even know his name. Mercy, that was the least of what she didn't know about him!

She did know, however, that for a little while she had nearly lost the upper hand, and been lucky that was all she'd lost. Why, he could have robbed her blind before she could even get to the umbrella stand!

MacRorah poured herself another cup of coffee and wondered what was keeping Teeny and the midwife. Perhaps she should have hitched up and gone around for Dr. Meyer. Polly had complained of a backache, not a . . .

Where *did* one ache when one was about to have a baby?

The midwife, Mrs. Squires, bustled in and was quickly admitted to the sickroom. MacRorah followed right on her heels, but her entry was barred by Mrs. George.

"Go set the kettle to boiling."

"But it's already hot."

"Then set the wash pot on to boil!"

MacRorah tried to peer around her shoulders into the room, where noisy, mysterious things were occurring, but Teeny came up behind her and took her arm. "You don't want to go in there, Miss Mac. You come and have another cup of coffee."

If she drank any more coffee, she would float right out of the kitchen, but she went nevertheless, knowing she was helpless against the massed forces of her staff.

Unable to concentrate on the chores of the day, MacRorah allowed her mind to drift back to her hazel-eyed, dark-haired mystery man. It hadn't been a total loss, she mused. She had learned something . . . although just what it was, she still wasn't certain. Her one real regret was that the cad had fallen asleep before she could cut him down to size. He was everything she despised in a man—weak, arrogant, insensitive, and immoral. Just like her father, in fact. She would have enjoyed the privilege of telling him so.

By nightfall, Polly's baby had still not been born. Both Maudie Squires and Mrs. George had been in constance attendance, and Dr. Meyer had been sent for late in the afternoon. MacRorah had been banished to the front of the house, where she was trying unsuccessfully to concentrate on Mrs. Espy's repair list. Leaking roof, smoking chimneys, and seven broken windowpanes this week alone, the latter probably a result of being situated between two waterfront saloons. At least there'd been no more fires lately.

Flinging down her pen, she rose and strode to the open hall doorway. "Teeny, will you *please* stop pacing? You're going to drive us all mad and wear a hole in the carpet besides!"

"Miss Mac, I'll buy you a new rug, that I will, but them old bats won't even let me in to see her! That ain't fair!"

"You and Polly have been at daggers drawn since the first time you laid eyes on one another. Maybe Polly doesn't want you to see her at a time like this, did you ever think of that?"

When she saw the effect of her words, MacRorah could have bit her tongue off. She laid her hand on the arm of the burly, one-legged ex-seaman. "Oh, Teeny, I didn't mean that, you know I didn't. It's just nerves talking. I haven't been sleeping at all well, and now this . . ."

"Don't reckon that gen'leman I carted off fer ye t'other night had nothin' to do with it, did he?"

Shoulders sagging, MacRorah sank down on one of the twin velvet-covered side chairs in the front hall. It was a mark of his distraction that Teeny sat down in the other one. He stared morosely at the tip of his mahogany leg.

Teeny Gritmire, whose proper name was Munroe Q. Gritmire, and whose age he'd given as thirty-four years, although he looked considerably older, had hair the color of sun-bleached straw, a battered face that had been weathered to the texture of harness leather, and the innocent blue eyes of a child.

It occurred to MacRorah that Teeny—as with each one of these people her mother had taken into her life and into her home—had a history of his own. They all had families of their own, perhaps. Sorrows that she could only guess at.

"Polly, she'd never look at a man what ain't got but one leg."

"Teeny, that's not so! Polly's not one to judge any man by something so insignificant."

"'Sides which, I'm old enough to be her paw."

"She's fifteen and a half—sixteen now." But far older in experience than any child should ever be.

Teeny and Polly? she thought wonderingly. To her knowledge, they'd never exchanged a single civil word.

Hearing the sound of muffled voices coming from the far end of the hall—the clatter of a basin, the awful sound of Polly's screams—MacRorah tried to ignore the tears that were trickling down the gullies of Teeny's weathered cheeks. Instead, she stared at the umbrella stand and tried to concentrate on something else. It occurred to her to wonder what would happen if her father should walk through the door with his new bride just now. Mr. and Mrs. Chalmers Douglas.

Dear God, she had a stepmother named . . . Chartreuse?

Silently, she reached over and covered Teeny's ham-sized hand with one of her own. Perhaps, she thought with a sigh, if she went back to bed and woke up again ten years from now, things might begin to make sense.

It was only a week later that Mr. and Mrs. Chalmers Douglas returned from a wedding trip abroad. MacRorah was just coming around to the front door to collect the mail, an empty wash basket under her arm from hanging out a lineful of little Megan's diapers, when the livery stable carriage pulled up.

Too tired to be overly curious, for the baby had kept the whole household awake all night, she waited to see who had come calling so early in the morning.

And then she dropped the basket, which rolled under the mock orange bush, forgotten. "Father?" she whispered, staring at the back of the thin, gray-haired man who had turned to assist someone down from the carriage. Oh, my mercy, he looked so old!

The new Mrs. Douglas, resplendent in a purple taffeta calling suit trimmed in crystal beads, ruffles, with lace jabot and cuffs, emerged from the carriage, all five curled and dyed ostrich plumes on her purple satin turban swaying precariously in the late October breeze.

Stepping down onto the granite mounting block, the woman paused to survey her new kingdom. "You sure this is the right place, Dobby? Don't look near as big as I remembered."

Dobby? *Dobby?*

By suppertime, it was plain as chalk that it wasn't going to work. MacRorah simply could not live under the same roof with that woman!

Dobby, indeed! Her father's name was Chalmers Dobson Douglas. And a gambler and womanizer he might be—and yes, a brutal and insensitive man, as well. MacRorah had still not forgiven him for leaving the country while his own wife lay dying, and for marrying so disgracefully soon after her death.

Even so, she could almost find it in her heart to be sorry for him after seeing the way his henna-haired Chartreuse led him by the nose.

First it had been her room. The new Mrs. Douglas preferred a westerly exposure to one where the early morning sun came through the windows. Nor did she care for the restrained decor of any of the five second-floor bedrooms. Something in purple or rose would suit her quite well, thank you, and Dobby, poor defeated man, had promised to see to it right away.

The staff, of course, would all have to be replaced. Who ever heard of a maid with a baby?

And that frightful, crude person who was forever clumping up and down the stairs—surely they could afford a butler with two legs!

Then, of course, there was Mrs. George, whose rather remarkable hair still showed traces of its former glory. Mud and marigold was her own way of describing it. She happened to favor rather startling gowns, in shades that were not particularly subdued, and she still indulged herself in a bit of rouge, but she was a fine cook, and she was kindhearted, and honest to the bone.

"Absolutely not, Father. If Polly and Teeny and Mrs. George go, then I go, too."

"Don't be stupid, girl. You got no place to go. Now, I know you're disappointed in me, and to tell the truth, I'm some disappointed in meself, but your stepma is a fine woman. Not quality, like your mother was, but then, comes a time in a man's life when comfort means more than quality."

"Comfort! She runs you ragged! You've lost so much weight I hardly recognized you!"

"Yes, well . . . there's comfort and then there's comfort. Leastwise, my Chartreuse ain't delicate, like your mama was. A man has his needs, Daughter. Not that you're old enough to know about such things."

She was eighteen and some months, as he knew very well. He'd tried hard enough to marry her off just this past spring!

The two of them, father and daughter, practically came to blows every day for a week as first one complaint and then another by the new Mrs. Douglas sent an indignant MacRorah striding into her father's study.

"I will not have that creature insulting Polly, Father! She's barely out of childbed. She's in no condition to be told to pack her things and get out, and to take her squalling brat with her! Little Megan can't help it if she has a rash! Now, if you can't manage your wife, then I will, but I refuse to dismiss the very ones who stood by me while Mama lay dying, while you were off gallivanting all over creation with that—that—painted whore!"

For that impertinence, she'd received a resounding slap, and knew she'd deserved it.

But every day it was something else. MacRorah was beginning to feel like a lone war-weary soldier, besieged on every flank by enemy forces. If she'd had anywhere else to go—if she could have afforded even the smallest cottage of her own—she would have left the very first day, and taken her friends with her.

Where was Seaborn when she needed him?

Gone traipsing off to Connecticut to some cousin's wedding, like the fair-weather friend he was.

What she really needed was someone to hold her and comfort her and tell her she was within her rights to stand up for what she believed in, and that the house that painted harridan was intent on ruining had belonged to her grandfather and was as much MacRorah's home as it was her father's.

Veering from anger to despair, MacRorah told herself that if she was to salvage anything at all from the ruins of her life, it would take both means and determination. Determination had never been a problem. The problem was means.

And unless she permitted Mr. Marshall to break the lease on 41 Pecan Street and turn all those poor unfortunate souls out into the streets again, which she had vowed on her mother's grave not to do, she could see no way clear to gain those means.

How on earth had she come to this in so short a time? To think that less than six months ago, she and her mother had been packing and making final preparations to leave for the cottage at Nags Head.

The cottage . . .

Grandfather MacRorah's cottage, where they had spent almost every summer for as long as she could remember. It was shuttered for most of the year. Occasionally it was rented out to select family parties at Mr. Marshall's discretion, but certainly not in October.

Did anyone live at the beach permanently?

Well, of course, a handful of fishermen and their families did . . . and probably a skeleton staff at the beach hotels. Maybe a few hardy souls, would-be hermits seeking to get away from it all.

Fired with fresh determination, MacRorah stood and brushed the dust from her tartan skirt. "Gordy!" she called through the back door. "Bring the gig around, will you? Hurry!"

Chapter Eight

TEN YEARS LATER

In an elegant stone mansion centered in the privacy of forty-seven acres of Connecticut hardwoods just north of New Haven proper, Courtland Adams gazed out the window of his study at the gathering dusk, his mind ranging back in time.

That had been . . . what? '80? '82? God, had it truly been that long?

It had been that long. Sometimes it felt more like a hundred years. At other times, it might all have happened yesterday. Funny, how certain memories could stick in a man's mind as fresh as the day they'd been made.

Or, in this case, the night.

The letter he had just received from his Cousin Seaborn, more personal than the usual brief business transmission, had brought back the rush of memories before he could slam the door on them.

After that last trip south just before his marriage,

once he'd come to his senses, Court had gone to his father with the idea of putting young Wiggins in charge of the southern properties that were centered in Elizabeth City, North Carolina, convenient to rail and seaway. Wiggins was smart and ambitious, and by then Court had no longer trusted his own judgment. Not with that delectable morsel of temptation lying in wait.

His father had been ailing, even then. Court had accepted the inevitability of his own marriage, and Diana's family had already begun making plans. By the time he'd reached home after that last memorable journey, he had made up his mind that in one respect, at least, he would never follow in his father's footsteps.

The little whore would have to find herself another protector. Given her assets, he shouldn't think the search would be a long one. As for him, he would simply put her from his mind and get on with making the best he could of a bad bargain. Reluctantly, he made up his mind to do without the comfort of a mistress. For Rick's sake, he owed this marriage his best shot.

It wasn't Diana's fault that he couldn't love her. She was certainly beautiful enough for any man. Impeccable manners, unquestioned position in society—not to mention the fact that she stood to inherit old Andrew Snelling's entire estate after Junius Andrew Jr., had died.

Court hadn't married her for any of those reasons. His own situation was comparable in every respect—

except perhaps in the beauty department. He'd never been above average there.

He had married his late brother's fiancée because his father's fondest wish, as well as that of old Andrew Snelling, had been to see the firm consolidated through the marriage of their two offspring. And because after his father's last stroke, shortly after Court had returned from that his last trip south, he had no longer been able to hold out against the irascible old gentleman.

Originally, the anointed pair had been Rick and Jay Two. Snelling's son, Junius Andrew Jr.—called Jay Two by his friends—and Rick, ambitious, capable, the image of his father in all ways, were slated to assume the reins when their elders decided to step down, with Rick's marriage to Snelling's daughter the icing on the cake.

The triumvirate, as Court had called them. Always odd man out, he'd been secure in having finally escaped the cold comfort of his family's bosom to make his own way. At the time, he'd been in his second year at law school.

On that particular weekend of the race, he had scheduled the trip home to take part in an ongoing competition, secretly amused that, much to his father's disgust, he was still the only decent sailor in the family. From the time when they were boys, racing in the club's junior events, Rick had never come in more than a poor fourth behind his younger brother.

Unfortunately, on this particular day, with the

company's honor at stake, Court was out of the running, sidelined by a severe head cold. The *Ariel*, jointly owned by the two families and representing Adams-Snelling in the annual regatta, had won three of the last five annual races, with Kellerman Wheelworks taking the remaining two. A tie was unthinkable. *Ariel* had to race, and dammit, she had to win, according to the two old men, scowling over scotch and water in the clubhouse.

In that one fateful afternoon, those two old men had watched their entire world come to an end.

By the time his train had pulled into the station the previous morning, Court had known he wouldn't be racing. Because he was far too groggy from the doctor's nostrums, the honor had fallen to Rick and Jay Two. Only at his father's insistence had Court even gone along to lend moral support. When the firing gun went off, he'd been sprawled in a deck chair, nursing the prescribed hot rum toddy and wishing he were home in bed.

To this day he despised the taste of rum.

The weather had been unseasonably warm, even with an army of tall thunderheads marching along the horizon. A brilliant sun had glinted blindingly off spanking white hulls and polished brass, the glare adding to Court's misery.

It had been a perfect day for a race, in fact. Quartering a light northeast wind, the nine contenders had set out from the starting line to the tune of cheers, toasts, and a chorus of irreverent advice.

By the time the last entrant had rounded the

fourth buoy, the sky had turned nasty. Still, with the wind freshening to near thirty knots, the race would be over before the weather closed in. That had been the consensus among the officials.

No one could have predicted that single isolated bolt of lightning that streaked down through the sky, its target a certain thirty-five-foot New Haven sharpie flying the Adams-Snelling colors.

That had been one of the few occasions when Court had drunk himself insensible. Losing Rick, the brother he had idolized all his life, had been bad enough, but seeing his father, aged a lifetime in a single day, turn on his own wife and demand to know why it had been Rick and not *her brat* that had been taken, had nearly killed him.

At the time, he hadn't understood. Yet, on some deeper level, perhaps he had. At least, he'd understood why he'd never felt secure in his father's love. His father had never loved him. It was that simple, though Court bore the man's name. Though he'd lived his entire life in his father's house, cold and formal though it was, worked summers for the firm his father owned jointly with old Andrew Snelling, and celebrated family birthdays and holidays along with an assortment of cousins, aunts, uncles and Snellings.

In the years after that tragic summer, he had tried not to think about it. Your brat. What had he meant? Not *our* brat, but *your* brat.

Court hadn't wanted to know then, nor did he now, although he'd always had his suspicions. There's been those love letters, written to his mother before he'd been born, that he had come across after both his parents had died ... they'd been signed, your Lawrence.

Your Lawrence. That proved nothing. All the same, it would explain a lot. He had vowed a long time ago that if he ever married, and if he should ever have children, they would never doubt that both their parents loved them above all.

And now, God help him, he had broken that vow.

He spread the pages of the letter out and scanned them again. The heading was his cousin's address in Elizabeth City, the date the eleventh of May, 1892.

My dear Courtland [he read]. *I must say, your Wiggins has a real flair for this business. He secured that parcel in question at half the cost I had anticipated. Papers, etc., will be in your hands shortly.*

It grieves me to learn of your latest bereavement. Although I don't suppose, judging from what little I knew of Mrs. Snelling, that you were ever truly close to Diana's mother. Still, her passing seems to have burdened you with sufficient to occupy you for years to come.

I have not, as you will remember, seen your little Iris since she was knee high to a cricket, but Sally Lee and I have bracketed your single achievement with our boys. Robert E. is seven now, Andrew all of nine, and up to more

mischief than I can deal with in any given day.
Reminds me of my own misspent youth.

As it has been more than four years since Diana's
tragic passing, might I inquire if there is a
second Mrs. Courtland Adams in the offing?
A woman's hand is most definitely needed in dealing
with a child of either gender. In the event you
and your daughter would wish a vacation in
which to become better acquainted, may I offer
our family place at Nags Head? You will consider
it quite primitive, I have no doubt, yet it's quite
comfortable and privately situated on the
sound side, away from the hotels and gathering
places, yet not so far as to be isolated. There are
only a few other cottages on this particular stretch
of shore, as the storm of '89 damaged many
beyond repair. Ours survived, as did the
Douglases', for which Sally Lee and I are grateful,
as one of our dearest friends resides there year-round.

But I digress. Let me again repeat my
invitation to you and little Iris to make use
of our cottage for as long as you like. In a relaxed
situation, away from the scene of so much sorrow,
you may well come to know your daughter and
even get to be friends.

Sally Lee sends her best regards. I am both proud
and embarrassed to confess that once again, she's
increasing. I must say, I'm rather pleased at
my success in that field, although I believe
Sally is rather less so. She had hoped to be done
with such onerous duties.

*Do consider our invitation. The cottage,
while it's a far cry from that museum-piece
you live in, is in the hands of a caretaker and
can be opened up, staff hired, et al., at a moment's
notice.*

Sincerely yrs, etc., etc.,

Yr. cousin, Seaborn Adams

Court grinned at the letter that had arrived in the morning post. The old son of a gun! He might have lost his hair, but evidently that was all he'd lost.

From the bottom of his heart, Court envied his younger cousin. His own life seemed a desolate wasteland by contrast. And yet, he had a child, even if she was practically a stranger. For four years he had had a wife. When she was sober. Perhaps it wasn't too late to start over.

For years he had blamed Diana for the alienation of his only child, and yet, in that he hadn't been fair. If he hadn't chosen to bury himself in his work, his harpy of a mother-in-law might not have moved in and gained a foothold in his home after old Andrew had died.

Poor Diana was gone now, as were both her parents. And his own. From a big noisy enclave, the joint families had somehow shrunk over the past ten years to one embittered widower and a single silent child, who stared at him with her mother's beautiful eyes under her father's thick black brows as if he were an ogre come to bear her off to hell.

Raking his fingers through his hair—hair that was

still dark, but which was well laced with silver at the temples—Court wondered if perhaps Sea was right. Away from all this, they might be able to forget the past and start fresh. It was worth a try. God knows, things couldn't go on as they were. The child hadn't spoken to him in four days, not since he'd barked at her for knocking over a particularly hideous urn Diana had set great store by.

As if he gave a good damn in hell about an urn! Or any other of the costly junk his late wife had stuffed their home with. Diana preferred things to people.

At least she had until she had come to prefer the bottle to all else.

Meanwhile, in another part of the country, another letter was being written.

> Thursday, 25th of May, 1892
> Nags Head, North Carolina

My Dear Sea and Sally,

I do wish you would move to the seashore! I envy you your two lovely boys, and would like nothing better than to have them for the summer. You must promise me that this next one will be a girl, for I do so long for another goddaughter, as I see little chance of ever having one of my own. But more about that later. I'm working on a SCHEME!

Do you remember all the wonderful times we had here as children? I still fish and sail and

*even wade about with my crab net, and of course,
I wouldn't miss my daily "dip." I'm quite determined
to teach Teeny to swim before another year is
out. (How many times have you heard me say
that?) But with so few friends about to play with—
this early in the season, there's only Teeny, Polly,
and little Megan—I'm afraid I even talk to
the seagulls, who aren't a particularly
intelligent lot.*

*Yesterday we built a sandcastle of such
monumental proportions that it took all
morning and earned me a bad sunburn and
an aching back. Megan, of course, could have
stayed on the beach forever. She's brown as an
acorn, and I am afraid the same can be said
of your friend, Miss MacMischief.*

*Did I tell you that Polly has joined me in Good
Works? We hand out pamphlets whenever we see
the Python Begin to Rear his Ugly Head. (You
do recall our classes in Ladies' Hygiene with
Miss Harvey, don't you, Sal?) On the first
Wednesday morning of each month, Polly gathers
her little group in my front parlor to sing
hymns and consume great quantities of
lemonade and cake while they denounce their
erstwhile lives of sin, although I prefer to call
it more tragedy than sin, for what woman
would willingly allow herself to be used in
such a manner? Sally, you would not believe the
pitiful condition of some of these poor creatures.
Whoredom, and you will please both pardon*

my plain speaking, but calling a boil a beauty
spot does not lessen the pain—whoredom is
truly a degrading profession, and dangerous as
well! Most of these women were coerced or lured
to such ends by an unspeakable cad named
O'Brian or Briant, or somesuch, professing to
have their best interests at heart. Some of them
are little more than children, lured from their
homes by what wicked promises I can only
imagine. I do what I can, conducting classes
in reading and mathematics. Polly gives classes
in domestic work. One of the hotels has been very
good about hiring our young "graduates" as
maids and kitchen helpers, although I'm sorry
to say, there are always a few backsliders.

But enough about that. Really, I'm not half
the crusader I once was. For the most part,
Polly has taken over for me here at Nags Head,
and Mrs. Espy, as you probably know, has proved
invaluable back in town. Moving our little rescue
mission away from all the saloons and oyster
houses was a most intelligent step. Sea, I thank
you for your advice. Things go well at our new
"Retreat," according to my weekly reports from
Mrs. Espy.

In answer to your question, yes, someday I
may move back, but even now, I cannot visit town
without recalling those sad days right after our
home burned down when I brought Father
back here to nurse him through his final
weeks. I don't suppose we'll ever know what caused

the fire that took poor Chartreuse's life. Sad to
say, I don't believe in the end Father even
remembered the woman. He spoke often of
Mother. I believe he truly loved her—or
perhaps I only want to believe it. I must say,
however, he had a most peculiar way of showing
it.

Teeny is building the most exquisite
furniture. Really, the man can do wonders with
even the most humble of our native woods. He
has been working with a boat builder part of
the time, although he's always around when
we need him. I was fortunate that he was, for
just last week my porch caught fire. How, I can't
imagine, as we're situated so far out over the
water, but one of the pilings underneath the
westward corner caught fire in the night and burned
up through two of the deck boards and a part
of the rail before Polly smelled smoke and
aroused the household. Teeny said it looked
almost as if it had been set, which is foolish, of
course. I asked him if he thought perhaps someone
could have tied up there for a spot of night
fishing and left a lighted cigar or lantern
lodged in the underpinnings.

I suppose we'll never know. Another of life's
little mysteries. Lately, they seem to happen
more and more frequently, but then, the longer
one lives, the more strange experiences one collects,
I suppose.

Now that Teeny and Polly are married, my

greatest fear is that they will decide to move
out on their own. I do believe, for in my old
age—and there are days, my friends, when I feel
quite old—I have become quite selfish, that if
they left little Megan behind, I would deem
it a fair trade. The child is bright beyond
belief, and truly a joy. I tell you quite frankly,
my dear friends, that I am actually considering
entering into the dreaded state of matrimony
simply in order to have a child of my own.

But as I said, more about that when my
SCHEME has had time to mature. Perhaps
curiosity will lure you to the beach when all
my pleas fall on deaf ears.

Ever your loving,
MacRorah MacMischief MacLonely

MacRorah waited until she had sealed her letter
and sent it off by Teeny to post before joining Megan
on the sound shore.

"You're not going out there in that hot sun without
a bonnet, Miss Mac!" Polly, her flat feet encased in
high-topped canvas shoes, her sturdy little frame surrounded by a snowy white apron, held out the broad-
brimmed straw with the frayed and faded ribbons.
"It'll take more buttermilk than that ol' cow's got into
'er to bleach them freckles!"

The cow was kept over in the small fishing village
in a fenced lot, along with several others. Teeny
brought the milk and eggs and whatever produce was
in season when he drove the cart home each eve-

ning. "Then I suppose I'll just have to stay freckled, won't I? It didn't seem to do you any harm," MacRorah teased.

After more than ten years in the Douglas employ, Polly still retained her freckles, as well as her sharp tongue. "Don't you two young'uns stay out all day, now, y'hear me?"

"Yes, ma'am," MacRorah said meekly, her eyes sparkling. If she'd thought to miss Mrs. George after that woman had married one of the men from 41 Pecan Street and moved to Perquimans County, she needn't have worried, for Polly had taken over bossing her around as naturally as a fly took to a sugar bowl.

It was already midmorning by the time MacRorah had finished her own chores and hurried down the long boardwalk that stretched between cottage and shore, dodging drying canvas shoes, buckets, dip nets, crab lines, and an assortment of cane poles.

Stepping off onto the warm pink sand, she scanned the shoreline in both directions for a sign of Polly's child. A sensible little thing, she knew which activities were allowed and which forbidden. She was not to wade out above her knees alone, nor was she to wander past the big dune to the south or the Adams cottage on the north. Most importantly, she was not to speak to strangers, and if accosted, she was to go straight home.

MacRorah told herself she was being overly cautious, for who in this sunny, friendly community of honest fishermen and summer vacationers would threaten a small child?

All the same, she had heard too many horror stories from those pathetic girls of Polly's, some of them little more than children themselves.

Besides, accidents happened. Just last week, MacRorah herself had been nearly frightened out of her wits when a drunken reveler from the nearby hotel had nearly run her down with his cart and knocked her off the boardwalk on her way back from her daily dip in the ocean.

Shading her eyes from the sun, she spied two small figures in the distance and began walking along the hard-packed sand near the water's edge. Megan had evidently found a friend. Soon families would be coming down for the season. Church camps brought hordes of children; the beach fairly teemed with them. But on the last day of May, they were still a rare delight.

"Good morning. Will you introduce me to your new friend, Megan?" Goodness, the poor child looked as if she were suffocating under all those ruffles and flounces! Who in his right mind would dress a child for a tea party and then send her out to play on the shore?

"This is Iris. She's eight and a half years old and she's come to stay for a while. Her nanny is named Jonesy, and she can't walk very fast."

MacRorah leaned over and braced her hands on her thighs. Staring down into that solemn little face, with its enormous blue eyes and those funny dark brows, she felt something warm and somehow sad come over her.

Her sister Rosa had had eyes like that. Not the heavy brows, but those summer-sky blue eyes, round and glistening with wonder. Even before fever had struck, Rosa had always been frail. This child looked even more delicate. How strange that they'd both been given flower names.

Megan, on the other hand, if she resembled a flower at all, was much more like a hardy little dandelion.

"Good morning, Iris. My name is MacRorah Douglas, but my friends call me Miss Mac. Do you suppose Jonesy would allow you to take off your shoes and go paddling in the shallows with us if we promise to hold hands and not wander far from shore?"

She turned to smile at the elderly woman seated in a canvas chair under a big black umbrella. The woman eyed her suspiciously, and MacRorah plowed through the soft sand to her side.

Camphor and liniment. Heavens, what an unpleasant aroma to bring to the beach!

Well, someone simply must rescue that poor waif. MacRorah had never been one to back down from a challenge—and besides, something about this particular child drew her in a way she hadn't been drawn in years.

Chapter Nine

I n the days that followed, Megan and Iris came to be close friends. MacRorah watched over them as they played together while Jonesy, the elderly nursemaid, sat well up on the shore under her cumbersome black umbrella, extending her limbs to bake her aching joints in the sun. Once satisfied of MacRorah's reliability and respectability, she was quite content to nap, refusing to join them in their picnic lunches.

It was Polly who packed the picnics for the trio to share. "My mommy makes cookies every day," bragged Megan. "She maked me a birthday cake that had six whole layers, and candles, too!"

But it was MacRorah who entertained her two charges with stories of Old Sophronia, who was rumored to be one hundred and twenty years old and who could hoo-doo warts off a body sight unseen. And of Big John James Jimson, whose grandfather had been a king in Africa and who had once single-

handedly saved an ox from drowning when the creature had backed its cart too close to the edge of the
wharf and followed it overboard. And of the sand hill
that swallowed hotels.

"Do you see that big pink sand hill way over there,
just under the cloud that's shaped like a pig? To this
day that hill is called Hotel Hill, and somewhere
under all that sand is a perfectly beautiful hotel, all
filled with lovely things just waiting to be rediscov-
ered when the sand hill moves on."

"Does it have people in it, Miss Ma—Marora?"
Iris's eyes were round as marbles.

"I'm sure not, dear. All the people had plenty of
time to pack their bags and move out. My mother
used to call me Rorie. You may call me by that name
if you'd rather."

"Could I call you that, too, Miss Mac?" Megan
chanted.

Laughing, MacRorah agreed that they could both
call her by any name that pleased them. She was having the time of her life with her two darling charges.
Would that summer would never end!

"If we dug up the hotel, could we keep it, Miss
Rorie?"

"Silly, it's too big to dig up," retorted Megan, who
had heard the tale many times before.

"Then could we paint with your watercolors?"

"Perhaps this afternoon we'll all paint a picture of
Hotel Hill, shall we?"

Iris's solemn little face fell. "Papa makes me take
a nap in the afternoon."

"Then perhaps after your nap," MacRorah suggested.

"After my nap I have to bathe and dress and play with my dolls until it's time for dinner. Papa lets me take dinner with him now, because he says it's only proper, but I like picnics better."

To MacRorah's way of thinking, Papa sounded a perfect prig. She knew by now that the poor little mite didn't have a mother, but surely someone in the family knew better than to dress her in silks and lace, with white stockings and patent-leather slippers to play at the seashore. Megan lived in her little denim bathing costumes and went barefooted from morning till night. Living as they did, it was only practical.

At night, long after Megan was asleep in her bed and Polly and Teeny had settled down for the night in the corner room downstairs, MacRorah lay awake in her bed up under the eaves, with a cool offshore breeze blowing in through the open windows.

Dreaming. And scheming. Narrowing her already shortened list of prospective candidates down to the last two.

And, in her weaker moments, summoning up the image of a face, the sound of a voice—memories of a man she had never quite managed to forget.

Court came awake with the sound of pitiful cries echoing in his ears. Groggily, he sat up and swung his legs over the side of the bed. His knees struck the wall. He stood up and his head bumped against the sloping ceiling. Only half awake, he'd forgotten for a moment that he was not at home in his own spacious bedroom, but in Seaborn's quaint cottage, surrounded by the smell of juniper and salt air and by the constant roar of the nearby Atlantic.

The sound came again—the sound that had awakened him. "Iris," he muttered, fumbling for the lamp. The Jones woman was deaf as a post when she chose to be, which was more and more often. He should have pensioned her off before he left New Haven, but he'd thought the child deserved at least one familiar face to turn to in times of stress. God knows, his own offered little reassurance. He was doing his best, but he had about as much notion of how to deal with a child as he did how to sprout wings and fly.

"There, there, princess, it's only a dream," he murmured, tying the sash of his bathrobe as he tiptoed into the moonlit room. He knelt down, awkwardly touching her shoulder, and tried to think of how Diana would have comforted her.

But then, Diana would have hired any number of nursemaids—and had—to see that her own sleep remained undisturbed, he thought with time-leavened bitterness. Even in the early weeks of their marriage, Diana had not been inclined to put herself out for the comfort of anyone else.

The small body felt hot under his hand. Was she feverish? God have mercy, he didn't have the least idea how to locate a physician in this benighted place! He should have asked more questions before he'd ever brought her down here.

She whimpered again, and Court felt like weeping. He was thirty-six years old, head of one of the largest lumber concerns in the Northeast, with branches as far south as Georgia and as far west as Arkansas, yet never in his life had he felt more helpless.

"There, there, sweetheart, it's only a bad dream. Tell Papa what's wrong, and he'll fix it, I promise. There, now, princess, it's only a dream."

Or a bellyache. Orange ices on top of two slices of cake and all that gooey fudge that had refused to harden had probably been too much, but she'd begged, and he hadn't the heart to refuse her. Jonesy had given him a sour look that had made him feel like a ten-year-old who hadn't yet learned to lace his own boots.

"Paa-pa," Iris whimpered. "My tummy hurts."

"I'm sure it does, Princess, but then, it's not a very big tummy, so it can't very well hurt too bad, now, can it?"

For his clumsy attempt at humor, he got a watery smile. The poor mite had inherited his eyebrows. With a mother as beautiful as hers had been, she should have been given a choice of features, at least.

It was with an increasingly familiar sense of inadequacy that Court gathered the small child in his arms and settled himself on her narrow bed. She weighed no more than a minute, which was probably the reason he could never forbid her the extra treats she begged for. She was so damned frail, so delicate—like one of her own dolls all dressed up in a tea party frock.

He couldn't bear the thought of her being ill—or being hurt or lost or sad. She was all he had in the world, and heaven help him, he loved her so much he ached with it.

"Papa, why can't I have a mommy? Megan has one. Megan's mommy makes cookies and cakes out of crabs and puts them in our picnic basket. First I thought they tasted funny, 'cause they're not sweet at all, but then I 'cided I liked them. Could we have crab cakes for breakfast tomorrow?"

Crab cakes on top of all the sweets he had allowed her tonight? No wonder the poor child had had nightmares.

"Can I, Papa?"

"Have crab cakes? For lunch, perhaps. First I'll have to—"

"No, I mean can I have a mommy? I'd rather have a mommy than a crab cake."

Sweet Jesus, how did a man deal with something like this?

Court felt the sweat break out on his forehead. "Now, sugar—well, you see, the thing is—"

Iris buried her small face in his chest and wailed pitifully. "My tummy hurts, Papa. Please make it stop."

"Maybe we'd better wake Jonesy so she can give you a dose of—"

"Don't want Jonesy! She smells funny! I want a mommy! Mommies never let tummies hurt. . . ."

"Shh, there, there, precious, if you want a mommy, then we'll just have to see about finding you one, shan't we? As soon as you're feeling better, we'll talk about it."

The sound of soft sniffle broke the warm dark silence. "I'm feeling better now, Papa. Can we talk about my mommy?"

Court suddenly felt as if a noose were tightening about his neck. "Umm, perhaps you'd better get some sleep first. Finding mommies, is, uh—pretty serious business."

Finding his daughter a mommy was the very last thing he wanted to do, but at a time like this, with her soap-scented hair tickling his chin and her skinny little arms wrapped around his neck, he would have promised her the stars and then done his damnedest to deliver.

Half a mile away, in a cottage very similar to the Adams place, MacRorah lay awake, taking apart her plan and examining it from all angles. Did she dare attempt it?

But if she didn't, what then? Go on as she was, growing older each day, watching other people's children as hopes for her own dwindled away?

Despite all her youthful condemnations, MacRorah was beginning to wonder if marriage was always so dreadful. Teeny had turned out to be a wonderful husband once he had finally convinced

Polly that he didn't look down on her for her past. And once Polly had managed to convince him that she didn't hold his age or his one-leggedness against him.

Of course, the fact that Teeny had doted on Megan from the day she was born had helped, but if those two, who had sparred like two prizefighters, could make a go of it, then she certainly should be able to choose herself a suitable mate in order to provide herself with a child and conduct a sensible, civilized marriage. It was purely a matter of selecting the proper candidate, setting out a few sensible rules at the very start, and not allowing emotions to muddy the waters.

It would be an equal partnership. That would have to be understood from the first. She might no longer be young, but she had never been ill a day in her life. She had all her own teeth, her eyes were as sharp as ever—she had no bad habits, and what's more, she was an heiress. That ought to count for something.

The field had been narrowed down to Reuben Albright and George Meeks, manager of the finest hotel on the beach. She rather preferred Reuben, who was a merchant and reasonably successful, though far from wealthy. Like herself, he was a year-round resident. Not everyone had the grit to endure the bleak winters on the Outer Banks.

Besides which, Reuben was even-tempered— might even be termed docile, which was all to the good. He still possessed all his hair and teeth, and his father, now in his seventies, appeared to be a vigorous, good-natured man.

They would have a boy first, and then, as soon as she regained her strength, a girl. That would be a nice arrangement. She had always longed for an older brother. Perhaps if she'd had one, she wouldn't have gotten into so much trouble.

On the other hand, perhaps she would have. . . .

The only fly in her ointment, MacRorah thought sleepily, was the fact that she would have to marry the man. It was a child of her own she wanted, not a husband. However, she knew far too well what happened to those poor unfortunates who had the one without the other. Too many of them were abandoned by their families at a time when they needed them most.

Between her two young friends and Reuben Albright, MacRorah scarcely had a minute to call her own for the next few days. On Monday she invited Reuben to take supper at her cottage on the following Friday evening. And then there were the bed linens to be washed and blankets to be aired to pack away for the summer. Polly fussed, as she always did, telling MacRorah she should hire someone to do the heavy wash instead of ruining her hands in a washtub.

"I enjoy it," MacRorah said simply, and that was that.

That done, she went through her wardrobe and selected a dress to wear for her supper engagement.

Her white voile was several years old, but it had always been a favorite. She sewed on new lace, hoping she wouldn't look too much like mutton trying to pass for lamb. With all in readiness, she had only to pass the time.

The next morning, she took the two girls out in her tiny sailboat, christened years ago by Seaborn as the *MacMischief*.

"Don't you have any bathing shoes?" she asked Iris, who had met them at the appointed place wearing white dotted swiss with a satin sash, white cotton stockings, and black patent shoes.

MacRorah knew for a fact what happened to black leather shoes once they'd been exposed to salt water. She only hoped the child's father was a forgiving sort. In two short weeks she had come to love the child and despise her papa for caring so little for his daughter that he left her in the care of a dotty old woman who moved at a turtle's pace when she moved at all, and whose notions of what was proper were fifty years out of date.

"We could take my shoes off," Iris suggested timidly. "Jonesy won't mind, she's sleeping."

"Then why don't we remove your pretty dress, as well. That way it'll stay nice and clean."

Megan, prancing around in her little denim bathing costume, tossed the paddles into the boat and clambered over the side. The boat stayed tied up beside the cottage except when MacRorah took it out or when Teeny used it to catch their dinner.

* * *

Later that same evening, a sunburned and beaming Iris informed her papa that she had found her new mommy. "Her name is Rorie and she can sail and swim and catch crabs and everything, and she smells good. She likes little girls; she told me so," she added shyly.

Court groaned inwardly. He needed a new wife about as much as he needed another hole in his head, but in a weak moment he had promised the child. "I'm afraid it isn't quite that simple, Princess. The lady might already have a—a papa."

"No, she doesn't. I asked Megan, and she said Rorie doesn't have anybody 'cept her and her mama and papa. If you asked, maybe she'd take us, too, so will you ask her, Papa? You promised!"

Court felt a twinge of heartburn that had nothing to do with the fried mullet his cook had served for dinner. How had he gotten himself into this mess? Dammit, he was a grown man! How had a child not yet nine years old managed to back him into this awkward position?

"We'll just have to see, then, won't we?"

"Can we see now?"

"Tomorrow. It's too late to go calling now."

"First thing in the morning!"

"After your nap, perhaps."

"Megan doesn't have to take a nap 'less she wants to."

"Megan is not my child." Thank God. One was enough!

"Will Megan be my real sister?"

Court, a panic-stricken look in his eyes, turned gratefully as Mrs. Jones hobbled into the room. "Time for bed, Princess," he cried heartily. "Give Papa a kiss and run along with Mrs. Jones."

MacRorah was an early riser, and for a change, there was a brisk early morning breeze. It was a perfect day for a sail. Megan and little Moses Brown were raring to go. Moses's father supplied them with oysters from his bed just offshore from the cottages. Claimed they were the biggest, fattest oysters in the sound.

"Just a little bitty sail, Miss Mac," pleaded Megan. "Moses's papa won't mind."

Polly's Wednesday ladies wouldn't be coming until ten. There was plenty of time. "All right, then, shall we see how quickly we can reach the channel marker? Moses, hoist the main, and Megan, you may man the jib."

Her willing little crew scrambled about the twelve-foot vessel while MacRorah cast off and settled herself at the tiller. The sails filled nicely, and MacRorah forgot she hadn't even taken time to eat breakfast. This was one of the joys of being entirely independent.

They had nearly reached the channel marker when they spotted Iris on the shore, leading a tall man by the hand. Her papa?

MacRorah was half tempted to turn back. She had a bone to pick with that gentleman! "You're luffing,

Megan," she called out, and it was just that moment when the tiller slowly began to sink under her arm.

It was such a ludicrous sensation that at first, Mac-Rorah didn't understand what was happening. Bewildered, she stared down as the rudder assemblage separated from the stern and drifted out of reach. Before she could quite grasp her predicament, the boat heeled over, causing the boom to swing wildly to the leeward.

"Hang on tight!" she cried, scrambling forward to grab a child under each arm.

It was already too late. The main sheet slipped from Moses's small hands. Yelping, he lunged after it, nearly oversetting MacRorah, and in all the excitement, the swinging boom dragged through the water, filling the sail. With chilling majesty, the *Mac-Mischief* rolled onto her side and began to sink.

There was never any real danger. A wooden boat didn't actually sink to the bottom—not right off, at least. Besides, they weren't out all that far. The water came only to MacRorah's shoulders.

But she couldn't help but think, even as she organized her charges, what if it had happened out in the channel? Dear Lord, what then? She was a strong swimmer, but with two children clinging to her, she would have been hard-pressed to stay afloat, much less reach shore!

By the time she was halfway in, half carrying, half floating the two frightened children, a crowd had gathered on the shore. Wouldn't you just know it? Here she had sailed all her life with nary a speck of trouble, but just let her run into a streak of bad luck, and the whole world gathered to watch.

Big Mo Brown waded out to take his son in hand. "What done happen, Miz Mac?"

"I haven't the least idea," she said, shaking her wet hair away from her face. "The whole steering apparatus seemed to come loose in my hand for no reason at all. By the time I realized the thing had fallen off, it was too late to retrieve it."

"Bracket done rusted out, I 'spect."

"It was a wooden bracket. Perhaps the screws—"

He shook his head, lifted his young son onto his shoulders, and waded off toward where he'd left his cart.

"Iris!" Megan sang out. Slithering out of MacRorah's arms, she went galloping away through the shallows. "Guess what happened to us! We got shipwrecked!"

Oh, my mercy, she could have lived a lifetime without this, MacRorah thought miserably. Not only was her hair in ruins, her old blue chambray wash dress was clinging to her like a second skin. If she'd known she was going bathing, she would have dressed accordingly. How was a body supposed to deliver an effective set-down looking like a drowned puppy?

But then, what she had to say to that gentleman would have to wait. It was most decidedly not fit for his daughter's tender ears. She wouldn't hurt Iris for the world, but it was past time her precious papa heard a few home truths. Naps and party dresses and all the sweets she could eat, indeed! What the child needed was bushels of love, dispensed with a dab of discipline and a large dose of common sense!

Megan had already splashed ashore, none the worse for her dunking. "I'll go find Papa to fetch the boat," she called over her shoulder.

"Rorie, Rorie, I've brought Papa!" MacRorah nodded absently to Megan and turned toward the child, who was pushing her way through the crowd, a slightly overdressed man at her side. "Rorie, this is my papa, and he says—"

"Not now, Princess," the man muttered. "I think the lady and I will discuss the matter later, after she's had time to make herself presentable."

That voice! Blinking through the salt-drenched lashes, MacRorah wiped the hair from her face and stared up at a man she had never thought to see again.

She had to be dreaming. Such things simply didn't happen outside the covers of a novel. Her *ice wagon hero*? The phantom of all those foolish dreams? The man who had given her one sweet taste of the kind of power that could enchain a woman before she even knew what was happening?

"You," she gasped.

"You!" he roared.

Looking from one to the other, Iris wailed, "Papa, what's wrong?"

"Not now, Princess," Court said distractedly, never taking his eyes from the half-drowned figure before him. Even in this condition, the woman was devastating. Judas priest, what had he let himself in for? "As for you, madam, I'll deal with you later!"

As the small crowd began to disperse, he turned and strode off down the beach, dragging his daughter behind him until he realized what he was doing. Slowing his steps, he looked ruefully down at the small child. "I'm sorry, Princess. I didn't mean to tug your arm from its socket, it's just—"

"But Papa, what's wrong? Why are you so angry?"

"I'm not angry, sweetheart, I'm simply—" How much lower could a man sink? Now he was lying to his own child. "Yes, sugar, Papa is angry, but not with you."

"But Rorie couldn't help it if the boat got sunk. She can sail real good, Megan told me so. She can catch fish and crabs and tell stories and everything, so don't be mad at her . . . please, Papa?"

Court was angry with the woman, but he was even more angry with himself for being attracted to a woman—a common whore—who could blithely endanger her own child. The same little Megan he'd been hearing about for days.

His anger was deflected momentarily by another thought. What if it had been his daughter out there? God, she could have drowned, and it would all have been his own fault! He'd been so wrapped up in his own affairs, going over all the land records and reforestation plans he had brought down with him, that he had allowed that creature free access to his most precious possession!

Without breaking stride, he swung his child up in

his arms, holding her tightly until she protested. "Sorry, Princess—Papa didn't mean to squeeze."

The wench had obviously been using his own daughter to get to him. It wasn't the first time Court had found himself to be the object of such tactics— Diana's female friends had been only too willing to offer him comfort, from the very day of her funeral!

To think that Iris's precious Rorie was none other than his own perennial virgin from that blasted waterfront bawdy house!

Oh, she'd been smart, all right. He'd have to give her credit. Cultivating the child as a means to the father. Or the father's bank account. No doubt she'd had it all planned—the audience, the perfect setting, the perfect pose—she'd come rising out of the water like a Botticelli Venus, the heroine of the hour, with two clinging children in her arms to heighten the effect.

And that, she had no doubt thought, plus his daughter's pleas, would be enough to melt the heart of any man.

Instead, he had seen her as she truly was, ten years older, brown as a common laborer, her eyes red-rimmed and her once-glorious hair dangling like seaweed about her shoulders.

Just let her try to work her wiles on him again, Court told himself, coldly amused. Ten years ago she had happened to catch him at a vulnerable time, but he was no longer the gullible fool he had once been.

At the foot of the boardwalk, he set Iris on her feet and smoothed her lace-trimmed pinafore.

"There you are, sweetheart. You run along now and tell Jonesy to give you a cookie and a glass of milk, all right?"

"But what about Miss Rorie? You promised—"

"I'll speak to your Miss Rorie after she's had a chance to recover. She did take quite a dunking, you know. She might appreciate a few days to recover."

"But Rorie never—"

"Run along, Princess."

Watching her thin legs pump their way up the sloping boardwalk, Court struggled to contain his fury. He would talk to her, all right. Only God knew what he would say to the conniving creature. Order her to stay the hell away from his daughter, for starters.

The real problem was what he was going to say to Iris.

He could bribe the woman to disappear, but even if he paid her off, she would likely just keep turning up again and again. Her kind always did.

The sensible thing to do would be to uproot them all and head north again immediately. Only somehow he didn't think Iris was going to be put off with a trumped-up excuse. He was beginning to discover that his small daughter, despite her fragile appearance, was more like him than he had thought. Once she got a notion in her head, it stayed there come hell or high water.

Chapter Ten

ℭ

Court could still hear Iris's tearful pleas and
Jonesy's placating tones ringing in his ears as
he let himself out the front door of the
eight-room cottage. He would have to deal with his
daughter later. God knew how he was going to do it
without upsetting her even more.

First, however, he had more urgent business to
take care of. That conniving little tramp had had
long enough to dry off and touch up her war paint.
What he had to say to her wouldn't take long, but it
needed to be said now, before she could regroup her
forces and attack on yet another front!

The thing that still mystified him was what she
had hoped to gain by insinuating herself into the
confidence of a vulnerable child. If she'd thought to
collect a payoff of some kind, she was in for a disappointment. He'd see her in hell first.

Or back in that cheap waterfront whorehouse,
which was the next best thing.

It wasn't Court's ability to deal with the woman that worried him, although he'd rather it had been anyone else in the world.

The rough part was going to be dealing with Iris without hurting her any more than necessary, and without having to explain more than an innocent child could understand.

The strumpet had done her work well, he would hand her that. All week long it had been Rorie this and Rorie that, wonderful, beautiful Rorie, who painted pictures of funny boats and funny birds and funny cottages that looked like long-legged birds— who made lovely picnics and told enchanting tales about walking sand hills.

Walking *sand hills*?

Court's anger turned inward. If he'd been any kind of a decent father, he would have investigated his daughter's new playmates immediately, before it was too late. Now she was going to be hurt—there was no way now to avoid it—and it was all his fault.

He would simply have to make it up to her somehow. God alone knew what he'd end up promising her this time. It would not be a mother, though. They would just have to muddle through together as best they could, because he'd had enough of marriage to last him a lifetime.

Marching shoreward along the boardwalk to the tune of his own turbulent thoughts, Court was oblivious to the clear sky overhead, the brilliant sun sparkling off the pale green waters of the sound, the snowy sails offshore and the graceful seagulls wheel-

ing and keening overhead. He should have had sense
enough to stay home in Connecticut where he belonged!

On the other hand, how could he possibly have
known the little witch would be lying in wait for him,
ready to finish the task she'd begun ten years ago?

He whipped off his tie and crammed it in his
pocket. Not up to her standards, indeed! Not even to
himself did Court dare admit that seeing the little
amber-eyed witch again after all this time had left
him badly shaken. By all rights, she should have
been a raddled old hag by now, her wickedness
etched in every line of her face. Instead of which,
she'd looked—

Oh, hell.

A pulse throbbed insistently at the side of his
throat, reminding him of the need for a cool head.
After years of maintaining a tight control over his
temper under circumstances that would have tried
the patience of Job, he'd gone storming off the minute he'd handed Iris over into Jonesy's care, ready to
beard the lioness in her den without even knowing
where her damned den was located, and then been
forced to retrace his steps to ask Jonesy if she knew
where the woman lived, which had only stoked the
fires higher.

She was staying in the third cottage down the
shore, similar in appearance to all the rest save for
the color of the shutters and the row of shoes, cane
poles, and other beach apparatus littering her boardwalk.

What the hell was she even doing in a respectable place like this? He'd have thought a woman of her stripe would have chosen one of the fancy beach hotels over a family neighborhood. But then, she was probably under the protection of some bald, paunchy businessman who used the place for his fancy piece when his family wasn't in residence.

Not that he really gave a sweet damn in hell who her protector was, Court fumed. For all he cared, the little tramp could be spreading herself for the chief justice of the Supreme damned Court, but if she thought for one minute she was going to use his daughter to worm her way into his life again, she'd picked the wrong dupe!

Failed to meet her standards, had he? For two cents he'd show her a thing or two about performance!

The pulse in his throat was throbbing again, and once more Court reminded himself that whatever had once been between them—not that anything had, at least nothing that he could remember—Iris's welfare took precedence now.

Damn and blast the rackety female, anyway! With roughly a million whores in the country, why did he have to keep tangling with the same one?

Having covered the distance of some quarter of a mile within mere minutes, he was halfway along her boardwalk, his mind coldly assembling the ultimatum he was about to deliver, when he heard the ragged chorus earnestly delivering a melody that sounded almost like "Rock of Ages."

"Rock of Ages"?

* * *

Having hastily bathed the salt off and buttoned on her coolest summer frock, her hair in a damp braid down her back, MacRorah willed herself to put the entire episode out of her mind. Small boats got swamped every day. It wasn't exactly headline news. You'd think the bluefish were running, or the scallops were in, the way the crowd had gathered so quickly.

But of all times for *him* to show up. What was he doing here, anyway? She hadn't thought of him in ages—at least hardly ever. Practically never, in fact. And to think he had to barge back into her life just in time to catch her wading ashore, looking like the cat's breakfast.

It wasn't as if she weren't a good sailor, either. She was an excellent sailor. It had to be some sort of judgment against her for past sins that the one time in her life she had capsized a boat, she'd had to go and do it before at least a dozen witnesses, not to mention the one man in all the world she had hoped never to see again.

But perhaps it wasn't the same man. It had been a long time. People changed. And besides, didn't they say that everyone had a double somewhere in the world?

She sighed as the ragged strains of "Rock of Ages" dwindled off, to be replaced by the clink of china. It was the same man, all right. She would have recognized him in an Amazon jungle wearing a loincloth and a bone through his nose. There was also the inescapable fact that he had recognized her, too.

"Oh—peepee!" she muttered.

Inside the house, Polly exhorted her wayward girls to put their sordid pasts behind them. Well, if they could do it, so could she, MacRorah determined. Hiking her skirt, she climbed up to her favorite perch on the wide rail that surrounded the cottage and set up her painting gear. Grimly, she dipped her brush into a teacup of water, then dug it into her sticky palette. Scowling, she swept it across the paper.

The sky was blue? She painted it a fiery red. The water was calm? She painted a raging tempest. Under the furious daubings of her brush, a royal tern that soared gracefully overhead was transmuted into a ferocious white eagle.

Actually, it looked more like a chicken, but it definitely had the soul of an eagle!

How *dare* he look at her as if she were a bit of rotten fish cast up on the shore!

How dare he even *be* here on her beach? He was supposed to remain a quiet, well-behaved phantom who turned up only on rare occasions in her daydreams.

Well . . . not so rare, perhaps. And not so well behaved, either, but that was another matter.

Probably it wasn't even the same man. They'd only thought they recognized one another. The man she remembered had dark hair—not quite black, but near enough. The eyes she remembered were green, streaked gold with flashes of sheer deviltry laced by a strange nuance of sadness that had lingered in her mind long after she'd forgotten the exact definition of his features. This man was older, his hair going gray at the temples.

But then, it had been a long time. Ten years, to be exact. Ten years, almost to the day, in fact, since she had dashed out of Mrs. Baggott's shop after her mother, been accosted by poor Chartreuse outside the shop, and pulled herself free, only to be caught in the arms of a stranger with a remarkably sweet smile and a pair of haunting eyes.

He was no longer smiling. And if those were indeed the same eyes, they were no longer sad. The eyes that had glared at her when she'd waded ashore had been absolutely furious!

Recklessly, she splashed orange and rose in wet puddles on her paper sea, determined to block the disturbing stranger from her mind until she could think how to deal with him. Because if he was indeed Iris's father, she was going to have to deal with him. For the child's sake, she could do no less.

With fresh determination, MacRorah focused her attention on her painting while inside the cottage, Polly's Wednesday girls cut loose with a spirited rendition of "The Old Rugged Cross." MacRorah never joined them in their sessions, for they seemed inhibited by her presence, but she always preferred to be close by in case she was needed for something.

The meeting would be coming to an end before much longer. Once it did, she would help put away the leftover refreshments, if there were any—usually there weren't—and dry the dishes while Polly washed. It was one of the few times she was allowed to help out in the kitchen.

Unable to make her shipwreck look like anything other than a grizzly bear walking on water, MacRorah impatiently flung her still damp braid over her shoulder. She hiked up her skirt, absently scratched a mosquito bite, and muttered a mild obscenity. Over years of associating with a less privileged element of society, her vocabulary had grown rather impressive.

"I don't know what the devil is going on here, and I don't want to know." The voice came unexpectedly from so close behind her that she nearly went sailing off the rail into the sound. "I have one thing to say to you, madam, and if you know what's good for you, you'll listen well!"

"I *beg* your pardon!" Her mouth fell open and stayed that way until she remembered to shut it.

"Stay away from my daughter!"

". . . the em-blum of suff'ring and sha-a-ame," came the doleful chorus from inside the cottage.

Frowning, he glanced over his shoulder and toward the open window. "What the—Madam, I don't know what your game is, but I promise you, if you so much as come within a mile of my daughter, I'll see you locked up in the nearest jail and I'll personally throw away the key. Do I make myself clear?"

MacRorah fought the urge to swat that superior sneer off his damnably arrogant face. How could she ever have doubted his identity for a single minute? "I have a few things to say to you, sir. You'll kindly oblige me by listening. In case you hadn't noticed, I live little more than a quarter of a mile from the cottage you rented, and as I have no intention of moving, it's entirely likely that Iris and I will be sharing the same beach. Furthermore—"

"We'll just see about—"

"*Furthermore,*" MacRorah stressed, "if you had half the brains of a sand flea, you'd know what Iris needs—"

"Don't even mention my daughter's name, you—"

"Hush your mouth, sir! I'm not finished with you!"

"Indeed you are, madam. I've warned you, you're to stay away from my child! I don't know what you've told her or how you've managed to worm your way into her confidence, but I'm warning you for the last time, I will not have her contaminated by the likes of any two-bit—"

"Contaminated! *Contaminated?*" MacRorah screeched. "If anyone is contaminating that precious lamb, it is you, you selfish, overdressed prig! You don't deserve a child like Iris! All I can say is, she must have taken after her mother, which is fortunate indeed, because heaven help her if she'd taken after you!" Smirking in a manner deliberately meant to provoke, she added, "Are you quite certain she *is* your daughter?"

It was all Court could do to keep from knocking her off her perch. Never in his entire life had he struck a woman, but this one tempted him almost beyond resisting. Under a layer of golden tan, her cheeks flushed with color, making her look—

Making her look too damned beautiful for any man's peace of mind, he thought rancorously. Even knowing what she was, he could feel his body begin to react with disgusting enthusiasm to her clean fresh scent, to the sun-blessed velvet of her skin—to that full, gleaming lower lip of hers.

Mortally embarrassed by his body's growing sexual interest, he glared at her.

She glared right back.

"Just remember this," he warned, fists knotted in his trousers pockets against the temptation to reach out and shake the living daylights out of her. "You're to stay the hell away from my daughter, madam! She's too young to understand what kind of woman you really are, but I'll tell her something, believe me, that will give her a disgust of you she won't soon forget."

"What kind of woman I *really am?*" MacRorah was mad enough to spit nails. To think he would hold one teeny-tiny mistake against her for ten long years! Was he so perfect that he'd never made a single misstep? She knew for a fact that he had once turned up uninvited and drunk on the doorsteps of a perfect stranger, which no true gentleman would dream of doing, and as if that weren't bad enough, he had done any number of wicked things to her person.

"One small mistake does not make me a pariah," she informed him haughtily, more injured now than angry.

"Pariah or not, madam, you've made your one mistake. And had to live with the consequences, obviously. But one more and you'll hear from my lawyer."

His *lawyer*?

But before she could question him further, Polly's meeting broke up and the porch was suddenly flooded with women who could best be described as colorful.

As well as embarrassingly frank. "Oooee, ain't he the lovely man, though?" The woman, a new recruit to the cause of righteousness, did all but feel his muscles while the lovely man in question stared at her in growing horror.

It was all MacRorah could do not to laugh, and truly, the last thing she felt like doing was laughing.

"Here, now, you let Miss Mac's gentleman alone, Maybelle. He ain't int'rested in what you're peddling, and you're not peddling it no more, less'n you've forgot!"

The gentleman sidled away as warily as if a cage full of circus animals had opened up right beside him. From the railing on the side porch, MacRorah watched him hurry down the boardwalk, his shoulders rigid under his gray worsted coat, his long, muscular legs covering the distance with no regard whatsoever for the poles and buckets and shoes littering the path.

Halfway down the boardwalk, he turned and glared at her. "By the way," he said in a voice that carried quite clearly over the water, "if that abomination is your best effort, I'd advise you to do the art world a favor and throw away your paints!"

MacRorah looked down at her colorful mishmash of a painting. She looked at the stiff back of the man striding down her boardwalk. Well! she thought, hurt all out of proportion to the insult to her artistic ability. There was one foolish dream that hadn't stood the test of time. Good riddance!

Later that day, Court had a teary-eyed Iris to deal with. He'd known it would be bad. He hadn't known just how bad.

"But Papa, you *promised*!"

"Iris—Princess, I—"

"But you did! I heard you! You said if I picked out a new mommy, you'd get her for me, and I picked Rorie."

Court tugged loose the knot of his gray silk four-in-hand. "Now, sweetie, if you'll just let me explain— Say, do you think there's any of that chocolate cake left? What do you say we go out to the kitchen and see what we can find to go with it? Maybe after your nap we might walk down to the hotel and treat ourselves to a great big—"

"I don't want a nap! I don't want to go to the hotel. I want *Ro*-rie!"

In desperation, Court made what he recognized too late as a tactical error. He promised the child that if she went along like a good little girl for her nap, later on he would do his best to find her Rorie and . . . well, they would see.

"Can I go with you to find her, Papa?" Iris was

practically dancing around him, but this time, Court stood firm.

"Not this time, sweetheart. You run along and wash those tears off your pretty little face and take your nap like a good girl, and I'll see if I can find Miss—ah, Rorie."

"Her real name is Miss Marora, and I know where she lives, Papa, she lives in the house with the green shutters."

Court knew, too, to his sorrow. He had only hoped to postpone the inevitable. "Fine. Now you run along with Jonesy, and I'll go make myself presentable, and later on this afternoon we'll see what we can do, shall we?"

By the time he showed up with Miss Marora, or whatever she called herself, he would have come up with a story that would convince Iris she never wanted to see the creature again. He would think of something. He had to! And if Iris wouldn't accept it from him, she would have to hear it from the horse's mouth.

Or, in this case, the whore's.

Reuben came early for supper. MacRorah had invited him for five in order to have time to talk. Reuben didn't care to stay out after dark. Too many strangers wandering around now that summer was getting under way, he said. Reuben was a sensible man.

So he came at four-thirty, resplendent in his best

white linen suit, his sandy hair parted in the center and plastered down.

He wasn't really an unattractive man, but with an image fresh in her mind of a lean, sardonic man with deep-set hazel eyes, poor Reuben suffered in comparison.

"Balderdash," MacRorah muttered. She loosened the sash around her uncorseted waist just a smidgen. Her waist was no longer eighteen inches around, it was almost twenty-one, but any man who took her would take her as she was, for she refused to torture herself for the sake of fashion. Long drawers, chemise, petticoat, and ribbed cotton hose were enough for any mortal to wear in hot summer weather. All that, plus her newly refurbished white voile with the sprigged overskirt, was surely sufficient.

They sat out on the front porch and drank lemonade while Polly put the finishing touches on supper. Teeny had brought home a peck of clams, a nice flounder, and a mess of greens from over in the village. Hardly party fare, but then, Reuben was hardly a party sort of man. Which was one of the reasons she had written his name on her list in the first place.

"Reuben, tell me about your mother's people. Were they all as healthy and long-lived as your father?"

Obligingly, Reuben discussed his maternal heritage at length. At great, tedious length. After some twenty minutes, MacRorah was more than satisfied that any child begat by Reuben Albright would inherit a sturdy constitution, at the very least.

Which brought her to the crux of the matter. The begetting itself. At nearly twenty-nine years of age, with a wealth of experience in such matters, all of it admittedly secondhand, MacRorah was not about to make the mistake of putting the cart before the horse.

Or in this case, the begetting before the marriage license. She had heard too many tales of how a single mistake had led an innocent girl straight down the primrose path.

However, she did know that although babies didn't come from kissing, kissing was often the first step. Before she could marry any man, she had to know if she would be able to endure the intimacies of the marriage bed.

Which meant that kissing was the next logical step. If she couldn't stand Reuben's kisses, she probably wouldn't be able to endure The Other.

"Reuben, would you like to kiss me?" she asked, startling him into dropping his lemonade glass.

By the time they had mopped up the mess, Reuben was backed up against the railing. MacRorah, handing Polly the dripping cloth, found herself standing practically toe to toe with her victim—that is, her intended victim. That is, her intended!

"M-m-miss Douglas, I—"

He was sweating. Was that a good sign or a bad sign? She should have thought to ask Polly. "It occurred to me that it might be a pleasant thing to try.

After all, we're both mature adults." Reuben was a good five or ten years more mature than she was. "It couldn't do any harm, could it?"

He gulped noisily, and fascinated, she watched his bow tie jiggle. Leaning forward just a bit, she came up against his nice, soft, squishy body and lifted what she hoped was a suitably besotted gaze to his perspiring red face.

She almost wished he would take the initiative, but this was probably the best way. At least this way she would remain in control of the situation. The moment she decided she'd had enough, she would simply back off and send him packing.

But nicely. She would think of some excuse. Reuben was a nice man, and she wouldn't hurt his feelings for the world. And he did smell rather good. Actually, he smelled like vanilla extract, and as vanilla was her favorite flavor, she counted it a mark in his favor.

"Reuben," she whispered, "shut your eyes. This won't hurt a bit." And slipping her arms around his neck, she mashed her lips against his and waited for the fireworks to begin.

From the foot of the boardwalk, Court watched, unable to believe his eyes as two pale figures merged. Both were wearing white, one obviously female and the other just as obviously male.

From this particular vantage point, it appeared to be the female who had done the merging. As a blindingly brilliant sun sank slowly toward the waters of the Roanoke Sound behind the cottage, he watched in angry disgust as a pair of tanned feminine arms slipped around the shoulders of the white suit. The white suit appeared to be far too busy bracing himself against the railing to cooperate.

The woman was obviously making all the moves.

And then, suddenly, it all fell into place. The hold he needed over her. If she was staying at the cottage under the protection of one man and seeing another, that was ammunition enough. If the bloke in the white suit was her current keeper, then he could threaten to tell him all the sordid details of that night ten years ago—she could have no way of knowing that he couldn't remember much past seeing her in that fetching bit of yellow temptation—but by threatening to upset her sweet little love nest, he should be able to put her in her place.

As a defensive maneuver, it was somewhat flawed, but for lack of something better, it would have to serve. Iris would simply have to understand that in a far from perfect world, disappointment was a part of life.

Somehow, he vowed silently, he would make it up to her. A new doll, perhaps. A dozen new dolls!

Anything but a mommy.

Chapter Eleven

𝒞

He couldn't sleep. Despite all he could do, once he had managed to settle Iris for the night with some vague promise of a delightful surprise on the morrow, Courtland lay awake for hours, reliving every detail of that single episode ten years ago.

Or, at least every detail he could recall.

Funny that he should remember parts of it so clearly—the scent of her skin, the dusky tint of her nipples, the way her pupils had widened when he'd cupped her breasts and brought them to his lips—only to forget the main event.

As if it had happened yesterday, he could still see her dressed in those few wisps of yellow gauze that had been deliberately designed to inflame, with her honey-colored hair drifting about her shoulders and those wide amber eyes luring him into her web. . . .

Court's brief moment of euphoria vanished like a soap bubble as he remembered that damnable note he'd found on his dresser the next morning, with a handful of bills accompanying her caustic appraisal of his "performance"!

He owed her for that.

Court's marriage had been a miserable failure from the very first, the child the only good thing to come of it. Not that he hadn't tried, for he had. He wanted to believe that Diana had tried, as well. At least, so far as he knew, she had never actually been unfaithful to him.

But then, Diana had never cared for the physical side of marriage. After a rather lackluster honeymoon in Vienna, they had returned to Connecticut, two strangers sharing a house, the one burying his troubles in work, the other seeking comfort in the bottle. Diana had stoically endured his lovemaking until pregnancy intervened, after which she had moved into a separate bedroom and installed her maid in the dressing room.

Iris's birth had been a difficult one. Court had waited a suitable length of time before attempting to approach his wife again, only to be told in no uncertain terms that his touch disgusted her.

From that day forward, he had remained largely celibate, resorting to prostitutes only when his natural urges got in the way of his concentrating on work, and even that not until after Diana's death from liver disease.

Which made it all the more difficult to understand how a single encounter some ten years ago had more power to hurt him—not to mention infuriate him—

than all the years of misery he had endured before, during, and after his brief marriage.

The Nags Head piers were bustling, carts plying back and forth between packet and hotel, hauling baggage and livestock. Now that summer was well under way, families were arriving daily. The shore that only a week ago had been largely deserted now rang with the sound of children's noisy play, with barking dogs, and with cows and hogs, not to mention chickens and geese, protesting as they were herded into encampments for the benefit of the families who had come for the summer season.

Iris would soon find diversion, Court assured himself. Another day or so and she would have made new friends, forgetting all about her precious Rorie. This time, he vowed silently, he would make it his business to meet those friends before she formed any more unsuitable attachments.

Bathing on the oceanside was the treat Court decided upon to make up for her disappointment. Iris didn't swim, of course. Few females of his acquaintance did, and he himself had gradually fallen out of the habit of swimming and sailing, preferring to spend his time working, despite the fact that his staff were all perfectly competent men.

Another of the sound-side restaurants had opened just this week. Perhaps he and Iris would dine out one evening. But the main activity was on the oceanside, where hotel guests and cottage residents alike could enjoy band music, dancing, bowling, and socializing at a seaside pavilion.

He'd have to watch himself, or he would end up promising her far too much, Court thought. She was such a solemn little thing. Hers was not the total lack of interest in anything outside her own comfort that had lent Diana her spurious air of composure, but instead, a half-hopeful, half-fearful sort of gravity that never failed to touch him deeply.

It was a subdued Iris who took her father's hand and set out for the boardwalk that stretched across the dunes to the oceanside. The third time he caught her glancing back at the cottage where that woman was installed, he wracked his mind for something to divert her attention. "We'll have to see about buying you a bathing costume, Princess. How would you like that?" Jonesy had dressed her in her plainest frock, but compared to the other children scampering around, he could see now that she was greatly overdressed for the occasion.

"Rorie has a pretty red bathing costume. She goes swimming almost every morning in the ocean before breakfast. She says it's not even very cold once you get used to it."

A pair of city-pale, barefooted boys in bathing trunks went racing past them, complaining about the burning-hot sand.

"Megan doesn't mind hot sand. She goes barefoot all day long," Iris confided, clutching his hand. "Rorie says it's only sensible."

Rorie says. Court still had a score to settle with

that woman, and he was not going to wait much longer. Perhaps, after all, he should try bribery. For a large enough settlement, she might be induced to leave the area until he was ready to go back to Connecticut.

"Tender feet are better off wearing shoes, Princess."

From the dune overlooking the sea's edge, Court scanned the modest crowd. According to Jonesy, who had it from one of the nursemaids staying at the hotel, most guests enjoyed a dip in the ocean before breakfast, then opted for bowling, strolling, riding, or fishing for the rest of the morning, after which they enjoyed luncheon at the pavilion or one of the restaurants and then napped until time to dress for dinner.

He had counted on the beach being largely deserted at this time of day, most of the bathers having already moved on to other activities. In that he was disappointed. Aside from a few strollers, there were several bathers, the men daring the waves that splashed halfway up their knee-length trunks, the women squealing and darting back as the spent surf threatened to dampen the soles of their high-buckled bathing sandals.

Court's gaze was drawn to a noisy quartet, bolder than most, who were standing waist-deep in the waves. Three men and a woman. They were laughing uproariously as the petite woman, clad in a scarlet costume, grabbed hold of a towheaded giant and

cried, "Jump, jump! Oh, yes—now use your arms!"
just as a big wave threatened to sweep over them.

"Look, Papa, there's—"

But Court wasn't listening. Instead, he watched
the wave knock the pair of revelers under. They
bobbed up sputtering, still laughing like a pair of
drunken sailors. The woman found her feet first, and
then she and the other two men tugged the blond giant to his feet. The two other men slipped in beside
him, one on either side, and the woman turned and
began wading ashore, still laughing.

Oh, God, not again. Court stood stock-still, unable
to believe his eyes, although just why he should have
been surprised he couldn't have said. He'd known all
along what she was.

But three men? In broad daylight? Had she no
shame at all?

"Papa, that's—"

"I know, Princess. On second thought, I believe
the water's too rough today. Why don't we come back
later on, when the tide's not quite so strong, shall
we?"

Without waiting for her to protest, he headed back
up the beach. God knew he hated to break yet another promise, but what else was a father to do? He
had to end this fascination with that shameless creature, even if it meant leaving before Sea and his family came down, and returning to that big empty
house with all its bitter memories.

Court didn't wait to see the cozy foursome emerge
from the water to huddle together on the beach, one

man supporting the blond giant while the woman knelt and unwrapped a wooden leg, and a third man strapped it on. He didn't wait to see the look of adoration on the weathered faces of all three men as she swaddled herself in a faded men's bathrobe, tugged the hood up over her streaming hair, and led the way back over the dune, her small bare feet churning through the hot sand.

MacRorah was exhausted, but it was a wonderful kind of exhaustion. She'd been threatening for years to teach every member of her household to swim. Living on the water as they did, it was only sensible. The real mystery was how any man could have made a living on the sea without ever learning how to swim, but she'd discovered that many sailors never did.

She had made it her business to teach Megan almost as soon as the child could walk. Polly still refused, but when two retired seamen from the Retreat had turned up this morning with a half-day layover before heading back on the packet, both had added their arguments to hers. One of them had lost his hearing and was no longer considered employable, the other had been nearly blinded in a shipboard explosion. But as it happened, both men could swim.

"You promised to learn last summer," she'd reminded Teeny just that morning. "Now no more excuses. You have two friends here today to see that you don't back out, so you may as well go put on those bathing trunks we gave you for your birthday."

The sound would have been calmer for swimming, but it was far too shallow, unless one waded half a mile offshore. They could have gone out in the boat, except that the boat was still laid up for repairs.

"Craziest thing I ever heard, a one-legged man floundering around in the wash like a beached porpoise," Teeny grumbled now as he came out of the bedroom wearing his usual canvas workclothes, but MacRorah could tell he was proud as punch of his accomplishment.

"At least you got your head wet and lived to tell the tale. The next time will be easier." One way or another, she was determined that he know how to stay afloat and propel himself through the water. He could probably manage now, but unless he *knew* he could do it, he would panic and sink.

Shortly after the two retired seamen left, the three Gritmires set out for Manteo aboard the *Annie Beasley* to stock up at Hollowell's store and buy fresh produce from Mr. Tillett, if that gentleman could be found. They were to return before dark if the weather didn't close in, otherwise they would stay overnight and return first thing in the morning.

Before she left, Polly had dished up a plate of cold boiled drumfish and potatoes and ordered MacRorah to eat every bite and not to dare wash a dish. MacRorah had crossed her fingers and promised, then slipped outside to give Megan twenty-five cents to spend on a gift for her mother's birthday, which was coming up in only a few days.

There, she thought as she watched her beloved

adopted family out of sight. Another project well under way. Teeny's swimming lessons. How could she ever have thought she would grow bored living here all year around? With so many people depending on her, she scarcely had time to get on with her own project of finding herself a father for her children.

With an empty afternoon looming ahead of her, perhaps it was time to pay Reuben another call. He hadn't been around for a few days. Orderly by nature, MacRorah decided it would be best to finish her business with Reuben, who had originally been number four on her list, before tackling number five.

Number five was George Meeks, the manager of the Hotel Alexina over on the oceanside. He was single and personable, and had been most understanding when she had explained her mission of rescuing prostitutes from their unfortunate circumstances.

The funny thing was—although it hadn't seemed funny at the time—that right at first he had mistaken her for one of that sisterhood. They'd both enjoyed a good laugh at that!

MacRorah blotted a bead of perspiration that was trickling down between her breasts. On the other hand, it could wait another day. She really didn't like this weather. It looked as if it might storm before night, in which case, she would be here alone. Though she was completely commonsensical, without a fanciful bone in her body, she had never felt entirely safe perched up like a lightning rod on pilings when one of the frequent lambasting squalls swept past.

Should she go and risk a soaking? Or should she cower here all alone, chewing her nails to the quick while she waited for lightning to strike her dead?

She would go.

On the other hand, she rationalized, Reuben might need a bit more time to think about her proposal. He had looked none too happy when he'd hurried off after the kissing experiment. Perhaps she should give him more time.

Which left Mr. Meeks. But then, that might complicate matters with Reuben.

What she needed was a list of things to be done, numbered in the proper order in which they needed attention. Number one on that list would be little Iris, because if ever a child needed her help, that one did. For two cents, she would forget all about Reuben and Mr. Meeks and march herself right up to that man's door and demand to know why he insisted on treating his daughter as if she were as fragile as a porcelain doll, dressing her accordingly.

And while she was at it, she could demand to know why he no longer allowed her to play with Megan.

And why it was somehow all *her* fault. What was it he'd said? That she had made a mistake?

She'd made a mistake, all right, and the mistake was not slamming the door in his face all those years ago! The man had been so inebriated he could hardly stand.

Thunder rumbled in the distance, but for once, MacRorah didn't even hear it. She was no longer a silly impressionable eighteen-year-old girl, out to prove something to the world without the least notion of what she was getting herself involved in.

Nor was she about to turn her back on that innocent child. Someone had to protect the poor mite from her insensitive clod of a father! Imagine plopping a child down on the beach every morning on the dot of ten all dressed up like a French doll, and expecting her to stay that way. Didn't the fool even realize that children at the beach were supposed to splash and dig and get gloriously dirty and wet? What else were beaches for?

MacRorah glared at the cold luncheon Polly had set out for her. In a little while, Iris would be taking her nap, which was another thing—the child was all of eight years old! Was he so anxious to be rid of her that he forced her to sleep her vacation away?

MacRorah told herself that it would serve him right if she marched herself right down to the Adams cottage and gave him a piece of her mind! Digging her fork into a cold boiled potato, she tried to pretend it was the neck of a certain pompous, heartless stuffed shirt!

They met halfway just as the dark clouds that had moved in over the sound began showing flashes of lightning. The water was as calm as glass, the air completely breathless. In deference to the oppressive heat and humidity, MacRorah had dressed for the occasion in her coolest outfit, which just happened to be her most becoming. She had twisted her braid up on top of her head, not in any attempt to look her best—although she had happened to catch a glimpse in her mirror before she'd marched out of the cottage and was not displeased with the results—but because the added height lent her added courage.

While she had been washing the plate and fork Polly had ordered her not to wash, she had rehearsed every word of what she planned to say. Every scathing set-down, every accusation. By the time she was done with that gentleman, he would know precisely what she thought of a man who would ignore his own child, leaving her in the care of a dotty old woman who couldn't have moved out of her chair to escape a rampaging herd of elephants!

What if Iris should wade out too far and need rescuing? she would demand. What if some ruffian accosted her? It had been known to happen. Girls little older than Iris and Megan, fresh off the boat from the country come to work in the hotel, had been known to disappear and turn up later working for some degenerate who preyed on such innocents.

Although, to her knowledge, it hadn't happened lately. At least, not since she and Polly had started handing out pamphlets and letting it be known that they would help any woman who wanted to escape that pimp person's evil clutches.

Oh, she would tell him off, all right, for not taking better care of his precious child. And while she was at it, she would take up the matter of all those layers of ruffles and flounces. Any dolt knew that a child at the beach should be dressed for the occasion in cool, washable, practical clothing that lent itself to digging for coquinas and splashing about in the shallows.

Heels digging into the damp sand, MacRorah marched along the shore toward the Adamses' cottage, and incidentally, toward the man who was marching to meet her. "And furthermore," she muttered aloud just as he came within range. "Furthermore . . ."

One look at the stern expression of the man striding toward her, lightning flashes illuminating his lean, angular face, and she clean lost her train of thought.

In the preternatural darkness, he was bareheaded, barefooted, his gleaming white shirt open at the throat, the cuffs of his dark trousers turned up halfway on his muscular calves. If he'd appeared before her in his underwear, she couldn't have been more startled.

He was beautiful. Oh, my mercy, he was shockingly handsome!

Court was ready for her. He had worked up a full head of steam, and nothing was going to induce him to blow it off prematurely.

Only why the hell did she have to wear yellow? Was it deliberate? Had she worn it on purpose to remind him that he had once made a fool of himself under circumstances he preferred to forget?

Not that it would have mattered a damned bit if she'd waltzed down the beach strip stark naked!

"Madam, I have come to the conclusion that this island is not large enough for the two of us."

"Don't you mean the three of us? I assume this is about Iris."

In the cool light of the impending storm, her face looked unusually pale, her eyes enormous. If he didn't know better, he would have sworn she was no more than twenty years old. To have lived the life she had and still retain that dewy look of innocence, she must have made a pact with the devil. "How much?" he demanded coldly.

"How much what?" Her gaze fell to his naked feet, making him acutely self-conscious. Dammit, he should have known better than to lower his standards!

"How much is it going to cost me? Has the going rate dropped since we last did business together? Twenty dollars, I believe I left then—not to mention the bill you so generously left on my dresser with your brief message."

Had he thought her pale? If he hadn't seen it himself, he would never have believed that a whore who had been practicing her trade for as long as this one had—who had actually borne a child—could still manage to summon up a blush.

Cynically, he told himself she could probably cry on cue, as well. Between her blushes and her tears, she must have managed to accumulate a bloody fortune by now. It was a wonder she hadn't collected herself a husband.

"How much?" he repeated. It was difficult to speak when one's jaws were clenched.

"Look, Mr.—What is your name, anyway? If I'm going to rip your blasted heart out and feed it to the fish crows, I'll need to notify your next of kin."

"It's Adams, and you're not going to do one damn thing but shut up and hear me out! Now—as I said, I'm willing to pay you to go elsewhere for the rest of the—"

"Adams? But that's Seaborn's cottage you're staying in."

"I do know where I'm staying, madam. Now, will you—"

"But if your name is Adams, then that must mean you're one of his Yankee cousins."

"*Aha!* Then you do have a grain of intelligence! That should make it all the easier for you to understand that if you don't accept my offer and leave quietly and immediately, I'll have you brought up on charges of—"

"You're the Connecticut part of the family! Oh, my mercy, just wait until Sea finds out about—" Slapping a hand over her mouth, she stared at him wide-eyed, and Court, exasperated beyond his meager limit, raised his eyes heavenward.

All he got for his petition was a spash of cold rain on his brow.

"Oh, my, we'd better get inside, the bottom's about to fall out," she said breathlessly, wheeling away toward her cottage.

"Hold on there, I'm not done with you, madam!"

"Then come with me," she yelled, starting to run as the rain commenced coming down in a solid, wind-driven sheet. "Polly and Teeny have gone to Manteo and taken Megan with them, and I left all the windows open!"

She left him no choice. He wasn't finished with her. But at least he had started, and he'd just as soon not have to go through the preliminaries again. So he jogged along behind her on the hard-packed sand until they came to the boardwalk, the two of them pounded along the cypress planks, drenched to the skin and deafened by the roar of rain on water.

MacRorah burst through the door first, her thin voile dress clinging to her like transparent tissue, escaping tendrils of hair plastered to her face and her neck. Breathless, she said, "Just let me close these on the west side and I'll get you a towel. Would you mind running up and closing the ones upstairs? Just the west ones. It probably won't rain in the others."

He wasn't churlish enough to refuse. After all, her landlord didn't deserve to have his floors ruined just because he had unwisely let his cottage to a woman of loose morals. Or to her protector. Court was beginning to believe she had more than one. Every time he saw her, it seemed she was with a different man. She might even be one of the stable of whores pimped by that flashy-looking character he'd seen hanging around the hotel just the other day.

Unable to suppress his curiosity, he shut the last window and then glanced around at the bedroom, which was not unlike the one where he slept. A dormer affair, it had the same sloping ceiling, the same double windows, and the same bare wood paneling, smelling sweetly of juniper . . . and of something else. Lavender, he rather thought. Lavender with a hint of citrus.

Nice. . . .

Scowling at the wet floor, he grabbed what appeared to be a large bath towel and found that it was a man's terry-cloth robe. One that was curiously similar to the one hanging in the master bedroom at his own cottage, only older and more faded. This one, too, was monogrammed with the initials s.s.a.

Good God. Not Seaborn, too!

Steeling himself to say what had to be said and leave before he fell under her spell again, if he had to swim home through the rain, Court clumped down the steep, narrow stairs.

She was setting out food. She glanced up, and he could have sworn that not a day had passed since he had caught her in his arms as she dashed heedlessly out into the street. She had looked at him then in much the same way—pale, wide-eyed, so damned beautiful he'd wanted to—

Yes, well . . . never mind what he'd wanted to do. He had done it a few weeks later, for all the good it had done him.

"There's some chocolate cake left. There usually isn't after a session with Polly's girls, but this time, two of them were absent, so . . . You remember the girls? They were here the day you insulted my artistic ability, remember?"

Court nearly strangled.

"Sit down, Mr. Adams, we need to talk."

"We need to talk, all right, madam, but I'll do the talking and you'll do the listening."

"It's Douglas." At his blank look, she added, "My name. It's MacRorah Douglas. Iris calls me Rorie. My mother did, too, but most people call me Mickey, or Miss Mac."

Again he attempted to speak, but she plopped a plate of cake down before him, sat down at the other side of the table, crossed her arms, and launched into her topic, which had to do with ruffles and flounces and white stockings and patent-leather shoes.

"It simply won't do, don't you see?"

Court saw, all right. Distractedly, he wished to hell she would change out of that wet gown. Through whatever layers she wore, he could see the hard peaks of her breasts, if not their actual color. That, his imagination filled in all too clearly.

He groaned.

"I think we need coffee, don't you? Something hot? I'll just set the pot on. Polly so seldom allows me in her kitchen, you wouldn't think I knew how to brew a decent cup, but I assure you—"

"Miss Douglas!" he thundered.

She glanced over her shoulder, and once again he was struck by the sheer perfection of her features. Her nose had a tendency to lift at the end, unlike Diana's more classical one. Her mouth was full and wide instead of the currently fashionable cupid's bow, but it was her eyes that—

Catching himself up, he scowled. "Miss Douglas!" he said sternly. "Sit *down!*"

Chapter Twelve

ℭ

M r. Adams, I did not invite you here to read me a lecture."

"I have no intention of reading you a lecture, Miss Douglas. What I intend to do is to issue a simple ultimatum, and that, madam, will conclude our association. Is that clear?"

He was angry. In fact, he was sizzling like spit on a hot stove! Was he always this way?

MacRorah answered her own question. Oh, no, indeed he was not. She had an all too vivid recollection of an earlier occasion when he had been anything but angry. She fought back the urge to smile, being fairly certain he would not appreciate her amusement, and her gaze was drawn to a pulse that beat visibly at his temple.

"I'm sure it isn't healthy to hold your emotions too tightly in check, sir. I have it on good authority that rage denied can lead to damage of the internal organs."

Abruptly, he pounded the table with one fist, causing his fork to clatter against his plate. Ignoring him, MacRorah picked up her own fork and cut into her cake. "Yes, well . . . as I was saying, you must know that Iris's clothes will never do," she said calmly. "One would think the child was—"

"What do you mean, they won't do? My daughter's clothes are the very finest—"

"—on her way to a fancy wedding instead of an outing at the seash—"

"—the finest available! Furthermore, if that young ripsnorter of yours is an indication of—"

"As I was saying, you dress the poor child as if she were on her way to a tea party rather than a day at the seashore, and I'm sure I don't know any ripsnorters. If you're referring to Megan, she happens to be—"

Court leaped to his feet, nearly toppling his chair. "Megan—Pagan! Madam, I neither know nor care what your daughter's name is, but I warn you, I will not allow—"

Guilelessly, MacRorah gazed up at him. "My daughter? But Megan's not my daughter. Although I suppose in a way she is. She's my goddaughter, and I'd claim her in a minute if Teeny and Polly would allow it, but—"

Leaning forward, he braced his knuckles on the table and glared down at her, and MacRorah was struck all over again by the beauty of his deep-set hazel eyes. Reminding her of a sudden squall sweeping in over the marsh, they flashed green and gold and slate gray in a face that was angry and bitter, yet remarkably attractive for all that.

Attractive? Truly, she mused, there was no accounting for tastes. The man was a barbarian. She'd seen better manners in the meanest waterfront neighborhood. And yet, she was drawn to him. Oh, yes, indeed, fool that she was, she found him dangerously fascinating. To think that those very same lips that were clamped so tightly together were the ones that had once—

"Have you looked your fill, madam? Then perhaps you'll allow me to continue."

"With your ultimatum?" She sighed. "No, I'm afraid I'm not done yet, and as your ultimatum will conclude our association, I simply must beg your indulgence for a moment longer." Calmly, she forked a bite of cake into her mouth and chewed. "Mmmmm, this really is excellent cake. You should try it. It's the same recipe Polly always uses for her Wednesday gatherings. You were here the last time, remember? We had the last two slices. It's one-two-three-four cake. One cup of butter, two of sugar, three cups of flour, and four eggs. Plus the flavoring, of course. Polly soaks out her own vanilla beans."

Court dropped back into his chair, staring at her as if she'd been spouting gibberish. "One, two, three," he repeated dazedly. "Gatherings?"

"Wednesdays. But we were speaking of Iris's clothes. You really must do something soon, Mr. Adams, else once the hot weather gets under way, and it won't be long—July and August are the worst months, you know—she'll probably fall prey to all sorts of summer rashes. I'd advise cotton. No more than two layers, the looser the better. Pinafores over a little shirtwaist would serve well enough, I suppose, although I really recommend a plain bathing dress. But no bathing shoes. Not for a child Iris's age. Bare feet are healthier than going about all day in wet hose and sandy shoes. Now, as for—"

Court continued to stare at her as if mesmerized until she broke off. And then she smiled at him in a way that completely shattered the put-down he'd been about to administer.

When was the last time he'd seen a woman smile with her eyes that way?

Had he ever?

"You wanted to say something?" she prompted guilelessly. "I tend to rattle on sometimes, but I was afraid if I surrendered the floor, I might never regain it."

He shook his head wordlessly, unable to come up with a single sensible response. Somehow, he seemed to have misplaced his anger.

"Well, then, that's enough about clothes. A word to the wise, as they say. Next, I really must insist that you consider hiring a younger woman to look after your daughter. Mrs. Jones may be all very well, but she can't begin to keep up with an active child. You might suggest she try ginger tea for her joints. It works wonders with Mrs. Espy, and I believe they're about the same age."

When he continued to look at her with that dazed

look, she went on to explain, "Mrs. Espy manages the Retreat. It's a sort of retirement home for, um, people who are unable to work at their professions. For one reason or another. My mother established it—although, actually, the house my mother established was on Pecan Street, down by the waterfront, but after the last fire, we moved. My mother had died in the meantime, you see, and Mr. Marshall . . ."

The girl was unbelievable. For sheer brass, he had never met her equal. "Do go on, Miss Douglas. I find all this absolutely fascinating. Cake recipes . . . children's welfare . . ." There was a muscle twitching near his temple. "Might I inquire if the, um—ladies I met here the other day were from this retreat of yours?" Her mother had been a madam. Evidently, the little witch had taken over the reins, enlarged the operation and then moved the whole bloody wicked empire to the shore.

God, what kind of a hornet's nest had he blundered into?

"Oh, no indeed," she exclaimed earnestly. "Those were Polly's girls. You see, the Retreat is in Elizabeth City, but when we moved here, we saw a need— well—" She laughed a bit self-consciously. "I'm sure that wherever there are men and women, one will find much the same conditions. At any rate, Mr. Meeks at the Alexina Hotel has been most cooperative in letting us know when our services are needed, and things are progressing quite nicely, as you could see from the little group that gathered here the other day."

Court couldn't think of a single thing to say. If he valued his sanity, he would leave this house before another moment passed, pack up his daughter and her arthritic nanny, and catch the next boat out. The next boat going *anywhere!*

Because for reasons that totally escaped him, despite her wet hair, her bedraggled gown, her unfashionably suntanned face, and a nose that was just a bit red on the tip—not to mention her unsavory profession—MacRorah Douglas was at one and the same time the most maddening and the most dangerously seductive female it had ever been his misfortune to meet.

And heaven help him, he was no saint. For his sins, he was a very ordinary, very harried, completely out-of-his-element male who didn't believe in striking a woman, and who hadn't bedded one in so long he'd damn near forgot what part went where!

Although his body seemed determined to remind him.

"I could help you interview applicants," she offered, rising to pour the coffee. The rain had slowed to a steady drone as the storm moved off over the ocean.

Help him interview applicants? Were they still talking about Polly's girls? Her girls?

God help him, this interview was getting completely out of hand!

Ignoring the aroma of freshly made coffee that

mingled enticingly with the scent of juniper, salt water, and the woman's lemony-lavender fragrance, Court stood abruptly and moved to the door. "The rain's almost over. I'd best be—"

"Oh, but I wasn't finished yet."

He turned then and leveled a look that had MacRorah's toes curling in her damp canvas slippers. "Indeed you are, madam. Quite finished. Because I suspect you mean well, I'll not insist you leave, but I warn you—if you make any effort whatsoever to see my daughter again, I assure you, you will regret it."

On that deadly, if soft-spoken threat, he stalked out into the driving rain to stride down the boardwalk, kicking aside shoes, cane poles, and whatever other paraphernalia got in his way. Her boat, the small sailboat she obviously didn't know how to manage, had been dragged up onto the shore, bottom up, its steering apparatus laid on top.

For good measure, he kicked that, too, on his way past.

Seaborn arrived the following day. Alone. Iris was crushed. Court had promised her a pair of cousins just her age for playmates, and a brand-new baby that, if she was a very good girl, she might be allowed to hold.

"Colic," Seaborn explained. "Noisy little dickens. Kept us up every night for the past week. Old Doc Meyer says give her another week or so and she'll be right as rain, but I wasn't sure I could go one more night without sleep. Poor Sal—she said to go along, she'd be fine, but I feel like a dog for running out on her. You ever feel like a dog, Court?"

"Frequently."

Seaborn shook his balding head. "Ain't a feeling I enjoy, but then, women have all the patience. Natural-born saints, if you ask me."

Court looked his skepticism, but said nothing.

"Looks like most of the cottages are filling up. Pooles came down last week, Stevenses due in to-morrow. My pa-in-law's place went down in that last storm, so they'll be moving in on us 'fore the season's over. Expect the old man'll be down before that, looking to rebuild. Pilings still standing, though— most of 'em, anyway. Told him I could make him a real good deal on siding and shingles." He grinned.

They were out on the porch that surrounded the cottage, which was built in a style similar to most of the other structures along the sound side. Near the foot of the boardwalk, Iris, dressed in a white muslin dress with pink satin trim, white hose, and patent-leather shoes, sat on a blanket, quietly arranging sea-shells in neat rows, while farther down the beach, half a dozen children, boys and girls alike, splashed through the shallows, skipping shells and tossing sticks for a great shaggy beast of a dog to retrieve.

The niggling feeling that his daughter ought to be romping around with the rest of the youngsters in-stead of sitting all alone off to herself made Court feel guilty, and feeling guilty made him angry.

And dammit, he was tired of feeling guilty! Granted, he had been an unsatisfactory son and a failure as a husband. He was certainly no expert at being a father, but he was doing his best. He was trying, dammit! Nor was he too proud to accept advice, even when he disapproved of the source.

"Hey, there's Mickey!" Seaborn exclaimed suddenly. Stabbing his cigar in a clamshell on the railing of the porch, the younger man loped down the boardwalk, waving and yelling as if he were one of the boys racing that shaggy dog out into the water instead of a sedate, thirty-four-year old businessman, father of three.

Thinking of a certain bathrobe he'd found lying on her bed—evidence, as if he'd needed evidence, of what she was—Court watched as his cousin, friend, and business partner jogged across the damp sand, dodging children, dogs, and a single stray chicken. Watched as the brown-haired woman in the spring-green gown tucked up well above her ankles flung down her basket and started running toward Seaborn, arms outstretched. He would've recognized her as far away as he could see her. Something about the blasted female never failed to set his teeth on edge.

Court watched as the pair met halfway between the two cottages. Seaborn swung the woman up in his arms, twirling her about until her bare feet were flying level with his waist.

This was the woman whose advice about child-raising he had lain awake far into the night considering? This hoyden? This outrageous baggage? This . . . whore?

The whole world had gone 'round the bend.

When he saw that they were headed his way, Sea's arm draped over her shoulders, her own around his thickening waist, Court abruptly called to Iris, "Better come in now, Princess, before you get too much sun."

"But Papa, that's Rorie with Uncle Sea. They're coming to visit us." First cousin once removed was too complex a relationship. The Adams children had settled on aunt and uncle status for their elders.

"Then you'd better go in and ask Jonesy to wash your hands and brush your hair, hadn't you?"

"But Rorie won't—"

"Iris."

"Yes, Papa."

Court sighed. There wasn't a reason in the world why he should feel as if he'd just kicked the family dog off the porch. Nevertheless, he did. As the doleful child disappeared inside the house, head hanging despondently, the pink sash of her ruffled dress trailing after her, he was once again swamped with feelings of guilt. Grimly, he turned to watch as the chattering pair made their way along the shore, and then up the boardwalk to where he waited, arms crossed over his chest.

"Have you taken up the trade of Trojan horse, cousin?"

Behind his wire-rimmed glasses, Seaborn blinked. "What kind of horse?"

MacRorah's mind was far quicker. "I asked him to bring me, Mr. Adams."

At her polite response, Court's dark eyebrows lifted in contemptuous amusement. He couldn't believe Seaborn had sunk so low as to bring his fancy piece to meet his niece and cousin. "I'm sure you did, madam. But as I'm also sure you won't want that grizzly bear on the beach eating whatever is in your basket, perhaps you'd better go back where you came from."

"Hey, Court—that ain't even polite!"

The wary smile he'd glimpsed in her amber eyes fled, but her gaze never faltered. Court gave her full marks for courage. "It's only clams. Chessie's an awful oyster thief—he finds them underwater and crushes the shells in his mouth, but he can't manage clamshells. I'm not sure if it's the shape or the hardness or the smoothness."

Court didn't give a damn if the dog chopped them up and made chowder. All he wanted to do was snatch the small, maddening female up in his arms and take her somewhere where he could plow her sweet body until he got her out of his system once and for all.

About a week should do it.

Maybe a year.

"Mickey says she's been helping you with Iris. She's great with kids, isn't she?"

"A regular pied piper," Court jeered softly.

"I'd have arranged an introduction right off it I'd thought of it, but I see you two didn't stand on ceremony. That's my Mickey. D'I ever tell you about the time—"

His Mickey?, thought Court. Now, why did that ring a bell? "I'm sure Sally Lee will be glad to have you back home again. How long did you say you were planning to stay, Sea?"

"Who, me? Oh . . . just until Ida Ann gets over the colic, I reckon. The packet had a vacancy, and I was caught up at the office. I told Sal I'd be back in time to bring her and the boys and the baby out for the Fourth of July dance at the hotel."

"And I'll hold you to it," MacRorah declared, turning her back on Court. "I'm dying to see her again. I hope she remembers to bring those books I asked for. One of the things I miss most is a library."

The two of them discussed books and Seaborn's new daughter, whom, he informed Court in an aside, he had wanted to name for MacRorah, only his in-laws had had other ideas.

Court watched, increasingly puzzled, as his cousin's Mickey—his daughter's precious Rorie—advised Seaborn on the use of fennel for Ida Ann's colic, daily walks to restore Sally Lee's constitution, and patience in dealing with his sons' more outrageous pranks.

"Patience, huh?" Seaborn grinned, his blue eyes twinkling behind his gold-rimmed spectacles. "I don't recall Chalmers ever having much patience when you were that age."

A shadow passed over MacRorah's face, which Court found intriguing, but just then a nut-brown girl in a blue denim bathing dress called up from below the porch, where she stood in waist-deep water.

"Rorie! Rorie, Papa says if you want chowder for supper, he needs to shuck those clams before he goes back to work, and you're to dig about six more big ones," Megan called up to the group of adults. "Want me to dig 'em for you? I can do it. I can find clams real good."

Hearing the voice of her playmate, Iris raced breathlessly out onto the porch, hair half braided, one shoe still unbuckled, "Papa, Papa, could I go help Megan? *Please?* I know how to find clams, too. All you have to do is look for the little keyholes in the sand, and Rorie says since Megan and I are closer to the ground than she is, we can see them even better than she can."

Thus the gauntlet was flung. MacRorah eyed Court, daring him to disappoint his daughter. Court scowled, but he knew when he was licked. "Buckle your shoe first so you won't trip," he said, grudgingly admitting defeat.

"Better yet," suggested MacRorah, "why not leave your shoes and stockings here, Iris? Even at low tide, we'll have to wade out a little way." When Court didn't object, MacRorah tried unsuccessfully to hide her triumph. For the child's sake, she couldn't afford to provoke the man now. He had a dangerously short fuse, as she knew all too well.

A moment later, the two men stood on the porch and watched the trio swing along down the beach, chattering a mile a minute. "Does Sally Lee suspect?" Court asked, rage simmering as he thought again about that damned bathrobe.

"Suspect?"

Court's fists clenched as he fought the urge to land a hard left on the jaw of his cousin and best friend. "Am I mistaken in thinking that Iris's Rorie and your precious Mickey are one and the same? And that you've stashed her down here at the beach for your convenience?"

"Me? Stash Mickey? What's the matter, old boy, been out in the sun too long?"

"Dammit, Sea, I saw your bathrobe!"

"Well, devil take it, I've seen yours, too. So's Sal, when we went north for Uncle Frank's funeral. Fact is, you're the reason I'm wearing silk now instead of good ol' Carolina cotton. First thing Sal did when we came home was to have one made up for me. She claims it gets her all hot and bothered, seein' me walk around in black silk with dragons crawling all over it. Feel like a damned fool, but women take these strange notions, you know. Usually best to humor 'em."

Court shoved his hands in his hip pockets and turned away, glaring out at the cheerful, sun-washed seascape. "Dammit, quit trying to change the subject. Is Miss Douglas or is she not the same female you've been blathering on about for the past ten years? The woman you once admitted you were in love with—the woman you're having an affair with, even now?"

Seaborn's jaw dropped. His glasses slid down his nose, lending him a sightly foolish look. "An affair! With *Mickey Douglas*? Man, you *have* been out in the sun too long! Sure, I love her—so does Sally. Heck, it's impossible not to love her, even if she is the world's worst scamp. Used to be, at least. Reckon she's calmed down some by now. None of us is gettin' any younger."

Court turned suddenly and leveled an accusing look at the younger man. "If you're not sleeping with her, then what's your bathrobe doing in her bedroom? And don't deny it, because I saw it there!"

Suddenly Seaborn's face didn't look quite so foolish. "What the devil were you doing in Mickey's bedroom?"

"Never mind that now, just answer me one question. Are you or are you not involved with MacRorah Douglas? And don't bother to lie. You never were any good at it."

"Involved? I reckon I am, if by involved you mean have I known her all her life, practically lived in her pocket—rescued her from some of her more harebrained schemes before old Chalmers could tear another strip off her hide."

"That's *not* what I mean and you damn well know it!"

"All right, then. I'll admit I used to be in love with her. I might even've married her, but she wouldn't have me. Then, too, Dad convinced me she'd ruin my reputation. You know Dad—he's always been big on appearances."

"My opinion of Uncle Henry just went up several degrees," Court said dryly. "Are you telling me there's nothing between you? In that case, how do you account for your bathrobe being found in her bedroom?"

A big grin broke out on Seaborn's plump, pink face. "Has she still got that old thing? Sal gave it to her for her men—you know, the old guys down at that place she runs? But Mickey took a liking to it, says it's just the thing to wrap up in after her morning dip."

Which might or might not be the whole truth. Court wished now he'd paid more attention all those years ago when his cousin had been rattling on about his wonderful Mickey. At the time, his mind had been occupied with his own problems. Such as Diana. Such as his father. Such as whether or not his mother had actually had an affair early on in their marriage, of which he was the unfortunate result. It would explain the coldness his father had always displayed toward him, and the feeling of despair he'd always sensed just under his mother's impeccable facade.

He hadn't wanted to know then, and he didn't want to know now. He had problems enough dealing with the future without wasting time on the past.

It was largely at MacRorah's urging that Seaborn agreed to cut short his visit. She managed to convince him that even though Sally had sent him away, she needed his support. "If you had to run away, the least you could have done was bring the boys with you. They could have stayed with me until you could bring Sally and the baby down later on."

"Ha! And have you teach 'em all you know about getting into trouble? That pair does well enough on their own, believe me!"

MacRorah had walked down to the Adams cottage to collect Iris to attend an open-air Sunday school meeting being held by a church group in a tent on Hotel Hill. The Gritmires were waiting, Polly braiding Megan's hair while Teeny brought the cart around.

To her surprise, Seaborn and Courtland were dressed to attend as well. Iris was beside herself with excitement. "Will it be like a circus, Miss Rorie, with elephants and chickens and all?"

"Chickens? No, dear, it's simply Sunday school, only as we haven't a real church yet, at least not one large enough to hold the summer crowd, it's being held in a tent."

"What's a Sunday school like? Do they have slates and books, like a real school?"

MacRorah glared at Courtland, who glared right back. If his daughter was unfamiliar with organized religion, that was hardly his fault. Diana had been a backsliding Presbyterian, and her mother had had a falling out with the minister, with the result that she had never introduced her granddaughter to the church.

Court had always considered religious training the responsibility of the distaff side of the family.

Teeny, with Polly and Megan dressed in their Sunday best, drove the cart along the shore to the Adamses' place, and they all walked down the board-

walk together, the two men leading the way. "Sea,
you know Polly and Teeny, of course. And this is
Miss Megan, all grown up. Mr. Adams, Mr. and Mrs.
Gritmire and their daughter." MacRorah smiled
grimly through the introductions. She could hardly
wait to see how the dignified Courtland Adams dealt
with riding in the back of a mule-drawn farm cart.
The beach didn't lend itself to fancy gigs and buggies, but most people considered roughing it a part
of the charm of a seaside vacation.

He dealt with it just fine, his dignity not one whit
ruffled from sitting between Seaborn and MacRorah,
with his feet dangling over the tail end of the weathered old wagon. It irked MacRorah no end to see
how his lean, hard body swayed gracefully with the
movement. Poor Sea had to clutch the sides as they
plodded along the rutted track, but then, physical
dexterity had never been among Seaborn's many attributes.

The enormous yellow tent was crowded, the plank
seating such that Courtland and his party found
themselves separated from MacRorah and the
Gritmires. Court had recognized the blond giant
with the wooden leg right off as being the same man
MacRorah had been hanging on to out in the ocean.
He had yet to figure out the puzzling relationships,
but under the circumstances, he was forced to admit
that perhaps the man had been hanging on to Mac-
Rorah instead of the other way around.

The trouble was, there was still far too much he
didn't know about the mysterious Miss Douglas.

While the Reverend Mr. Bricklaier, come to the beach for his annual family-vacation-cum-revival-meeting, expounded on a wide variety of sins and the slim chance of salvation, Court was able to enjoy a clear view of MacRorah in her pink-figured swiss muslin and her white straw cartwheel hat. With her sun-kissed cheeks, her tilted nose, and a hoard of sun-bleached curls tickling her delicate nape, she looked innocent as a newborn babe. And hardly any older.

The woman was a witch, pure and simple. She had bewitched them all—even Sea, who should have known better—into believing she was something she obviously was not.

Beside him, Iris fidgeted. "Papa, when can I go sit with Megan?"

"Shh, in a few minutes, Princess."

"Papa, I have to use the potty."

"Didn't Miss Jones take care of that before you left home?"

"She forgot."

That did it. He was going to pension off Mrs. Jones and hire himself a combination nursemaid-bodyguard, and then he was going to wring somebody's neck. At this point, he didn't even particularly care whose!

"The meeting's about done, Princess. We'll be home before you can blink an eye."

"I don't have to blink an eye, Papa, I have to—"

Fortunately, at that moment the congregation stood and began gathering up reticules, parasols, hymnals, and offspring. Iris's attention was distracted from her immediate problem as Megan hurried up with an invitation to share their picnic dinner.

Evidently, thought Court, an al fresco luncheon was a part of the meeting, which explained the large baskets in the back of the cart. They could have told him, dammit! How the hell was he supposed to know how they did things down here? He'd be damned before he would beg food like a stray mongrel, even for his daughter's sake!

And then the Wednesday girls descended upon him, and he actually resorted to prayer, something he hadn't done for more years than he cared to remember. *God, get me out of this mess, and I swear to You, I'll make it up to You!*

"My, if it ain't Miss Mac's nice gen'leman friend. Dearie, I don't do business on the Lord's day, but if you was to—"

"Hetty! Behave yourself!"

"I were only teasin', Polly. I might've reformed, but that don't mean a girl can't keep her hand in."

"Papa, Papa—I have to go real bad!"

Now, Lord. Right now. I don't even care how You do it.

Chapter Thirteen

Two men leaned against the trunk of a gnarled live oak overlooking the new beach pavilion, sharing the contents of a Mason jar. "Damn near ruint me, she has," muttered the eldest of the pair, a dapper man wearing a flashy plaid suit and matching spats. "Can't hardly find a girl no more what ain't been sedooced by them blasted leaflets her an' that woman o' her'n hands out! I burnt a whole bundle o' the things back in May, but it didn't do no good. Damned pair o' harpies, meddlin' in a man's business so's he can't hardly make a decent livin' no more!"

The younger man took a deep swallow, grimaced, wiped his mouth on his arm, and handed over the jar. "Heard tell you tried to burn more'n leaflets," he said slyly.

"Where'd you hear that!"

"Word gets 'round."

"Yeah, well—I ain't sayin' I did and I ain't sayin' I

didn't. All I'm sayin' is, I come damned near to puttin' her outta business back in town ten years ago. She come out ahead that time—moved her whole operation to a new place an' went right on a-grabbin' ever' girl I had my eye on afore I could even get 'em set up in business. Weren't hardly a decent whore left in Lizzy City 'tween her'n that old lady o' her'n. Business got so thin on the ground I took to spendin' summers down here to take advantage o' all the Yankee money comin' down, an' then, damn if the little bitch didn't foller me!"

"You gonna go after 'er ag'in? Happen, I'm real good wi' a knife. Silent-like, y'know what I means?"

"Fire's cleaner. It don't leave nothin' behind 'ceptin' ashes. Trouble is, half th'time the damn fire goes out afore it can turn the trick."

"Coal oil, that's the secret. Shoulda soaked 'er in coal oil first."

"Not her, ye bleedin' bonehead—'er house. It's got to look accidental-like."

"Hmmm. Tree might could fall on 'er if a body was to saw through mostways and then give it a shove at the right time. How 'bout drownin'? Place like this, folks wouldn't give it a second thought."

"Swims like a damn fish. Paid a feller to rig 'er boat so she'd lose her steerin' and take on water soon's as the wind hit 'er, but the damn thing fell apart while the bitch was still in shalley water. Way she waded ashore, draggin' a pair o' young'uns wi' half the world lookin' on, you'a thought she was a bleedin' hero-wine!"

"Forget 'er boat. Go after the girl 'erself. Trick is to lash 'er to a anchor, haul 'er offshore, an' drop 'er overboard. Like to see 'er swim home wearin' forty pound o' cast iron."

Darcy sighed. With his luck, some frigging fisherman would drag her up in his nets. Next thing he knew, all hell would break loose and every bleeding sot on the beach would be flapping his tongue and snooping around where he'd got no business.

It had been Darcy's experience that once a man got the wind up, he clean forgot his poor pecker. Business fell off, his girls got lazy and started reading leaflets and listening to preachy females.

So no anchors. And no coal oil. Nothing that would cause a flap that would knock the starch out of a gentleman's cock.

On the other hand, a simple robbery—maybe even one that got a mite rough—now, that might be good for business. Damned shame, the high-arsed bastards would say to one another, and the hotel would blow off about setting up a guard. The bleeding sots would get all excited and order up a fresh round, pinch the barmaid's tits, and first thing you know, they'd be looking around for a place to dip their wicks.

Yessirree, just the right touch of excitement could be downright good for business. Not too much—not too little.

Darcy stroked his jaw, took another swig of Buffalo City swamp juice, and looked through the wide windows at the well-heeled crowd inside the pavilion.

He still had a few good girls left, he thought proudly. Catch 'em young, train 'em up right, and set 'em down in high cotton, that was his motto. He looked after his girls real good, and they appreciated it. Steered them clear of the rough trade except for a special now and again. Demanded cash on the barrel head, and they got to keep twenty percent of the take once he covered expenses and took his share. Couldn't do fairer than that.

"I work real cheap," the eager young conspirator confided. "Twenty dollars, a gallon o' this here firewater, an' maybe a few free tumbles, and she'll be outta yer hair permanent-like."

Permanent. Darcy sighed. He'd like nothing better than to see the damned twit planted so far under, her ass would be hanging out in China, but it just wasn't smart. A man didn't last as long as Darcy O'Briant had lasted in this business by making stupid mistakes. "Ten dollars, two quarts, and no tumble. But nothin' permament, y' hear? The bitch's got money, and where there's money, there's lawyers. I don't need no damned lawyers messin' around my territory."

"Fifteen, six, and one tumble wi' that blonde that just come in on the packet boat, and it's a deal. Nothin' permanent, just real discouragin', ye might say."

Darcy O' Briant took out an ivory toothpick, proceeded to remove a string of yesterday's roast pork from between his yellow teeth. He studied it for a moment, then wiped the toothpick fastidiously on his sleeve and dropped it back in his pocket. "Twelve an' six, an' ye can keep yer drawers buttoned up. That little blonde's going to make me a mint o' money, so long as that Douglas bitch don't get to 'er first."

"Deed's as good as did, mate. You leave it to ol' Willy. I'll see she don't go handin' out no more leaflets no time soon." Damn skinflint. Had more women than a dead croaker had flies, but no, oh, no—not a one to spare for poor old Willy.

So maybe Willy would just lift the Douglas bitch's skirts and have himself a little game of poky-poky before he "discouraged" her. Man had to make his own luck in this world.

They were going to leave her, sure as the world. MacRorah knew she should be pleased that Teeny had found regular work over in Manteo with a boat builder, doing what he loved best, but the thought of losing her little family after all these years was enough to break her heart.

Perhaps by the time they got home tomorrow, they would have changed their minds. It was a big decision, after all. Working for a stranger after all these years would be different.

Instantly, MacRorah was ashamed of her own selfishness. A man had his pride. Hadn't it been her father's pride that had led to his downfall?

Ever since they had set out that morning right after breakfast to look over the house Mr. Willis offered along with the job, she had tried her best to stay too busy to think, but no amount of staying busy could ease the ache of impending loss.

She had offered to keep Megan and allow Teeny and Polly more time to look over the situation, but Megan had been every bit as excited as Polly. "Papa says there's a real dollhouse right in the yard, Miss Mac. Mr. Willis built it for his little girl, only she's all grown up now, so he says I can have it."

"And a garden, Miss Mac. You never seen such nice rich dirt, and fig trees so full, I'll be preservin' from here to kingdom come! Why, I've not had a garden o' me own since I left home back when I was a girl." Tears had threatened both women at the reminder of Polly's early misfortunes.

MacRorah might have managed a dollhouse, but living in a cottage perched out over the water, there was no way she could manage a garden. Not so much as a posy at the foot of the boardwalk.

In the end, she'd had to content herself with reminding them all that if things didn't work out, they would always have a home with her. Teeny was so proud of being able to support his family with his boat-building skills that she could only be proud for him, pretending to be every bit as thrilled as they all were.

"If self-pity was mud and you were a hog, MacRorah Douglas, you'd be in absolute heaven," she muttered, mopping her eyes and blowing her nose. She never cried. Never!

Besides, it wasn't as if she had nothing better to do. It must have been providence that had directed her to ask Mr. Meeks about the dance at the hotel. She'd been hearing the band practicing all week long, and with Reuben all but scratched from her list, MacRorah had decided it was past time to get on with her scheme.

Mr. Meeks had promised to collect her at eight. A quick glance at the wag-tail clock showed barely enough time to hang out her dress to air, wash and dry her hair, which took forever, and try to bleach a few layers of suntan from her face with a cucumber and strawberry paste.

While her beautifier did its work—LaFrance Murphy had sworn it would remove warts, moles, freckles, and liver spots—she might as well take the time to dash off a note to Mrs. Espy explaining her need for someone to take Polly's place. Perhaps an older woman with a child. She couldn't imagine being without a child in the house, not after all these years. Megan had been almost like her own daughter.

MacRorah's thoughts immediately flew to Iris. But Iris wasn't hers—not like Megan had been. Besides, Iris would be going home at the end of the season. Possibly sooner, if her father had anything to say about it, and of course, he had everything to say.

Selfish, arrogant, evil-minded prig! It had finally dawned on her, right in the middle of the Reverend Mr. Bricklaier's benediction, just why the man was so dead-set against his daughter's having anything to do with her.

To think that after all these years, he still held her one single indiscretion against her!

Well . . . perhaps not her *single* indiscretion, but certainly the only one in which he had been involved. She'd been little more than a schoolgirl at the time, and besides, the town had long since forgiven her for the cemetery affair. And for the cats she'd let loose in the First Baptist Church in the middle of a wedding. And for pinning a gentleman's union suit on old Miss Spencer's clothesline. And for the rumor about the private investigator that had had every man in town on his best behavior for weeks. And for the—

Oh, for pity's sake, the truth was that she had been dull as ditchwater ever since she'd come of age and moved to Nags Head. Other than handing out a few leaflets when the packet boats came in bringing fresh girls from the country to staff the hotels and restaurants, and sledding down Jockey's Ridge on a copper wash pot, with her skirts blowing up over her head, she hadn't lifted any eyebrows in years.

Well . . . there was that letter she'd written to the editor of the paper about that awful man who made a practice of entrapping innocent young farm girls and leading them into lives of wickedness. That had caused a brief stir, but other than that she had led an exemplary life.

Polly certainly didn't consider her a bad influence, and she'd stack Polly's righteousness against Courtland Adams's any day.

As dusk fell and the last few children ran home to

supper, leaving the sound side once again calm and peaceful, MacRorah sealed her letter to Evelyn Espy, propped it on the mantel all ready to go out in the mail tomorrow, and paused to gaze out the window. There was a lamp lit upstairs in the Adams Cottage. She wondered if Courtland was getting ready to go to the dance.

According to Iris, who had told Megan, who in turn had told MacRorah, the man never did anything but bury himself in his dull old paperwork. But Sea would be leaving in the morning. And Sea had always enjoyed socializing. Perhaps he would drag the old stick-in-the-mud away from his desk for a few hours.

Not that she cared one way or another. Not for herself, at least. But if he ever did unbend, his daughter might reap the benefit. It couldn't be much fun, being stuck away in that gloomy old place with Mrs. Jones and her flapping black gowns and her camphor and liniment, and a grumpy old papa who was afraid to smile for fear his face might crack right wide open.

Funny how a child with blue-gray eyes and golden curls could stir such a longing in her heart, making her feel lonely and a bit sad even before Teeny had mentioned the prospect of moving his family to Manteo.

"Silly old maid, you're hardly alone," she chided, thinking of the hordes of visitors who appeared every summer without fail like a noisy, cheerful flock of migratory birds.

And took flight again just as soon as the days began to grow shorter, she reminded herself as she stepped outside to bring in the gown she had hung out to air away any lingering scent of camphor she used to keep away the brown crickets.

The last stain of color was fading from the western sky when MacRorah heard the first faint strains of music drifting across the dunes, borne on the warm offshore breeze.

Dabbing a glass stopperful of scent behind each ear, she sniffed appreciatively and dragged the stopper between her breasts for good measure. Subtlety, she suspected, would be lost on a man like George Meeks.

Pausing, she tried hard to dredge up a bit more enthusiasm for the last remaining candidate on her list. He had started out as number five on a list of five, but when number one had been caught cheating in a card game, the list had been shortened. Marshall Dingall had been a handsome scamp, with more charm than the law allowed. Unfortunately, he'd also been crooked as a snake on a hot rock.

Then there had been Alec and Peter, two perfectly lovely men who had jointly managed the hotel dining room. She'd had a hard time making up her mind which would be the better bet, for they were both perfect physical specimens, but when they had suddenly decided to move to Norfolk and buy a florist shop, her list had been reduced to two: George and Reuben.

And now there was only George. He had never actually made any move to promote a more personal relationship, but then, MacRorah was used to taking charge. Preferred it, in fact. She had never been a particularly good follower.

Lifting her chin to admire her reflection in the salt-clouded mirror, she made up her mind that tonight she was going to dance and flirt and drink at least one glass of champagne. Maybe two. She hadn't had champagne in years!

Tonight she fully intended to enjoy every single minute of the evening, even if Reuben had been crossed off her list and she was down to her last candidate.

Actually, Reuben had crossed himself off her list. She hadn't seen hide nor hair of the man since she had fed him his supper and then kissed him. Which had been a distinct disappointment.

The kiss, not the supper.

She didn't know what she had expected—well, yes, she did, too, but that was neither here nor there. Nothing had happened. As a kiss, it had held all the wild excitement of stepping into a pair of wet shoes.

Some forty-five minutes later, MacRorah fastened on the pearls that had belonged to her grandmother. Then she slipped on the salmon-pink taffeta over a corset she had dug out of her trunk. The thing was pinching her in two, but the dress wouldn't fasten without it. She only hoped the result was worth the agony.

Without Polly's skilled assistance, she had done her best to sweep her hair up into a pompadour style, complete with a psyche knot that was mostly a snarl of artfully arranged tangles, patting the last one in place just before she opened the door to her escort.

And his *companion*?

"Good evening, Miss Douglas, may I make known to you Miss Brown? Miss Brown is here visiting with her parents. Elizabeth, Miss Douglas is a familiar figure at the hotel. She, uh—takes an interest, you might say, in certain members of our staff."

Elizabeth Brown's Cupid's bow mouth tightened visibly. She extended two limp fingers and withdrew them almost at once. "How very . . . extraordinary," she murmured.

"Yes, isn't it?" MacRorah said through clenched teeth. "How lovely to meet you." She was suddenly conscious that her gown was two years behind the fashions, her best slippers pinched, and if she drew a full breath, there would likely be stays and buttons flying in all directions.

As for the mess she had smeared on her face, it had been an utter waste of perfectly good food.

Had she misunderstood the arrangement? Or had Mr. Meeks? Perhaps Miss Brown was a cousin. Or somehow connected with the owner of the hotel, which was why he had explained about her own connection with the staff.

"Let's not waste time in any more chitchat, ladies, a hotel doesn't run itself, you know."

Mentally, MacRorah added "stuffed shirt" to the other attributes under George's name on her list.

The trip to the hotel in one of the establishment's neat blue buggies took all of ten minutes, during which time MacRorah remarked on the weather, the likelihood of rain, the possibility of a storm sweeping up from the Caribbean, and smiled until her teeth dried up.

"I do appreciate your calling for me, Mr. Meeks. And how very thoughtful of you to bring Miss Brown along." *And do you know, Mr. Meeks, that though Cupid's bow lips are all the rage, a small mouth can be an indication of stinginess? But then, yours is none too large, either, is it?*

Unconsciously, MacRorah pursed her own mouth, which was too wide and too full, and entirely too prone to get her into trouble.

"You're fortunate that I was able to get away, Miss Douglas." George handed over the reins to the cart boy and assisted first MacRorah and then Miss Brown down from the high seat.

His hands, she couldn't help but notice, lingered longest on Miss Brown's waist, which couldn't be more than fifteen inches around.

"Yes, I suppose I am," she agreed, feeling like a walrus by comparison. "I could have gone alone, of course, but I would have felt so self-conscious. I've always shied away from putting myself forward."

She hoped he was too much the gentleman to remember the day three weeks ago when she had gone to leave a stack of leaflets with the housekeeper to pass out to any young maid who looked as if she might be headed for trouble. The lobby had been filled at the time with attractive couples, some with children, some obviously newly wed. Suddenly her own life had struck her as terribly drab and uninteresting. Reminded of her increasing years and her rapidly dwindling opportunities, she had impulsively asked Mr. Meeks about the new band. And then she had asked him if he danced, and if he ever attended the hotel dances as a guest, and whether or not it would be considered dreadfully improper for a single woman to attend unescorted, for she couldn't help but hear the music all the way out to her lonely cottage, and she did so long to watch people dancing and enjoying themselves again before she grew too old.

Which was how it had come about that he'd offered to collect her. She had made it impossible for him not to. Only it hadn't worked out quite the way she had planned.

"If you'd care to refresh yourself, Miss Douglas, Elizabeth will show you to the ladies' retiring room, won't you, my dear?"

His dear. "Perhaps later. The band sounds wonderful!"

"I suppose they're adequate, but lately they've been getting rather demanding. I've hired a smaller group for the rest of the season. Now, if you'll excuse me, ladies, I have several things to attend to. I'll join you, shall we say in half an hour?"

High and dry, like a tide-stranded minnow. Mac-Rorah stared at her escort's retreating back, then turned with a determined smile toward the pretty young thing he had foisted her off upon as if she were of no more interest than last week's newspaper.

"Don't mind me, Miss Brown, I know my way around so well. I do live here year around, you know."

The tiny Cupid's-bow lips pursed until they almost disappeared altogether. "Yes, I believe George mentioned something about your being a local. How . . . quaint. Are your people fishermen, Miss . . . um, Davis?"

Before MacRorah could come up with a suitable retort, someone called her name. She spun around and almost fell into Seaborn's arms. "Sea! I hoped you hadn't left without saying good-bye! Oh, but you're just the man I was longing to see!" She ignored the ladylike sniff beside her. Lifting her chin, she tucked her hand through Seaborn's arm and steered him determinedly as far away from Elizabeth Brown as she could get.

"Leaving first thing in the morning. I already told you that, don't you remember?"

"Oh, silly me!" She tried fluttering her eyelashes but gave it up when he stopped in his tracks to stare at her.

"Got something in your eye? Better come sit down and let me take a look. We found the only place in the house that has a breeze. We'll each stand you to a lemonade, whaddya say to that, scamp?"

"I'd much rather have champagne. Who's we?"

"I managed to pry Old Sobersides loose from his desk. Don't know why I put up with the two of you

all these years—one of you wild as a buck and up to
every rig, the other one stodgy as a turtle."

MacRorah dabbed at her eye, which was perfectly
all right, with her lace-edged handkerchief. "There,
it's fine now," she murmured. There were several
things she could think of that she'd rather do than
have a drink with Courtland Adams. Being staked
out on an anthill was one of them. Walking barefooted over an oyster bed was another.

"Hey, Court, look what the cat dragged in! Order
us another round, will you? Lemonade for my little
friend here. She's not old enough for anything stronger."

"Wretch," MacRorah muttered under her breath,
but rather than make a scene, she sank gracefully
into one of the hotel's deep lounge chairs across a
low table from the man she had once thought of as
her ice-wagon hero.

Some hero he'd turned out to be!

With a strangely detached sort of curiosity, Mac-
Rorah watched as one woman after another strayed
past their little group and lingered to gaze at the
lean, well-dressed gentleman in the stark black and
white, who scowled as if he were angry at being
dragged out against his will. Though he seemed on
the surface to be relaxed, there was a sort of tension
about him. He reminded her of a watch that had
been wound to the breaking point.

"So what brings you out tonight, Mickey?" Sea exchanged his empty glass for a full one and angled his
chair to take advantage of the breeze that blew in off

the ocean. "I thought you'd long ago outgrown this sort of frivolous affair."

Before MacRorah could reply—not that she had any intention of explaining about her list and her candidates, and where the process of elimination had led her—he turned to Courtland and said, "Hey, would you believe this old gal is nearly thirty? What are you now, Mick—twenty-eight? Twenty-nine?"

MacRorah grimaced. Courtland actually grinned.

"What I am is wondering how Sally Lee has put up with you all these years without doing anything more drastic than lifting your scalp. If you were mine, I'd have long since wrung your pudgy little neck."

"I know that. Why'd you think I was so quick to take no for an answer that night I dared you to run off to South Mills with me? Hey, Court, d'I ever tell you about the time I asked—"

"Would you care to dance, Miss Douglas?" Courtland asked, rising and extending his hand.

"I'd be delighted." Gliding smoothly into his embrace, MacRorah called herself a fool, but she was past caring. There was an odd tingly feeling in the air tonight—the same feeling that sometimes assailed her just before an electrical storm struck. A sort of fearful kind of recklessness. Yet as far as she knew, there wasn't a cloud in the sky. "Actually, I'm more relieved than delighted," she confided after half a turn about the room. "No woman cares to be reminded that she's growing old."

If she'd expected him to make some tactful denial,

she would have been disappointed. But then, nothing tonight was turning out the way she had planned it. Just when had she lost control?

She honestly didn't know how or when it happened, but at the moment, it was easier to blame Court Adams than to blame fate. Fate was too impersonal. Fate didn't have a face. It was much more satisfactory to blame something one could glare at and curse—or perhaps even strike a bargain with.

He was a surprisingly good dancer. Not fancy, but firm and decisive. Even though he wasn't holding her tightly, MacRorah was acutely aware of his body. He was warm and solid. He smelled good, too. Like wool and starched linen and expensive tobacco. His hands were cool, yet her skin burned where he touched her, which was downright scary if she stopped to dwell on it.

And, of course, she did. Like poking a troublesome tooth.

Strange, the way he'd always affected her. She hardly even knew him. He wasn't the handsomest man she had ever met. Peter and Alec had been far better looking, with an elegance Courtland Adams didn't even pretend to possess.

He certainly could never be accused of being charming. He was rude, abrasive, insensitive, unfair—in short, he was everything she had ever disliked in a man. As for his morals, she had only that one occasion to go by, but if that was any indication, he was no better than most men. Possibly worse.

Although, on reflection, she realized he had probably not been married at the time. Still, he had married shortly thereafter. Which meant he'd been engaged.

Suddenly, for no real reason, she felt like crying again.

"Miss Douglas? Mickey?"

"MacRorah," she said stiffly. "If you feel you must."

"What's wrong, MacRorah?"

"What could possibly be wrong? The music is lovely, the night is young—I'm dancing with a personable gentleman. What more would any woman want?"

"Granted. So why do I have the feeling you're about to cry? Or curse—or possibly both?"

She offered him a syrupy smile. "I'm sure I don't know, Mr. Adams. Perhaps it's because you're such an extremely poor judge of character."

His soft crack of laughter took her by surprise. "Am I?"

MacRorah pushed herself at arm's length, which was a mistake, because he reacted by drawing her closer, holding her so tightly she couldn't escape without making a scene. She was having enough trouble drawing breath without this added complication!

"Your hair looks nice tonight."

"Thank you," she said through clenched teeth.

"That windblown style suits you."

"It's not supposed to look windblown, it's supposed to look—oh, never mind."

He was smiling. And a smiling Courtland Adams was something she was unprepared to deal with.

But before she was called on to deal with him, the music ended and he led her back to Seaborn, who had reached the garrulous stage. As a drinker, Seaborn had always followed a predictable pattern.

After seating her, Court took his place across the low table. Sea grinned foolishly at them both. For the next twenty-odd minutes they were treated to a rambling discourse on the probable effect the rebuilding of the Dismal Swamp Canal would have on lumber shipments, interspersed with comments about colic and unhousebroken puppies.

Through it all, Court continued to regard her steadily, as if he couldn't quite make up his mind what species she belonged to.

At this point, MacRorah wasn't entirely sure herself.

As if on cue, Seaborn drifted into the melancholy stage, mourning with equal dolefulness the aphids on his precious roses, the dismal state of the economy, and the stain on his new necktie.

MacRorah knew from past experience that unless they got him outside into the fresh air quickly, he would fall asleep right where he sat. In a public place, that would be a problem.

She leaned forward and laid her hand on his knee. "Sea, if Sally Lee's expecting you tomorrow, don't you think you'd better head back to the cottage now?" It was purely habit, worrying about him. He had looked after her for half their lives, saving her from the worst of her mistakes, comforting her after all those dreary and painful battles at home, giving her moral support throughout her father's awful last few weeks.

Now it was her turn. When a waiter came by with three drinks, MacRorah ignored the pink lemonade and reached for Seaborn's drink before he could. Sea protested.

"You promised me champagne, remember?" She took a large swallow, shuddered, and took another. It wasn't champagne; but then, she was in no mood to quibble at this point.

Courtland, seemingly as relaxed as a green snake on a waterbush branch, looked from one to the other. If he was thinking anything at all, it didn't show in those enigmatic eyes of his.

"Will you please take him home, Mr. Adams? I assure you, it's either that or book him into the hotel, and they might not have an empty room."

"What about you, Miss Douglas?"

MacRorah stood, a bright and, she sincerely hoped, convincing smile fixed in place. "Mercy, it's past time I was getting back to my escort. Poor George, he'll be wondering where I am."

Seaborn, struggling to his feet, blinked owlishly, and said. "George, hmmm. He part o' your gran' scheme, Mick? How many lef' on yer list?"

She vowed on the spot never to confide another thing to either of her dearest friends. "Never mind that now. Are you going to be all right? Did you walk over? Shall I ask George to have a buggy brought around?"

"Georgie Porgie, pud'nin' pie, kissed the gals an' made 'em cry. D'old Georgie kiss you, Mick? Member that time in the grape arbor? Court d'I ever tell you 'bout the time Mickey held me down an' kished—"

"Go home, Seaborn. I'm sure Mr. Adams doesn't care to hear any more of your tall tales. Nor do I."

She walked with them to the door and then watched as Court half led, half dragged his cousin down the graveled path. Perhaps she should have insisted they take a buggy.

Although she could insist until she was blue in the face and it wouldn't do a speck of good. Court had declared the walk would do them both good. MacRorah was beginning to suspect she had finally come up against a will every bit as strong as her own.

Just before she turned to go back inside to find George and tell him she was leaving, in case he wished to see her home, Court turned and glanced over his shoulder. For the longest time—mere seconds, probably, yet it seemed an eternity—they stared at each other in the dim light of the lanterns scattered around the periphery of the hotel grounds.

And then he gave her a brief half salute, looped an arm under Sea's, and disappeared into the darkness.

Suddenly, MacRorah felt tired. The evening had scarcely gotten under way, yet as far as she was concerned, it was over.

She really should go find George.

On the other hand, who needed the humiliation of begging a favor from a man who obviously wasn't interested? She'd been taking care of herself for a good many years now. It was beginning to look as if she was fated to go on doing so for whatever years remained to her.

So much for candidate number five. He hadn't even bothered to ask her to dance, yet she'd seen him waltz past twice with Miss Cupid's Bow in his arms, holding her at arm's length, as if she were a paper full of fish scraps he was taking out to the trash.

He wasn't a very good dancer, either, she thought with a satisfying streak of pure meanness. Who wanted to marry a man who waltzed as if he had a plank strapped to his back?

She sighed, remembering the way a certain pair of hazel eyes had smiled down at her as she'd been led firmly and gracefully across the dance floor.

Impatiently, she waved away a mosquito. Who wanted to marry a man, anyway?

Chapter Fourteen

H ow strange that she should still feel so rest-less, MacRorah thought as she paused at the end of the hotel walkway and waited for her eyes to adjust to the darkness. There was no storm in the offing. A zillion stars gave witness to that fact. The sea sounded calm enough as it whispered to the nearby shore.

Perhaps it was the lemonade. Polly's version consisted solely of lemons, sugar, and water. The hotel's lemonade was flavored with a dash of bitters and enough syrup of grenadine to turn it a delightful shade of pink. That had been Peter's creative touch.

Perhaps, she thought with a tense sort of amusement, she was allergic to bitters. Or to grenadine.

Or perhaps she was allergic to Courtland Adams. Tonight she had actually been in the man's company for more than an hour without suffering the urge to crown him with the nearest potted plant.

Pausing, she balanced herself on one foot as she

emptied out the sand from a slipper, then impulsively slipped off the other one, peeled off her stockings, and tucked them into her reticule. The sand felt delicious, still slightly warm under the soles of her feet. How many ladies over the age of fourteen would dare allow themselves to enjoy such a sensuous delight?

Holding her taffeta skirt up over her ankles, MacRorah deliberately slithered her feet through the silky peach-colored sand. Amazing, how sensitive the arches on one's feet could be!

Hiking her skirt up even higher, she executed a gliding step as the faint strains of a waltz drifted through the still night. All her life she'd been called outrageous—she might as well enjoy it.

Not that she had ever set out to be outrageous, not even as a child. In fact, she rather thought if her father hadn't made it so plain that he was disappointed that she was only a girl, she might even have followed her mother's early pattern and become a perfect model of propriety.

But once she'd realized what a disappointment she was, her pride had been stung and she had struck back the only way she knew how. By the time it had occurred to her that the whole town considered her outrageous, she'd been too far out on a limb to back down, with the result that she had responded by becoming even more outrageous.

Only now, at the advanced age of twenty-eight and some months, was she beginning to wonder if the game had been worth the candle. How many times had she—

She cocked her head. What was that, a night bird? Probably just an owl.

To bolster her courage, she began listing aloud all the night birds she knew, wishing she hadn't been so quick to send Sea and Courtland on ahead. "Saw-whet, Chuck-will's widow . . ."

Not that she was nervous. "Whippoorwill, night hawk—um . . ."

It could be a wild beach pony. It could even be a stray cow, escaped from one of the brush-fenced pens.

The noise came again from quite nearby. It was definitely not a cow.

"Helloo—who's there?" Her voice sounded thin in the soft warm stillness.

There was no answer. She hadn't really expected one.

"Really, Miss Douglas, you're getting dreadfully fanciful in your old age," she whispered. Drat Seaborn, anyway! Why did he have to go and remind her of the passage of time? And in front of Courtland, too!

Not that she—

The blow came swiftly, unexpectedly. One instant she was trudging through the soft sand, pausing now and again to listen to whatever small creatures scurried through the night—the next moment she was sprawled out facedown, her mouth full of sand, while several constellations revolved lazily around her head.

When she felt the hand on her ankle, her heart froze in her breast. Whimpering, she tried to kick it away, but her will seemed strangely detached from her body.

Something tugged at her skirt, and she kicked out again.

"Don't fash yerself, girlie, ye're gonna love it." The guttural whisper exploded like cannonfire inside her head as she felt the rough hand slide up the sensitive back of her leg.

And then she felt herself being flopped over onto her back by hands that made no pretense of gentleness and those same hands began tearing at the ribbons at the knee of her drawers.

This wasn't happening to her. It was a nightmare—she was only dreaming. Paralyzed with fear, she tried to scream, but the only sound that emerged was a pitiful whimper.

Her head throbbed. Her arm tingled. Futilely, she struck out, but her tormentor only laughed and pinched her breast.

When he began tearing at the neck of her gown, she lashed out again, horrified when her palm came in contact with sticky hair and sweaty flesh. Before she could do him any damage, her assailant cursed and slapped her hard, causing the stars to fly in circles all over again.

And then, suddenly he was gone, his weight lifted from her as neatly as if he'd been plucked up by a giant fish hawk. As her gaze gradually focused on the dark figure looming over her, she cringed. "Oh, no—oh, please!"

"Mickey, say something!"

"It wasn't a cow," she whispered, and burst into tears. "I never cry," she sobbed, ashamed, frightened, more shaken than she dared admit. "I could have managed," she muttered through tears. "I—I was just getting ready to scream." She rubbed her eyes and got them full of sand, which only made the tears flow faster. "S-someone from the hotel would have heard me and come to help."

Someone *had* come to help. The last man in all the world she wanted to see her like this. Weak, helpless, embarrassed—at the mercy of any night-crawling predator who happened by.

He drew her up into his arms, and she wailed noisily. It was true—she almost never cried, but when she did, it was no quiet, ladylike endeavor. She sniffled, sobbed noisily, and gasped for air.

Awkwardly, he patted her back. He stroked her hair—her lovely psyche knot, all full of sand and tangles and probably sandspurs, too. "There, there," she thought he murmured, but she was making so much noise herself, she couldn't be certain.

He felt good, that much she did know. She was suddenly quite certain that there was no place in all the world she would rather be than in those strong, sheltering arms. The same arms that once, a long time ago, had saved her from walking into the side of a moving ice wagon.

A few feet away, something stirred. She heard a wheezing sound, then a string of foul oaths, and then Court lowered her gently to the ground again. "Excuse me a moment," he said politely. The next sound she heard was the sickening sound of flesh striking flesh.

A few feet away, Court cursed, nursing his injured knuckles. He'd forgotten how painful fighting could be, even for the victor. "Shh, don't cry, love—he won't hurt you again," he said softly, unaware of the endearment that had slipped out.

"I'm n-not crying," she mumbled. "Hit him again!"

"I would, but I'm not sure he'd even feel it." What concerned him more at the moment was how to immobilize the thug until he could be carted away to the nearest jail. Ripping off his necktie, Court tied the man's hands behind him. For good measure, he dragged the man's feet together, knotted the laces of his boots so that they couldn't be easily removed, then tied the laces of the two boots tightly together. "There, you degenerate son of a bitch, let's see you try to run away now," he growled.

Given a choice, Court would have strung the bastard up from the nearest tree. Unfortunately, he had studied just enough law to suspect that the ensuing trouble would more than likely outweigh any momentary satisfaction.

Wiping his hands on his handkerchief, he turned back to the woman. "Come, now, let's get you home," he said firmly, in what he hoped was a comforting tone. He was new to the business of comforting females—new and not particularly good at it.

Lifting her up into his arms, he mentally set a course through the darkness, leaving the meandering path to cut directly across the dunes toward her cottage. "Shh, don't cry now. We'll be home before you know it, and your girl—Polly, is that her name?"

She sobbed something, and Court felt his gut twist painfully. Whatever else she was, he'd lay odds she hadn't been lying when she'd said she never cried, otherwise she'd have done a better job of it. Diana had cried beautifully. A few crystal tears, a quivering chin, and a ladylike sob or two, guaranteed to give a man a lifetime load of guilt.

MacRorah was not so constrained. But then the poor mite had reason to cry. If that bastard had hurt her—

"Hush, now, love, I'll explain everything to your girl. She'll look after you while I go back and take care of a bit of unfinished business. You'll be fine, you'll be safe, I promise."

"Why did you come back?" she whispered, adding a gulp and a sniffle. "Is Sea all right? He didn't get sick, did he?"

"He's fine. Dead to the world by now." Court hadn't a clue why he'd felt compelled to race back as soon as he'd dumped his cousin onto the sofa. Evidently, there were still a few atavistic survival instincts that hadn't yet been bred out of the human male. The notion might have been intriguing if he'd bothered to dwell on it. At the moment, however, he had more important matters on his mind.

Aiming for the pale shape of her overturned boat, Court continued downhill, cradling MacRorah's slight weight in his arms and trying to ignore her trembling and the residual shuddering sobs. She was so small, so vulnerable.

But small or not, at the moment she was also damn near choking him to death, clutching the front of his shirt with both fists as though she feared he might dump her out at the foot of her boardwalk.

"I don't see a light," he said as they approached her place.

"I n-n-never leave a lamp lit. I'm afraid of f-fire."

God, she didn't even sound like the same woman. What had happened to all that abrasive independence that invariably sent him around the bend? Where was that flash of spirit that had captivated his imagination the first time he'd ever seen her? If he lived to be a hundred and ten, he might possibly come to understand her.

"Where's your girl? Polly whatsername?"

"Gritmire. They all left for Manteo early this morning, but you d-don't have to worry about me, I d-don't need anyone."

She'd stopped crying. Now she was shaking like an aspen in a hard wind. "The devil you don't," he growled.

Shouldering open the door, which the stupid twit hadn't even bothered to lock, Court felt his way through the darkness. By the time he had lowered her to her feet and lit a table lamp, he knew he couldn't leave her here. Not alone.

"Would you like to, uh—wash your face and . . ."

Seeing where his gaze had been drawn, MacRorah stared down at the torn bodice of her gown. Her beautiful, ruined taffeta. "I'm sorry," she whispered, almost as if she expected her father to come to life and punish her for having lost her sash or ripped the hem of her pinafore.

And then she simply stood there in the middle of the room, not knowing where to go or what to do. Nothing like this had ever happened to her before. And of all the people in the world to have witnessed her disgrace, *he* had to be the one.

"Would you care for some refreshments?" she asked in the stilted voice of a polite stranger.

"Judas priest!" Court bit off the oath, then wheeled around and began rummaging through her cabinets. "Where do you keep your brandy?"

"With the vanilla and lemon extract."

His anger didn't surprise her. From the first moment he'd barged into her life again after ten years, he'd been angry about one thing or another.

Although, for just a little while tonight, she had hoped they might become friends.

He found the bottle of brandy Polly used to baste fruitcakes, poured a third of a tumbler full, and closed her fingers around it.

"Drink," he commanded.

"No, thank you," she whispered.

"Dammit, drink the stuff before you fall on your face! Sip it. Don't gulp it!"

And because she was too numb to think—or perhaps because she was used to reacting to orders that way—she downed it in two big gulps.

It hit her stomach like a bomb, exploding and spreading fire in all directions. Not until he whacked her on the back did she remember to breathe again. Tears streamed down her face, and when she rubbed her eyes, she got even more sand in them, and then she started to cry again.

"Oh, Christ," Court intoned, and he truly meant it as a prayer.

Once she caught her breath, MacRorah lowered herself cautiously to the settee, with Court hovering over her like a big, predatory hawk. "You needn't stay, sir. I assure you I'll be perca—percafly all right."

Oh, blast. Her tongue had gone numb! She couldn't talk—she couldn't think—what was worse, she had a terrible suspicion that she had just lost control of her life.

"Percafly," he repeated sarcastically. "I'm sure you will, madam."

Court felt like grinding his fist into that bastard's face all over again. Unfortunately, that pleasure would have to wait. "Would you like to change into something more—ah, more appropriate before we go to my place?"

He watched her eyes widen. Those magnificent amber eyes that were now wet and red-rimmed, the thick, golden brown lashes caked with sand. He could hardly take her there in this condition. If Iris happened to wake up and see her before Jonesy could get her cleaned up, there'd be hell to pay.

"Let's wash your face, then, and I'll find you something to put on. Do you want to select something, or shall I?" He remembered the location of her bedroom all too well, having made a fool of himself over the bathrobe he'd found there.

"You. I don't have any feet."

He cut her a swift look, then nodded knowingly. The brandy. Evidently, it had hit her hard, which was just as well. Better than shock, at least. The less she remembered about what had happened tonight, the better off she'd be.

He rummaged through her wardrobe and found a simple day dress that shouldn't be too much trouble to fasten onto her. It had been so long since he'd helped a woman dress—or even helped one undress—that he wasn't sure he was up to the task.

She was talking to herself when he came back downstairs with an armful of clothes, a hairbrush, and a pair of shoes. Sitting upright, hands folded in her lap, her voice as calm and reasonable as if nothing at all had happened to her tonight, she was going on about a list of something or other—and some guy named Reuben.

"Shall I bring a basin of water and wash you up here, or can you manage?" She was making him nervous. And because there was no way he could help noticing the way her torn gown sagged over her breast, exposing a bit of ribbon and one small, brown nipple—noticing and remembering another time when he had kissed that same nipple—he felt guilty. And feeling guilty made him feel angry and defensive.

"D'I ever tell you 'bout Reuben? He was next to th'las' one on my lis'. Poooor Reuben. Worse'n wet shoes."

Sweet Jesus, I don't need this!

By the time Court found the kitchen, poured a basin of water, grabbed a bar of soap and what he hoped was a washcloth, and hurried back to the sitting room, she had discarded poor Reuben of the wet shoes in favor of George. George, it seemed, had something wrong with his lips.

None too gently, Court grasped the back of her head and began scrubbing her face. Feeling the grit of sand under his fingers, he could only imagine what it must be doing to her delicate skin.

"Ptui!" She spat out the cloth and blinked up at him. "D'I ever tell you 'bout the time m'father washed m'mouth out with soap? Wanna know what I said?" She stared up at him owlishly, and Court felt a dangerous tremor in the region of his heart.

Finishing her face, he went to work on her hair, removing pins and combing out the worst tangles with his fingers. "No, Miss MacMischief, I do not want to know what—"

"Miss *Chiff*! Tha's what Sea calls me! How'd you know that?"

Court was beginning to think he knew far too much, and nothing at all about this maddening, tantalizing woman. According to Seaborn, whom he'd pumped shamelessly for information, her father had been a brute, ruling his family quite literally with an iron fist. He'd been a gambler and a womanizer, taking money from his wife to support both habits. Eventually, when it was almost too late, according to Sea, his wife had found the courage to defy him.

As for MacRorah, the more miserable Douglas had made her life at home, the more outrageous she had become.

"You could always tell when Chalmers had come down hard on her. He wasn't a big man, but he was mean." Seaborn had been amused that the two of them had met and taken an immediate dislike to one another. Court hadn't bothered to mention the fact that he had first met her ten years earlier. "Mickey was more than a match for him, though. Never complained. Never shed a single tear, s'far's I ever saw. She'd just get this mulish set to her jaw, and her eyes would start glinting fire, and then it was Nelly, bar the door! Lord knows how many times that little gal set the town on its ear."

And she was still setting the town on its ear, thought Court as he toppled her over against his chest and dragged a brush through her hair.

Why was he even bothering to clean her up? It was her safety he was worried about, not her pride. All he knew was that he couldn't just walk out and leave her here, all dirty and tattered and frightened. Not even if he locked every door and window in the house. He had no intention of involving himself in her problems, whatever they were, but for Sea's sake as well as Iris's, someone had to take care of her until she was on her feet again.

God knew how long that would take. At the moment, she was giggling and rubbing her nose against the front of his shirt, which wasn't helping him keep his mind on what he was doing.

"Stop that!" he snapped, shoving her hands away when they strayed up to his ears.

"D'I ever tell you 'bout Reuben's ears? Teeny-tiny, itsy-bitsy ears." She lifted her face until her nose was practically brushing against his. Her eyes slowly crossed and uncrossed, and she whispered, "D'you think all our babies would've had teeny-tiny, itsy—"

All our babies? All whose babies?

"MacRorah, kindly shut up. Now, if you can stand up long enough, I'll see if I can shuck you out of that ruined gown and then we'll see about making you decent again. All right? Then here goes."

Laying aside the hairbrush, he stood and slipped his hands under her arms. She grinned up at him and allowed him to help her to her feet. Cautiously, he removed his hands, and with a sigh, she slithered silently to the floor.

"Oh, hell, what now?" For two bits, he'd leave her there. He might even go so far as to throw a blanket over her. He could lock all the doors and windows and leave a lamp turned down low in case she woke up and didn't know where she was. . . .

"Come on, MacMischief, let's go." Kneeling, he

lifted her limp form into his arms. She hardly weighed much more than Iris.

Snatching her clean clothes from off the arm of the sofa, he rolled them into a bundle, blew out the lamp, and let himself out the door.

"Damn clutter," he swore as he dodged his way past bamboo poles and canvas shoes.

His toe struck a bucket, sending it noisily over the side of the boardwalk, and MacRorah's head popped up from its comfortable resting place on his shoulder. "D'you know that George has a teeny-tiny, itsy-bitsy mouth?" Her tone implied it was a matter of grave national concern. "Our babies . . ."

She fell silent, leaving him wondering what all this business about Reubens and Georges and babies was all about. Halfway between the two cottages, she began to snore. Not a loud, disruptive snore, but a soft little purring sound.

It occurred to Court that he had never known anything quite so intimate as the sound of a woman's snore.

Quietly, he began to swear all over again.

Chapter Fifteen

❦

Sea was on the sofa, dead to the world. Not even pausing, Court headed for the stairs. Ten to one, Jones would be out like a light, too. Sometimes he wondered about her "rheumatics medicine."

In case he was mistaken, he rapped softly on the nanny's door. Then, not wishing to wake Iris, who slept in the next room, he continued on to the end of the hall, where his own room was located. At least the bed was made up. He could dump her onto the bed, cover her up, and settle down in Sea's bedroom. From the looks of the poor guy, he wouldn't be able to navigate the stairs anytime soon.

"M' head hurts," MacRorah said sleepily when he lowered her to the bed.

"I'll see what I can find for it," he muttered. He'd felt a distinct lump on her crown when he'd combed the sand from her hair. He only hoped the skin wasn't broken. He was no expert on scalp wounds, and he had yet to locate a physician in this be-nighted place.

When he returned from the kitchen a few minutes later with one of Mrs. Jones's headache tablets and a tumbler of water, MacRorah was struggling to reach the buttons at the back of her gown.

"Here, let me," he muttered, setting the tray aside.

What she needed was a maid. Someone like Diana's gorgon, whose sole duty, he'd often suspected, had been to keep him away from his wife's bed.

That was precisely what she needed, he thought with grim amusement as he released the scores of small covered buttons to reveal a shoulder so soft and pale it cried out for his lips.

"How'd you ever get them all done up?" he grumbled, embarrassed by his body's enthusiastic response.

"Button hook. Long-handled one. Do you think I could have something to drink now?"

"No more brandy for you, madam, you've had quite enough."

"I meant water," she said with a tired sigh, and then, be damned if she didn't close her eyes and lean on him, her head falling back against his shoulder.

Alarmed, he caught her in his arms, wondering if the blow to her head was more serious than he'd thought. Was she asleep? Unconscious?

"MacRorah? Rorie?" His arms tightened around her waist and he peered around to see that her eyes were closed. Not so much as a flutter from her lashes.

God, how could she possibly trust him enough to fall asleep in his arms? Didn't she realize how much he despised her?

He *did* still despise her ... didn't he?

"MacRorah, wake up, now," he growled. With every intention of pushing her away, he found his arms tightening around her instead. "Judas priest," he intoned despairingly. "The sooner we get you settled for the night, the better."

Her response was a sleepy mumble of gibberish.

"What happened to your shoes?"

She giggled, a soft, husky sound that affected him in a totally inappropriate way. "Lost 'em. Up on the hill, I 'spect. Oooh, my head hurts. D'I drink too much champagne? I promised myself two glasses—maybe even three. To celebrate."

"Celebrate?" *Don't ask,* he thought. If he was smart, he would get a tablet down her throat, get her under covers, and get the devil out of range, because even knowing what she was, the woman affected him in a way he couldn't begin to understand. She plain scared the living hell out of him.

"George," she murmured lugubriously. She was still leaning against him, her back against his chest, her rounded bottom nestled too cozily against his crotch for comfort. The last time he had held her like this ...

Had he ever held her like this?

That was the damnable part—he couldn't remember!

"George," she repeated, heaving a sigh that Court

echoed feelingly. "I didn't even get to kiss him. D'you s'pose George is like wet shoes, too?"

What was this obsession she had with wet shoes?

With a little wiggle that set off all sorts of unsuitable repercussions, she cried, "Currants! All puckered and tiny and hard. I never really cared for currants, you know . . . I never did. D' you think I could have a cold cloth for my head?"

This time, Court succeeded in putting her away from him. She swayed, but then righted herself, and he was struck all over again by how very small she was. How vulnerable any woman was against a man's brute strength.

Someone should have taught her self-defense. Her father—only, according to Sea, her father was the last man she could look to for protection.

All right, dammit, he would teach her himself! "Here, take this tablet, drink all the water down, and then you're going to bed, madam. I'll get you a nightshirt—you can hardly sleep in what you're wearing."

He would get her a nightshirt, but he damned well wouldn't put it on her. A man could take only so much, he told himself.

But, of course, he did. It was like dressing a rag doll. And because of some misplaced desire to protect her modesty—as well as his own sanity—he draped the nightshirt over her head before he began removing what was underneath it, to the effect that everything got all tangled up before he had halfway begun.

Court swore under his breath as he yanked on a recalcitrant sleeve. MacRorah giggled.

"Woman, if you know what's good for you—" he grasped her hand and shoved it through the sleeve of his best muslin nightshirt. Personally, he never wore the things, because they had a tendency to twist and bind whenever he spent a restless night.

And lately, he'd been restless more often than not.

He managed to get both arms in the proper sleeves, and then he considered how to remove the gown and petticoat which had settled somewhere around her hips. By now, she was seated on his lap, making the task even more impossible.

"Stand up," he ordered.

She grinned at him. Her mouth was shiny wet from the tumbler of water she'd tossed back like a seasoned drinker. He couldn't seem to look away from her lips.

"I'd better not."

"Madam, unless you want to sleep as you are, you'll do as I say!"

"You have a lumpy lap, d'you know that?"

"I have a *what*?"

"Lappy lump. Right here. . . ."

Face flaming, he caught her hand as it crept in between their bodies, and jerked it out again. "Dammit, woman, behave yourself!"

"Ouch," she said plaintively, her amber eyes as big as chestnuts. "That hurts."

He dropped her fist like a hot potato. Standing abruptly, he steadied her, then swept her up into his arms and whipped back the counterpane. He dumped her on the bed in a tangle of bedding and clothing. Glaring down at her, he wished her a good night and was halfway to the door when something made him look back.

Oh, God. Oh, sweet Judas, she was hopeless.

And so was he.

"What the devil are you trying to do to me?" he demanded hoarsely.

She was sprawled on her back, the nightshirt caught somewhere about her shoulders, her own torn gown down about her hips. Something white and thin and beribboned hung in tatters, exposing one pale, perfect breast above an expanse of tightly laced stays. Below that, a pair of shapely limbs sprawled in abandon, bare from the knees down—bare and unfashionably tanned.

Bare and incredibly enticing!

Court groaned. Reluctantly retracing his steps, he tugged the nightshirt down over her torso, grumbled something under his breath, and then headed for the door again.

Despite a headache, brought on in part, she suspected, by her own intemperance, MacRorah was not completely sozzled. She might be mildly disguised, but that was hardly enough to keep her from acting sensibly.

Or as sensibly as one could, given the circumstances.

She wondered idly how Court's kiss would compare to Reuben's. It had been so long, she was afraid her imagination might have exaggerated its attractions.

She wasn't at all sure she even liked the man—Courtland, that is, not Reuben—nor did she fully approve of him. There was no denying, however, that she liked the way he made her feel. Liked it enormously.

Oh, my mercy. What if she had already fallen in love with him? Courtland, that is—not Reuben. She certainly did feel *something* for him.

The brandy, she told herself. It must be the brandy, because if there was one thing MacRorah was sure of, it was that love of that sort had no place in her future plans. How could any woman remain in control of her life if she was foolish enough to fall in love?

Court was almost at the door again when she called him back. "My corselet," she said apologetically, flinging the nightshirt up around her shoulders. "I can't sleep in it. I can't even breathe properly."

He blinked once and then hastily averted his gaze. "When have you ever done anything properly?" he grumbled, but obligingly, he returned to the bedside, rolled her over onto her stomach, and tackled the laces.

Dammit, the wretched things were wrapped around her waist, crisscrossed and tied in the front. Which meant that he had to roll her back over again, only to be confronted by a smile so guileless, so damned bewitching, that he lowered his face in surrender, swearing softly.

"You win," he said, his voice muffled by crisp muslin, delicate lawn, and sweet, fragrant flesh.

Without meaning to, he tasted her skin with the tip of his tongue, and felt her immediate response.

She caught her breath. Her hands moved to his head, but instead of shoving his face from her breast, she tangled her fingers in his hair and pressed him closer. It was all the encouragement he needed. Come tomorrow, he would probably denounce himself for taking unfair advantage, but tonight he was without conscience. Court told himself he owed her something for that wretched, mean-spirited note ten years ago.

And she damn well owed him, too! She should have known a man in his cups would be in no shape to perform. If she'd been at all smart, she would have sobered him up first.

Or at least stuck around long enough the following morning to allow him to make amends.

Not that he would have been in much better shape, if memory served, he thought ruefully.

"MacRorah," he whispered, "are you sober now?"

"Mmmm," she replied. Her fingers had strayed from his scalp and were now examining his ears. Ears were for hearing, he told himself desperately. And for holding up spectacles. So how come his ears were connected directly with his groin?

Lifting his head free of her exploring hands, he wrestled the nightshirt over her head and flung it aside. He finally managed to deal with the corselet and flung the small rigid thing across the room. Then he tackled the remnants of her gown and petticoat, dealing roughly with the various tapes and buttons.

Breathing heavily, he was about to shift his position in order to slide the garments down her limbs when she stopped him with a single request.

"Court . . . would you kiss me, please?"

Would he kiss her?

Dear God, would a drowning man reach for a life ring? Would a starving man refuse a banquet?

He kissed her. Lying half on the bed and half on top of her slight body, he kissed her as he had never before kissed any woman. Giving, taking— demanding her very soul.

She tasted of brandy and her own sweet, salty self. She smelled of some exotic wildflower essence he couldn't quite identify, but it was right for her. Wild and spicy and incredibly sweet.

His body throbbed insistently, and he shifted his position, urged on by her small, surprisingly strong hands, until he was lying fully on top of her, twisting his hips to part her thighs.

He kissed her nose. He kissed her eyes. He kissed her ears and reamed them with the tip of his tongue, his body leaping frantically at her reaction.

My God, she was incredibly sensitive! She was genuinely aroused, as eager for him as he was for her. Somewhat to his own amazement, Court was deeply touched.

Eagerly, he fumbled with the buttons on his trousers. When his hand tangled in the sheets, he swore

fervently. He was sweating, he was shaking—eager as
a green kid at his first attempt.

Slow down, Adams, he told himself. *The lady isn't
going anywhere, and neither are you. Slow down, or it
will all be over before you're even inside her. Performance,* he reminded himself.

He would show her performance!

"MacRorah," he whispered. "Tell me how you like
it. Slow? Fast? Rough or gentle? Tell me, Rorie—I
want to please you, sweetheart." His hand cupped
the slight swell of her belly and then moved lower.
As he felt the brush of her pubic curls, his heart rate
roughly doubled.

Dear God, he wanted her! He had had many
women since his first contact at the age of fifteen.
Never before had he felt this way about any woman.

Bewitched. He had to be bewitched. He had
wanted her for ten years, thinking all the time he despised her. "Tell me your pleasure, Rorie," he whispered, lowering his head to take her sweet, soft
nipple between his lips. He grazed it gently with his
teeth, laved it with his tongue, and waited for her to
express her preference. Perhaps she was waiting for
him to lead the way. Perhaps she wanted to be dom-
inated . . . although he could have sworn that would
not be her style.

And then she told him.

"Rorie?" Court frowned, lifting his head disbeliev-
ingly. "MacRorah?"

There was no mistaking the sound. He had heard
it while he was bringing her from her cottage to his.

It was a snore. Not a loud snore—hardly more than a purr—but unmistakably a snore.

Reluctantly, Court rolled off her body. It was a wonder he hadn't crushed her, although even in the throes of passion, he had remembered to spare her his full weight.

Furious that he had allowed himself to be so easily seduced—a man of his years and experience—he straightened his clothes, and then straightened hers. Reluctantly, he took a lingering last look at her sleeping body before he dragged the spread up to her chin. She owed him, he told himself, for all those years when she'd persisted in coming between him and Diana.

Diana, who had dutifully submitted to him in the first year of their marriage, waiting impatiently for him to finish his business and leave her bed. Diana, to whom he'd been faithful in body, if not in mind.

Deliberately, Court turned and gazed down at the woman sleeping in his bed. The truth was, he admitted reluctantly, she looked as innocent as any child. As innocent as his own daughter. Yet ten years ago she had advertised for a lover, hadn't she? She had led him into her parlor and allowed him to make love to her . . . hadn't she?

And hadn't he woken up the next morning, thickheaded and filled with a tangle of confusing memories that had haunted him for years afterward?

He had. For his sins, he most surely had.

Despite what Seaborn had said about her, Court knew for a fact that it was this same woman who had invited him into her room to make love to her all those years ago, and then rated his performance in a terse little note afterward.

And paid him off. That had been the crowning blow. She had paid him off as if he were—well, as if he were no better than she was!

"Well, my sweet, meddlesome little witch," he whispered to the peacefully sleeping woman. "This time you managed to escape, but I'm a patient man."

Downstairs in the kitchen, he splashed water on his face, straightened his clothing, and let himself silently out the door. He had some unfinished business to attend to up on Hotel Hill.

Chapter Sixteen

℃

It was some time before MacRorah dared open her eyes, even longer before curiosity forced her from bed. The glare from the windows was fearful, especially as her head was threatening to explode. It took only a single squinty glance to tell her that she was lying in the southeast corner bedroom of Sea and Sally's cottage. She had seen all the bedrooms at one time or another, as the Douglases and Adamses had been beach neighbors forever.

Now all she had to do was figure out what she was doing here.

And why her head felt like a pumpkin that had fallen off the wagon onto the cobblestones.

"Are you up yet, Miss Douglas?"

The sound of the unfamiliar voice jarred painfully, reminding her for some strange reason of camphor and liniment. Which made about as much sense as anything else since she had first opened her eyes to gaze up at the sloping ceiling that had been painted a pale sea green.

In bits and pieces, the memories crept back. No wonder her head throbbed! Someone, probably in an attempt to rob her of Granna MacRorah's pearls, had hit her good!

But then Court had come along. He had carried her all the way home in his arms. She distinctly remembered explaining why she never left a lamp lit when she went out. He had lit one, brushed most of the sand from her gown, and then scoured her face with the tea towel. He had fed her a tumbler full of Polly's brandy and brought her here, and . . .

Oh, my mercy.

And then came the questions. Where had Sea been all this time? He would have had something to say about . . . whatever.

Or had Mrs. Jones been the one to put her to bed?

Where *was* Court, anyway? Was she truly a ruined woman now?

She didn't feel particularly ruined. A bit sore in places—her head and belly especially—but hardly ruined.

Before she could decide on her precise condition, there was a knock on the door, followed by the entrance of a sternly disapproving Mrs. Jones bearing a heavy service tray.

"Up and down, up and down," she panted. "Me knees don't take kindly to all this salt air. Here." MacRorah lifted her hands to fend off the tray the woman shoved at her, then grabbed it in self-defense. "Oatmeal, prune juice, and coffee."

Eat it or do without, MacRorah interpreted, reluctantly amused. One look at the older woman's glowering face and she began to wonder just what Court had told her about last night. If she weren't already ruined, Jonesy's lumpy oatmeal should probably do the job.

And then Iris burst in, her small face unusually animated. "Rorie, Rorie! Papa said you were visiting, and I wasn't to bother you because your head hurt, and I said I wouldn't, but I'm not bothering you, am I? Does your head hurt real bad? My mama's head hurt a lot, too. She took—"

"Miss Iris! Stop bouncing on the bed!"

MacRorah grabbed the tray as it began to slide. "Careful, let me set this aside."

"You're to eat all your breakfast, Miss. Mr. Adams said you'd had your head stove in by some wicked murderer. I told him all along this was a heathen place, not fit for decent folk. Biting flies big as a blackbird—sand that gets in a body's bed until she can't sleep a wink! I told him, I said—"

"Oh, do hush," MacRorah cried impatiently. Iris's eyes had grown round as buttons.

"Did a murderer hit your head?" she whispered.

Glaring at the black-clad nanny, MacRorah shifted the tray to the marble-topped bedside table and gathered the child in her arms. "Of course not, dear. I fell last night, coming home from the dance at the hotel. I must have struck my head on one of the conch shells that line the path, because I didn't see another soul," she said soothingly. Which was not a very big lie. She really hadn't seen the man who struck her.

"Does it hurt very much?" the child whispered.

Like the very devil! "Would you like to feel my goose egg?" MacRorah tilted her head and placed the small fingers on the lump that had formed there.

"Oooo, it's big! Will it always be there? How will you pull your bonnets on? Will you have to cut a hole in them? I saw a horse once who wore a straw hat, and he had holes cut in it for his ears. His name was Sugar Boy."

"Humph!" That from Jonesy, who stood, arms akimbo, glaring at MacRorah as if she wore one of Mr. Hawthorne's scarlet letters tattooed on her forehead instead of a lump on the back of her head.

If there was one thing MacRorah could do without, it was censure. She had already heaped more than enough of that commodity on her own head. "Thank you for the tray, Mrs. Jones. I'll bring it downstairs as soon as I've finished."

Which would be as soon as she could find a place to dispose of everything except the coffee. Prune juice and cold, lumpy oatmeal were a bit more than she could face at the moment.

With a last snort of disapproval, the woman closed the door firmly, then opened it again. "Come along, now, Miss Iris. Miss Douglas don't need company."

Which, roughly translated, MacRorah thought as the child slid off the bed and meekly followed her nanny from the room, meant that no unmarried woman lying in any man's bed was fit company for an innocent child.

Where was Court? Was he truly so depraved as to feed her brandy, take advantage of her, and then leave her to be discovered by that camphorated old gorgon?

Or had he merely brought her here and left her in Jonesy's care? "Remind me to stick to lemonade from now on," MacRorah muttered. She sipped the coffee, found it to be weak and no longer even hot, and sat it aside. Better no breakfast at all than one that would undoubtedly finish her off.

Draped in a sheet, she prowled silently about the room, searching for her clothes. Her pearls were on the dresser, and gratefully she fastened them about her neck. The small, matched string had belonged to her mother and to her grandmother before her, and she would have been heartbroken to have lost them.

Her clothes were a mess. She grimaced at the torn bodice of her salmon-pink taffeta. As she searched for her shoes and stockings, another few pieces of the puzzle came together. Amused, she pictured some stranger finding a pair of white kidskin slippers and silk stockings on top of the hill. She could just imagine what wicked thoughts that would provoke!

Her amusement quickly fading, MacRorah proceeded to make herself as presentable as possible with the aid of a few pins and the hairbrush on the dresser, a silver-backed brush that was already beginning to tarnish from exposure to the salt atmosphere.

Oh, her head ached! If memory served, she hadn't been the only one who had overindulged last night. Had Sea been awake when Court had brought her here? Probably not, else he would have had something to say about her condition. All she needed was to have him go back and tell Sally that Court had brought her home drunk as a lord, taken her upstairs, and kept her there for an entire night.

Not that Sea would tattle on her. At least, not intentionally. But never in his entire life had the man been able to keep a secret, and this time, the facts were fairly damning. For the sake of her reputation, which had never been entirely above reproach, the sooner she scurried on back to her own place, the better.

Praying she could escape without having to answer any awkward questions—as if she knew any answers—MacRorah made her way down the narrow, steep stairs to the pine-paneled living room, where her luck ran out.

A groggy-looking Seaborn was nursing a cup of black coffee on the sofa where he had obviously spent the night, if the clutter of coat, vest, shoes, and bedding was anything to go by.

"Mick? What the deuce are you doing here this time of day?" he demanded blearily. "Come to take Iris out fishing?"

Mercy, a last-minute reprieve! "I wanted to say good-bye before you got off," she said primly, which was only a minor stretch of the truth. "So . . . good-bye, Sea, and give Sally and the children my love.

You'd better not miss that packet, either, or Sal will tear a strip off your hide."

Gentle Sally Lee had never in her life so much as raised her voice. Nevertheless, Sea liked to consider himself henpecked, and so they all went along with the pretense.

"Where's Court?" he mumbled, blinking painfully at the bright streak of sunlight that slanted through the east-facing window.

"I have no idea. I haven't seen him since last night." Nor did she wish to. At least, not until she could figure out exactly what had—or had not—gone on in that bedroom upstairs.

Court strode along the shore, his bare feet splashing in the incoming tide. He'd been walking since just before sunrise. Walking and thinking. And thinking was a hell of a lot more painful than even the shell cut he'd collected on his left foot.

Last night he had come within an ace of seducing a woman who was not only inebriated, but who was temporarily under his care, a thing no honorable man would dream of doing. He'd been wound up so tight it had been all he could do to pull back. Fortunately, some residual shred of decency had overcome the fierce demands of his body at the last minute.

Thank God. He'd have felt like the very devil this morning if, after plying her with brandy, he had used her like a whore.

Which she was not. He still wasn't entirely certain just what she was, other than Sea's beloved Mickey.

His own daughter's Rorie. The same bewitching little baggage who had led him such a merry dance ten years ago, and then turned up unexpectedly when he had all but forgotten her.

The sun had barely measured its own diameter above the horizon when Court turned back toward the cottage to roust Sea out in time to catch the boat. It was then that he saw her emerge. With his back to the sun, he watched her glide down his boardwalk and step gingerly off onto the sand. She moved as if she were balancing a stack of plates on her head.

Even hungover, she was a sight to behold! Her hair, which seemed to take on all the color of the sunrise, was hanging down her back, tied with what looked suspiciously like one of his neckties. Her gown was no longer gaping open—she had worked some sort of magic on it, making her look almost respectable.

And then, as she came closer, he noticed that her feet were bare. Small, tanned—naked as a child's. Just why a pair of bare feet should excite him when sex was the farthest thing from his mind was a mystery he would probably never solve. The bloody truth was, everything about the little witch excited him!

"Good morning," he said quietly when she came within range. If her expression was anything to go by, she was feeling wretched. "I'd hoped you would at least stay in bed long enough to recover. Your people aren't back yet. I passed your place half an hour ago and there was no sign of life."

Overhead, a pair of gulls swooped, searching the incoming tide for morsels of fish. Dozens of pink and gold clouds drifted past in a pale turquoise sky. Oblivious to the splendors of an early summer dawn, the two stared at one another hungrily.

"They'll probably be in on Mr. Tillett's boat," MacRorah murmured after several long moments had passed. "He'll get in late this evening."

"Rorie?"

There was a question in his voice, even though he knew this was no time for questions. Indeed, it would be better if certain questions were never asked, much less answered. Better for all concerned if he simply packed up his entire retinue and caught the packet to Elizabeth City with Seaborn, and the first train headed north. Given time—another ten years or so—he might even forget what she looked like.

"Well . . . thank you for—for everything," she said politely.

Court had an idea she was wondering just what the devil "everything" included. The thought made him smile. "You're most welcome, MacRorah. I'd do as much for any friend of Sea's and Iris's. By the way, you should know that the man who attacked you last night is in police custody. He won't be bothering anyone again for a long, long time. It seems he's wanted on several counts in Virginia Beach."

"Oh. Well, then. My pearls are safe."

Her pearls, Court thought as he watched her turn and walk away. Should he have told her that someone had hired the man to do away with her? God, the very thought made his blood run cold!

He wouldn't tell her—not just yet. Instead, he would tell that giant watchdog of hers. The one who was leaving her to move to Manteo.

"Ahh, MacRorah, what am I going to do about you?" he whispered as he watched her grow smaller in the distance. "What am I going to do about *me*?"

She skirted the edge of the water, allowing the tide to wash over her feet the way a child would. The way he had himself.

Something told Court that his life had changed irredeemably since the day he had stepped off the packet some three weeks earlier onto the rickety dock, surrounded by Iris and Jonesy and enough baggage to fit out a platoon. Since then, along with his shoes, coat, and tie, he seemed to have shed every ounce of common sense he possessed.

MacRorah half expected Court to show up at her door as the endless hours crept past. Not that there was any reason why he should. She was perfectly safe. The man who had tried to rob her was no longer a threat. Besides, she had been looking after herself for years.

It must be the silence, she told herself. A body simply needed to be around people occasionally, if only to remind her that she wasn't entirely alone in the world. She missed the cheerful sound of Polly in her kitchen, of Megan's chatter and the noise of Teeny's hammering on whatever he had taken it into his head needed repairing. The ever-present sound of lapping water, of old wooden timbers creaking as the sun began to heat them up, and the constant squawking of feeding gulls was not enough to fill the emptiness that threatened to engulf her.

It was only the knowledge that her family would soon be leaving her, she told herself. She would adjust soon enough to the change. If there was one thing she was, and had always been, it was sensible.

But soon, even Iris would be gone, and she would miss her, oh, she would! As for Court . . .

MacRorah refused to think about Court. No woman with half a grain of sense would allow herself to fall in love with a man whose moods were even more fickle than the ever-shifting winds along the Outer Banks. No woman who wanted to call her soul her own would fall in love at all.

There was one sure antidote for the dismals, and that was to stay busy. If Teeny had thought to set the boat overboard before he'd left, she could've gone fishing. The house, thanks to Polly, was spick-and-span, and she wasn't quite desperate enough to mop clean floors.

She could try her hand at cooking something. Her head no longer ached quite so much, and her stomach had almost recovered from the insult of champagne, brandy, and the hotel's famous version of lemonade. She wasn't quite certain, however, that it could withstand the assault of her own cooking.

As it turned out, she spent the morning mending and washing, trying to keep her thoughts from stray-

ing too far afield. The salmon-pink taffeta was
ruined, but the material from the full skirt, she decided, might be salvaged by Mrs. Espy's sewing
class.

Later on, feeling considerably improved, she
cooked the fresh turnip greens Polly had sorted and
washed before she left, and then set out to make
herself a pan of biscuits. She had watched Mrs.
George a thousand times. How difficult could it be?

Iris came just after noon. She was alone, which
surprised MacRorah, as she was seldom allowed out
without supervision.

"Does Mrs. Jones know where you are?"

"I told her I was going to see if Megan was home
yet, but I'm not sure she heard me," the child said
diffidently.

"She'll be home late this evening."

Iris picked up a silver-framed miniature of Rose at
age nine. "Is this your other little girl?"

So MacRorah explained about Rose, who was
in heaven with Mama and Father. "My Mama's in
heaven, too. Do people from here go to the same
heaven as people from Connecticut?"

MacRorah bit her lip, torn between laughter and
tears. "I'm not sure, love, but won't it be fun someday to find out?"

While she set another place at the table, Iris
replaced the miniature and picked up a headless de-
coy that was being used as a doorstop. "Jonesy says
she's leaving just as soon as Papa can find her passage on a boat," the child confided. "She said she

doesn't hold with loose women. What's a loose woman? Is it someone whose knees aren't all stiff like Jonesy's?"

MacRorah buttered a biscuit, spread it with enough strawberry preserves to disguise the burned flavor, and set it on the plate beside a small serving of greens.

"These smell funny," Iris said, poking at the soggy green mass with her fork.

Indeed they did. MacRorah had seldom been allowed the freedom of her own kitchen. "Try a taste. They're good for you. Has your father found someone else to look after you?"

Iris shook her head, still eyeing the greens suspiciously. "I told him I wanted a mommy, and he promised me I could have anyone I wanted, but when I told him I wanted you, he said no."

"A mommy?" He said *no*?

"I could be your little girl, and you could be my mommy, and Megan could be my sister . . . sort of."

He said no?

"Dear, it doesn't quite work that way," MacRorah temporized.

"Why?"

"Well, I'm not sure . . . only I think your father should be the one to choose a new mommy for you."

"But he said I could pick out any mommy I wanted, and I picked you, so will you talk to him?"

"Here, have another biscuit. Did you know Megan helped pick the strawberries to make the jam? Isn't it about the most scrumptious jam you ever tasted?"

He said *no?*

Well . . . *blast!*

Chapter Seventeen

ℭ

C ourt watched for a glimpse of the stubby little Wanchese packet boat late that afternoon. The moment he caught sight of her
gray sails, he headed for the dock, leaving Iris sulk-
ing in her room and a dour Jonesy in the midst of
packing her trunks.

This had been the very devil of a day, nor was it
over yet. He had come in from his earlier walk with
a sore foot, only to be confronted by the nanny, who
had all but accused him of—so far as he could tell—
debauching children and wallowing in sin.

He had listened just long enough to get the gist of
her sermon, then written out a bank draft, adding a
more-than-generous bonus, and promised to secure
her passage on the very next boat out and hire a cart
to haul her and her baggage to the packet dock.

After which he had heaved a sigh of relief. Funny
thing, he had never noticed just how disagreeable
the woman was back home in Connecticut.

But even worse than Jonesy's gloom and condemnation had been Iris's questions. Why had Rorie come to stay and then left so soon? Wasn't she happy there? Didn't she want to be a mommy after all? Was it because Iris had bounced on her bed? Perhaps if Papa were to go ask her again, and say please?

It struck Court that his daughter was younger in many ways than her years, which was probably his own fault, too, although he couldn't quite figure out why.

Damn all, why should he feel guilty? Hadn't he looked after her to the best of his ability since the day she was born, hiring the very best nannies? Actually, Diana's mother had selected Mrs. Jones from among several applicants, but Court had never had cause to question his mother-in-law's judgment. And after Iris became solely his responsibility, he had done his best to give her everything she could possibly need. She had demanded he find her a mommy, and in a weak moment, he had agreed, but that didn't mean he had to settle for the first candidate she selected, did it?

The last thing he needed or wanted was another wife. Even so, given a reasonable period of time, Court fully intended to look around for a suitable woman. One who would meet his exacting requirements for the position. Someone Iris liked.

Someone *he* liked. Certainly not someone who habitually made herself a target for every wagging tongue on the Eastern Seaboard.

Which ruled out MacRorah Douglas. Even Sea, who had known her forever, and at one time even claimed to love her, had admitted that MacRorah had kicked up her heels more than a time or two.

Precisely how high, Court wondered now, had she kicked in her high-kicking days?

As if he needed to ask. He, himself, had been one of her "high kicks," and judging from what he'd seen so far, she was still kicking. There was George. And Reuben. Not to mention all those babies she kept talking about. It was perfectly clear that living alone and unchaperoned all these years, she had grown even more ramshackle than when he'd first encountered her.

So why, he mused, did he like her so much?

Because he did. The little witch grew on a man before he even knew he was in danger. For all her faults, she was a warm woman—genuine and direct.

More direct than was comfortable, at times.

Not only that, she liked children, nor was she afraid to get down on their level. And children, including his own daughter, adored her. The trouble was, the woman was a blasted female pied piper! Given half an opportunity, she could lead an innocent child into more trouble than a hapless parent could handle.

And then laugh about it. Oh, yes, that infectious laugh of hers was definitely a danger. It started in her eyes as a tiny sparkle, escaped first as a low, husky gurgle, and then bubbled over, affecting everyone within hearing.

It occurred to Court as he dusted the sand from his left heel and peered down at the angry red flesh around the small shell cut he'd received just that morning, that he could never recall hearing Diana laugh. She had been totally devoid of a sense of humor.

MacRorah, on the other hand . . .

"Watch it, Adams," he muttered gruffly. "If you're not careful, you'll find yourself hooked, gaffed, and landed!"

As if any man with half a brain would consider for one moment marrying a woman who had once posted a notice at a men's club advertising for a lover. Even if that man had been one of the applicants.

Worst of all, Court fumed as he hobbled along the shell-littered shore toward MacRorah's cottage, was the fact that he still couldn't remember all that had happened that night when he'd bearded her in her den, so to speak. He recalled only that she had worn yellow. And that they'd been lying on what he'd thought at the time was a sofa, but what must have been the bed in that godawful room of hers. And that her nipples were a rosy shade of brown, not pink.

Which brought on another set of memories, of far more recent origin.

"Judas priest," he whispered aloud as he limped the last few yards to the Douglas place. His nurse-maid was leaving him flat, the cook had come down with a fever two days before and they'd been roughing it ever since—his foot was throbbing abominably, and all he could think of was a wicked, beguiling little female who was more worried about losing her pearls than she was about losing her life!

Her virtue, unfortunately, was already long past redemption.

Teeny was attempting to launch the mended sailboat when Court reached the foot of the Douglases' boardwalk. Without asking, Court threw his weight into the task of log-rolling the flat-bottomed craft down the gently sloping shore and into the water. By the time she was floating and secured fore and aft to the mooring stakes, he was wet to his waist.

"Much obliged," the older man said gruffly. The two men eyed one another warily, like a pair of strange cur dogs.

"Is Miss Douglas at home?"

"Inside. She don't need no aggravation, neither, if you take my meanin'."

"Then I'll not bother her. Are you aware that she was attacked last night?"

The man seemed to swell before his very eyes. Massive shoulder muscles flexed. Hamlike hands became fists. In a face that could have been carved from Honduras mahogany, Teeny's eyes narrowed to cold blue slits.

Court stepped back involuntarily. "Not by me, I assure you," he said hastily. He went on to describe the happenings of the night before.

Teeny interrupted with a few terse questions, not to mention a string of the foulest oaths Court had

ever been privileged to hear. "O'Briant," he said flatly.
"The bleeding barstid, I knowed he wouldn't quit trying!"

"O'Briant who? Quit trying what?"

And then it was Teeny's turn to explain. By the time
he had finished describing the fires at 41 Pecan Street,
a near miss when MacRorah's horse had suddenly
spooked crossing Long Bridge over Charles Creek, her
move to the cottage after her father had married his
mistress, and the unexplained fire soon afterward that
had taken her stepmother's life and injured her father
fatally, plus several more recent events that had
aroused Teeny's suspicions, one thing was clear to both
men.

MacRorah Douglas needed a keeper.

And both men were equally determined that she
would have one.

Beyond that, Court decided as he limped off toward his own cottage to deal with whatever new ca-
tastrophe awaited him there, he was not prepared to
go. First he would send Jonesy on her way. Then he
would do his best to placate Iris. After that . . .

Well, after that, he would see. But one thing he
promised himself: He would give Miss Douglas a
dressing-down she'd not soon forget. Ladies—and he
used the term loosely—did not hobnob with whores
and their pimps. Not if they hoped to be accepted in
polite society!

By suppertime, Megan was still bubbling over with
excitement over her new home with the swing and

the dollhouse and a pen in the yard that could hold either geese or a puppy.

MacRorah suspected it would be the latter.

All Polly could talk about was the garden she planned to have. "There's plenty of time to set out onions and collards. Come winter, we'll have us many a good mess o' greens," she said as they waited for Teeny to return from some mysterious errand in the village. He had gone out to put the boat overboard, then called through the window a short while later to say he had an errand to run over in the village and would be back in time for supper.

MacRorah tried her best to be as happy for the Gritmires as they were for themselves. Hadn't this been her mother's dream? To pluck poor unfortunates from the brink of doom and set their feet back on the path of righteousness?

Not that Teeny had ever been *un*righteous. In fact, from the look on his face as he came inside more than an hour later, he was feeling a bit more righteous than usual.

Fixing MacRorah with a lowering glare, he said, "I had a word with Mr. Adams."

"Sea? But I thought he left this morning. Oh, don't tell me he missed the boat!"

"Not him. T'other Mr. Adams."

"Court. Oh. Then I suppose he told you about my getting into a tad of trouble last night." She might have known Court would waste no time in handing her care over to Teeny.

Dutifully, she listened to the familiar lecture. Al-

though he'd been in her employ for more years than
she cared to recall, Teeny never hesitated to speak
his mind when he thought she had overstepped the
bounds of propriety.

Which she invariably did. Sooner or later. Not deliberately, but because she simply couldn't be bothered to abide by all the stuffy rules that were
supposed to apply to ladies and gentlemen.

To ladies, at least. Gentlemen made up the rules,
and then blithely disregarded them when their own
pleasure was involved.

Little Moses Brown, the oyster boy, came with a
message the next morning, before MacRorah had
even had her second cup of coffee. "It's from that
there Yankee ge'man staying in Mr. Adams's house.
He done gimme a penny to bring it and said if you
wuz to send a answer, he'd gimme another one."

MacRorah was half tempted to give the child a
nickel and send him on his way, but she didn't dare.
Iris had said Jonesy was leaving. If the child needed
her . . .

But it was not Iris's pale image that drifted before her mind's eye as she ripped open the envelope.

The handwriting was exactly like the man. Stiff,
upright, firm, and unyielding.

Although his lower loops were surprisingly volup-
tuous. . . .

Hastily, she unfolded the single sheet of vellum.
"Madam," he wrote. Oh, dear, they were back to

that. "I have asked Gritmire to escort you to my cottage at your convenience for a brief conference. I would appreciate your prompt attendance."

"Well . . . blast!" MacRorah swore softly. Propping her chin on a knotted fist, she stared out the window toward the Adams place.

Moses fidgeted. Taking pity on the impatience of youth, she fetched a nickel from her reticule, handed it over, and told him there was no response. Grinning, he jammed the coin in his pocket and darted out the door.

If Court wanted to confer, he could bloody well come to *her* house!

An escort! As if she hadn't had the run of the entire area for ten long years and more!

Moses poked his head back inside to give her another message. "Miz Mac, Pa says if you want some oysters, he done took up a mess this mornin' from the inlet."

Everyone knew that inlet oysters were the saltiest and tastiest of all. "Oysters? Oh . . . a peck, then, if you please."

"Yes, *ma'am!*" Grinning widely, the boy spun away again, leaving MacRorah to reread the brief note and ponder the nature of the "conference."

She wondered if Jonesy had already left. And then she wondered if Court had some notion of hiring her to take the woman's place.

In a pig's eye! For pure, pithy arrogance, he took the cake!

* * *

It was not until midafternoon that MacRorah took pity on Teeny's impatience and let herself out the door. "You didn't have to wait," she said. "I can certainly find my way a quarter of a mile down along shore without a guide. I've been doing it since I was three years old."

He favored her with a curdled look, causing her to smile. They both knew that there was ample reason for concern. More than a few times she had set out for someplace or other, only to be diverted so far off course that she forgot her original destination. A friend—a stray dog—word that the blues were hitting over on the oceanside—it didn't take much when one lived by the sun and the tide instead of the clock and an engagement calendar.

"Are you going to stay here and guide me back home?" she teased as they neared the foot of the Adamses' boardwalk.

"I'll be around some'eres," Teeny said gruffly, and she knew he would. Hadn't he been keeping an eye on her for as long as she had known him?

Court came out to greet her, his expression coolly shuttered. Actually, he looked drawn. Almost as if he had slept no better than she had these past few nights.

"How is Iris dealing with Jonesy's leaving?" she asked, sinking onto one of the canted benches built into the railing.

Court propped one foot on the lower rail beside the bench and stared out toward the streak on the horizon that was Roanoake Island. "I'm not sure. She hasn't said much."

"But then, she never does, does she?"

He turned to glare at her. "What are you implying? That my daughter is not happy?" He commenced to pacing, and MacRorah noticed that he was limping.

"I didn't say that, but children sometimes draw inside themselves when they're not happy. Court, have you sprained an ankle?" He was wearing his shirt and tie again, but the laces on his left shoe were left dangling.

"No, dammit, I have not sprained my ankle! Iris has no reason in the world not to be happy. She has everything any child could wish. She knows all she has to do is ask, and I'll do everything in my power to give her whatever she wants. She *knows* that!"

"Then she must be happy, mustn't she? How could she possibly not be?"

After one long, suspicious look, he hobbled over and dropped down beside her. "Jonesy left just after noon yesterday. Iris hasn't said much, but I don't think she likes the meals I make for us. Did I tell you the cook went home sick? Some sort of belly complaint. I expect she'll be back next week, but so far, I haven't been able to find anyone to fill in until then."

"Do you want me to ask around? Or are you jiggering for an invitation to supper? If you're about to suggest I hire on as your temporary cook, I'd advise you not to. I've been told my kitchen skills constitute a lethal weapon."

He actually smiled at that. At least, his lips twitched. "What if I were?"

"I wouldn't cook for you, but I might invite you and Iris to supper before Polly leaves. Moses brought by a sack of oysters. Tonight we're having fritters and stew."

His lips twitched again. It really was a smile, she decided with a painful little throb in her chest. "Iris discovered she liked Polly's crab cakes. Oyster fritters aren't all that different. Court, is this what you called me over here for? There are restaurants, you know."

"Yes, I know. Were you aware that Iris had mentioned you as a potential mommy?"

"Oh, my mercy, did Sea tell you about my list? I'll wring his neck!"

"Your—uh, what list?"

"My list of husbands. Potential husbands, that is. Actually, not so much husbands as potential fathers for my child, because if there's one thing I swore I would never have, it's a husband."

"Your . . . child?"

"My, um—potential child. Or children."

When he continued to stare at her as if she had suddenly sprouted horns, she hurried to explain. "You see, there comes a time in a woman's life when in spite of all her youthful declarations, she—well, she craves children. Of her own. Naturally, I would never have the one without the other. Children without a husband, I mean."

Under his steady regard, she was beginning to gabble like a turkey.

"You'd like to have a child?"

"Well, of course I would. What woman wouldn't? More than one, if possible, although I'm not getting any younger."

"You mentioned a list—would that list by any chance include a George and a Reuben?"

"You know George and Reuben? It's George Meeks at the hotel, not the George who hires out oxcarts. Oxcart George has a wife and a swarm of children. I'd never, ever dream of breaking up a happy home."

"Oh, no. No indeed," he said dryly. "Never, *ever.*"

She slanted him a searching look. Arms crossed over his chest, he was scowling at a tea towel that hung limply from the back porch clothesline. She was beginning to suspect he was teasing her. "Well, I do have my standards," she said stiffly, wondering just when she had relinquished control of the situation.

"This list of yours—what does it include besides names? Ages and incomes, I presume. Any candidate would need to be of breeding age, as well as able to support whatever size family you settle on."

"I have more than enough money to support my own children. But since you asked, a meek disposition is my first requirement, because I'll not have a husband who would try to interfere with my—well, my independence."

"Oh, no, of course not—that would be unthinkable."

Was that a gleam of amusement she saw in his eyes? Probably not. To her knowledge, men were remarkably lacking in humor. "A healthy constitution is extremely important. Nice teeth, and parents who lived to a ripe old age would be good, too, because those things can be passed on to one's offspring. I haven't quite made up my mind to go through with it, but I must admit, there are times when I'm sorely tempted. The thought of growing old all alone no longer seems quite so . . ."

But Court was no longer listening. So she had money of her own and wasn't just casting around for a wealthy husband, he mused. He dimly remembered Sea's having mentioned her family connections—something about an old tyrant who owned half the town and, with the connivance of a crafty judge, left his money tied up so that only his daughter and granddaughter profited at his death.

". . . but of course, I could never marry a man who expected to manage me."

Damn. He had missed half of what she'd been saying. Probably nothing important. The important thing was, she was available if he should decide to take her on.

"Tell me, then—is there any room on your list for another candidate? One who already has a child but wouldn't mind having others?"

MacRorah's palms were suddenly sweaty. Her heart was pounding a mile a minute. She felt as if she'd been out in the sun too long. "Another candidate?" she asked weakly.

"I believe I mentioned that Iris is shopping for a mother?"

"She, um . . . you did say something to that effect."

"And that she had selected you as a likely prospect?"

Oh, my mercy. It was one thing for her to make lists of candidates. Making lists was something she'd done all her life. But this was different. Someone else was making the list!

"Of course, there would have to be certain agreements on both sides. If I were to ask you, that is."

If he were to ask her? "Assuming I were to agree!" she snapped. As if any woman would be such a fool.

But what, MacRorah wondered reluctantly, if she were to take him up on his dare—for surely, that was all it could be. What if she were to add Court's name to her now defunct list of candidates?

He would come out far ahead of all other contenders in every category save one. Control. Control was crucial, and she wasn't at all certain she would ever be able to control him. Even worse, what if she had already fallen in love with him? As much as it pained her to admit it, she was beginning to suspect it might be a distinct possibility.

She tried to remember her mother's warnings and found, to her surprise, that they had grown dimmer with the passage of time. Marriage alone was difficult enough. A marriage that included a one-sided love would be impossible. She shouldn't even consider it.

"I think we should consider it," he said. "For Iris's sake, you understand." He had slung his left leg up over his right knee and loosened his shoe so that she could see some sort of lump underneath his black silk hose.

"Of course . . . I mean, naturally it would only be for Iris's sake if— That is, if you were to . . ."

"Ask you."

"Yes. If you were to ask me." She was about to wring her fingers right off her palms. Wiping them on her skirt, she clasped them tightly on her lap. "And *if* I were to agree. Although it would probably be best all 'round if I simply helped you find another nanny and perhaps a temporary cook."

"You're probably right." Absently, Court stroked his ankle, running his fingers down into the heel of his shoe. Feeling her eyes on him, he looked around to see her nibbling her lower lip and promptly forgot all about his throbbing heel.

Feeling absurdly guilty to be caught lusting at such a time, he said stiltedly, "I only mentioned it for Iris's sake, you understand. The way she's been moping around lately . . ."

"I hardly thought otherwise. Court," MacRorah said without pause, "what have you done to your foot? It's all swollen up. Are you sure you haven't sprained something?"

"I nicked it yesterday morning. On a shell, I suppose." He smiled, but it lasted only a moment. "You'd think a man my age would know better than to walk barefoot outdoors."

"Let me see."

"My foot?" His eyes widened as if she'd suggested he disrobe right out in public, in broad daylight.

"Well, hardly your elbow. Take off your shoe and sock, and whatever you've bundled around it and let me see. Shell cuts can go septic before you know it. You could lose a limb."

"Good God, it's only a small cut—barely half an inch long."

"Fine. Be stubborn, then. I'll ask Teeny to start turning you a wooden leg."

"Oh, for crying out loud," he muttered. Wrenching off his shoe, he ripped off his sock to reveal a linen handkerchief wrapped untidily around the wound and knotted at one side. "You don't have to do this, you know," he said, sounding embarrassed as she took his foot in her hand.

He had nice feet. It occurred to her fleetingly that elegant bones, just as dark hair or hazel eyes, could be handed down to a child. "Tell me where to find a tub."

"How the devil would I know where to find a tub? I'm not a bloody washerwoman!"

And temper. Mentally, she added that to her list of inheritable traits. She was tempted to drop his foot, heel and all, onto the deck and march down that boardwalk without even looking back, but of course, Iris would be left then with no one at all. The child, at least, deserved better.

Did the child deserve the mother she had chosen?

"Don't ask for trouble, MacRorah," she muttered. She located a washtub hanging on the wall outside the kitchen door, dropped in a large lump of salt and a dollop of vinegar, and dragged it out onto the deck. "I looked in on Iris while I was inside."

"That wasn't necessary. She's napping."

"No, she's not, she's playing a game of checkers with her doll."

"Hell."

"You swear too much. It sets a bad example for a child."

"You're a nice one to talk," he sneered.

"I never swear except in the case of direst emergency. Roll up your pants leg while I go fetch a pail of water."

He rolled up his pants leg, and MacRorah returned, poured the water into the tub, and instructed him to put his foot in it.

"Are you sure you're not trying to poison me?"

Standing before him, she braced her hands on her hips. "Now, why on earth would I do that? You're doing a good enough job of it without my help."

"With me out of the way, you might be planning to steal my daughter and claim her as your own. With Sea as her next of kin, you might even get away with it. The damned fool is still half besotted with you!"

"I think you must be feverish." She laid a hand on his forehead, and Court caught her fingers before she could back away. Looking her straight in the eyes, he drew her closer until she was standing between his thighs, one foot on either side of the tub.

It was awkward, to say the least.

"What about it, MacRorah? Would you consider it?"

"Would I consider what? Poisoning you?"

"Marrying me. Strictly for Iris's sake. To be quite honest with you, I'm at my wits' end. I haven't always been the most attentive of fathers, you know. One way to make up for it would be to give her the mother she wants."

If MacRorah weren't clutching his hand with one of hers, his shoulder with the other for balance, she might have toppled over in a dead faint.

Would she marry him? Would she claim Iris as her own daughter? Would she forsake all her ambitions, her dreams of independence, of making a difference in the lives of others?

But what of making a difference in the life of one small, lonely child?

Oh, my mercy, it was tempting.

Dare she commit herself to spending the rest of her life with a man who didn't love her—a man who had inhabited more than a few of her dreams—a man would probably insist on taking her a thousand miles away from all that was dear and familiar?

"Do you know what I think?" she asked, tilting her head to one side.

"I'm afraid to ask." His hand tightened on hers. In the elegant, arrogant arrangement of features that she had memorized so long ago, his eyes glowed like live coals.

"I think that must truly be the most extraordinary proposal any woman has ever received."

It was as though some tightly wound spring inside him had suddenly been released. He toppled her onto his lap. One of her feet bumped against the tub, sloshing water over them both, and suddenly, they began to laugh.

Chapter Eighteen

ℭ

Oh, my mercy, she had gone and done it now, MacRorah thought hours later, lying in her bed up under the eaves. She had promised. She had accepted Court's proposal. She had honestly tried her best to think clearly, but given the fact that he'd been holding her on his lap at the time, her face pressed against his shoulder, his hands warm and hard on her body, she was very much afraid she had made a hash of it.

If she'd thought lemonade, champagne, and brandy were an intoxicating combination, it was nothing to the few moments that had followed. She had been kissed before—even kissed by Court before. But never in quite so exhilarating a manner. She'd felt like a stick of green kindling tossed on top of a heap of glowing coals. For a few moments, it would only twitch and sizzle—then, all of a sudden, whoosh! It would burst into flames.

Which was exactly what she had done. Burst into

flames. Privately, she sincerely hoped, because if Court had any idea of the feelings rushing through her at that moment—of the wicked, delicious things she had wanted to do to him—he would have dropped her flat on her behind and leaped over the railing.

And quite properly, too.

Fortunately, Iris had joined them before things could get entirely out of hand, which was a good thing, because by then, the beach was beginning to grow crowded with strollers, waders, and fishermen. She would have been disgraced all over again.

"Why are you holding Rorie, Papa? Is she sick?"

A red-faced Court had cleared his throat. MacRorah had smoothed her hair and her shirtwaist, buttoned her two top buttons, and tried desperately to think of something innocuous to say to distract from the wild flush on her own face.

"Your Papa's hurt his foot," was the best she could come up with, although it hardly explained why her breast was still tingling from the pressure of his exploring hands.

"Are you fixing it for him?"

Which had prompted her to stand and say sternly to Court, "You might as well take your foot out now, it's soaked long enough. Iris, dear, do you think you could find a towel?"

MacRorah headed directly for Sally's medicine chest, glad of the excuse to escape. A few minutes later, feeling somewhat restored, she hurried out again, carrying a bottle of Porter's Healing Oil, to find Iris blotting her father's foot and chiding him for going barefoot on the beach when he'd refused to allow her the same privilege.

MacRorah had no intention of mentioning Court's proposal and her own acceptance. It was still too new. Besides, once she was away from his immediate influence and she came to her senses, the fewer people who knew about it, the easier for all concerned.

She hadn't counted on Court's conniving turn of mind. "You'll be pleased to know, Princess," he'd announced without even glancing her way, "that Rorie has agreed to be your new mommy."

MacRorah could have crowned him with the washtub, water and all. After that, of course, there was no backing out. Iris, usually so solemn, was beside herself with joy, hugging them both, dancing back and forth, bubbling over with plans for the future that included picnics, puppies, and a party with crab cakes and Polly's one-two-three-four cake.

MacRorah watched as a lifetime of doubts and dreams fought for ascendancy. Was she truly committed? Was it was too late to back out? *Did she even want to?*

Perhaps not, but that didn't mean she intended to get all gooey and misty-eyed about it. No, indeed. She had no intention of giving up her life's work. All she had agreed to do was to trade her services as a stepmama for the opportunity to further her own plans.

Or so she rationalized.

* * *

It was decided that the Gritmires would delay their move until after the wedding. Deliberately, MacRorah tried to take advantage of Polly's romantic streak. "I'd thought perhaps a spring wedding?" she suggested, thinking to postpone their leaving.

"I've got to get me collards and onions set out. The first of August, that's me final offer."

Iris wanted the wedding held that very day, but it was Court who finally settled the matter. "A week from today. Sea and Sal will be here by then. When I get the license, I'll see about importing a justice of the peace to do the job."

To do the job.

MacRorah would think of those words a hundred times during the following week. It was certainly the right description of the circumstances, but even so, she wished he wouldn't be quite so businesslike about the whole procedure.

Not that it wasn't a business arrangement, because it was. Iris needed a mommy. Something more permanent that a mere nanny. Someone who could be counted on to stay around even if her knees hurt and she didn't care for the climate.

"At least this nanny will have a long-term contract," MacRorah whispered to herself, trying bravely to look on the bright side.

The next day, Court brought Iris to her while he took a short business trip. "Look on it as a dry run, in case you want to back out before it's too late."

Which was, of course, the wrong thing to say. "I

gave my word," MacRorah told him, pride adding a glint to her light brown eyes.

"Fine. Then I'll be back in plenty of time for the wedding," he said. "By the way, do you happen to have a yellow gown?"

A yellow gown? MacRorah was puzzled. Was she to wear some sort of a uniform? If so, she much preferred yellow to black. "I have a mustard-yellow wool shirtwaist. Will that do?"

"Don't worry about it, then—I'll bring your wedding gown when I come."

"My wedding gown! You'll do no such!"

Capturing her face in his hands, he grinned down at her. She hadn't seen such a look on his face since he had swung her off her feet a moment before she would have walked into the side of a moving ice wagon.

"Tsk, tsk, tsk! Not even married yet, and already you've forgotten your vow of obedience."

With those deep-set hazel eyes laughing down at her, MacRorah was having trouble remembering her own name, much less a vow she had yet to make. "Since you brought up the matter of obedience, Courtland, there are a few things we need to get straight."

"Indeed we do, MacRorah, but it'll have to wait. My boat's leaving in less than an hour, and if I miss my train connections, I might not make it back in time for the wedding."

He still held her face between his hands, one thumb straying over her lower lip, which made it almost impossible to think. "Perhaps that would be best, after all. Court, please let go of my face."

"Not until you kiss me good-bye. And don't even think of backing out, by the way—I'll not allow it."

Jerking her face free, she glared at him. "I think you're suffering under a slight misapprehension, Mr. Adams."

Court's brows shot sky-high. He grew very still. "Oh?"

"I agreed to marry you and look after Iris, and I have no intention of going back on my word. But let's be clear about one thing. I fully intend to be a good mother, because I love your daughter very much. I'll do my best to be a dutiful wife, as well, but there's one thing I will *never* be, and that's a doormat."

Court looked as if he were going to speak, but MacRorah wasn't finished. "I do have a mind of my own. A perfectly good one. It's served me quite well for any number of years, and I intend to go on using it."

"Meaning?" he prompted. Gray was the predominant color in his hazel eyes at the moment. A deep, stormy shade of gray.

MacRorah pressed a hand against her heart, which had lodged somewhere just under her chin. "Meaning that I'll continue to make my own decisions and you may make yours. One thing, though—I'd very much prefer it if you wouldn't take a mistress—at least, not until Iris is old enough to—to understand."

"Damn it, MacRorah!"

"Hush. You said you were in a hurry, and I'm not quite done yet."

"Oh, there's more?" he inquired in a silky tone that made her vaguely uneasy.

"Just this. If you ever—*ever* lift a hand in anger against either Iris or me, I'll leave and I'll take Iris with me. I'll see you in hell before I allow you to hurt that child."

To say Court looked thunderstruck would be understating the matter. "Are you quite done, madam?" he asked quietly after a long, charged silence.

Hands knotted together, MacRorah forced herself to stand firm, hoping her skirts hid her quaking knees. *Thinking* an ultimatum was one thing. Delivering it in person was quite another. "I—I believe I am."

"Good. Then you might as well hear what I have to say before I take my leave." He didn't add *and good riddance,* but it was understood. "Firstly, once we're married, you may hire all the nursemaids you wish, but understand this—both Iris and any children we might have in the future will take precedence over your social life. Is that agreed?"

She nodded, thinking distractedly about those other children. Thinking even more distractedly about the begetting of them.

"Secondly, you must agree to spend a minimum of two hours a day with the children, except when there's a special reason. Is that agreed?"

Again she nodded, knowing she would be spending far more of her time with the children than any measly two hours, and not because he demanded it, either.

"Thirdly, if you drink at all, it will be in extreme moderation."

She grimaced, thinking of the unfortunate results of her recent indulgence, and thought for a moment she saw his eyes soften in shared understanding.

Evidently, she was mistaken. "Last of all, there's this matter of your extracurricular activities."

"My what?"

"This business of hobnobbing with the lower classes."

"Now, see here—"

"No, madam, you see here! I'll not have a wife of mine—the mother of my child—consorting with whores, pimps, and other forms of lowlife. It's one thing to endanger your own neck, but it's quite another thing to expose my daughter to danger."

"Why, I never!"

"All those unexplained fires? That near disaster of some years ago when your horse bolted in the middle of a bridge? That business with the broken steering apparatus on your boat? Those were no mere accidents. Nor was that attempted rape the other night. Someone badly wants you out of action, madam, and we both know who and why."

"Oh, but I—"

"If Polly wishes to carry on in your absence, more power to her. She's Gritmire's problem, not mine, thank God. But I'll have your word right now that you'll have nothing more to do with this—this blasted crusade of yours!"

"But—"

"Promise me, MacRorah," Court insisted grimly.

"But if I—"

"Now!" he roared.

Clapping her hands over her ears, MacRorah cried, "All right, all right! If you want to stand by while innocent children are sold into slavery, while wicked, wretched old men pass on every kind of disease known to man, then on your conscience be it! I take it you have no objection to my composing the occasional flier?"

Court sighed. "I'll even agree to pay for the damned things, but if I ever catch you handing them out personally, I'll wring your scrawny little neck, is *that* understood?" Raking his long-fingered hand through his windblown hair, he swore softly. "Judas priest, what have I let myself in for?"

Before MacRorah could even think of enlightening him, he caught her by the shoulders and jerked her hard against him, kissing her startled mouth with bruising force.

Long before it ended, the kiss gentled. Long before it ended, MacRorah's arms had gone around his waist. As furious as she was, she couldn't seem to get close enough. And that, too, she held against him: the fact that he could make her feel this way when all she wanted to do was rail at him and force him to see her point of view—to strike out at him when he refused to agree with all her notions.

No, she didn't, either; that wasn't at all what she wanted to do, she thought sadly as she watched him stride down the boardwalk a moment later.

Court returned the evening before the wedding date. By that time, MacRorah had changed her mind a dozen times, only to change it back again.

Megan and Iris had run wild the entire week. It occurred to MacRorah that Iris bore little resemblance to the pale, overdressed child who had first wandered outside to gaze wistfully at the children playing along the beach. Her arms were quite tanned, her little face was freckled, and she had discovered an unexpected talent for skipping seashells on the water. Four was her current record. Megan's was three. MacRorah's was five, but she modestly kept that achievement to herself.

The children were outside catching lightning bugs when Court came to call. "Did you think I'd taken a flier on you?" he asked.

MacRorah, who had lingered outside to watch the first few stars appear, said, "I wasn't worried. After all, I have Iris."

Mercy, she had forgotten how handsome he was! Those lean, aristocratic features, that tall, wiry body. The smell of him that she had always particularly liked—starched cotton, good woolens, a hint of tobacco, and some light, crisp masculine scent.

He sat down beside her and placed a large, flat box on her lap.

"What's this?"

"Open it later. How've you been, MacRorah?"

"Fine. Iris can skip a clamshell four times. She'll want to demonstrate, and you must be patient— nothing goes the way you want it to go when you care too much. The first dozen or so will probably sink like a rock."

She was babbling. In the near darkness, she could feel his gaze on her. It had the effect of dispatching her wits. Her fingers gripped the box in her lap, wondering what was in it. Wondering even more just what had happened to the peaceful, orderly life she had planned.

From nearby on the shore came the sound of squeals and giggles.

"That's Megan and Iris. They're catching lightning bugs in one of Polly's canning jars."

"Isn't that a bit strenuous for this time of night?"

"It's hardly even dark. Besides, they'll be good and tired when they go to bed; otherwise, they talk until all hours."

"They sound as if they're getting too excited. Jonesy always insisted—"

"They're just fine, trust me," she said, and he sighed and looked away.

Which made her heart sink. That was part of the trouble. He *didn't* trust her. After all this time, he still held against her that one foolish prank she had involved him in. "Court, do you remember—

He cut her off impatiently. "MacRorah, I've been thinking. I believe what we're doing is the right thing, under the circumstances, but it's occurred to me that you might have misunderstood, um . . . certain aspects of our relationship."

"Misunderstood?"

"About our marriage tomorrow."

"You've changed your mind?" She felt as if the earth had just crumbled under her feet.

"No, no—that is, of course I haven't changed my mind, else I wouldn't have brought you a wedding gown. All the same, it might be best if we clear up certain matters right from the first."

"But we've already done that, haven't we? I listed my requirements, you listed yours, and we both agreed? You won't tell me what to do, and I won't drink alcohol. And naturally, I intend to spend most of my time with the children—with Iris, that is. That's why I'm—that's the only reason you're marrying me, isn't it?"

If she'd hoped he would deny it, she was to be disappointed. "I just wanted to be sure you understood—" He cleared his throat and frowned out at the gathering darkness. "Don't you think it's time you called those girls in?"

"Sure I understood what, Court?"

He stood and turned away, his lean frame silhouetted against the gray-purple sky. "I don't love you, MacRorah."

He didn't love her. Well, of *course* he didn't love her! Nor did she love him! All the same, MacRorah could not but wonder why she should feel so stricken.

"Frankly, I don't believe I'm capable of loving any

woman, nor am I sure such a thing even exists outside the realm of dime novels. However, I fully intend to be a good husband to you," he declared, turning back to face her. "You'll not want for anything, nor will I make a nuisance of myself by—that is, in a personal way. I would like to have another child—I believe that's also your reason for agreeing to this arrangement—but I assure you, I'll not force my attentions on you until you indicate your readiness."

Fortunately, it was quite dark now. He couldn't possibly see the color that burned her cheeks. Rising abruptly, MacRorah clutched the box to her bosom and leaned over the railing. "Megan! Iris! It's time to come in now," she called, her voice commendably steady in spite of a heart that had cracked right through.

A notice of the marriage of Miss MacRorah Douglas, daughter of a prominent local family, to one Courtland Adams, president and owner of Adams-Snelling Lumber Company, appeared on page one of the Elizabeth City daily paper. On an inside page of the same issue there was a brief account of a body, identified as one Darcy O'Briant, that had been found behind a notorious brothel, a pair of dressmakers' shears in his throat. Other than the weapon, a common item almost impossible to trace, there were no clues as to the identity of the murderer.

The Douglas-Adams wedding, choreographed by Sally Lee with Polly's assistance, was held at one in

the afternoon in the parlor of MacRorah's cottage.
On that she had held firm. Court had wanted to use
one of the hotels, but MacRorah's home represented
generations of family. She desperately needed that
feeling of support.

Caroline and her husband, Joe Bill Culpepper,
were there. They were staying at his family's place a
few miles down the beach. Sara Ball was living
somehere in the wilds of New York with her second
husband, in the advanced stages of her first pregnancy. Sally Lee had gotten in touch with as many
friends as possible, and there had been a regular av-
alanche of wedding gifts.

MacRorah read and reread the letter that had
come along with an enormous Waterford candelabra
from Frances Gilbert, and thought about the changes
that had taken place in all their lives since those innocent afternoons at her father's ice-cream parlor.

Sea, of course, served Courtland as best man. Iris
and Megan, dressed in their new wedding finery,
flung flower petals wildly in all directions, and a
stern-faced Teeny gave MacRorah away.

She was afraid for a moment he was going to refuse. In the end, after five paces that took them from
the foot of the stairs to the center of the parlor
where Polly and Sal had arranged a bank of ferns and
white gladioli, he glared fiercely at the bridegroom,
planted her hand on his arm, and stepped back to
frown at the poor minister, who had been brought in
from Manteo for the occasion at Polly's insistence.

There was no music, although Polly had offered

her girls to sing a selection of hymns. The ceremony took all of three minutes from start to finish. By the time Megan and Iris, who had swept up the petals already thrown, began to fling them all over again, MacRorah, acutely conscious of the man at her side, was examining her own emotions wonderingly.

She was married.

She was a wife.

After all the years of swearing she would never wed, all the later time spent scheming and making lists, she had gone and married a man who, more than any other man ever had, threatened her vow of independence.

"There, that's done. Well, Mrs. Adams, shall we take a few minutes for refreshments before we begin our wedding journey?"

Chapter Nineteen

𝓒

Second thoughts? Court could have sworn he'd considered things from every possible angle before he had ever proposed marriage. Now, the longer MacRorah kept him waiting, the more he was beginning to wonder if he had not just made the second biggest mistake of his life.

However, it was too late now for second thoughts. Against all expectations, he had taken himself a bride.

Or rather, he had taken his daughter a mother. There was, he told himself, a definite difference.

He'd ordered the wedding supper to be delivered some twenty minutes earlier. It was now growing cold. Not that he was hungry—at least, not for food.

What the devil could she be doing in there all this time?

He poured himself a drink, set it aside, and began to pace the large, well-appointed room. He'd been fortunate in acquiring accommodations on such short notice at the finest hotel on the beach, which was also the hotel farthest from their own cottages. Ordinarily it would have been impossible to find anything at all, much less the bridal suite, at this time of year, but thanks to the recent outbreak of a virulent stomach malady, the ranks of vacationers had thinned considerably.

Passing the side table for the third time, he lifted his glass and then set it down again, remembering a certain night some ten years ago, and a certain note pertaining to his disappointing performance.

A performance he couldn't even remember.

This time he would remain sober if it killed him. This time he would show her a performance they would *both* damned well remember!

His bride had been holed up in that blasted dressing room for nearly an hour now! Surely an hour was time enough to divest herself of a wedding frock and a few petticoats.

A slow smile began to kindle in his hazel eyes. She had truly been a vision in the pale yellow creation he had shopped all over Norfolk to find. She'd been wearing yellow both times he'd encountered her all those years ago. For some crazy reason he didn't even try to fathom, it had been important that she wear yellow again when she gave herself into his keeping.

He had half expected her to refuse to wear the gown he'd chosen—it wouldn't be the first time he had come up against that mule-stubborn pride of hers—but she'd surprised him. He had almost swallowed his Adam's apple when she'd come down the stairs, looking as fresh and innocent as a buttercup in a spring meadow.

The smile faded from his eyes as he wondered just how innocent any woman could be after running a house for retired whores. Or after she had consorted with females of loose morals to the point where she had become a serious threat to the most successful pimp on the mid-Atlantic seaboard.

Second thoughts? Second childhood, more likely! He'd been crazy even to consider marrying again, but the deed was done. Now it was up to all concerned to make the best of it.

Scowling at the closed door, Court took another turn around the parlor. Surprisingly enough, the wedding itself had gone off without a hitch, although some of the guests had been forced to remain outside on the deck, the parlor being far too cramped to contain them all. After a round of congratulations and advice, Gritmire's having been largely paternal and Sea's largely irreverent, they had imbibed the requisite champagne and sampled Polly's crab cakes and watermelon-rind pickles, topped off with slices of a delicious, if decidedly gaudy, wedding cake. Then, while his bride had gone upstairs with Polly and Sal to finish packing her valise for the short trek across to their hotel, Court had stepped outside for a breath of air, only to find himself being pelted with rice by a flock of giggling bawds.

Polly's girls.

Or were they MacRorah's girls?

He had nearly bolted right then. Only the thought

of Iris, her grave little face aglow with happiness, had driven him back inside.

"Balder-bloody-dash!"

From behind the closed dressing-room door came the muffled sound of cursing, MacRorah style. *Balder-bloody-dash?* Her vocabulary was certainly colorful. He'd better warn her about small pitchers with large ears.

"Are you all right?" he called through the walnut-paneled door.

"Yes! It's my—never mind!"

Her never mind. He grinned, took a cautious sample of scotch, and commenced pacing again, his black silk dressing gown slithering softly around his legs. He should consider himself lucky to have had a honeymoon at all. MacRorah had suggested they take the two girls along with Sea and Sal's two boys to Raleigh for a look at the state capitol.

Sal had managed to look horrified and embarrassed at the same time. Sea had nearly laughed his fool head off, but it was that woman of hers—Polly—who had grabbed her by the wrist and taken her into the kitchen for a good talking-to. Through the window, Court had overheard most of the housekeeper's lecture concerning the pitfalls awaiting undutiful wives and unsatisfied husbands. Although Mrs. Gritmire had stated the case in rather more elementary terms.

On his next turn about the room, Court paused to gaze out at an ocean that reflected the dying colors of the sunset. Somewhat to his own surprise, he was

growing rather fond of this benign section of sea-
coast. Iris reveled in it. Diana had considered New-
port tolerable, anything south of Cape May beyond
the pale. He wondered what she would have made of
Nags Head's unassuming atmosphere.

Court's first wedding trip had taken them to the
south of France, followed by an extended shopping
spree in Paris. As a honeymoon, it had been an un-
mitigated failure. He took cold comfort from the
thought that this one could hardly be worse.

God, he was tense! Sweating like a greenhorn
about to lie with his first woman! which was crazy in
light of the fact that neither one of them was precisely inexperienced.

Dammit, that was part of the problem! Even today,
while Sal helped Polly pass out refreshments to the
guests out on the deck, Court had caught Sea gazing
at the new bride with a bit more interest than was
appropriate under the circumstances. When he'd
charged him with it, his cousin had confessed that
even now, he couldn't help but wonder how they
would have gotten along had he married MacRorah
all those years ago.

"She would've wrung you out and hung you up to
dry," Court had told him.

Sea had lifted his glass and grinned. "Might've
been worth it, though. Pity Pop wasn't more broad-
minded." He gazed warmly at MacRorah, who was
laughingly kneeling so that Megan and Iris could
tuck rose petals into her headdress along with the
silk narcissus. "You better take good care of her, old

man, y'hear? My little Mickey's not nearly as tough as she tries to make out."

His little Mickey be damned! Court fully intended to take excellent care of his bride, if she would ever quit hiding in that blasted dressing room! The more determined he'd been all day not to think about tonight, the more he'd thought about it. By now, his nerves were tuned tighter than a three-dollar fiddle.

It didn't help that he couldn't even remember the last time he'd had a woman. Judas priest, what if, at the crucial moment, he froze up? What if he let her down for the second time?

At least this time he was stone-cold sober.

After donning the lacy ivory gown and negligee that had been a gift from Sally Lee, MacRorah hung up her yellow wedding gown, wondering again why Court had selected it. Wondering even more why she had accepted it. Surely it wasn't the thing for a groom to buy his bride her wedding gown?

Not that she'd ever been a stickler for protocol. Still, she had always pictured herself, when she'd thought of marrying at all, in white. But Court had chosen the palest shade of yellow, and so she'd worn it. He obviously didn't know the first thing about all the traditions connected with weddings, even though he'd been married before. But then, men didn't hold with such sentimental claptrap as white for brides and something old and something borrowed and all the other lovely superstitions.

Such as the something blue that Polly had labored

so lovingly over all week, stuffing it out of sight whenever MacRorah had entered the room. The beribboned satin garter was the brightest shade of blue imaginable, embroidered with red rosebuds, with gold- and silver-colored glass beads and three rows of lace—two purple and one black. MacRorah had slipped it on above her knee under her wedding gown, praying it wouldn't slip down around her ankle before the ceremony was done. It itched, but she would have cut out her tongue before she'd have said so.

And then Polly had insisted she wear it the first night, as well. "I laid a spell onto it so it'd make you a baby right off," she'd declared, her blue eyes earnest and red-rimmed from hours of intermittent weeping.

Touched, MacRorah had embraced the earnest, energetic little woman who had been her closest friend for ten years, and promised not remove the wretched thing until morning.

Absently now, she slid a finger under the garter and scratched her thigh as she stared at her image in the mirror. Should she take down her hair? She had worn it teased over a rat, with silk flowers tucked into the crown and a wisp of a veil floating down over her shoulders.

Well. She could hardly wear a veil and half a dozen silk blossoms to bed. Nor even her rat. It would all come undone during the night and she'd look like a fright come morning.

Mercy! Imagine waking up with a man in her bed.

Imagine going to bed with one!

MacRorah couldn't. Her imagination led her right up to the very brink, and left her dangling there. Here she was, a woman who had sworn never to put herself under a man's power—a woman who had read countless books, and even written tracts about birth control, self-respect, disease, about nearly every aspect of a man-woman relationship. Why, she'd be laughed right off the face of the earth if any of her converts knew she hadn't the least notion of what actually happened, save in the most basic biological sense.

At the moment, it was that very same biological sense that frightened the bejabbers out of her.

"MacRorah?"

Her eyes widened. She clutched her hairbrush protectively to her bosom. "Yes? I—I'm coming."

"Your supper's getting cold."

And so am I, she thought despairingly, bracing herself for the coming ordeal.

It took almost more courage than she possessed to open the door to the parlor. Ever since they'd been led up to the bridal suite, she'd felt as if everyone in the hotel must know exactly what they were doing.

Or what they were about to do.

"Are you cold?"

She realized she was shivering, her arms wrapped around her body. "No. I'm nervous, that's all." She attempted a smile, but it was a brittle affair, at best.

"No more than I am," Court said, and she noticed then that he looked paler than usual, his angular features more sharply honed. Perhaps it was that wicked-looking garment he was wearing. There was a feverish look about his eyes that made her wonder if he might have contracted the illness that was making the rounds.

"Court, do you feel all right?" she asked anxiously. "I mean, other than being nervous? I mean, you're not coming down with something, are you?"

"Nothing that I'm aware of." He still stood at the window, although he'd turned when she'd entered the room. MacRorah hovered in the doorway. They stared at one another while the ornate clock on the mantel ticked away the minutes with agonizing slowness.

"Your foot!" MacRorah blurted. "Oh, don't tell me it's turned septic again!"

"MacRorah, this has gone far enough. We're acting like a pair of love-struck adolescents instead of two mature, reasonable adults. Now come and eat your supper and we'll take things as slowly as you wish. I promise you, I'm not an ogre."

"No," she whispered, edging closer to the table that had been set up over by the window. "I—I didn't think you were."

Much later, she would wonder how they had gotten through the next hour. The champagne, which neither of them had touched. The elegant supper of shrimp in aspic, celeried oysters, chicken croquettes with green peas, braised asparagus, stuffed flounder, bride cake, and the hotel's famous charlotte russe, most of which they had left untasted.

The window was open, allowing the soft salt breeze to blow through the room. Evening strollers could be heard outside calling out, laughing—a few even singing.

"Do you play basketball?" she blurted. Basketball had been the favored remedy for the relief of sexual tension in one of the books she had studied in an effort to better advise her girls. "When the python rears its ugly head, play basketball, girls, play basketball!" exhorted its author.

Court looked puzzled. "Not in years," he said. "Shall I send downstairs for a deck of cards—or perhaps a chessboard?"

"Oh, no! That is, I'd probably beat you, anyway. I've always been good at games," MacRorah said guilelessly, and then flushed at the thought that he might think she was bragging when she was simply stating a fact.

"Then I'll make a point of offering you an opportunity, but not tonight, I believe." His deep-set eyes were in shadow, so she couldn't tell whether or not he was teasing her. "MacRorah—we have to get this business over and done with, you know. The longer we put it off, the more awkward it will be for both of us."

She sighed, rubbing her arms as if she were freezing. In fact, she was quite warm. In fact, suddenly she was uncomfortably warm. And her thigh itched. "I know, I know. And I do want a child, Court. Besides Iris, I mean. Although if she's to be our only child, why, then, I'll not be too disappointed. I al-

ready love her as if she were my own. And just look
how much she's—"

"MacRorah."

"Well, since Jonesy left and she started wearing
more appropriate—"

"MacRorah! Dammit, don't you have another
name? What the devil were your parents thinking of,
giving you a name like that?"

Before she could stop them, tears formed in her
eyes and overflowed. She never cried. She really
never did, almost never. "I was named for my grandfather. I'm sorry if it displeases you."

Court was out of his chair in an instant, fumbling
in the pocket of his dressing gown for a handkerchief. Not only didn't he have a handkerchief, he
didn't even have a pocket. He'd bought the damned
outfit on a whim just after he'd bought his bride's
wedding gown.

He should have stuck to a blasted nightshirt! "I'm
sorry, my dear, MacRorah is a fine name. Honestly, I
can't imagine a finer one."

MacRorah mopped her eyes on her sleeve and
glared at him. "My father hoped it would soften
Grandpop MacRorah into loosening the purse
strings. It never did, but by the time Father found
out it wasn't going to work, it was too late to call me
anything else."

"It's a nice name. I could always call you Mickey.
Or Rorie."

"Don't forget MacMischief and MacTrouble." Her
lips twitched in a watery grin.

"Dearest, please don't cry. I didn't mean to hurt you. I would never do that, it's just that . . ."

"I know," she said, meeting his gaze head-on with typical directness. "You're nervous. I am, too. But I already told you that, so why don't we just get it over with so we won't have to suffer through another wretched evening like this?"

Warm light from a pair of cut-glass lamps played over her glistening pale brown hair, over skin the color of old ivory, reflecting tiny dancing flames in her enormous wet-lashed eyes. Court took a deep breath and held it while he tried to figure out whether his best course would be to walk out here and now, collect his daughter, and head for Connecticut—or toss his bride on the nearest bed and have his way with her.

How could any one woman be so utterly desirable and so utterly maddening at the same time? He had never known anyone like her.

There had never *been* anyone like her.

Moving abruptly, he swooped her from the chair and strode through to the bedroom. She was right. The best thing for all concerned was to do the deed and get beyond it. Perhaps tomorrow, when he was able to think of something other than his blasted male appetite, the two of them could sit down and work out a few ground rules.

Her slight weight in his arms made him feel protective, which took him by surprise. But before he could make sense of it, he caught a drift of a delicate scent which nearly buckled his knees. Warm woman and some clean, wildflower scent. Lemon and lavender?

God, he felt like a rutting stag!

What *was* it about this woman that had haunted him for ten long years? That had caused him, to his everlasting shame, to imagine—to dream—to fantasize about her more than a few times, even on the rare occasions when he made love to his own wife?

Reaching the bedroom, he dropped her like a hot coal, praying the loosely gathered silk trousers he wore concealed his rampant erection. She fell onto the thick feather mattress, her diaphanous garments drifting up over her thighs, and Court stared down at her in awe. "Great Scott, what is that—that *thing* you're wearing?"

Her head popped up off the pillows and she stared down over her thinly clad body to her bare limbs. "It's, um—well, it's my something blue."

"Blue! It's a bloody bawdy-house rainbow!"

"Polly said it was also a—a sort of fertility thing? Not that I'm one bit superstitious, you understand, but I thought it wouldn't hurt to . . . to wear it?" Her tentative statements emerged as questions.

Court swore softly, and then he began to laugh. MacRorah jerked her gown down over her legs, but he swept it back up again, grinning down at a pair of the shapeliest legs he ever remembered seeing— even though their lower extremities were a bit too tanned to be considered strictly fashionable.

She had scratched a pink ring about her left thigh under the garter. "From the looks of it, I think blood poisoning is more likely than pregnancy. Shall we hang it on the bedpost, instead? I promise, it'll work just as well from there. And if it doesn't—" His eyes twinkled down at her, relieving to a surprising degree the knot of tension in her belly. "Well, we'll just have to try twice as hard, won't we? I'm willing if you are."

He was more than willing; he was downright eager. The sight of his bride in her pale yellow wedding finery had kindled the first flame. He'd been reminded all over again of the way she had looked the night she had opened the door and invited him into her rooms.

The sight of her now, sprawled in deshabille across his bed, his for the taking, was just about to do him in. If he waited much longer, he was going to go off like a blasted geyser, and she'd have cause all over again to complain about his performance!

MacRorah could hardly breathe. Only now did she dare admit that as dangerously foolish as she had been all those years ago, she would probably have made love with him then if only he hadn't fallen asleep. In fact, for a long time, she thought they had made love, but of course, she was far wiser now. In theory, if not in fact.

"MacRorah?"

At the sound of her name, spoken in a hoarse whisper, MacRorah opened her eyes to see Court standing over her, bare to the waist, a pair of baggy black silk trousers hanging low on his narrow hips.

He had hair on his chest. A small, densely furred diamond of dark hair that spread between flat, copper-colored nipples and pointed down to the gathered waist of those strange, exotic trousers. He was, she thought, quite the most beautiful man she had ever seen.

Swallowing hard, she bravely met his eyes, awaiting the inevitable. Polly had said it hurt the first time, but after that it got better. And with the right man and a bit of practice, it could be much, much better.

"I'm not afraid," she whispered.

"MacRorah—I want you to know that whatever you've done—I mean, the past isn't—" He looked away, raking a hand though his hair. The hand, she noticed, was unsteady. "Let's forget the past, shall we? We'll both start fresh, and this time, I promise you, my sweet MacLovely, you won't have cause to complain." He knelt beside her on the bed and gathered her up in his arms, his breath warm on her face.

"This time, perhaps you won't fall asleep," she teased.

His hands cupped her chin, tilting her face up to his. With his mouth mere inches from hers, he smiled crookedly. "Did I fall asleep? Ah, well . . . it's hardly any wonder. I expect I was exhausted." His thumbs strayed over her lips, parting them. "I have a feeling neither of us will be getting much sleep for the next few days."

And then he lowered his mouth to hers, and the world instantly telescoped into a small place that was exceedingly hot, exceedingly sweet, incredibly exciting.

He kissed her mouth, teasing her lips apart, the thrust of his tongue echoing the beat of two hearts and the thrust of his hard masculine length against her belly. MacRorah did her best to follow his lead. Her hips shifted restlessly. Daringly, she drew his tongue into her mouth and sucked, savoring the sensations that coursed through her body.

The skin of his back was like warm, wet silk under her exploring hands. Her palms drifted down over his taut buttocks, and she felt him leap against her. Her thighs trembled with the need to part—it was the strangest sensation! The things he was doing to her with his hands and his mouth were certainly not included in any book she had ever read!

Her *ear?*

Oh, my mercy. His hands were kneading her breasts even as his lips left her ear for her throat. She shuddered uncontrollably as lightning streaked through her body, stabbing again and again the woman's parts that were hidden between her thighs.

He had removed her garter, but still she itched, only this itch was different—sweet and hot and hungry. And in an entirely different place. She longed to scratch, only she didn't quite know where or how.

Breathing harshly, he removed her negligee and slipped her gown down over her shoulders. Her breast felt cool where his tongue had wet the filmy cloth. When he lifted her hips and dragged the wispy garment down, she heard it tear and wanted only to tear off his sleeping trousers, too. As decadent as the garment looked—as wonderful as he looked wearing it—she wanted to see all of him. Touch all of him.

Oh, she was shameless, an utter wanton. If this was the price a kept woman paid her keeper, why, then, she would be willing to be kept for the rest of her life, wedding ring or no wedding ring!

His tongue, then his teeth, raked her nipple, and she groaned. "Ah, Court—I'm afraid—"

Afraid she would truly burst into flames. This aching, throbbing hunger deep inside her was like nothing she had ever experienced. Surely it couldn't be . . . safe?

And then his hands slipped lower, cupping the slight rise of her belly, circling, then dipping into her navel. Pleasure stabbed through her again and again, shrill, like the sound of a telephone bell.

Desperately, she reached for the drawstring at his waist and tugged at it. "Please," she gasped. "I want—"

"What do you want, MacRorah?"

"I want—I don't know what I want!" she wailed.

But Court knew. Rising, he stripped off his single garment and stood before her in the dim light of a single lamp, fiercely male, boldly aroused, so beautiful she felt like weeping.

But even more, she felt like touching. And so she did.

"Ah, sweet—" He gasped as her hands clasped his erect penis, her fingers measuring his length and lingering on the satiny crown.

"I never knew—I never dreamed," she whispered.

It was more than curiosity, it was a compulsion—surely the strangest compulsion any woman had ever known. But before she could come anywhere near satisfying her curiosity, Court covered her hands with his own and drew them away.

"But I want to—"

"Not now," he gasped. "I'm beginning to understand why I got such an unsatisfactory report the last time. If you touched me the same way then . . ."

But MacRorah wasn't concerned with reports, satisfactory or otherwise. Lying beside her, he had turned onto his side and laid his palm over the mound at the base of her belly.

She felt as if molten honey flowed through her veins, robbing her of her wits, her will—everything except the sweet, throbbing urgency that had settled somewhere between her thighs.

And then, even as his mouth covered hers, his fingers began to move. Her groan was lost in his kisses—her mind went with it as he began a slow, rhythmic circling motion.

His fingertips were moist—or she was. Glowing circles of the most unimaginable pleasure began to wheel over her head, growing closer, closer—until suddenly she cried out, her thighs tightening on his hand.

"That was for you, love," he rasped, his voice low and thready. "This time, we'll share." And he mounted her, making a place for himself between her trembling limbs.

She was damp all over. Her heart was pounding,

and she gazed up at him wonderingly. "Wh-what was it?"

But Court was beyond speech. The instant he broached her soft, hot body, he closed his eyes, his face a harsh and unfamiliar mask. *Patience, patience,* he warned himself, but after ten years, he had no patience left.

He plunged home. MacRorah screamed and bucked. Startled, he tried to withdraw as the horror of the truth overcame him. With the sound of her pitiful whimpers ringing in his ears, he told himself he was mistaken. He had to be mistaken! He distinctly remembered—

He remembered nothing. Not one blasted thing.

"MacRorah," he whispered rawly. "Darling, please—"

"Is . . . that all?"

His laughter sounded more like a sob. "I think it had better be all. We have some talking to do. Tomorrow." He was still inside her, still turgid and aching with need despite the shock of discovering that she had been a virgin.

Reluctantly, he began to withdraw, but she held him there. "Please—Court, do you have to leave now? Did it hurt you, too? Polly said it only hurt the first time, but you've done it before, I suppose— well, of course, you have."

"MacRorah—" He groaned.

"But I'm ready to do it again if you want to. I liked the first part—I'll probably learn to like the second part, too, once I get used to it, but it's rather strange, you know—having someone else inside your body. Of course, I've read all about it, but I didn't know it would be so—so awfully personal."

It was sheer, bloody-minded selfishness, but Court knew he was going to take advantage of her offer. Sweet, misguided, deceiving little wretch, he should wring her neck!

Instead, he kissed her, and the kiss deepened, and her body began to move. It was all the invitation he needed. Slipping a hand down between them, he found the pearl he was seeking, and to his amazement, she gasped and began to convulse around his shaft mere moments after he touched her.

Twice more he brought her to her pleasure before he allowed himself to come home. Long afterward, as she lay in his arms, Court thought he must have lost consciousness for a while. Never, not even in his carefree college years, had he experienced such a release. Even now, it throbbed deep inside him, like ripples on a warm lake, kissing the shore again and again in ever decreasing circles.

"Are you still awake?" he whispered. There was no answer. She lay limp and damp beside him, his amazing, contradictory little bride. How was it possible? How could he not have guessed?

More to the point, how was he going to manage living with a woman who had married him only for his reproductive services? She had made no bones about why she was marrying him. She wanted a child. She wanted *his* child—his daughter.

She stirred beside him, and he kissed her closed eyes. For someone who was so soft, so feminine, she was surprisingly strong. Sailing, fishing, climbing sand dunes—that sort of activity would do it, he supposed.

Even so, she was going to be sore tomorrow. Perhaps if he helped her bathe—a long soak in warm water and a slow, sensuous massage with scented oils afterward should turn the trick.

Court grinned up into the darkness as his mind launched into a seduction scene right out of the *Kama Sutra*. One part of him wondered briefly what had happened to the sober stick who had brought a year's worth of work with him on a beach vacation. The man who had forgotten how to smile, much less laugh.

A man who had been so careful to explain to his bride that he didn't love her.

Chapter Twenty

❧

Opening her eyes, MacRorah lay quietly for a long moment, wondering where she was. Wondering why she felt as if she'd spent the day riding an ox without benefit of a sidesaddle. Slowly, it came back to her. What she had done. What *they* had done together.

"So this is what love feels like," she mused. Oh, my mercy. All those strange, shivery feelings? The sudden, unexpected pain? And then what had happened after that. . . .

It had been the most singular experience of her life.

Had she told him? Surely she wasn't so lost to all reason as to confess her feelings. Lust was one thing—lust was merely a commodity.

But love? Surely she hadn't been so foolish! Not after he had taken such care to point out that he didn't love her.

She would simply have to *un*love him, otherwise,

she would be no better off than her own mother had been. Still, there was a bright side. Iris was now her child. In time, she might even be fortunate enough to have another child.

But then, she reminded herself, her mother had had children, too. It hadn't been enough to make up for a life of misery and degradation.

"MacRorah?" Court spoke quietly from the door of the bathroom. It was a private bathroom, one of the few private baths in any of the hotels on the beach. "I've drawn a hot bath for you. I thought you might like to soak a bit. Are you terribly sore?"

"Mmm, a bit. Did you ever ride an ox?"

His dark brows shot skyward. "No, I can't say I have."

"Well, don't. They're not built for riding. I'm beginning to think I'm not, either."

Court was half amused and half horrified by her plain speaking. He had woken up feeling as relaxed as if he'd just spent hours in a steam bath, followed by a vigorous session with a Swedish masseur. The few times since his marriage had ended, when he'd sought temporary relief of a sexual nature, he had felt only depression afterward.

Last night he had been stunned by the innocence of his bride, by her untutored sensuality. Just before he'd fallen asleep, she had asked him diffidently if he had felt any pleasure in the act.

God, if he'd felt any more pleasure, he would have evaporated on the spot!

Now, steeling himself against the temptation to

dive back into bed and take her again, he handed her her negligee, watched while she wrapped it around her and rose, clutching it tightly under her chin. He averted his gaze from the sight of her warm flesh glowing through its translucent folds. "I believe you'll find everything you need," he told her. Briefly, he considered helping her bathe, and then following where that activity led, but something warned him that he rather desperately needed a long, brisk walk on the beach. A solitary walk on the beach. He had some serious thinking to do. Or rather, some rethinking.

He cleared his throat. "Take your time. I plan to— that is, if you don't need me, I plan to take a walk along the beach. Shall I order breakfast on my way out?" At her nod, he said, "Good. I'll see you in an hour, then. I'll have a pot of coffee sent up right away, shall I?"

MacRorah nodded. Mutely, she watched him go. Freshly bathed, his hair still damp, he looked stern and pale and formidable. A stranger, in fact.

Had they truly done all those wonderfully wicked things together last night?

She supposed one shouldn't talk about it. One probably shouldn't even think about it in broad daylight, only she couldn't seem to help it. She was just now coming to terms with the fact that for nearly thirty years she had inhabited this body without once realizing what it was capable of doing—of feeling.

Forty-five minutes later, MacRorah was putting the last touches on her toilette when someone rapped sharply on her door. Her breath caught in her throat and she could feel the heat rush to her face as she prepared herself to greet her new husband without blurting out her feelings.

"Cour . . . T-Teeny?" Puzzled, she peered past the worried-looking man to the empty hallway beyond.

"Miss Mac, I'm sorry to bust in this way, but you gotta come with me right now!" He looked frantic.

"Oh, dear God, it's Court, isn't it? What happened? Has he been hurt? Where is he? Tell me, Teeny!" Without waiting for an answer, she pushed past him and raced for the stairs.

"It ain't him, Miss Mac, it's them young'uns. And Polly, too. They're all a-heavin' and a-squattin', and I can't do it all alone. I'm right sorry to have to bother you at a time like this, but I need help, Miss Mac."

Gripping the newel post with clammy hands, MacRorah tried to sort out the message so that it made sense. "The children, you say—"

"Polly, too. She come down with it this morning, afore daylight."

"They've got whatever it is that's been going around?"

"Yes'm, I reck'n so. All I know is, I can't fetch and empty three buckets at the same time, and I don't dare ask Miz Sally to help out on account of the baby."

"I should think not! Wait just a moment, Teeny, and I'll write a note for Court."

"I got the cart right outside."

"You can collect my things later—no, I'll ask Court

to bring them. No, he shouldn't be exposed. Oh, mercy, let's just go! I'll think later, when I've had time to sort it all out."

The next few days were a nightmare. Court had insisted on moving in and helping out in the emergency and MacRorah had insisted right back. "You'll catch it, sure as the world, and I simply can't deal with another patient," MacRorah called to him from the deck. She had placed a straight chair halfway down the boardwalk to bar the way. He came that far several times a day, and they talked over the intervening distance.

"You look tired," he called softly the second morning. "Are you getting enough rest?"

Enough rest? She wasn't getting any rest at all. How could she when her three patients were timed to go off in sequence at fifteen-minute intervals, twenty-four hours a day? In between bouts, it was all she could do to coax ginger tea and soda biscuits down them, and snatch a bite for herself.

"I'm fine," she assured him gently. "You don't have to worry about me, Court, I never get sick. I believe Iris is coming out of it. She's a real little trooper."

"I finally located a doctor," he told her on his next visit. "Unfortunately, he's been ill since Sunday."

"We don't need him, but thank you. Court, go home and go to bed. You look awful." There were shadows under his eyes as dark as muscadine jelly, and he had forgotten to shave. He hadn't worn a necktie in days, and half the time, he forgot to wear shoes.

"Gone plumb native," Polly had said that morning just before she'd grabbed the bucket again.

To MacRorah, he looked beautiful. She loved him so much she ached with it, which was far worse than aching temporarily with stomach cramps and the headache. Those would pass.

Not that she let on. He was concerned, which was only natural. She was now his wife—the mother of his daughter. But he hadn't asked for her love, and she had no intention of forcing it on him. To hand him her heart would be to surrender all control over her life.

"How are you holding up?" he called the next morning, his gaze moving over her, making her miserably aware of her uncombed hair, her soiled apron, the shadows under her own eyes. She had lost track of time. How long now had she been a wife?

So far, the position hadn't a lot to recommend it.

"I'm tired, but well enough."

"Your—uh, stomach?"

"Cast iron. I've been taking a spoonful of vinegar in honey every day. I have it on good authority that it helps ward off the influenza."

She had it on the authority of no less an expert than LaFrance Murphy, who had caught every disease known to man; but then, LaFrance was a pessimist and MacRorah was an unregenerate optimist. She was convinced it made a difference.

"Sea and Sal and the babies left yesterday," said Court.

"I'm glad. Who's taking care of you?"

"I take care of myself. I don't need anyone."

Or if he did, MacRorah thought, he would never admit it. He had arranged with one of the restaurants to prepare box meals, which Teeny collected, leaving Court's at the foot of his boardwalk and bringing theirs home with him. If it weren't for Teeny's enormous appetite, theirs would have been largely wasted.

She'd insisted that Teeny sleep outside in a hammock and that both men take a dose of vinegar in honey three times a day. She was counting on those measures, plus her prayers, to keep them both well.

"Well . . . I'd best get back inside," she said reluctantly. "Iris is definitely on the mend, but Megan and Polly are still feeling wretched."

"I could take Iris home with me—there'd be one less for you to look after."

"I wish you would leave her here. She's company for Megan."

Court backed down the boardwalk, unwilling to end another brief, frustrating contact. How long could he live this way? He'd been frantic when he'd returned to the hotel three days earlier, to be greeted by an empty suite and a brief note from his bride saying she was needed at home and that Court was to pack her bag and leave it at the foot of her boardwalk.

Teeny had met him there and explained, else he

would have stormed the place and no doubt made an ass of himself in the process. The ex-seaman had nailed up a quarantine sign and then rigged up a bell with a pull cord that extended halfway down the boardwalk so that Court could signal whenever he needed to see MacRorah.

Which was constantly, if only to assure himself that she was still all right. Gradually, it had dawned on him that what he really needed was to hold her, to comfort her—to promise her the moon and stars if only she wouldn't leave him.

It was downright scary. Having guarded his feelings for so many years, he was unsure how to deal with them. Walking slowly back to his own empty cottage, he tried to remember a time in his life when he had felt this way about a woman.

He couldn't. But then, he had never known a woman like MacRorah.

Early on the fifth day, MacRorah removed the chair and the quarantine sign from the boardwalk. By nine o'clock, she had scoured every bucket and chamber pot in the cottage and set them out to sun. By ten she had thrown open every window to allow the brisk southwest breeze to blow through, and had set a tubful of bedding to boil with a bar of lye soap on the big cast-iron range. By the time it came to a boil, threatening to boil over, she was almost too exhausted to get up and close the damper, but knowing the end was in sight and she could sleep for a solid week, she forced herself to drag out the washboard.

Outside, a haggard and still-shaky Polly was directing Teeny as he draped mattresses over the railing to sun. Iris and Megan were squabbling over the paper dolls they had cut from the latest copy of the *Delineator*.

The siege was ended.

Court came twice before noon. She refused to allow him inside, even though she was sure all danger of infection was past. "Let me do this my own way, in my own time," she said, and he went away, muttering something about managing women.

Which she was. Always had been. But over the past few days, MacRorah had had a great deal of time to think about the man she had married in such haste. Things she had observed had come together in her mind with things she had heard, painting a far different picture from the one she had first imagined.

According to Sal, who had it from Sea, Court's father had been a lot like her own. He had treated both his son and his wife shamefully. Court's first wife had been no better. She had married for all the wrong reasons and then proceeded to drink herself to death, ignoring her child and husband alike.

It was no wonder he couldn't love her. First he would have had to trust her, and trust would not come easy to a man like Courtland Adams.

That afternoon, MacRorah bathed and dressed in her best gown, which now hung on her like a tent, and set out to meet her husband. He usually came several times a day. This time, she intended to meet him halfway. It was the only way she could think of to gain a modicum of privacy.

Choosing the place where the tide had cut away the shelving beach, leaving a cliff some three feet high, she sat, spread her skirts becomingly around her, and waited. The sun felt glorious. If it had rained all week, she wasn't sure she could have gotten through the ordeal, but fortunately, it had remained fair.

Her hair was still damp. She had scrubbed herself and her hair, along with everything else in the cottage, feeling as if she'd just emerged from a house of pestilence. Now she unpinned her braid and loosened the strands, allowing the wind to blow through it. It never looked quite neat, no matter how hard she tried, but surely Court would forgive her a bit of untidiness, under the circumstances.

Court was almost upon her before he saw her. Dear God, how could any woman look so beautiful and so awful at the same time? She was lying back, sound asleep, her shapely little feet dangling several inches above the ground. Even though she had managed to avoid the influenza, she had lost weight. Her cheekbones stood out sharply. Her eyelids looked almost translucent. The only specks of color in her face were the shadows around her eyes and the slight flush caused by sleeping in the sun.

How long had she been here? He'd taken pains to bathe and dress so carefully, hoping that at last he'd be able to take her back home with him.

"MacRorah?" he whispered, sitting beside her on the sand bank. The tiny, embroidered handkerchief she had spread to protect her head from the sand was inadequate for the task. She would have sand on her pillow tonight.

On his pillow, he sincerely hoped. Even if he couldn't make love to her—even if he could only hold her until she regained her strength—he never wanted to spend another night apart. This last week had been sheer hell.

"Darling, wake up. You're getting too much sun."

Slowly, she opened her eyes, those clear amber eyes that had captured him so long ago. And then she smiled, and Court knew in his heart that what he had long feared had finally come to pass.

She yawned, rubbed her eyes, and then beamed up at him. At the sight of her familiar, contagious smile, he melted another few degrees.

"I told you it would work," she said, her voice husky from sleep.

"What would work?" He was transfixed by the sight of her hair, lit through by the sunlight, glowing like molten bronze.

"Vinegar."

"Vinegar." Caught between tenderness and desire, Court willed himself to patience. He tried to recall if patience had been one of the requirements on that infamous list of hers. According to Seaborn, she had vowed never to allow herself to come under the control of any man. Something to do with the way her father had treated her mother.

He didn't want to control her, he merely wanted to possess her, body, heart, and soul.

"Come home with me?" he invited.

"For a little while," she agreed.

He suspected they were skirting around the issue foremost in both their minds. Their marriage. Their interrupted honeymoon.

A thought occurred to him as he took her hand and drew her to her feet that made his blood run cold. Did she think— Surely she didn't think that just because the marriage had been consummated, she was finished with that part of her wifely duties?

"MacRorah—" He matched his pace to her slower one, turning over and rejecting several pat phrases. "My dear, I know you're exhausted. If you want to, uh—postpone— That is, for a few days, if you'd rather not . . ."

"Do you know what I'd truly like to do? Go to bed and sleep for a week. After that, I'm ready to take on whatever task you see fit to assign me."

Task? Duty was bad enough, but *task*?

"Court, about Iris—she's really too old for a nanny. I think we can do without another Mrs. Jones, but a cook—I must tell you that I've no notion at all of how to manage a kitchen." She yawned, and Court fought against the frustration of wanting her desperately and being afraid of frightening her off.

"We'll talk about it later, once you're feeling strong enough."

Her answer was that same old slow, sweet smile that never failed to melt his small store of resistance.

He served her hot chocolate, which was something he had learned to make for his daughter, and she fell asleep on the sofa before she'd even tasted it. For a long while, he simply watched her sleep.

And then he carried her up to his bedroom, smoothed out the rumpled sheets, and laid her down. She murmured something without once opening her eyes, and Court fought against the temptation to strip off his clothes and join her there.

Instead, once he was certain she was sleeping soundly, he went back to the Douglas cottage. Iris hurled herself at him in a way that startled him, for although she'd always been obedient, she had never until recently been a particularly demonstrative child.

He put it down to the influence of MacRorah and the Gritmires, and decided it was not a bad thing. Actually, it felt rather nice. "Hello, Princess. I've missed you terribly."

"Have you come to take me home? Papa, could I please stay just until Megan has to go? We made buggies for our paper dolls from spool boxes, and Teeny taught us to make cat's cradles and whirligigs with a string and a button, so can I please stay a little while longer?"

It was Polly who settled matters. With half the bossiness wrung out of her wiry frame, she still had enough to manage two households with one hand tied behind her. " 'Pears to me it makes sense. You look after Miz Mac, and Iris'll keep my girl outta mischief whilst Mr. Gritmire and me packs up to move. If Miz Mac was here, she'd get in the middle of things and wear herself plumb to a frazzle, not but what she ain't already wore out."

It made sense to Court, too. In fact, he couldn't have been more delighted. After bidding his daughter to behave herself and mind Mrs. Gritmire, he hurried back to his bride.

His hollow-eyed, plumb-wore-to-a-frazzle bride.

Chapter Twenty-one

∾

MacRorah slept until sometime after dark. She couldn't say what had awakened her—perhaps hunger. Perhaps the feeling that she was no longer alone.

Court had dragged a chair close beside the bed, and he slept there, his head falling over at an awkward angle, the guarded look he habitually wore for once absent.

The windows were open to the balmy night air. She was glad he wasn't one of those fearful souls who thought that shutting themselves up inside an airless room would ward off summer miasma.

She looked to her heart's content, studying this man who was both a stranger and her husband. It occurred to her that the first time she had seen him, she'd been struck by a sense of sadness in his eyes, in spite of the way he had teased her.

Was it still there? She thought it had been, at least until after their wedding. Actually, she wasn't sure just when it had disappeared, because after Teeny had come for her and taken her away from what was to have been a three-day honeymoon, she'd been too busy to look.

Surely no bride had ever had a stranger honeymoon, she thought with tired amusement. Still, it was entirely in keeping with the reasons for her marriage. Court could have no cause for complaints, for she had certainly taken her place as his daughter's mother.

The trouble was, she thought now, her gaze moving hungrily over his lean face, with the deep-set eyes, the arrogant nose, and the mouth that could look surprisingly sweet when his stern mask slipped, she wanted to be far more than Iris's mother.

He came awake suddenly, silently taking stock of his surroundings in the instant before he opened his eyes. MacRorah watched the barriers slip back in place, and sighed. For just a moment, she had hoped—she had thought perhaps . . .

"You'll have a crick in your neck," she said.

He tilted his head experimentally. "Not a bad one. I only slept for a few minutes." Judging from the angle of the moon, he had slept a few hours. They both had. "Are you hungry?"

"Starving. Did you bring me up here? I don't remember that."

"You fell asleep on the sofa in the middle of my brilliant discourse on the more fascinating aspects of the lumber business."

His wry look drew forth that husky, affecting giggle

of hers that should have seemed out of place in a woman her age, yet didn't. Once more he resisted the urge to gather her in his arms and kiss her senseless.

Patience, he cautioned himself. He had every intention of having his way with her—all his ways, in fact—but it wouldn't serve to rush his fences.

"Oh, I meant to bring you something," she said, leaving him to wonder what she meant.

"Supper? I have it delivered at six every evening, remember? It should be downstairs now."

"No, it was something else, but food is even better. I hope you ordered enough for a dozen men."

"Half a dozen, at least. Cold roast chicken, potato salad, and whatever sweets the hotel thought to include. The bathroom's right through there, although you already know that."

He stood and stretched, and MacRorah was struck all over again by what a remarkably attractive man her new husband really was. It was not that he was the handsomest man she ever known—Alec and Peter, numbers two and three on her list, had been handsomer in the strictest sense, but there was something about Court—a guarded strength, a depth, perhaps—that made him stand out among all the men she had ever known.

She wished she was more experienced. Or that he was less scrupulous. What would have happened if he'd decided to nap in bed instead of in a chair?

Her pulses quivered at the thought.

They dined on cold chicken, a variety of salads

and fruits, followed by a Lady Baltimore cake that was good, but not quite so rich as Polly's plain one-two-three-four cake. Afterward, MacRorah lay back in her chair and relaxed, replete, and allowed her gaze to feast on the man who had served them both. He hadn't allowed her to lift a finger, saying she must take care to conserve her strength.

"I'm perfectly strong," she declared, hoping he didn't think she was the kind of woman who was forever ailing. She had good cause to know how very little patience men had with illness.

"You lost too much sleep to make it all up in a single nap."

"But I'm not sleepy now. I thought I might go home and——"

"This is your home, MacRorah. At least, for as long as I choose to remain here."

She realized that he meant the beach, not this particular cottage. "Oh? And if I choose to remain longer than you do?" Here it was, then. The first test of wills.

"We'll just have to work out a compromise."

"A compromise." So far, so good, she thought. Only why did she feel just a niggle of disappointment? "I suppose that's reasonable enough. But you must remember, this has been my home for the past ten years."

"I'm aware of that." Court rose and took the plates out to the kitchen, to join several stacked haphazardly on the countertop.

"Well, then, what do you suggest?" she asked.

"I've considered buying a place of our own here. Sea could be of help there. I'm sure he has—"

"I already own a perfectly good cottage."

He regarded her warily. "Yes, of course. I thought perhaps you might like something, uh—larger? More elaborate? With separate quarters for a small staff? I assure you, I can afford—"

"Yes, I know. I can afford, too," she snapped. "Courtland, I think you'd better understand something right now. You didn't marry some poor waif who'd be grateful enough for any crumbs you tossed her way to allow you to walk all over her."

Court looked as if he'd just been handed a live firecracker. MacRorah almost backed down, but if there was to be any hope for this marriage—and she had every hope for it, even if it didn't offer much beyond the basics, which was all she'd thought she wanted at first—then they might as well lay all cards on the table.

"Court, I married you because you offered me a family—that is, the chance to be a mother. Just as you married me because you needed a mother for Iris. Neither of us was looking for more than that...." She waited, hoping against hope that he would argue, but he didn't. Instead, his eyes took on that narrowed look, that guarded look that warned her she was treading on dangerous ground.

Fool! You're going about everything in precisely the wrong way! Honey and vinegar might ward off disease, but honey alone works better with men.

"But you're tired, and so am I. I suggest you see me home, and we'll talk about it tomorrow."

"MacRorah," Court said softly, his eyes glinting with a steely determination she had seen before, to her sorrow. "You *are* home. I thought we'd settled all that. Now, you may keep your cottage if you like—it will serve very well for our annual visits—but for the moment, wherever I am will be your home. And I'm here, dammit!"

Her mouth opened and closed several times. Not a sound issued forth.

"We'll go back now and collect whatever you need for the night and the next few days, and then we'll come back here. Is that clear?"

It was more than clear. MacRorah had had years of experience. There were times when a direct confrontation was in order, times when a flank attack was more effective.

The walk along a moonlit shore was actually quite pleasant. Court took her arm when she stepped back suddenly to avoid the incoming tide and kept it, tucking it under his elbow.

"Did you ever watch the phosphorous glow in wet sand at night?" he asked.

"Oh, yes! And did you ever sail at night and watch the fish swim out from under your boat? Isn't it amazing how they glow in the dark?"

"Only when conditions are just right," he murmured.

Conditions, MacRorah thought, were perfect. She could easily glow in the dark, if only there'd been time to establish some sort of a relationship before they'd been interrupted.

A drift of his crisp, masculine cologne captured her attention. Reuben had smelled exactly the way his store smelled, of dry goods. George smelled of bay rum and pomade. Neither man had excited her one bit. She hadn't loved them. She wasn't sure she had even liked them overly much.

Was it love that enhanced the senses? That made her feel like dragging her feet through the sand and leaning her head against Court's shoulder?

She wanted him to kiss her again. Wanted him to lay her down on the warm, dry sand and make love to her again. She hadn't the least doubt that if he did, she would glow in the dark as much as any phosphorescent fish.

The girls were asleep. Polly sat at the kitchen table, stringing beans while Teeny whittled her a slotted cooking spoon. He was forever making her things. She had more crochet hooks than a body would ever use. MacRorah thought it was sweet. She envied them their quiet, close relationship as she packed a small bag with enough to last her a day or two.

By that time, she figured, she and Court would either have come to blows or come to some agreement. She wasn't about to pack her trunk, only to have to haul it back and unpack it if things didn't work out.

But she did remove a small package from her dresser drawer, one that had come in the mail the day before her wedding. Unwrapping it, she gazed down at the dear, familiar face of a child she had feared losing. A child who was now, if all went well, her own.

She'd borrowed a photograph of Iris several weeks before and sent it to one of the men at the Retreat, who had copied it onto ivory. A skilled artist, he had captured that very quality that had reminded her so much of her own sister, Rosa, and at the same time, reminded her of Court.

She had thought to have a memento when summer ended. Now, if things worked out—if she could just learn to compromise—summer might never end.

She waited until they were back at the Adams cottage, until after Court had put her bag in the room he was using, to give him her gift. "I had it done for me," she confessed candidly. "To remember this summer by. If you like it—that is, I'd like you to have it. If you want it. It's not a perfect likeness, but I think he captured her true nature, don't you?"

Court had unwrapped the small rectangular parcel cautiously. He didn't want her to give him a wedding gift. He hadn't given her anything, and he should have. Women set great store by such things.

"Do you like it?" she asked anxiously.

Oh, God, he felt like weeping! He was incredibly touched that she would do such a thing. Not that she would offer him the miniature she had meant for herself, but that she would have had it painted in the first place.

No matter how he tried to remain aloof, Court

could only believe that she truly loved the child and that her love was completely unselfish. He could almost feel jealous of his own daughter.

Abruptly, he turned away to stare out the window. When he had blinked several times to clear his vision, he saw her reflection in the glass. She was still standing there, her arms at her side, her face completely unguarded.

He'd thought he was good at reading people. Now he searched for some sign that she wanted more from their marriage than just his daughter.

"It—it's beautiful," he said, his voice rough with unfamiliar emotion. "Thank you."

"You gave me Iris. And a wedding gown. I wanted to give you something, too."

Now was his chance. If only he could reach her— reach behind that prickly independence of hers and get underneath her guard . . . "I've never been particularly good at expressing my feelings," he said, still waiting for some sign.

"No, I don't believe you have."

"Yes, well—what I'm trying to say is that I might have misled you. About my reasons for wanting to marry you, that is."

If possible, she grew even more still. "No, that's wrong," he corrected. "I didn't mislead you." Was that disappointment he saw in her eyes? "Actually, when I asked you to take on the role of Iris's mother, I didn't know—that is, I wasn't aware . . . although I probably should have been. I should have guessed that . . ."

Breathlessly, she whispered, "Guessed what?"

Court clasped the tense muscles at the back of his neck and massaged them briefly. He was thirty-six years old. He'd been married, for God's sake! Yet here he was, head of a successful business, stammering around like an eighteen-year-old kid trying to work up enough nerve to steal his first kiss!

"Dammit, I want to hold you—I want to kiss you," he blurted. "That's not even all I want! Ah, hell, this isn't working."

The corners of her mouth twitched, and he caught a gleam of mischief in her amber eyes. "Do you want to go to bed and do . . . well, I'm not sure what you call it. That is, technically, I know, but it doesn't seem quite right, now that I've actually done it."

"MacRorah . . ."

MacRorah. Was there another woman on the face of the earth with the same mixture of sass and shyness? A woman so outspoken, so outrageous—so maddeningly obstinate—and at the same time, so sweetly generous?

"If you don't want to do it some more, then that's all right, too. I could always wash the dishes, instead. Although you did promise me that we could make a baby of our own, but I don't know where Polly's garter is, so perhaps we shouldn't even waste time trying."

"MacRorah—" His voice sounded a warning note.

"But then I expect you're tired if the only nap you've had was in that miserable chair."

"Dammit, woman!"

He wasn't good with words—at least, not the flowery kind of words a woman would want at a time like this—but he did know how to make babies. He would make her a dozen babies if that was what she wanted.

"Starting right now," he muttered.

MacRorah didn't even try to avoid him. She had finally come to know this man she had married. He might not look the part, but he was far more a man of action than of words.

Taking the lead, she headed for the stairs. Court caught up with her near the sofa, and that was as far as they got. What happened next was more a case of spontaneous combustion than a kiss. His fingers tangled in her hair, while hers went straight for the buttons on his shirt. He fell back onto the sofa and pulled her down on top of him, settling her between his thighs, and then proceeded to kiss her senseless.

Then, somehow, she was on the bottom, one foot on the floor, the other limb sprawled against the cushions. A sense of déjà vu flickered through her mind when she felt his lips on her breast.

But unlike that memorable night ten years ago, this time no one fell asleep at the critical moment. This time, there was no turning back.

"Do you know how many times I've dreamed of this?" Court whispered.

"Of making babies?"

"Of making love. With you. Of making love and waking up to do it again and again, and then waking up in the morning with you in my arms, in my bed. Forever. Does that frighten you?"

She shivered, but not from fright. "A—a little. I don't remember anything in your rules about—about that sort of thing."

"Nor in yours. Perhaps," he said as he deftly reached under her petticoat to unbutton the waistband of her drawers, "we should change the rules?" His hand slipped over her belly, and then down to the warmth between her thighs. "What about it?"

MacRorah drew in a shaky breath. "Don't distract me, Court, this is important!"

"What's important? The rules?"

"Not the dratted rules—*this!*" She wiggled her hips to settle him more firmly in place.

Court's bark of laughter was muffled against her damp throat. "You mean *this*?" he suggested, with a deft movement of his hand.

She breathed a sigh. "I think I'm beginning to glow like a fish. Do you see anything?"

His voice was so deep it was nearly inaudible. "Oh, yes, I see something. I see something so incredibly lovely . . ."

It was awkward on such a narrow space, but neither of them even considered moving. Somehow, Court managed to remove several articles of clothing, both his and hers. By the time he thrust into her, he was trembling with need, overflowing with an emotion he could no longer deny.

He pierced her sweet, hot depths, trying desperately not to move too quickly. When she cried out, he thought he had hurt her—she was so small, so tight. "God, I'm sorry," he groaned.

"Oh, my—oh, Court, I do love you so," she gasped.

It was more than enough to push him over the edge. Moments later he shuddered hard and collapsed, one knee on the floor, both her legs gripping his hips.

When he could speak again, he said, "We're going to have to find a wider sofa, my love."

"I've a perfectly good bed."

"And I've a perfectly good kitchen table. In time, I expect we'll try them all."

Her soft gurgle of laughter ran through him like a bolt of lightning. "Next time, though," she whispered, "I really should remember to wear my garter."

Court was already anticipating the next time. "On the other hand, we could lose the confounded thing and simply try harder."

The mantel clock chimed eleven times. Outside, the sound of water lapped against the shore. MacRorah hugged her happiness to her and vowed to be the best possible wife and mother, so that Court would never regret marrying her.

"What was that sigh all about?" he asked, shifting them both to a more comfortable position.

"Oh, nothing . . . only I thought tomorrow I might start on a list of ways to change so that I can set a better example for our children."

Court's laughter rang out in the warm stillness. "Promise me one thing, beloved—no more lists. You

may change anything you like about my house as
long as you don't change a thing in the woman I
married—the woman I fell in love with before I even
knew her name."

Closing her eyes, MacRorah savored the moment.
She would change, and so would Court. Change was
inevitable. Iris would grow up, and they would grow
old, and they would quarrel—frequently, most likely.
They were both opinionated people.

But where there was enough love on both sides,
there was security. And she was convinced that there
was more than enough love on both sides to last a
lifetime.

Epilogue

ℰ

MacRorah was folding diapers in the formal dining room under the noses of some half dozen illustrious Adams ancestors when Court got home. The laundry was not her responsibility, but when Laurence had cried, Hannah had dashed upstairs, leaving her laundry basket on the kitchen table. Rather than risk offending Mrs. Coltrane, who didn't care to have her kitchen invaded while she was preparing dinner, MacRorah had taken the basket into the next room.

"Why are you doing Hannah's work, love?"

"I like to smell clean laundry. What's that you're hiding behind your back?"

"If you need more help, we'll hire it," Court said, and then he smiled that smile that still had the power to make her knees grow weak. "I've got 'em," he declared, fanning a sheaf of train tickets under her nose. "We leave on the nine-ten three days from today. I talked to Teeny—he'll arrange for Polly and

Megan to open up the cottage and hire on staff. Sea and Sal and their brood will be down next weekend."

It had been nearly two years, what with her pregnancy and Laurence's birth. Court still insisted on treating her as if she were fragile. "Did you think to remind him to get the boat out of storage?"

Court's grin widened as he slipped his arms around her waist from behind. "For the children, yes, but I think you and I deserve something a bit more . . . ah, private."

MacRorah twisted around. "Courtland, have you been up to something?"

He assumed an innocence that belied what his hands were doing. "My, but you have a suspicious nature, Mrs. Adams."

"Only because I know you too well, Mr. Adams," she retorted, trying to sound stern, but succeeding only in sounding breathless.

Really, at their ages, one would think the novelty would have worn thin!

"It occurred to me last fall that with Sea's cottage full and ours running over, you and I might need to sneak away now and then for a bit of, um—adult conversation. I sent along a set of specifications to Teeny, and by now, *MacMischief II* should be all fitted out and ready to launch. Happy birthday, darling."

MacRorah turned in his arms, her cheeks blooming with becoming color. "Oh, my mercy, what am I going to do with you!"

A pair of deep-set hazel eyes, without a single

trace of sadness or bitterness, sparkled down at her. "You have to ask?" Court teased. His breath quickened as his hands dropped to her hips, pressing her against his aroused body. Her hands slipped inside his coat, and she lifted her face for his kiss.

From nearby came the sound of Hannah's footsteps as she brought his son downstairs to greet him, and Court swore softly. Iris's giggle rang out as she raced down the hallway, followed by the clickety-click of her new puppy's toenails.

He groaned. "Later," he whispered.

Sighing, MacRorah straightened her shirtwaist and smoothed her hair. Watching her husband greet their two beloved children, she beamed. Oh, yes, she promised herself. Now, and later—and forever.